THE DARKEST GLASS

OLIVIA DANSON

ODDWORKS PRESS, LLC

Cover illustration and design © Ashley Hankins, www.ashleydoesartstuff.com

Edited by Carrie Jones, carriejonesbooks.blog

Published in 2025 by Oddworks Press, LLC

ISBNs: 979-8-9996001-0-3 (e-book), 979-8-9996001-1-0 (paperback), 979-8-9996001-2-7 (hardcover)

First printed in the United States of America

*To my mom, thank you for everything. You truly are one of the best parents
ever and I'm forever grateful to have you in my corner.*

AUTHOR'S NOTE

Before our tale begins, a gentle reminder that this story contains dark fantasy and horror themes, including fantasy violence, emotional/physical abuse, body horror, murder, self-harm, blood, gore, toxic relationship dynamics, discussions of grooming between a minor and an adult (mentioned), suicidal ideation, panic attacks (on page), reference to suicide attempt, depression, drug use, alcohol abuse, consensual sexual content (off-screen), drug addiction, post-partum depression (mentioned), hanging (not by suicide), forced institutionalization, grief, parental abandonment, bullying (on page and past reference), cannibalism (mentioned/organ, source not on page) and kidnapping (mentioned). Reader discretion is advised.

Although inspired by events and culture from the Victorian era, this story is not historical fiction or historical fantasy, but a magical, reimagined world separate from our own. This book is not meant to serve as an accurate depiction of the aforementioned time period and should not be used as an educational source. To learn more about the historical Victorian era, please consult non-fiction sources and cited academic materials.

Now, for those that are ready, onward to the monsters, magic, and madness...

1

Julia

"The hunter who seeks the deer also, in turn, seeks the wolf." – *Unknown, engraved quote beneath a statue of Saint Martin of Healers*

In the sleepy town of Temmings, one warning was repeated more than any other: *terrible things happen to those who aren't careful.*

Standing in a field on the outskirts of town, far from the safety of the cobbled streets, crowded teahouses and second-hand dress shops she knew, those words ran through Julia Sheffield's head again and again. A bead of sweat slid down her neck as the forest loomed like a living wall before her. Trees crowded its edge like teeth, their needle-like branches beckoning her where the sunlight dared not reach.

She squeezed George's hand. "Ready?"

She looked down to see her youngest brother transfixed, lips slightly parted, as if captured by song. Panic tightened her throat.

"George? You ready?"

George blinked, shaking off whatever had held him. "Ready."

"And you're sure you trust Roger on this?"

George's nostrils flared. "He swore it on his grandmum's grave! He said Billie was right over there, near the forest edge. He's out there, Jules and he needs our help."

Julia wasn't so sure. No one had seen Billie Moore in six days. He was small for his ten years, and the runt of her brother's group of friends. Billie's father, a whaler from Portyard, was out at sea more than he was on land, so Julia had often seen Billie helping his mum and sister at the Moore's tailor shop on Blackwood Street. She recalled George telling her on more than one occasion Billie being the target of Marcus Campbell and his gang's viciousness. The same ruffians that made faces behind Father O'Malley's back and threw eggs (and on occasion filled inkpots) at horse cabs and ran away laughing. The same boys she'd overheard daring each other to go into the forest alone for sport.

Maybe they had chased Billie into the forest and lost track of him, only to grow bored and forget about him later. But it'd been six days. If hunger hadn't taken him, Julia was certain the wolves must've by now.

George dug the toe of his boot into the dirt. "Wendall and Melvin were just too scared to come with me, but I trust Roger. He doesn't lie."

Everyone lies, Julia almost said, but held her tongue. What Roger Aberton said he saw—Billie Moore standing at the edge of the forest, whole and healthy—sounded like a lie. But Roger's wide-eyed stupor and refusal to leave the house since the encounter spoke of a far more terrible truth. One most adults in Temmings were all too eager to leave out of their polite teatime conversation.

Billie was no different than Lovina Bauldry, Baxter Graham, Nan Smedley, or Timothy Winters. All children, Julia was told as she was growing up, that were naughty and wandered off when they shouldn't have. Only years later, during a market trip with her mum, did eleven-year-old Julia learn from Lilah Roan, the local apothecary and town gossip, that they each had gone past the fields and were never seen again or returned a muted shell of their former selves.

"The forest, it whispers things," Lilah had told Julia while her mum was busy comparing tinctures. "It's alive and all living things must consume. Never go near there, understand?"

Julia let out a shaky breath. She'd seen the white guiding candle burning in the window of Billie's room for the past six days. The old wives in town claimed it to be a beacon to guide the missing home, but Julia and her friends knew it as a marker of loss.

"When we go in there, you have to do everything I say, all right?" Julia kneeled so George was forced to look at her. She gripped his shoulders, her light blue eyes unblinking. "I'm serious, George. Run off and I'll tell Da and Auntie you cut class to come here alone."

"I promise, I won't run off." George crossed his chest. "But we'll find him right, Jules?"

As she was about to respond, the words of their older brother Frederick echoed in her mind.

"Don't lie to him, Jules," he had warned her that morning. *"It's cruel, giving him hope like that. They searched the forest already. Billie's gone."*

She knew Fredrick was right. Of course they wouldn't find Billie, but she also knew George would never be satisfied until he saw the truth for himself. Wouldn't it be crueler to deny him that chance?

She grabbed George's hand. "Come on, then."

As they crossed the field hand in hand, Julia looked over her shoulder. No one ran after them. No one called their names or tried to stop them.

No one noticed more children slipping away.

Julia and George crossed the field, feet unwavering, and entered the mouth of the forest.

The warmth of the sunlight fell away and a thick, earthen mustiness permeated the air. In the speckled canopies above, birds chirped and tittered to each other.

"Thanks again for coming with me," George said as he brushed back a branch.

He kept his eyes trained ahead, but Julia could see the traces of a smile. She marked the tree with a piece of chalk from her dress pocket and ruffled his short auburn brown hair, a shade deeper than hers, with her free hand. "Sure. Just stay by my side, all right?"

George giggled. "Okay."

Julia kept a lookout as she and George called out Billie's name. Halfway into their search, a flash of orange darted past them and disappeared somewhere behind a cluster of trees. George spun around, craning his neck to catch a glimpse of the creature, but the fox was long gone.

"Jules, aren't foxes supposed to be deeper in? Does that mean we're close then?"

"No, we're not." Julia swallowed hard, tucking a long strand behind her ear. A bead of sweat trickled down her freckled cheek. "But it shouldn't be running *towards* Temmings. That's ... death."

She turned back to the path ahead and let out a small gasp.

"George, does something look different to you?"

George frowned. "No, why?"

"I mean, the trees ... they look ..." *Like they moved.* Julia gripped the piece of chalk tighter. "Never mind. Let's go."

Two hours later, the pair sat down against a gnarled tree with sagging branches. Julia sighed with relief to be off her feet. She stared up at the canopy, watching the sunlight dance behind the leaves. It was almost peaceful enough to forget they were in a place not to be trusted.

George took a canister from his pack and gulped down a mouthful of water. When he didn't show signs of stopping, Julia snatched the canister away.

"Oi, don't hog it!"

"But I wasn't done yet," George moaned with a pout, wiping his mouth.

Julia managed a small swig before the canister emptied. "Brilliant. Now we have no more water." She tossed it to the ground and shot George a nasty glare. "Way to go."

George tucked his chin between his knees. After a moment, Julia picked up the canister with a sigh, dusting off her dress. "Just as well. We need to head back before Da catches on we're not at the market. Come on, we're leaving."

"No, we can't go yet!" George blurted. "Please, Jules. If we don't find Billie by tonight, they'll blow out his guiding candle and it'll be too late! Just a little longer, please?"

Julia sighed. "We've already looked everywhere. He's not here."

George got to his feet, not bothering to brush off the dirt sticking to his threadbare shorts. "He's here. He's got to be. I bet he's just hiding 'cause he's scared is all."

Don't lie to him, Jules.

"George," Julia said quietly, taking his hand, "it's been six days. Billie would've come back to Temmings by now, don't you think?"

George was silent for several seconds.

"What if it was me?" He pulled his hand away and looked down at her with a mixture of hurt and anger. "Would you give up on me then, too? Huh? Like Billie's parents? Like Mum?"

Julia flinched as if struck. *Does he really think I'm like* her?

"No, that's not—"

The low howl of wolves reverberated through the forest. Julia was on her feet in an instant. She grabbed George's arm and pulled him behind her.

"Do you see anything?" she whispered, trying and failing to keep her voice steady.

George shook his head. She could feel him trembling beside her, or was that her own fear besting her?

Howls echoed through the forest again. It was coming from behind them now. *Are we surrounded? But how?* Julia's heart thrashed against her chest. George grabbed Julia's hand and squeezed, jolting her back to her senses. They needed to move. *Now.*

"Let's go!" Julia hollered. They sprinted toward the nearest chalk-marked tree. Julia glanced over her shoulder but didn't see their pursuers.

Another howl. Closer this time.

Too close.

George leapt to avoid a tree root, but Julia's layered skirts and corset didn't afford her the same limberness. Her boot tip caught a root and sent her toppling to the side. George skidded to a halt.

"Jules!"

Julia raised herself up on her scrapped elbow and gasped.

Billie Moore stood behind them in his school blazer and shorts. Aside from a tear on his left jacket arm, his blond curls flecked with dirt and missing a shoe, he was as whole and healthy as Roger claimed.

George broke the silence first.

"Billie, i-it's me. G-George."

Billie didn't say anything. Julia gawked at him. How had a ten-year-old survived unharmed in the wilderness for six days? Could he even hunt? And why wasn't he reacting? Was he in some sort of shock?

A rancid smell lingered on the still air like meat left out too long. Julia wrinkled her nose, fighting against the nausea threatening to overcome her.

Billie tilted his head in one slow, wooden movement. "We can be mates." He extended his hand to George and smiled. A thin line of amber sap trickled from Billie's mouth but he made no move to wipe it away. "Come with me."

"What? We're already mates." George took a step forward. "We came to take you home. Your mum and sister are really worried about you." He turned to Julia with a wide grin. "See? I told you Roger wasn't lying!"

Julia's skin prickled. Something else was nagging at her …

Then it hit her. *The wolves.* Only minutes before they'd sounded so close, right upon them even, yet their howling had all but stopped. Even the birdsong and chittering of insects had died away. The forest had fallen quiet. No, not quiet.

Waiting to consume.

Julia's gaze slowly fell to Billie's feet. From where she sat, she noticed what George didn't—Billie's feet weren't fully touching the ground.

Julia screwed her mouth shut to bottle her scream. *Save George, save George, save George.*

"Come with me," Billie repeated to George, his brown eyes flat and unblinking. He paid Julia no mind as she slowly stood to full height. Because she was taller than them, she noticed a tree standing oddly by itself just to Billie's right. One of its branches hung curiously low, which Billie obscured from view. On the other side of the tree hung another low branch, slender as an arm, with smaller sharpened branches sprouting from it like fingers. Branches that looked sharp enough to cut skin and slim enough to dig into the back of a young boy.

Julia dove for George. She grabbed the crook of his arm and screamed, "Run!"

The siblings sprinted over rotted leaves and detritus as the mimicry howls morphed into guttural snarls. Julia struggled to follow her chalk marks as fear surged like wildfire through her.

No, no, not like this! We can't die like this!

Finally, the field came into view. Julia ground her teeth together and pushed through the searing pain in her calves. George followed suit just as the snarls gave way to Billie's impossibly measured voice repeating, "Come with me. Come with me. Come with me." Heavy footsteps thundered behind them, tearing out roots and underbrush with each pounding step, sending a flock of birds screeching into the sky.

"Jules!" George cried, wheezing. "It's gonna catch us!"

"Don't stop!" she screamed. "Don't look!" She wouldn't let the forest have them. Not like Billie. Not like that.

With one final sprint, they broke past the tree line and collapsed in the field. Every breath felt tinged in fire and spittle, but Julia didn't care. They were alive. When she mustered the courage to look back, no one was there. The trees stood unmarked and the undergrowth undisturbed. All was well and calm, save for Julia's wildly beating heart, sweat drenched skin and trembling hands. She gathered George in her arms and held him in a vice-like grip as their shaking sobs wove together into a terrible chorus.

"I'm sorry," she whispered into his hair, squeezing her eyes shut. "I'm so sorry."

This was her fault. She had let George believe he could still be the hero, still save his friend from an unspeakable fate. She'd worn the wrong mask. Told the wrong lies. Believed the wrong stories.

After all, such terrible things happened to those who weren't careful.

2

JULIA

"Fear not the Zealot, for they know no better; fear not the Mad, for they believe no better; fear not the Heretic, for they want no better." – *The Reverend Vicaress Helena Vowl of Glasshern*, By His Grace: Lessons of Our Saint Father

On the ninth day of Billie's disappearance, nearly the whole of Temmings crammed into the St. Kersey cathedral to attend the Moore vigil.

A stagnant air hung over the attendees, thick with heat and breath. Even as Father O'Malley approached the pulpit, his ring of white hair limp with sweat and his pale, papery skin hanging as loosely as his robes, latecomers continued to shuffle in and wedge themselves against those standing in the back. The Sheffields had been fortunate enough to claim their usual service seats in the third row on the right, in no short part due to Aunt Agatha waking everyone shortly after dawn.

"Really, it's just distasteful," Agatha whispered to her brother-in-law, Charles. Her lips pursed into a scowl. "Who arrives late to a vigil? Honestly, is there no decency left in this town?"

Charles nodded, swallowing a creeping yawn.

Agatha sat up straighter, opening her gilded copy of the *Book of the True Word*, the sacred text of Ascendism. "Julia, dear, straighten up. You're slouching." Agatha's penciled brows furrowed. "Julia. *Julia?*"

Julia's gaze broke away from the small wooden coffin at the foot of the pulpit wreathed in garlands of yellow and white pansies. She plastered on a smile and sat at attention.

"Sorry, Auntie."

She took a deep breath, but it did little to quiet the memory of Billie's stolen voice.

"Come with me. Come with me. Come with me."

A small hand brushed hers. Julia jerked back, garnering a few curious stares. Federick nudged George.

"Careful now, Georgie or she may faint," he chided with a smirk. "Need some air, Jules?"

"No, thanks," Julia replied with a mocking smile. She nudged George. "What is it?"

His downcast eyes held no focus. The brightness there only days before had waned into a vacant stare.

"This isn't right, Jules," George whispered. "He's still out there."

"Not now."

"But—"

Father O'Malley cleared his throat and a collective hush fell over the crowd.

"On behalf of Mrs. Moore and her daughter, Piper, I thank you all for being here today to join in collective remembrance of our very own Billie Adam Moore." Father O'Malley let out a rattling, wet cough. Only after dabbing his mouth and tucking his kerchief back into the breast pocket of his dark robes did he continue.

"Young Billie was a brilliant child loved by friends, family, and peers alike. It is on this day we come together to remember him and cherish his memory. He will continue to be loved and forever in our hearts, in peace always. It is during these times we are reminded to keep to the haven of Temmings and support each other."

Father O'Malley joined his pointer and middle fingers together, crossing them into an 'X' above his chest to symbolize the crossing of the staffs, when the worthy entered Paradise and spoke the Saint Father's true name to him.

"Come with me. Come with me." Julia's fingers dug into the edges of the *True Word*. Crossing into the forest let madness in. The hunter's madness. But despite the rumors, Julia had always been of the mind the hunter's madness was simply a strange fungal fever. Monsters didn't exist. Billie was dead.

It wasn't real, Julia reminded herself. *It wasn't real.*

"And now, let us have a moment of silence for young Billie."

As everyone lowered their heads, Julia lifted hers to the bronze statue of the Saint Father clad in simple robes. He stood positioned on an altar behind Father O'Malley holding the *True Word* in one hand and a jar of snake oil in the other. A large serpent hung limply around his shoulders—the basilisk of innovation, the first creature to be used to harvest snake oil and lead Halcyon into an industrial age. Inscribed in a bronze plaque above the statue was the quote: "The industrious shall know my name at the gates of Paradise and speak honestly this truth unto me."

A row of half melted white candles decorated the altar, their black wicks the last acknowledgement of Billie Moore.

Monsters only lived in stories whispered by old crones in their soothsayer shops at the edge of town and retold by children behind cupped hands. Talk of blood draining duskborns, soul snatching raven-eyed, demon magic-wielding fateshifters, and moon cursed blood wolves made great spectacle for tourists looking to liven their countryside stays. No one told better tales than Lilah Roan, the local apothecary and town gossip.

"It was my great-great grandmum who would say to salt your doorways and win-dowsills to keep out intruders. Jotted it all down in her journals, she did," Lilah told Julia once when she skipped class to wander the market. "She went on about keeping a bowl of water beneath your bed to anchor the soul at night. Light a white guiding candle for the lost for seven days and not a day more. Tie a stem of honeysuckle to your infant's crib to ward off changelings until they can speak." A scowl soured her weathered features. "Hmph, the good it did her. She died here in Temmings, you know. They accused her of being a fateshifter and burned her at the stake."

Julia never paid the stories any mind, but now looking upon Billie's empty casket, a creeping sense of dread overcame her.

You weren't listening. You weren't careful.

When Father O'Malley let out another phlegmy, wet cough Julia nearly jumped out of her seat.

"In honor of Billie Moore, I remind us of the journey of the Saint Father, fraught with danger and uncertainty in much the same way we now find ourselves. As verse three describes ..."

Julia's eyes glazed over the passage Father O'Malley began reciting. She noticed George wasn't reading either. She followed his gaze to Billie's coffin.

It could've been anything out there, she reassured herself. *We're safe here.*

"... and so the Saint Father gathered his disciples during those fiendish days in the Age of Demons and laid down his walking stick before them at the edge of the Silver Sea. 'My honored disciples, the way before us is not a simple one, but I beseech you to walk with an honest heart and an open mind. It is love that shall guide the worthy. Only those who have the courage to love can harness the power of the world.'"

We're safe here. We're safe.

Quiet murmurs of agreement rippled through the cathedral. Julia nodded along, but her mind was elsewhere. Sweat pooled on the back of her neck and under her arms. As she absently scratched beneath the black cuffs of her mourning dress, she noticed Frederick was smiling. She followed his gaze to Regina Mathers, a pretty girl from Norchester in the next row up who was visiting her cousins for the season. Regina returned a coy smile of her own before turning her attention back to her reading. Julia took this to mean that Susanna Rivers was no longer the shiny penny of her older brother's eye. In the row behind Regina sat Marigold Lanton, a tenth year at the Elmwood School. She exchanged whispers with fellow tenth year Lillie Posely, no doubt about Frederick's newest fancy.

And just like that, life was moving on from the world that knew Billie Moore as alive and well.

After the service let out, Julia caught up to her father.

"Da, can I visit Charity's? She's hosting a gathering this afternoon for the Elmwood girls." She lowered her gaze. "It'd be good to have that kind of support right now."

Charles gave her a weary smile. "Of course, love. Your aunt and I are here for you if you ever need to talk."

"Thanks, Da."

He kissed the top of her head. "Off with you then. Proper manners at Templeton House, young lady."

"Yes, Da."

As she stepped away, Julia noticed Frederick bidding Regina farewell with a forward kiss on the hand.

Saints, he can't be serious.

Regina slid Frederick her calling card and he openly watched her leave. Julia rolled her eyes and waded through the dispersing crowd.

"Really, Frederick? At a vigil?"

"What? I don't recall my affairs being any business of yours, dear sister."

Julia flashed a sickly-sweet smile. "You're right, I could utterly care less what my ratbag of a brother gets up to and with whom. But I need you to do me a favor."

"Is this about your little private prayer salon at Templeton House?" Frederick smirked. "Nice one there. Looks like little Billie's helping us both out today, bless him."

"Don't be an ass," Julia snapped, slapping Fedrick's arm.

"Ow, okay fine."

"I need you to keep an eye on George. He's not doing well."

"Well, obviously. His friend did just die."

"He's *missing*." The words tumbled from Julia's mouth before she could stop herself. Fredrick raised a brow. "I mean—never mind. Just keep an eye on George, okay? I don't want him doing anything stupid."

"Don't worry, I'll watch him."

"Thanks Fred."

Julia broke away from the vigil crowd and left Dowry Street. She walked a short distance to Chanton Street, the only street in Temmings wide enough to accommodate carriages from the train station the next town over. Tendrils of ivy snaked along the honey-colored stone shopfronts, twining around gas lamps and flowerboxes bursting with the pinks, whites and yellows of late summer. Julia often wondered how the reek of horse manure mixed with the damp, earthy air Temmings was known for could be any sort of remedy—was the smog of the capital that terrible?

A moment later, Julia recognized the weathered stone archway of Templeton House. A pair of crouching stone jackals perched on either side of the entrance as if guarding the sprawling manor from intruders. Julia cast a quick glance behind her.

Most people were still milling around the cathedral, heads bent and eyes glassy. They clustered in groups, touching shoulders and arms in hopes of easing the pain of a child lost too soon. No one was looking for another to slip out of their sights.

Julia disappeared down a narrow street between the courthouse and the courier's office. Once safely on Milner Street, she strode past the entrance to the large, open-air market—closed for the vigil—and traveled down the cobbled bend past the Seven Hells pub. When she finally reached Bybrook Trail, a cleverly hidden path bordered by half collapsed stone walls pot marked with lichen, she was ready to unlace her boots and corset.

On the other side of a cropping of trees, obscured from all but the most well-trained eye, she heard a group of girls chatting and giggling. As she got closer, she spotted them sitting beneath a large oak tree, lovely and untouchable. The Graces. Lake Promise was an arm's reach away, its mirror smooth surface freckled with lily pads.

Martha Malster, her blonde curls weaved into a loose braid halfway down her back, spotted Julia first.

"You made it!" Martha kissed her cheek, her large doe eyes gleaming.

"Took you long enough." Emily Colby cast her a playful smirk, her wavy, dark brown hair brushing her fair shoulders. She pulled a vial from her black gloves, revealing a warm amber liquid inside.

"Did you nick that from your da's bottles again?" Julia asked.

"Maybe. I can't believe he still hasn't noticed. Or he feels bad mum only lets me see the sun for school and prayer," Emily laughed, raising the vial to her lips. "Speaking of, tell me you didn't actually go to that Elmswood prayer circle, did you?"

Dorothy Atheron, a head shorter than the rest of the group, finished weaving a daisy crown and set it atop her halo of dark coiled curls. "That was her little brother's friend, Em. Don't be such a harpy."

"Am not. I didn't want our poor Jules falling in with the wrong crowd."

Martha, who was now laying in Emily's lap, giggled. "You're not really troubled are you, Jules?"

Julia laughed it off. "Of course not. He wasn't my friend."

She plucked the vial from Emily, who broke into a grin. "Oi, give it here, you thief!"

The sweet burn of whiskey coursed down Julia's throat. She tossed the empty vial back to Emily with a wink.

"You owe me," Emily chided.

"Right on it, then," Julia replied. "Dory, help me out of this thing, will you?"

Dorothy untied the knot of Julia's corset and slowly pulled the laces loose. After a deep inhale and wide arm stretch, she shimmied out of her underthings. Emily, Martha, and Dorothy stared at her wide-eyed.

"Oh saints, you wouldn't," Dorothy squealed.

Julia peered over her shoulder and flashed a wicked grin. She slipped out of her stockings and jackknifed into the water. The coolness slipped across her bare, sun-freckled skin and separated her long auburn hair into coppery tendrils. She hovered in the cradle of Lake Promise, suspended in its clear depths.

Seconds, minutes, hours may have passed. It didn't matter. She was far away from monsters and saints and mourners. A world away from the madness haunting the forest. She opened her eyes to the shimmering surface of the world she left behind. Feeling her lungs beginning to squeeze, Julia raised her arms and pushed herself upward in one stroke.

When she broke the surface, she smoothed back her waterlogged hair and rubbed her eyes. A sudden chill sent goosebumps across her arms, but then Emily's gaze found hers and warmth filled her once more.

"Have yourself a good swim?" Emily asked as her fingers lazily played with Martha's hair.

Julia grinned. "Best of the season."

Dorothy, who had hiked her skirts and moved to sit at the lake edge, shook her head. "You're absolutely mad, Julia Sheffield." She kicked her bare, tawny legs and sighed. "This water is splendid though." She closed her eyes and leaned back, unaware of Julia inching towards her.

"Then you should come on in!"

Dorothy squealed, pulling back her legs just as Julia's fingers brushed her feet.

"Saints, Julia, I swear I'll murder you if you drag me in!" she cried, half laughing as she kicked water at a giggling Julia.

"Come on, live a little!"

Dorothy stuck her tongue out. "Go prune already."

Julia chuckled as she pushed off, floating along the lake's surface. She stared at the pale blue sky but inevitably her mind wandered towards her uncertain future. If her da and auntie had their way, it was a terribly boring picture: graduation, finishing school, a well to do marriage—very poor yet exceedingly handsome Harrison Goldwell's face surfaced in her mind instead—children, and then housekeeping until the end of her days. She closed her eyes and sighed.

How dull.

"Oh, Dory that reminds me," Martha interjected. "I need to borrow your clasp tomorrow. You know, the dark green one?"

Dorothy sat up on her elbows and cast Martha a skeptical stare. "Is it because Mr. Harper is coming back from Hadderdale tomorrow?"

Martha smirked. "Maybe."

"You're not still on about him, are you?" Julia replied. "Honestly, Mar, he's not worth the fuss."

Emily curled a strand of Martha's golden hair around her finger. "And you're far too pretty for him," she added. "Besides, his wife's the niece of the Viscount of Rosedale. I heard he only teaches in Temmings out of pity for us poor, ignorant fools."

"Says you," Martha huffed. "He does fancy me, you know. He even said he'd bring me back a gift from his travels. And anyway, I hear his wife is a dull hag he was forced to marry. How dreadful is that?"

Dorothy ran her fingers through her curls, fiddling with her daisy crown. "I swear I'd rather drown myself in this lake than be forced to marry someone who didn't like me."

No one said anything, but Julia heard the unspoken fear in their collective silence. *As if we have a choice in who we'll marry.*

"He's like your da's age, Mar," Julia finally said. "I'm sure he's fancied other students before. You deserve someone special, not some creep."

Dorothy and Julia exchanged looks. It was the closest she dared to reveal to Martha that she'd caught Emily making advances on Mr. Harper after class the day before his trip. Worse, the creep had played right into it. She'd sworn Dorothy to secrecy to spare Martha's feelings, but it still rubbed her wrong. Emily knew how sensitive Martha was and still went ahead with her little game anyway.

Because of course every toy in the box must belong to Emily.

"What about you, Jules?" Emily's face gave away nothing, but retaliation sharpened her tone. "Do you think Mr. Harper is handsome?"

Before she could answer, Dorothy spoke up first.

"Julia only fancies Harrison." She cupped her face in her hands, batting large doe eyes and making a kissy face. Emily and Martha broke into a fit of laughter, Mr. Harper soon forgotten.

Julia glared at Dorothy, who smirked back at her. "Come on, Jules. Live a little."

Julia scoffed and splashed Dorothy again, laughing as she shrieked and dove out of the way. Julia slipped back beneath the water and let herself drift across the surface, drowning out the Graces' chatter. As she closed her eyes, the memory of Billie's glassy stare greeted her.

"Come with me."

Julia's eyes flew open. Her body jackknifed upwards, and her feet kicked furiously beneath her. The Graces turned to look at her, eyebrows raised.

"Jules?" Emily sat up straighter. "You alright?"

Julia nodded. "I'm fine. Just thought I felt something brush my feet."

"So, you'll be coming tonight then?"

"Tonight?"

Emily groaned. "Honestly, I love you to bits, but you've got a cloud for a head." She walked over and kneeled at the shore. "The gathering tonight at the Gafton Manor. Just sneak out. Everyone's gonna be there." A smile pulled at her lips, sharp as a knife tip. "Including your beloved Harrison."

Julia's heart fluttered. She hoped the water would hide her creeping blush. It would be the perfect chance for her and Harrison to finally talk away from the prying eyes of the teachers or the always open ears of Elmwood's halls. She would need to find a way to sneak out beneath her father and aunt's notice, but she'd figure something out. She always did. She looked up at Emily, eyes alight.

"Count me in."

3

TOBIAS

High above Higdin's pub, crumpled on the third-floor landing, Tobias Flemming finally regained consciousness.

A sharp ache shot through Tobias's head even before he opened his eyes. His muscles seared with pain as he struggled to sit upright, finally managing to half crawl and half push himself against a nearby wall. Tendrils of yellowed wallpaper long peeled off raked against his bare back, eagerly sticking to his clammy, freckled skin and damp, russet curls. He leaned back and let out a deep sigh, the stagnant air coating his tongue.

"Bloody hell."

Sunlight streamed through the grimy window across the landing. How long had he been out this time? No, it didn't matter. Swallowing hard, he raised his right hand in front of his face. He had to see it for himself.

The ropes he'd tied the night before had been severed. No, not just severed—torn. He stared at the frayed tails, the undersides of his wrists raw with rope burn.

A creak of wood snapped him from his thoughts. Standing on the landing was Higdin's owner, Hilda Cooke, fists balled at her sides. His headache immediately worsened.

"*You,*" she snarled.

She grabbed his arm and yanked him onto his feet, ignoring his cry of pain and the wallpaper flecks littering the floor.

"It happened again, dinnit? *Dinnit?*"

"No, it's not—"

She squeezed his arm harder. "Don't lie to me, boy. I already got enough of it from that ox of mine downstairs. I don't need it from you, too."

"I just was sleepwalking, is all," he finally managed to say.

"Sleepwalking?" Hilda scoffed, raising one of his bloody wrists between them. "You still think *this* is all just sleepwalking then, do ya?"

He rolled his eyes. "Damned if I know."

A sharp sting spread across Tobias's cheek. Hilda's brackish brown eyes locked with his, her glare sharper than any blade. She rested one hand on her wide hips and pointed an accusing finger at Tobias with the other.

"Oi, watch your tongue," she snapped. "One word from me and your head rolls through Iron Square. Remember that."

Tobias grinned despite himself. "And after the tale I'd have for the City Watch, yours'll be followin' right behind mine. We'll have ourselves a bloody fine race, eh?"

Hilda let out a long sigh as she reached into her pocket for a hand rolled kell and match box.

"I know you hate listenin' to me," she said, the kell tucked between her thin lips as she struck the match, "but I'm tellin' you now youth is a terrible blindness. I was sixteen once too, you know." She took a deep drag and exhaled a cloud of smoke. The reek of acrid pine unique to kellweed filled the air.

"Marcellus will only stretch his neck out so far for you," she reminded him. "Me even less. A gang's a business, love, in case you forgot. Those bloody coppers are always sniffin' around. If they hear some Market Streeter living here is sick with wolf bite, kid or not, Higdin's goes up in smoke and you're flayed in the street for sport."

Tobias's jaw clenched, his normally sandy complexion blanching.

"I'm not sick, all right?"

Tobias hated the words even before they left his lips. He hated the hollowness and whine in them. But he had to say them. Someone had to say them. Otherwise, it left room for fear to grow. And he couldn't afford that. Not if he and Lucy were to survive the coming winter.

"One of these days it won't be me here when you open your eyes." Her face softened ever so slightly. "Your sister, she's a clever one. You're a fool to pretend she's dull."

"Don't you think I know that?" Tobias snapped.

Hilda ignored him. "This is the last time, Tobias. I'm done. When it happens again, you and Lucy can house up with Marcellus and his boys on Market Street."

The pain in Tobias's skull throbbed anew. The hallway landing suddenly seemed too small, the damp air too thick.

"You know I can't take her there. It's not safe. Please, Hilda I promise it won't happen again."

Hilda shook her head. "Don't make promises you can't keep. Look, I'm a barkeep, not a nanny. Either sort yourself out or find somewhere else, but I'll be damned if a couple of orphans bring me down with them."

"Fine, I'll go, ok? I'll go, but just let Lucy stay here. Please." Tobias tried to grasp some convincing argument, but his head was too jumbled from the night before. "She can help Ari with dishes. But nothing behind the bar. And no patron favors."

Hilda was silent for a moment, then gave a curt nod. "Fine. She can keep to the kitchens for now, but the moment she's of age she tends bar." *And sells hollium with each drink* hung unspoken between them like a sword dangling over his sister's future.

"Deal," Tobias said through clenched teeth, extending his hand, revealing the skull and coin tattoo marking him as a member of the notorious Market Streeters. He shoved down the thought of Lucy anywhere near hollium—or honey, as it was often called—the most addictive drug in Halcyon.

I'll get us out, Luce. I promise.

Before she took his hand, Hilda added, "And I'm keeping my discounted protections around the pub courtesy of the Market Streeters. I expect no hassle from the Seadevils or the Barrel Boys. Make sure Marcellus gets word."

"Better to not make promises I can't keep, remember?" Tobias chided.

Hilda's lips curled into a mirthless smile. "This one you'll want to strive for." She squeezed his hand until his knuckles ached, but he refused to let the pain show on his face.

"Be out before sundown." Hilda spun around and headed back downstairs.

Tobias shook out his hand.

"Wench."

Silence filled the void Hilda left behind. Tobias doubled over, squeezing his eyes shut and letting the clamminess of the hall cling to his skin. No one in Lordhaven of any proper standing spoke of blood wolves by name, but their bestial shape and hunger lingered in stories and rumor, leaving fear to fester in the minds caught outside after dark. Whether or not any of it was true Tobias couldn't say.

What if the dreams are more than just sleepwalking? he wondered.

Since being bitten, his dreams had escalated from dreaming of wolves to becoming one, running through the narrow streets of Lordhaven overgrown with gnarled black trees splitting through empty rowhouses and snaking through shopfronts. He peered down at his wrists again as a sinking feeling clawed at his stomach.

"Saints, get it together, Flemming." He shook his head and pushed off the wall, heading up the stairs until he reached the fourth floor. He took a deep breath before opening the door.

The summer heat pressed against him first, cloying and viscous. Tobias crossed the small attic flat and pried open the single, newspaper-covered window. The cry of an infant, the shout of a constable and clattering hooves floated up from the street. The pungent, slightly sweet smell of burning snake oil mixed with the rot of pooling sewage slowly wafted in but Tobias didn't mind. It was a small comfort to be reminded life trudged on, even if he remained rooted in place, pressed between one bad hand and another. He grabbed a thin spun white shirt from the floor and pulled it over his head as a noise erupted behind him.

"Toby!"

Tobias's head snapped up to see his sister, one leg outside and the other draped over the windowsill, the corners of her speckled hazel eyes, mirrors of his own, crinkled with delight. A tattered blue scarf was tied tightly across her chest.

"The window was open, so I rushed back!" She swung her other leg inside and closed the window. Her two auburn braids whipped behind her, windswept and nearly undone. "Where did you go? I didn't see you when I woke up."

"I, um, had a bit of work to do with Ezra and Tavia this morning, but that's all done now. It's just you and me today."

"Really?" Lucy beamed. "You mean it?"

Tobias nodded. "Aye, we can have a whole adventure." He ran a hand through his matted, russet curls, only to feel a bump on the back of his head and winced.

"Are you okay?"

Tobias dropped his hand. "I'm fine." He nodded towards her scarf. "What'd you get there?"

She hurried over to the cot opposite his and untied her scarf. "Mr. Singh had this wonderful flatbread. It's a bit old, but it's really good! I got—" As he reached for the flatbread, he caught her staring at the frayed rope around his wrist.

Shit. He pulled his hand back and looked away, his fingers clenching the flatbread until it nearly tore in two.

After a moment of silence, Lucy spoke up.

"Did you have bad dreams again?" she said in a low voice.

"It's nothing to worry about," Tobias replied between chews, untying the rope ends and tossing them on the floor.

"Is that why you left last night?"

"I said *drop* it, Lucy."

She recoiled and shame boiled up inside Tobias, turning the flatbread in his mouth to ash. He swallowed hard.

"Saints, I'm sorry. It's not your fault, Luce, okay? It's not you. Just been a rough morning is all."

"It's okay," Lucy said quietly. She put her small hand over his and smiled. "I have scary dreams sometimes too."

Tobias grasped her hand and offered a shadow of a smile. "You tell me next time you do and I'll chase 'em away, all right?"

"Promise?"

"Promise."

Lucy smiled and took a bite of flatbread. As she ate, Tobias relished the brief and quiet moment of sharing a meal with his sister. His gaze lifted towards the window where, just on the other side, the capital city of Lordhaven dwelled, imposing and insatiable.

I won't let you take her away from me, too, Tobias silently cursed the city.

A pebble flicked against the window, pulling Tobias out of his thoughts.

"Stay there," he ordered Lucy as he crossed the room and looked out the window. Standing in the street was a young boy around Tobias's age of sixteen with shaggy black hair that fell across his light blue eyes and three scars across his right cheek.

"Oi, Toby! I've got news!" he hollered, then pointed to the alleyway.

Tobias sighed and ducked back inside. "It's Ezra. I'll be right back. Stay here."

"But I wanna say hello!"

Tobias crossed his arms. "Another time, promise. Now hurry on with that bread, hmm? We have the day together, remember?"

"Fine," Lucy said with a pout, nibbling her flatbread, but her jubilant kicks gave away her excitement for the day ahead.

Tobias slipped out the window and made his way down the rickety fire exit with practiced ease. The alleyway reeked of rot and urine. Roaches scurried through the cracks in the cobblestone and darted beneath tied waste bags. Clothing lines heavy with laundry crisscrossed between the crowded flats above, their quarters teeming with as many people as pests.

Ezra Molyns grinned and threw his arm around Tobias. "There he is! So, how do you feel about getting a bit richer?"

Tobias rolled his eyes, certain another one of Ezra's schemes was sure to follow. Tobias slid his hands deep into his pockets to keep his rope burned wrists hidden from view.

"Look, Ez, I really got other things to get on with today—"

"It's worth it, mate. I promise."

Ezra's clear blue eyes darkened as he leaned closer, lowering his voice to barely above a whisper. In Lordhaven, rumor ran that every rat had an open ear.

"Burrows Medical College will be hosting a surgical demonstration tomorrow night. Problem is their freezers are a bit empty and the District Coroner left the city two nights ago. Took off for the summer horse races in Burlington."

Ezra smirked. He pulled a folded slip of paper from his patchwork jacket and held it between his fingers. "Lucky for us, Burrows is only looking for one body. Fresh request this morning and now it's ours."

"Let me guess," Tobias ventured, "poor payout?"

Ezra frowned. "You know, you really do ruin all the fun."

Just then, the sunlight caught Ezra's face just right to highlight the three scars across his right cheek. Tobias's throat tightened. His own scar—a punctured half-moon on his left calf—ached at the reminder. It'd been almost a year since the attack, but the memory of the man's eyes was as vivid as if it'd been yesterday.

Unseeing.

Feral.

Clouded by the throes of blood wolf madness.

That'll be me one day.

Tobias cleared his throat. "Who do we need to get this time?"

Ezra leaned against the faded brick wall, blocking a constable recruitment poster. "Male, mid-twenties to early thirties. Fit sort. No wounds, not counting a knock to the head if needed." He winked. "Simple grab and run. We'll be back before you know it."

Tobias ran the calculation he always did. One hundred and fifty sterlings for his and Lucy's boat passage to the northern isle of Bronwen. Another five thousand for a one room cabin cliffside. From what he already had saved, freedom from Lordhaven and the Market Streeters was a little over three thousand sterlings away.

"I'm in," Tobias said.

Ezra beamed as he pushed off the wall. "Aces! Meet me tonight at the belltower. We'll strike the North Rim then."

4

JULIA

"I will always remain vigilant to correctly diagnose and treat the patient before me. I enter each instance with the understanding that the dosage determines what is medicine and what is poison."

– *Dr. Orwald Morosini, The Apothecarist Oath*

Tonight I'll see Harrison. Me, tonight!

Thoughts of dancing and banter at Gafton Manor filled Julia's head as she set the table. She had the perfect dress in mind—the green one from her birthday last year—and she knew enough dance steps to not embarrass herself if Harrison asked her to dance. Saints, would he ask her to dance? What if he didn't?

"My, you seem in good spirits." Agatha set down her famous dish of cottage pie in the center of the table, filling the cramped dining room with the smell of buttery potatoes, crisped beef and roasted vegetables. "Have a good time at Templeton House with your classmates?"

"Oh, yes it was lovely," Julia lied. "A great help."

"Splendid!" her aunt beamed, removing her oven mitts. "You're lucky to count Charity Greerson as a friend. Honestly it would do you well to run in her circles. I heard the Greerson's will be traveling to Pennyson end of the week after next. Perhaps you should suggest to Charity you both have tea at Walden Yard?"

"But we're not going to Pennyson. The cab fare alone—"

Agatha sighed. "Really, Julia have you no creativity? Girls in your station must *create* opportunities for yourselves if you ever hope to keep out of the gutter when you're older. If we don't innovate, how can we ever hope to rise to worthiness?" She massaged her knuckles as she spoke, mindful to rub each joint. "Imagine if the Saint Father had never slayed that basilisk and discovered all the wonderous properties of snake oil for machinery and medicine? Halcyon would still be a backwater fiefdom at the mercy of hedge god cultists. Find your snake oil, dear."

Julia held her tongue. She'd much rather take her chances in the forest again than have tea with Charity Greerson, let alone insert herself on their family trip in hopes of raising her social station, but appeasing her aunt's scheming was by far the easier road to take. It meant less chatter at supper and the faster she could sneak off to Gafton Manor. As she set the last plate, it suddenly hit her whose seat she was standing over.

Mum.

Julia gripped the plate until her knuckles hurt. Mary Sheffield's freckled face and guarded smile, so much like George's, rushed through her mind like a torrent.

Do you truly hate us this much, Mum? she wanted to scream. *Are we so easy to leave behind?*

The tears fell inward, trickling over the cracks and into the yawning hole Julia imagined tucked behind her heart. But her mask held in place, pretty and proper, free of troubles.

"Everything all right?" Agatha piped in.

"Yes, Auntie." Julia hurriedly set down the cutlery and took her seat just as her father and Frederick walked in, ushering in the smell of sweat and bark. Small dustings of sawdust clung to their overalls and boots. George trailed in behind them, a phantom on their heels.

"Smells divine, Agatha," Charles boomed, pulling out his chair at the head of the table. "Need a good supper after today. The shop was absolute madness." He let out a low whistle. "And a bloody fine cottage pie this looks to be."

"I do say I'm rather pleased how it turned out," Agatha admitted with a chuckle as she sat down across from Charles.

Fredrick cut a large piece for himself. "Better even than Mrs. Hargraves pie, Auntie."

"Oh that Mrs. Hargrave." Agatha set down her fork just as Julia shot Frederick a glare from across the table. "Turning down my offer to help her with Vanessa's debut gown because she thinks my hemming is a bit 'dated.' I know those were that spoiled tart's words! Saints only knows why she bows to that girl."

"Now, no need to fuss, Agatha," Charles interjected between chews. "I'm sure Florence meant no harm by it. You've both gotten on for years now. The Hargraves are a well-minded family."

"Ah, but you've spoken some ill words yourself, Da," Frederick pointed out, waving his fork. "Pub talk counts, too."

"Are you calling me a liar?" Charles held a hand over his heart in feigned hurt. "My own son, even! Oh, who could've spread such wicked lies about my name? Oh, saints forgive me!"

Julia snickered, but her aunt's glare reminded her it was unbecoming to do so. George, meanwhile, continued eating his food in silence.

"I never did care for that daughter of hers," Agatha continued. "Her voice is very disagreeable. Shame such a pretty face gone to waste. It's no wonder her mother held back her debut this season." Agatha dabbed the corner of her mouth with her napkin. "Speaking of which, Charles, perhaps Julia shall accompany me to see Mrs. Carraway tomorrow? I think it would be well for her to introduce herself now that she's sixteen and on the cusp of womanhood. Mrs. Carraway did a fine job with the Bryson and Pembleton girls. Their debuts were simply splendid."

Julia's breath caught in her throat. Her eyes darted to her father, but his face was unreadable.

"A bit early, don't you think, Agatha? Debuts aren't until eighteen. I want Jules to focus on her studies. She needs to be gettin' her marks up."

Julia avoided her father's gaze. Sure, her grades weren't *remarkable*, but she could hardly be blamed for slogging through such boring studies day after day.

Good marks only matter if you know what you want to use them for, she almost said, but kept the thought to herself.

"Nonsense," Agatha huffed. "Only the wealthiest and brightest get entry into finishing schools and the key is to prep as early as possible. Mary and I began prepping when we were sixteen. I'd have never met Albert otherwise, I'm sure." Her eyes glinted with a mixture of pride and sadness at the mention of her late husband.

Julia kept her head low and took another bite of cottage pie. It was a certain kind of cruelness for her aunt to have done everything right—finishing school, marrying a well off solicitor from Lordhaven—only to lose it all to the whimsy of disease and find herself in the countryside with children she couldn't have and a husband that wasn't hers. Julia often wondered if her aunt ever resented her sister, Mary, for turning Agatha's grief and widowhood into an opportunity to leave her own motherhood behind.

"In any case," Agatha continued, "one never knows who may stop into Temmings on their way to Lordhaven or Presdale. Best to be prepared, I say."

"But no one ever stops in Temmings anymore," George finally piped in. "That stupid hare cursed us all."

"George, manners," Charles warned.

"It's true, Da! No one interesting ever comes to Temmings. They're too scared."

Silence fell over the table. Frederick returned his attention to his cottage pie. Charles and Aunt Agatha exchanged a look Julia couldn't decipher.

Finally, Frederick broke into a chuckle. "So, are we just going to believe there really are mad hunters, monsters, and the like out there, then? Hiding in the forest, waiting to pick us off for sport and stop Jules from gettin' a husband?"

"Shut up, Fred!" Julia snapped.

"*Enough* you two," Charles bellowed. "I won't be having that kind of talk at this table. This is a sensible, saintly household and we behave as such; do I make myself clear?"

"Agreed. See, Charles? Clearly there is still much work that needs to be done." Agatha cast a withering glance in Julia's direction. "A young lady needs proper guidance, not the influence of her rowdy brothers. When the social season ends in Lordhaven, it would be ideal to have Julia attend etiquette training with Mrs. Carraway. This way she can secure a recommendation to attend Fairview in the spring. I'll arrange introductions tomorrow."

Charles sighed, caught between two battles and the waning chance of enjoying his cottage pie. "Agatha, we've been over this. We haven't the means to pay for finishing school. Julia will continue her education at Elmwood and when she graduates, she'll debut with the other girls during Maiden's Day."

Agatha scoffed. "Elmswood certainly won't give her the skillset to keep a home or prepare for the social season. She wouldn't last a minute in Lordhaven. The girl can barely manage a running stich."

Julia rolled her eyes and took a bite of pie. "Neither can Fredrick, but he wasn't suddenly outcast when he turned eighteen."

"Actually, all Halcyonion boys take a secret swordsmanship test at eighttee—" Frederick replied before getting a swift kick to the shin under the table from his sister.

Agatha's gaze cut across the table at Julia. "If you learn nothing else, dear, understand society respects those who respect themselves." Her painted lip upturned into a sneer as her attention swept to Frederick. "Make no mistake, there's a factory line waiting for both of you if you feel so inclined to stand side by side."

Charles cleared his throat loud enough to draw all eyes to him. "Julia's right, Agatha. What if she doesn't aspire for such high living in Lordhaven? Mary found peace here in Temmings."

"Mary found what she needed," Agatha quipped. "But as we all know, needs can be very fickle things."

Several agonizing seconds passed before Charles finally spoke again.

"Fine. George, you'll need to tend to your sister's chores tomorrow afternoon so she can prepare herself. She'll help you with yours the next day as is fair. Frederick and I will be taking the train to Bresbin tomorrow, but we'll be back by sundown."

Julia's gaze shifted between her aunt and her father. They carried on as if her life was no more than a garment to be handed off when the time was right. As if she didn't have a say in the matter at all.

"I'm sorry, Auntie, I do appreciate your help, really." Julia set down her fork, plastering on a sweet smile. "But I won't need to see Mrs. Carraway tomorrow."

"What is this now?" Her aunt's tone hovered dangerously close to a warning. "All well-minded ladies start their social training at sixteen. Finishing schools hardly ever accept anyone without it. Besides, Mrs. Carraway so rarely offers assistance to poor girls, may the saints bless us with her charity."

"I know, but I want to travel when I turn eighteen. See the world, and, I dunno, maybe take on an apprenticeship." The mask continued to hold, pretty and proper. "We'll be saving a lot of money if I don't debut, and Mum did the same thing when she turned eighteen."

No one spoke. Julia was certain her flagrant boldness would be met with equally swift disapproval.

To her surprise, her father said nothing. Her aunt, while splotchy with anger, held her tongue. Neither of them met her gaze.

"Da?"

"Julia, we talked about this already." Charles kept his voice even, but Julia sensed the tension beneath the surface. "Unless you intend to graduate from Penrose College as a traveling nurse like your mum, with sterling that I know for a fact you don't have, there is absolutely no point galivanting around Halcyon like some highborn on holiday. Your mum traveled to study her craft, not to laze about aimlessly. You're going to debut and find a respectable husband or be taken on as a nanny or seamstress."

Julia lifted her chin. "Mum would let me take on an apprenticeship."

"Your mother isn't here right now so this discussion is done. I'll speak to her about it when she eventually returns."

"Da," George interrupted, surprising everyone. "Isn't Mum returning soon? That's what you said her last letter said. That she'd be return before Harvestgrain starts. And summer is almost over ..."

"Don't you worry, scout," Charles replied with an air of nonchalance, returning to his pie. "Your mum will be returning as soon as she can. She still has patients to treat in Bronwen. Scarlet lung is breaking out nasty there, it is."

A brittle smile hung on Frederick's lips. "Two years now, Da ..." He shook his head. "That practically qualifies her for sainthood."

"Oi, you watch your tongue," Charles warned with a pointed finger. "Your mum is doing wonderful and important work helping those suffering from the outbreak. Not everyone is fortunate enough to have Lordhaven's modern hospitals at their disposal."

"But she hasn't visited once," Frederick retorted. "We haven't seen her since Uncle Arden died. She's a traveling nurse with a family, not the bloody vicaress. It's not fair."

Charles slammed down his fork.

"Don't be a child, Frederick," he snapped. "You've plenty family right here. How's it look to your brother and sister to whine over all this coddling? Hmm? You're nearly nineteen. Act like it."

"Sorry, Da." Frederick resumed eating but refused to look at anyone.

Julia spun her fork between her fingers, prepared for it to end at that, when George suddenly spoke up. "Is Mum too scared to return home because of the duskborn?"

Charles stopped eating. "George, what did you say?"

Julia stopped spinning her fork, her breath caught in her throat.

No no no no no.

"Is she afraid of the duskborn? That's what the older boys at school said took Billie, but it's not true. Jules and I saw him. There's no dusk—"

"Saw who?"

"Billie. In the for—" But he realized his mistake too late. Julia didn't need to look over at the end of the table to feel her father's gaze burning right through her.

"Julia, did you and George go into the forest?"

"No, Da, never."

"What have I told you both about going near there?"

"Da, I swear we didn't—" but one look at George and the lie was clear. His glassy eyes all but spelt out his guilt. Charles looked from him back to Julia.

"I just wanted to get Billie back, Da ..."

"Shut *up*, George!"

"That's it!" Charles roared, slamming his fist down on the table, "I will *not* tolerate the disrespect and lies at this table!" He shot a seething glare at Julia and George. "Both of you, go clean yourselves for bed. You're done with this meal."

"Fine." Julia pushed back from the table, her chair scrapping against the floor. She stormed up the stairs and fell back on her bed, muffling a scream with her pillow. Tears clouded her vision, but she dug her fingers into her pillow to stifle their fall.

"We should run away one day," Emily once told her when they were thirteen. *"Make them miss us."* The memory of laying on Emily's bed, bodies pressed close as they read fables and talked about vanishing and secrets stirred a yearning for the quiet of those simple afternoons.

Maybe she was right. I don't need Da or Auntie or Mum.

"Jules?"

George stood in the doorway, his face solemn. Julia propped herself up on her elbows. "What?"

"I-I'm sorry. I didn't mean.... I just—"

"Well, spit it out then. You had no trouble talking downstairs." When George said nothing, she groaned and rolled over. "Just leave me alone. I swear you're so damn annoying sometimes."

The bed opposite hers creaked beneath George's weight.

"I'm sorry," he whispered as he dug at his cuticles. "Really. I didn't mean to rat you out like that. I just thought that Mum—"

"I *said* I don't care."

George was silent for several seconds.

"Jules, why won't Mum come home?"

Julia's breath caught in her throat. Memories drifted before her like phantoms: the days her mother spent in bed without bathing; the vitality she had when scarlet lung called her away for work; the letters her mother wrote that sent her love but never a return date; her aunt's prolonged stay after Uncle Arden's death.

She didn't hate her mother. At least hate didn't feel like the right word. Maybe it was because she was old enough to remember her before her mask had slipped, before George was born and it cracked into tiny pieces too small to pick up and put back together. When her mother still showered brilliant smiles and kind laughter on her and Frederick. It was a rosy illusion to look back on. But what good had that done? Knowing the truth—that her mother loved her—had only hurt more. Because it meant sometimes loving someone wasn't enough. That sometimes, the ones you loved most would never be enough.

"Jules?"

As long as the mask doesn't fall, no one gets hurt.

Julia sat upright but kept her eyes trained on her feet, unable to meet George's eyes.

"She changed her mind."

"What?"

"Never mind."

Julia disappeared behind the changing partition next to her bed. She slipped out of her day dress and shimmied on her favorite dress, a dark green empire waist that swirled around her ankles. It had been her sole birthday present last year, and she cherished how it made her feel like a highborn from Lordhaven about to attend a ball.

"Jules, what are you doing?"

Julia ignored him. She opened their shared closet and lifted the loose floorboard near the back. Tucked away were her treasures, including a pot of red balm Martha had stolen for her during an outing to the market last month. She rubbed a pinch on each cheek and dabbed her lips.

"I'm meeting some friends, but you better not say anything. You owe me one and I need out of this house for a bit."

"But, Da—"

"It's fine. He never apologizes first, remember? And Auntie retires early. She won't meddle. Not when Da is right pissed." Julia popped out from behind the screen and slid into her flats. "So thanks for that I guess."

She opened the window and, satisfied no one was on the street, threw over one leg, then the other. Below was a stack of crates filled with wood Frederick and Charles had chopped just the other day.

She lowered herself down onto the stack with a quiet thud and slipped away into the night, never looking back.

5

—◆—

TOBIAS

"**M**ISSING:** Avery McDonall, Male, 45. Last seen at the Golden Crown Gambling Club. Please report any sighting to the City Watch. **REWARD:** 10,000 sterlings." – *Missing persons poster, the North Rim, Lordhaven*

In the shadow of St. Wyndolyn Tower, Tobias hoisted himself onto the third-floor balcony of the abandoned Wimberly Mansion.

Half torn advertisements and graffiti plastered the faded brick exterior. Inside, just beyond glassless windows, the muffled voices of squatters deep in their hollium dreams echoed in a chorus of addiction.

Ezra stood at the mildew-stained guardrail as Tobias approached. The dusky shadows hid his expression, but when Ezra dropped his hand from his mouth his thumb nail was down to the quick.

"Oi, what's got you?" Tobias asked.

Ezra nodded to the street below. "I, uh, think we may have a slight problem."

Tobias followed Ezra's gaze to Peddler's Bridge, the entrance to the North Rim. Although they didn't stand out at first, Tobias eventually noticed two men leaning against the spires on either side of the bridge. But it was the imposing, arm-length fishhooks hanging from their belts that made Tobias's stomach turn.

"What are Seadevils doing there?"

"Well, it *is* their territory...."

"You know what I mean," Tobias said, gently smacking Ezra's arm. "They've never patrolled this openly before. You sure you got the request right?"

" 'Course I did. Have I led you wrong yet?"

Tobias rolled his eyes. "You think Tavia got in okay?"

"Um, about that." Ezra scratched the back of his neck. "Tavia's not coming tonight."

"What you mean?"

"Well, you know how she's been lately. All priss and out of sorts, right? Stomping around base, slamming doors. Absolute menace really. And we, um, just didn't see eye to eye this morning, is all."

Tobias's eyes narrowed. "What'd you do?"

"You know, it's that kind of attitude that's really hurtful, mate."

"Ezra, I swear to the fucking saints, I will literally push you off this balcony right now."

"Fine, all right," Ezra groaned. "I may have mentioned at breakfast that Rhody sent word she'd be back 'round port soon."

Tobias rubbed his face and groaned.

"Ugh, you idiot!"

"I know, I know I'm the twat and it's a bit too soon, but I'm really not to blame here, Toby. Rhody's the one that went and pissed all over Tavia's feelings and ran out to sea on her. I'm just an innocent bystander. They're both my mates. I can't just *not* talk to one of 'em"

"Right," Tobias snapped, "but you don't piss off the one that's on land year-round and who lures in the marks that help us all get paid."

"That's a fair point. But listen, it's fine! We don't need her anyway. We can still make it into the Rim."

Tobias let out a long sigh. "Is this when I'm supposed to pray?"

Ezra slung his arm around Tobias's shoulders, his skull and coin hand tattoo a mirror of Tobias's own. "We can take Smithy's tunnel. He owes me a favor anyway. See? No harm, no foul."

Tobias burst into laughter. Only when Ezra's face remained unchanged did Tobias's laughter wilt. "Bloody hell, you're serious."

Ezra shrugged. "Smithy's a changed fellow. Right solid in the head now."

"He tried to hack my arm off last time," Tobias balked. "My *arm*."

"Eh, he was just cross is all. His lass was being difficult with him back then. Bad time and place."

"He's a *nutter*, Ez. The drink and tar salts and honey and saints knows what else have scrambled whatever crumb of mind his mum gave him."

Ezra sighed. "Look, I know it seems bad but he runs almost all the tunnels in the city. We can get in and get back out without the Seadevils even smellin' us." He looked out across the horizon to a city tinged in smoke and shadow.

"Deal was to be at Burrows College by midnight. If we're gonna do this, we gotta go now."

In the distance, a bell tolled the eighth hour. Tobias's weary gaze fell on Peddler's Bridge. He didn't like the Seadevils roaming the area, hooks at the ready. He'd seen a glimpse of one poor bastard on the wrong side of a Seadevil hook—a runt of the Barrel Boys—and it was enough to make him retch on the spot. But a two-way cut was larger than three. He took a deep breath and sighed.

Three thousand sterlings away from freedom.

"All right, I'm in."

"There he is!" Ezra cheered, mock punching Tobias's shoulder.

"And if I get bloody hacked to bits because Smithy thinks the moon is too bright, my spirit will hunt you down in the Infernal Plains."

"Deal," Ezra said with a wink.

The pair moved with light footwork down the balcony to a second-floor window, jumping across to the first floor door canopy and down again until they were in the tangled, overgrown remains of the once brilliant mansion gardens. Overhead, purplish-blue bled through the rose gold of sunset as nightfall grasped the sky.

Once outside the gardens, they slipped into the crowd of passersby, taking care to keep beside carriages that blocked them from the view of the Seadevils posted at the bridge. After a couple blocks, they slipped down a narrow alley sandwiched between a pub reeking of boiled meat and cigar smoke, and a closed cartography shop. A single gas lamp illuminated the shop's side door.

"You sure about this?" Tobias whispered.

"Trust me, it'll be fine" Ezra replied. "Smithy's our best way past the spotters. Just play nice and we'll be to the Rim in no time."

"Easy for you to—" Tobias was cut off by the groan of a swinging door on old hinges. A boy no more than nine or ten stood in the doorway with dark curly hair and a scowl.

"Smithy in?" Ezra asked.

"Who're you?"

"Tell him Ezra Molyns and Tobias Flemming are here."

The boy slammed the door in Ezra's face.

"Oi!" Ezra pounded on the door. "The little twat just left!"

"Pft, has the right idea ..." Tobias grumbled, shoving his hands in his pockets.

Several minutes later, the boy reappeared in the doorway. "Smithy'll see you. Head straight back."

Ezra glared at the boy as he walked past, but the boy ignored him. The backroom of Smithy's shop was crammed floor to ceiling with half opened crates the world over, bundles of maps, untranslated atlases, and reams of blank scrolls. Partially filled inkwells were strewn across every table, and the stale reek of ink, kell smoke, and paper permeated the stale air.

The boy brushed past them and sat down at a small desk. He dipped his quill in a blue glass inkwell and resumed his task in silence. On the other side of the room, a dwarven boulder of a man looked up from a map of the Avalon Isles sprawled halfway down his desk.

"Aye, whatta surprise we have here!" He removed his magnifier glasses and slid off his stool with an audible thud. "What're you lads doin' around at a time like this? Shop's closed Imma afraid."

Ezra gave a short wave. "Just comin' round to say hello." He elbowed Tobias. "Ain't that right, Tobias?"

"Mhmm."

Ezra nodded towards the boy at the desk. "Got yourself some new help, Smithy? A real delight."

"Aye, Bram's been here nearly a month now." Tobias noticed the boy stiffen under Smithy's gaze but said nothing. "Good with the quill and quick on the trace, that one. Me hands be givin' me a terrible time lately. Bloody rain only makes it worse." He pulled out a flask from his vest pocket and took a swig.

"Got some runts of me own runnin' around this blasted rathole of a city but, eh, not worth shakin' trees for honey. Bram here came from Chapman House, just like you lads."

Tobias's stomach clenched at the mention of their old orphanage. Home of misery and free labor.

"Right, cheers. Anyway," Ezra said, edging away from the topic. "We wanted to head through the tunnels. Got some business in the Rim tonight."

"Oh?" A single bushy grey brow arched upwards. Smithy took another swig from his flask and let out a loud belch. He nodded towards Tobias. "One of Marcellus's boys is like one of me own. How's the ol' bastard doin' these days?"

"Good, good," Ezra interjected. "Keeping busy. Says we may be ready soon to get bigger marks."

Tobias cleared his throat. "Sorry Smithy, but we really gotta run. Best leave before—"

Smithy slammed his fist onto his desk. The noise ripped through the shop with a brute viciousness. Tobias and Ezra both flinched. Even Bram paused in his work, electing to remain perfectly still. Smithy's bloodshot gaze held Tobias's for several seconds. Tobias never once looked away, whether out of fear or defiance he wasn't sure, but a cold sweat pooled on the back of his neck as the taut silence held his throat.

Then, as if a candle was blown out behind his eyes, all anger dissipated from Smithy's face and he belted out a hearty laugh.

"Right then, go on, get at it! But be wary ... Word is a lass was snatched straight off the street the other night. And not by no person. A *beast* they say." Smithy flashed a checkered smile. "Keep your wits about you, lads. Oh, and tell Kempsey when you see him the tiger's stripes are blue."

Tobias and Ezra exchanged glances. They quickly skirted around Smithy's desk and down the narrow staircase into the cellar. Behind the single door was a hatch embedded into the floor. Ezra leaned down and lifted it, revealing a tunnel illuminated just enough to see a finger or two ahead.

"Ladies first," Tobias grinned.

"And that's precisely who'll I'll be seeing first, so thank you."

Ezra swung his legs over the side and jumped down into the tunnel. Tobias made the short leap next. Just as he landed, Smithy appeared above them like a crooked god. His beard lay flat across his barrel of a stomach as he squatted down.

"The Rim's on alert since the Seadevils showed up, so be quick about it." He squinted into the dimly lit tunnel. "And if any spotters show up, this door ain't openin', got it? Cry and scream all you bloody want, it makes not a lick of difference to me. Saints blessings, lads."

The tunnel door slammed shut above them.

6

TOBIAS

"Careful of them Green Coats. Of all the gangs, they understand addiction best. The North Rim was a stockyard before they came with flashy ideas and hollium profits. Word is if you lean close, you can still smell blood in the bricks. But lean too close and you'll be smellin' your own." *– Johnie Ellis, letter to Harry Thornton, undated*

The tang of wet earth and snake oil permeated the dead air.

"Let's get on with it then." Ezra led the way. Tobias followed close behind, but his thoughts were worlds away, imagining the wanted posters that one day would show his face crudely drawn beside that of a blood thirsty beast.

"You're fouler than usual," Ezra said. "Everything all right?"

"Fine."

A chuckle in the dark. "Don't tell me that bit about the beast got your knickers soaked through."

"What? No, 'course not. It's just some pub tale anyway."

"I dunno. There's plenty of terrors prowling the Parlor District."

"Aye, and they're all drunks or peddlers. Don't be stupid, Ez."

"But can you imagine? A saint's honest beast like in the stories? Probably just another hairy brute like we saw at the carny show last year. You remember that one? Bloody seven feet tall?" Ezra chuckled, but Tobias said nothing as Hilda's voice wormed through his ears. *Think those dreams are just night terrors?*

He swallowed hard, willing down the nausea and panic bubbling in his stomach. What if there were others, worse off than him, hunting the streets of Lordhaven like lone wolves and killing people for food? No, he couldn't think like that.

I'm not sick. I'm not sick. I'm not sick.

Tobias cleared his throat. "It's probably just some drunk perv creepin' around in the shadows."

"Could be. Rather boring though." Ezra stopped and pointed up. "Oi, we're here."

A crude, makeshift sign read "DUNLY STRIT" on the left side of the tunnel. Beside it, a short ladder with dented side rails and missing treads was affixed to the wall. Ezra climbed up first and slowly opened the door above him. A faint yellowish glow cut across his eyes and nose. He motioned for Tobias to follow.

When Ezra was halfway out of the hole, a door swung open. A bald man clad in a tailored green vest and black trousers walked in and leveled a pistol at Ezra's head. Tobias froze, catching a momentary glint from the metal surface.

"What is the color of a tiger's stripes?" the man asked.

"B-Bla—"

"BLUE!" Tobias shouted from the hole.

The man peered around Ezra and locked eyes with Tobias, as if just noticing he was there. The pistol remained trained on Ezra.

"The tiger's stripes are blue," Tobias stammered.

Kempsey stored his pistol and stepped aside. "Welcome to the Rim, lads."

The boys hurried past him and found themselves in a long hallway. The thick parlay of voices and rattle of throwing dice filled the hall.

"I recommend you two make yourselves scarce. The Hound's Club is no place for children."

"Will you be 'round?" asked Ezra, a hint of shakiness still lingering in his voice. "So we can come back through the tunnel?"

Kempsey shot him a steely glare. Tobias grabbed Ezra's arm.

"Come on, let's go," Tobias urged beneath his breath.

They hugged the back walls of the Hound's Club until they spotted a side door for the kitchens. Leaving the tipsy patrons and betting theatres behind, they weaved past the confused waiters and sweaty line cooks and scampered out the exit door.

Once they were outside, Tobias sucked in a lungful of air.

"I'm *never* listening to you again."

Ezra's nerves boiled over into infectious laughter. "Bloody hell, you were brilliant, Toby! Saints, I've had some run ins before but that was ..." He laughed again and shook his head in disbelief. "Tavia's gonna piss herself when I tell her. She'll be so jealous she missed out."

"Twenty sterling you lose a finger."

Ezra mulled it over. "Aye, probably should give her another day. Maybe two. You think two?"

"Over there." Tobias nodded towards Crown Street, the main vein that snaked through the heart of the North Rim. "The Golden Queen has two Seadevils out front. The Pearl's got two, no, one spotter at the corner." He shifted his gaze to Peddler's Bridge. "All clear on the south end. But getting to Burrows might be a problem."

"Not if we grab a winner," Ezra said with a smirk.

"And you know who usually made that easier?"

Ezra rolled his eyes.

"Let's hope the drink is strong tonight."

The sharp smell of sweat, kell smoke, and perfume clung to the Rim like shadows. Cabbies with doorless, open carriages ferrying drunks and poor Burrows students ambled alongside curtained, lacquered carriages seen most often in the posh Garden District. Sidewalks teemed with young highborns, rosy cheeked from too much liquor, and red-lipped sallies slung on their arms, corsets sinched and lace fans fighting desperately to preserve well drawn makeup against the muggy night. Snake oil lamps lined the streets like stars, lending the Rim a golden, dreamy quality. It was easy to lose oneself in the sea of kitten houses and coin parlors. The promise of easy sterling and even easier pleasures was irresistible.

It was a dream inevitably dulled for Tobias after hunting marks night after night. Coin parlors let only the best paying patrons win, sallies only flocked to those who were as handsome as their family carriages, and pubs saved the strong ale for the first glass and watered down the rest. And yet a small part of him still wanted to believe in the Rim's illusion of pomp and ease.

Suddenly, a short man in his late twenties stepped out of pub and nearly collided with Tobias. He stumbled back and eyed Tobias over.

"Do I know you?" he stammered.

"Oi, it's me, from the other night," Tobias replied with practiced ease. Ezra quietly separated from the pair and disappeared down a nearby alleyway. As he rounded the corner, he pulled out a billystick hidden in his waistband.

"From the other night?" The man rubbed his prickly chin and mulled through his booze-soaked memories. "You look pretty young though."

Tobias slung his arm over the man. "You know, William? William Daugherty? Listen, don't trouble yourself. You played a round of Cradle with my brother's mates. Come join us at the flat. It's just a row over."

"Ah, with the mates …" The man bubbled with laughter. "Yes, we played Cradle …"

When Tobias and his companion were nearly upon the alleyway Ezra was hiding in, a woman's hand shot out from the crowd and grabbed the man's arm. "Ellis, wait, you're not really leaving, are you?"

Tobias came face to face with a petite ebony doll of a woman in a dark red corset and layered skirts. Her locs were woven into a onyx black crown dotted with pearls.

Her dark eyes locked with Tobias's. "And just where were you running off to with my Ellis?"

Ellis looked between the woman and Tobias.

"You know him, Marjory?"

"No better than you do." Marjory folded her arms. "Now get back to the table, Ellis. You promised to take me by the Emperium after this, remember? Their shadow theatre simply can't be missed."

"Ah, yes, yes." Ellis slipped from Tobia's grasp and held out his arm to Marjory. She led him back into the coin parlor without a second glance behind her.

"Dammit." Tobias ran his hand through his curls. He dipped into the alleyway and motioned for Ezra to follow him.

"What happened? He was right there!"

"His date happened," Tobias grumbled. "Let's just keep looking."

As Tobias scanned the crowd, he caught the eye of a tall, stone-faced man standing near the entrance to Haight Kitts, a boisterous pub across the way. He held Tobias's gaze for a breath too long, his scowl deepening. Tobias broke contact first, noting the large silver hook hanging on the man's beltloop.

"Head to Red Row," Tobias muttered beneath his breath.

Ezra didn't need to be told twice. They wove in between passersby, careful to keep each other in their sights, on their way deeper into the Rim. Eventually they came upon the bend at the end of Crown Street and into a quieter area free of pubs and coin parlors.

Red Row was notorious for its kitten houses, lodgings of ill—and pleasurable—repute marked by red cat statues in their windows. None was more famous than Vulpine, the oldest and most exclusive kitten house on the row. Nestled at the end of Crown Street, it was five stories of heavily curtained windows and no signage. Only a single black door marked it as the Vulpine. Tobias had heard stories of its member-only offerings, and each story was more outlandish and depraved than the last.

"Oi, over there. At Vulpine. Poor bastard can't get in."

A bearded man dressed in a patchwork jacket and frayed trousers was pointing and yelling at a broad shoulder gentleman in a burgundy vest. The latter stood behind a podium at the door with a bored expression on his face.

"My turn. Here, take this." Ezra handed Tobias his billystick. "Try not to miss, eh?"

"Try not to piss everyone off."

Ezra crossed the street as Tobias continued and abruptly turned down a darkened alleyway. He hid behind a pair of bins and waited.

"Da!" He heard Ezra exclaim. "There you are. How'd you get over here?"

The bearded man gave a startled response, but Tobias didn't catch Ezra's reply. A few minutes passed. Tobias's heartbeat pulsed in his ears.

"—sorry to trouble you," he heard Ezra say.

A soft chuckle, like summer rain. "Lost, perhaps?" A woman's voice. "This is a proper establishment."

"Yes, I did see the cat statue in your window ..."

"Get him home." A deep voice. The burly guard.

Footsteps coming up the way.

"It'll be grand. Lots of sallies. Hollium, too. Pipes of it."

"Down the honey road ..." the bearded man sung off pitch. "Down the honey road, sweetest you'll ever know ..."

"Aye, right down here," Ezra said.

Tobias watched the pair walk past him. A second later, he sprung up from his hiding spot and lobbed the back of the man's head with the billystick. The man stumbled as if surprised, then collapsed on the ground.

Tobias and Ezra each took a pocket.

"Aces, got our carriage money!" Tobias held up a coin purse, beaming. Ezra looked grim. He held up a residency card.

"I think we got a slummer."

Tobia's face fell. "What?" He reached for the card and turned it askance to catch the lamplight from the street.

It was a residency card for one George Cranton, age 32, married, and a certified resident of Stanton Trough, Lordhaven, Halcyon.

"Bloody hell, he's from Stanton Trough. That's in the Garden District. He's a damn highborn."

Ezra frowned. "He looks like a grifter from a rough night at Higdin's. Fooled me."

"That's the point." Tobias shoved the residency card into his pocket. "Forget it. I'll burn it later. Let's just hail a carriage and get him to Burrows. The sooner the better."

"And what happens when the City Watch come knocking on doors looking for him? Burrows will clamp up and Marcellus will have our arses."

"They won't have to know," Tobias countered, throwing Cranton's left arm over his shoulder. "We keep the residency card and Burrows keeps the body. By the time he's reported missing, he'll be bits in the Dorne anyway. They won't keep him past tonight if they're smart."

Ezra took Cranton's other arm and the two lifted him up.

"He's heavier than he looks," Ezra said through gritted teeth. They made it back onto the street and hailed down a carriage. The burly guard from Vulpine watched them but made no move to intervene. As were most guards in the Rim, he was paid well enough to keep his mouth shut to the happenings outside.

The carriage driver pulled on his horses' reigns and stopped beside the trio. Tobias spoke up first.

"Can you help us, sir? Need to head to Burrows Medical College. My mate's da here had a bit too much drink and dice tonight."

The coachman raised a brow. "He's not sick is he?"

"No, sir," the boys replied in unison.

"Fine. Fifteen sterlings. Twenty-five if he pukes."

Tobias paid him from Cranton's purse and squeezed into the back of the carriage with Ezra and Cranton. Not fifteen minutes later, they came to a halt in front of Burrows Medical College.

It was a modest campus nestled on the block between Meris Street and Aughton Way. On the side of the building was a small door partially hidden from view by surrounding shrubbery.

Ezra knocked twice rapidly, waited a moment, then knocked a third time. A few seconds later, the door cutout slid open and a pair of bespectacled brown eyes peered down at them.

"State your business."

"We have replenishments for the theatre."

The cutout slid shut. A fourth year in a white lab coat and wire framed glasses opened the door. Two larger men in matching black shirts and pants took Cranton from the pair. One opened Cranton's mouth and eyes while the other inspected his arms, hands, and neck.

After the examination, one of the men said, "Knot on the back of his head, but he checks out." The student nodded. He reached into his jacket and held out a burlap pouch. "Here you are then. A hundred sterling."

"The mark was for two and a quarter!" Ezra countered.

"And you would've had the full reward if you'd hit him a little less hard. He's needed tonight and we can't do much with that swelling."

Tobias nudged Ezra. "Let's just take it. We'll grab Tavia next time, eh?" Ezra contemplated a moment then grabbed the pouch from the fourth year's outstretched hand.

"Bloody crooks," he muttered loud enough for everyone to hear. The fourth year huffed and shut the door. Ezra opened the pouch and poured half into Tobias's hands. A golden phoenix was emblazoned on each side.

"Try not to spend it all in one place."

Tobias closed his fists around the coins and let their cold edges bite into his palm. Bodies in one hand, sterling into another. A vicious cycle for an insatiable garden. He tucked the sterlings into the coin purse sewn into the waist of his trousers.

"You up for a little celebration? Saved you some of Melda's meat pies from breakfast this morning. We can roast 'em up back at base."

Tobias recalled Hilda's steely gaze and the ropeburn on his wrists. How long would it take for the others to catch wind of his restless nights? And what if his nightmares got worse? What happened if his body began to change and he couldn't stop it?

What if, what if, what if.

"Sorry mate, I promised Lucy I'd read some stories with her tonight. I'll stop by base tomorrow though."

"Holding you to that."

Tobias waived Ezra off and then disappeared back into the Rim, embracing the garden's illusion if only for a moment longer.

7

JULIA

The Gafton Manor, surpassed in size only by the governor's mansion, perched on a hill overlooking the market square.

Julia had long dreamed of living in such a large house. What must it have been like to wake up each morning with breakfast ready, coffers full of sterling, and the day free of obligation other than one's own choosing.

It was rumored Judge Loch Gafton kept such a fine residence because the solicitor bribes outside of Temmings paid so well—far more than a judge's pittance—and Julia didn't blame him. Who wouldn't want to come home to a grand manor? She pushed open the cool iron bars of the gate, careful to close it behind her, and hurriedly made her way across the cobbled pathway leading to the front door.

A short gentleman with a curled mustache and a pressed navy jacket and gold piped trousers opened the door. A white hand towel was slung over his right arm.

"Ah, more guests for young Master Gafton, I presume?" Before Julia could answer, the man ushered her inside. "Right this way, miss. Any preferred refreshments for the evening?"

"Uh, tonic water please. With lemon." During her only visit to Lordhaven before Uncle Arden fell ill, she'd overheard a finely dressed woman order one at a dress shop her aunt frequented. The butler nodded and replied, "A fine choice, miss. The other guests are right through here."

The butler led her to a large seating room with fifteen-foot high ceilings and cast in the golden glow of snakelight. Snake oil carried a far stronger light than the regular lamp oil the Sheffield's could afford.

An upbeat dandy tune played from a nearby gramophone. Several young people lounged on the fine furniture while some kept to private corners. A few heads turned her way, but interest was soon lost and conversations resumed.

Julia knew most in the room as ninth years from Elmwood, but there were a few she didn't recognize. Amongst them were a handful of older kids that carried a posh air to them, a glossiness the damp fog of Temmings stripped away from locals.

"Julia?"

Standing before her was Martin Gafton. His short, cropped hair, edges finely tapered, framed light brown eyes and high, dark tanned cheekbones.

"Emily mentioned you'd be coming by. I'm happy to see you made it." He flashed his brilliant smile and Julia's stomach fluttered. "Wouldn't be a party without all of the Graces. But I've wondered something. There's only three Graces in the Saint Father's flock but four of you. How's that work?"

Julia smirked. "You tell me."

Was she Kaia of Charm? Sulmara of Beauty? Or Ineva of Creativity? In truth, she and her friends aligned with a different Grace nearly every other day, swayed by their moods and each other's whimsies. It was a game Emily created to tie the four of them together, a special garden for them alone. And it was this shared secret made as children that Julia held like a sacred treasure in her heart, even if somewhere along the way their rosy garden had become a thorn hedge too prickly to cross in either direction.

"We'll be the same Grace, Jules," Emily decreed when they were eleven. *"Look, our names fit together, see? Julia, Emily. Five letters. Only we could be the same person."*

Martin tilted his head back as if assessing her. "Well, Sulmara and Kaia are close guesses. Can you play piano? Flute, perhaps?"

"Don't strain yourself." Julia giggled. "So, is your mum or da around?"

"Mum's upstairs, but she hit the cabinet early, so she won't be up till morning. And Da's out on business. Criminals to pardon and all that."

"He must be very busy then."

Martin shrugged. "Suppose so. But make yourself comfortable. I got some of my mum's good stuff tonight if you can keep a secret." He lifted his glass and winked. "I'll be around if you need me."

As he slipped away to chat up a group of tenth years from the local rugby union, the butler reappeared with a tall glass of fizzling water. A lemon wedge was perched on the rim of the glass.

"Your tonic water with lemon, miss."

"Oh, thank you." Julia took a sip and found the bubbles to be oddly pleasant on her tongue.

Just then, she spotted Emily, Martha, and Dorothy huddled together on a velvet green sofa near the back of the room. Dorothy perched on the lap of a pretty blonde Julia didn't recognize.

"Jules, you made it!" Martha stood and threw her arms around Julia. Her smile stretched from ear to ear and a warm blush tinged her cheeks. "You look simply *marvelous*."

"Already enjoying yourself, then?" Julia said with a raised brow.

Martha brought her finger to her lips and giggled. "Pft, don't be cross, Mum."

A young man seated across from them glanced in Julia's direction. He was near her age, with the same warm brown skin, light brown eyes and high cheekbones as Martin. He watched the pair approach, but his gaze lingered on Martha.

Dorothy blew an air kiss to Julia and reached out and took her glass of tonic water. "Bless your heart, I'm parched."

Julia rolled her eyes and forfeited the glass as she sat down in the only empty seat. Emily linked her arm with Julia's and leaned in close.

"Thank the saints you're here," she whispered, lacing their fingers together. "I was afraid tonight would be dreadfully boring."

"Oi, Jules, I was sitting ther—" but Emily cut Martha off.

"Jules, you know Lucas, don't you? Martin's cousin?" Emily said, gesturing to the young man across from them. She leaned forward, twirling a strand of hair around her finger. "Lucas, didn't you mention earlier you and Martin traveled to Fiore this past spring? You simply must show us the tarentelli. Martha tells me it's *the* dance of the season."

"Well, if the audience demands it." He chuckled and reached out his hand to Martha. "May I have the honor, Miss Malster?"

Martha blushed, all annoyance about her taken seat suddenly forgotten. "Why, yes, I'd love to."

As Lucas led Martha along quick turns and nimble footwork she half laughed, half stumbled through, Dorothy laid her head on top of the blonde girl's.

"Well, maybe now she'll forget about Mr. Harper for a couple weeks," Dorothy said with a sigh. "I swear if I had to hear her pout one more time over him, I was going to drown myself in Lake Promise."

"Trust me, love, your friend doesn't want to tangle with Lucas Gafton," the blonde girl warned in a hushed whisper. "His family winters at Muxford Lodge where my sister works. She heard from another lodge girl he sends out duplicate letters to girls all over the countryside as a pastime for when the summer season comes around." She rolled her eyes and took a sip of Dorothy's stolen tonic water. "He'll only break her heart."

Emily chuckled. "He was never going to be anything serious. Martha just needs a distraction, is all. And look at that." She cocked her head to the side, smirking. "He's doing brilliantly."

"Oi, Em" Julia interjected, "have you seen Harrison?"

Something flickered across Emily's face, but it was gone before Julia could make sense of it. "You're not actually worried about him, are you?"

Julia shrugged. "No reason. I just thought he'd be here, is all."

"Saints, we're at *the* Gafton Manor. It's time to try something new." Her lips curled into a mischievous smile that sent Julia's heart fluttering with its promise. "So, who will it be tonight?"

"Em, come off it. Here?"

"Why not?"

They held each other's gaze with nothing but the thrill of their agelong bride game between them. Something old, something new, something borrowed, something blue, the winner gets a sterling in their shoe.

"Fine," Julia said after a moment's hesitation. "Something borrowed."

Emily's chin tilted ever so slightly upwards. Julia saw the glint behind her eyes. A mirror of her own.

"Deal."

"Have fun with my scraps," Julia teased.

"Jealous, are we?" Emily leaned in close. Too close. "Afraid they'll steal me away?"

Julia wanted to laugh. When had Emily ever belonged to anyone but herself?

"We'll always have each other."

There had been a time before Emily, before Martha, before Dorothy. A time when Julia was a little thing in Frederick's shadow, too scared to venture beyond its confines lest the bullies caught her. But that world had been quiet and colorless.

"Promise?"

"Promise."

Julia grinned and looked out across the room. She caught sight of a tall young man in a navy embellished blazer and the rigid stance one acquired from etiquette classes. He had fair skin smattered with freckles and shaggy red hair cut low on the sides. Her heart fluttered when their eyes met, and he gave her a small nod.

"Well, looks like I'll see you at midnight," Emily said, rising to her feet. Julia followed her line of sight to Donal Verlow, an eleventh year Julia had made out with after cutting class together in early spring. She hadn't spoken much to him since Charity had wormed her way onto his arm, but she had toyed with the idea of rekindling things. Now a small part of her regretted telling Emily about the fling. Donny was supposed to be her plaything to take off the shelf on a whim. A toy that was hers alone.

"Don't forget your souvenir." Emily giggled and grabbed a glass of honey wine from a nearby waiter's tray. And then she was gone, walking through a crowd that seemed to part for her.

Julia grabbed her own glass and downed it in one gulp. Let Emily have her fun with Donny. She would be sure to have a far better story by the end of the night anyway. Julia approached the young man in the blazer once his friends had stepped away.

"First time in Temmings?" she asked.

"No, but it's been quite some time," he replied. "Though I can't say I've seen you here before either."

"Oh, you wouldn't have. I only run in Temmings's top circles. Elite stuff I'm afraid."

"Oh, really?" He chuckled, flashing a charming smile dotted by dimples. "Well, I should say thank you for making an exception for me then." He dipped into a shallow bow. "Daniel Wells." His green eyes slid from her face down to her bosom, then buoyed back to her face. "And may I ask the name of my future sponsor?"

"Julia Sheffield." She reached for another glass of honey wine, emboldened by Daniel's charming smile.

"Are you a friend of my stepsister, Benjamina? I could've sworn I heard her mention you before."

The wine soured on her tongue. Of course she'd be talking to that tart's stepbrother. Why would the universe make anything easy? Surely anything Benjamina, one of the bullies that had kept her tethered to Frederick's shadow all those years ago, mentioned to her terribly handsome stepbrother was slick with snark, but Julia smiled all the same. Daniel would be a distant memory after tonight anyway.

"Of course, Mina is simply the best. Her poetry circles after class are brilliant. Has she read you any?"

"No, she hasn't."

"She's just shy," Julia lied. "But I swear her gift for words is unmatched. She hadn't mentioned her stepbrother would be starting at Elmwood."

"Oh, no I'm not," Daniel replied, almost too quickly. "I attend Moorwick Boy's Academy in Lordhaven." He raised a glass to her. "Perhaps you can visit me next time you're in the city."

A spark caught in her belly. How easy it all was. The thrill of slipping into a fictious life woven from the headiness of bubbling wine and a night rich with rebellion was intoxicating. The fight at dinner felt years, worlds, lifetimes away from her. But the shadows dancing along the manor walls cut at strange angles, crowded like teeth, beckoning her down a hall where the other party goers dared not go.

A shiver crawled up her neck as she hurriedly refocused her attention on Daniel.

"Certainly." She ran a finger along his arm. "You must know so many interesting places. Will you show me?"

"I'd be happy to."

Julia glanced past Daniel. Donny was chatting with Martin Gafton and Marcus Shelby, another tenth year. Her heart began to race.

Where is Emily?

"Shall we carry on in a quieter setting?"

Julia smiled, eager to be rid of the unease grasping at her.

"Of course."

Daniel had merely been a starting point.

Sure, his kisses were nice and he promised to take Julia to Burlington Commons the next time she was in Lordhaven (he'd be waiting a while on that one), but sitting with his

Moorwick Academy cufflink twirling between her fingers at ten o'clock somehow felt like a loss.

He'd been too easy to snare, and even easier to lift off from while they kissed. An hour later and he still hadn't noticed his cufflink was missing.

Emily had been right. This night was turning into a dreadfully boring affair after all. Julia took another sip of wine, her number something or another glass, and looked out at the swell of people. Blazers and polite chatter had at some point between Daniel's mouth on hers and her theft given way to loosened collars and unfiltered whispers.

She didn't see the Graces anywhere, but then again she'd only just surfaced herself.

Suddenly, the music shifted to a bar shanty from Bronwen and Martin was standing in front of her, hand extended. "Will you have this dance with me, Miss Sheffield?"

A heady bliss overcame her. Julia followed Martin out to the dance floor and let the music carry her feet. He slid his hand across her back, pressing her close.

"You're a splendid dancer."

"Liar," she half giggled, half snorted against his neck.

"Am not. None finer in Temmings."

"So not as good as those Lordhaven girls then?" she teased.

"You wound me, Miss Sheffield." His hand dipped to the small of her back. "Perhaps I can make it up to you?"

How boring.

She pulled away to reveal a tight, polite smile. "I'd love that. But you'll have to excuse me for a moment. I must visit the powder room."

"Oh, yes, um, of course. Just down the hall."

She gave him a kiss on the cheek and hurried down the hall. The walls shifted with each step. It crossed her mind that perhaps her drinks may have been stronger than she thought, but then the powder room door was within her sights, and the wooziness was soon forgotten. She slipped inside and locked the door behind her.

She studied her reflection. How lovely her mask looked tonight, rue eyed and pink lipped.

She finger combed her long auburn hair and straightened her dress. Martin would be waiting for her, but it was his party. Surely there was nowhere else for him to go. Her mind drifted to Harrison and his honey brown eyes and full mouth. She already had Daniel's cufflink, so why not have a little fun before midnight?

When she opened the door, she went left to explore the rest of the house. She hadn't seen Harrison on the dance floor, so perhaps he was on the balcony? He had never been much of a crowd pleaser and didn't pretend otherwise. It was one of the things she liked about him. He was entirely different from Daniel, Martin and Donny.

Something new.

A soft moan cut through her thoughts. In her sobering clarity Julia noticed a door partially ajar just up ahead. No lights were on inside, but as she crept closer, she heard a muffled voice groan a familiar name.

"Emily."

The voice was deep and breathy with passion. Or hatred. It was hard to tell when the ground beneath her shifted so much. As she leaned against the wall, she realized she knew that voice. Her mind may not have remembered in that moment, but her subconscious recognized the timber of it, the shape of its pitch. Her stomach roiled with primal energy. Anger was late to reach her, but when it did it was chiseled to a fine point.

Walk away. It's not Harrison.

Julia pushed off the wall. She'd be wrong—surely, she'd be wrong—but still curiosity drove her forward. Just as her fingers grazed the doorknob a hand grabbed her arm and jerked her back.

"There you are, Jules." Dorothy's grip held firm. "I've been looking all over for you. Martin's been asking 'round about you."

"Martin ...?"

"Let's get you some water."

"No, I'm fine." Julia tried pulling her arm back, but Dorothy wouldn't let go. "I need to see—"

"You're drunk, Jules," she said louder than necessary, glancing at the door. "Trust me, you'll want to go back to the party."

She held Julia's face in her hands and her warm touch felt oddly comforting. Julia abated and let Dorothy lead her back to the main room.

She squeezed Dorothy's hand, her voice barely above a whisper. "Dory, where's Emily?"

Dorothy hesitated for a second too long, but Julia didn't catch it.

"She probably stepped out for some air. You know how she is. Flighty and all that."

Julia wanted to argue she knew exactly how Emily was, thank you. That Dorothy only knew what Emily wanted to show her, how it was a joke really, almost pitiful to watch sometimes, but Dorothy had already led her halfway down the hall and Julia's mind wandered off again.

"Sit here."

Julia plopped down on the green cushioned sofa from earlier. Martha broke away from Lucas mid-kiss as Julia sat down.

"Find Harrison, Jules?"

Dorothy leveled a glare at Martha. "Don't be a twat."

"What? You can't keep her secrets forever you know." Martha shrugged. "But fine. Don't let me stop you."

"Piss off," Dorothy hissed, a blush crawling across her cheeks. "And keep your mouth shut for once."

Martha rolled her eyes as Lucas nuzzled her neck. "Aw, don't be cross, Dory. It's a party. We're supposed to be having fun." She snickered and resumed kissing Lucas.

"Dorothy?" Julia stared up at the ornamented ceiling, her arms splayed out on either side of her. "Do you think if I married Martin Gafton I could have a beautiful ceiling like this one?"

Dorothy nestled beside her and handed her a glass of bubbly, pale pink liquid.

Julia downed it in one gulp. "That's not water."

Dorothy smiled. "No, it's not, but tomorrow it's nothing but water until you marry Martin Gafton for his posh ceiling."

"I'd hate that." Julia frowned. "Maybe I'd come to hate this ceiling too."

Dorothy burst into laughter. "You're so bloody awful."

Julia smiled then, her head bubbly and her tongue loose. "The truth is really awful, isn't it?" She grabbed another glass of the pink liquid seated on the table beside her. "But it's a party. Cheers, I guess."

She trained her gaze on Martin. He was in conversation with another brunette, but when his eyes found hers, she knew she had him. A swell of heat rose in her chest as he approached.

"I believe I'm still owed that dance."

If Dorothy protested, Julia didn't hear it because Martin Gafton was sweeping her away in a shambling waltz. When he was close enough to kiss, Julia locked eyes with Emily.

She stood off to the side of the wall, neither near nor far from the hallway Julia had been a short while ago. She was alone, rosy cheeked and beautiful, standing in a lovely pomegranate colored dress. Her face revealed nothing, but it didn't need to. Julia wasn't

Dorothy or Martha. She and Emily didn't need words. She'd seen that look a thousand times before.

What's your next move?

A choice had to be made. Midnight was approaching.

When Julia pressed her mouth against Martin's, her mind was filled with Emily and breathy voices and sharp smiles and jagged shadows. She knew then her souvenir wouldn't be enough. She'd played it safe again. Emily had won. Again. Again and again and again. The thought drove Julia's body closer to Martin's, a sore loser for all to see. For *her* to see.

I hope it hurts you.

When Julia broke away from Martin at the dance's conclusion, the midnight chime echoed through the manor. Julia looked back, but Emily was gone.

The party was over.

8

NATHANIEL

"The divide between Man and Beast lies in the purely human pursuit of perfection and the absolute self." – *Dr. Richard Brendell,* The Principles of Predators

At the tender age of seven, Nathaniel Trevet came to understand kindness and cruelty were not, in fact, so different from each other.

He learned this lesson from his mother, a woman of a quiet disposition and good humor. Born into a highborn family, Priscilla Lethe was well versed in the classic works of Ardalle, Goberd, and Seys. She trained with the celebrated pianist Tullia Rivelli through her teenage years and graduated from Penrose College with honors. Once a Trevet, she often hosted tea for the founding members of the elite Tuss Muss Poets Society for Ladies and even counted the Duke and Duchess of Hetton as close friends.

To Priscilla's delight, her son carried her affinity for learning and fondness for the arts. Looking back, Nathaniel realized this had certainly made her efforts to ease the pain of his grim future far easier. For it was to her and her husband's horror their son had been bestowed with an appearance neither conversation nor charm could hide.

From what Nathaniel could recall, it came down to a matter of proportion—ears too small, jowl askew, eyes beady, nose misshapen, limbs oddly crooked. His health was equally poor; his lungs never held enough air and his joints throbbed most days, worse still when it rained. Some house staff whispered he couldn't possibly be a Trevet, aside from perhaps his father's thick brown hair and his mother's dark blue eyes; others openly suspected he was a fateshifter scorned by Azavith in a deal for magic gone wrong.

Nathaniel didn't know at the time what the word 'burden' meant, but he had felt the weight of the word's presence draped across his hunched shoulders for as long as he could remember. It threatened to break his scrawny neck if he moved, so he rarely did. He read histories and grand stories and studied languages spanning the world in the quiet of his room instead. He reasoned if he could mature into someone who was smart, witty, and well-spoken like his parents then maybe, just maybe, his mother wouldn't look so sad and his father would actually *look* at him. Sometimes he wished he could've called upon the other children he would see playing outside or attend school with them. But as the years wore on, he realized this was never to be. He would be forever surrounded by legions of tutors either too timid or too stern to be considered friends. And so, each birthday he would wish upon his lavishly tiered cake for a baby brother or sister to keep him company in the hallowed halls of Greybriar.

But Priscilla was a delicate creature, often susceptible to fits of utter fatigue. She was in no position to bear another child. The family line needed Nathaniel to be glorious and brilliant and worthy of the Trevet name. And so, one overcast morning, just four days shy of Nathaniel's eighth birthday, Priscilla did as any sound mother of aristocratic position would do for her outcast son.

She sought a tonic.

Shielded in the warmth of the Heathcliff Inn's finest suite, Nathaniel sipped a glass of sherry and privately relished his return to Lordhaven.

Outside his window, five floors beneath, the night was alive with celebration. The Seven Swords Festival was upon the Theatre District once more, celebrating Lordhaven's victory over a long dead empire that had been foolish enough to try and lay claim on the kingdom before anyone could remember. Celebrators packed into the narrow streets below, romping and drunk, migrating towards Eddleton Stage at the district's center. There the march would unfurl into a grand dance at the stage's foot and end with a performance from the traveling troupe, Brivley Yorn, who famously reenacted the siege in heady, comedic splendor until dawn.

Trumpets roared and drums beat feverishly around them as Lordhavians, young and old, clapped and sang into the night.

Nathaniel half-heartedly indulged in the idea of joining them. The whole event was a distasteful affair—there was certainly no disputing that—but somewhere deep down he found the raunchiness of it all somewhat comforting. He retreated from the window and stood in front of the fireplace. Hands in his pockets, his thoughts drifted back to the festival goers trouncing about with bright eyes and rosy smiles. How many would stray from the merriment and find themselves in his sights, alone and wanting, ripe with blood for the taking?

A knock at the door broke Nathaniel from his reverie. His dark blue eyes narrowed. Only one person knew he would be here, and even then, he had lied about the exact time to afford himself some privacy to mull over his next move. He put his drink on the mantle and opened the door.

Standing on the other side was a slim young woman in her early twenties whose smoldering hazel gaze was nearly at level with Nathaniel's. A thick braid of wavy black hair woven with golden ribbon fell across her pale shoulders and tapered down her bosom.

"My, my, Nathaniel Trevet in the flesh at last," she purred as she strode past him into the room. She paused in front of the mantel, eyeing the glass of sherry.

"Good evening to you, as well, Rose."

"I grew bored waiting for you to announce yourself. I wondered if you'd decided to sleep through the last rays of the season." Rose helped herself to a seat on the sofa, her garnet-colored skirts billowing beneath her. "Now do be a dear and pour a lady a glass."

Nathaniel's lips tightened into a thin line. He pulled out a spare glass from the room's cabinetry and poured just enough for Rose to wet her palette.

"So tell me, Nathaniel," she began, taking a sip of sherry, "what is your business in Lordhaven? I figured the air would be far too dirty for your liking after your jaunt through Emismore. Smog hangs on the heat in this city something terrible."

Nathaniel frowned. The air was foul, almost oily. Some trades had taken residence in the Theatre District after operation tariffs in the Iron District proved too expensive to maintain. Coupled with an already bloated population, the once exclusive Theatre District was quickly becoming a scene of overlabored children, poor sewage and backroom hollium markets.

"A change of scenery is pleasant every now and then," he replied, entertaining Rose's snooping with only the least bit of exertion. "The travel did me well."

"I'm certain it did. Perhaps you could tell me about it sometime."

Nathaniel's eyes briefly met hers before returning to the fire. Any longer and she would glean the truth from them, he was certain of it. But now was not the time. Claude was clear in his instructions—the others had to believe he had traveled to Emismore to recruit a new member for the Order of the Boar. He couldn't let the lie unravel now. He had questions of his own for Claude first.

Nathaniel pulled a gold pocket watch from the front of his blue silk vest. The face opened and revealed it to be close to nine. He snapped the watch closed and tucked it back in his breast pocket.

Rose took another sip of her sherry. Madams worth their salt were attuned to the whims of bored gentlemen as sailors were to the tides. He didn't have to wait long for her to take the bait.

"Surely, you must've heard of the new kittens I just plucked from the coast of Obello," she mused. "Even a few from the Charnai tea houses. Why not celebrate your return at the Vulpine instead, hmm?" She traced a slender finger around the rim of her glass and looked up at him with sultry eyes. "Festival blood is always so boozy and thin. You know I carry nothing but the finest."

"I don't doubt it would be a splendid time," Nathaniel replied, striding past her towards the hat rack near the door. "But Claude has summoned me this evening and I must leave now if I'm to be on time."

Rose finished off her sherry. "Ah, there it is." She snapped her fan open and got to her feet.

"Then spare a lady a moment for a story?"

"Rose, I needn't keep him wai—"

"Then I'll skip the dull parts." She closed the distance between them until she was nearly pressed against his chest. She lowered her voice to a whisper.

"Rumor has it a royal was amongst the cadavers used in Dr. Brennan's surgical theatre five nights ago."

"At Penrose College? You're certain?"

"I saw the body myself," Rose replied. "The old coot spared me no more than a glance, but I'm nearly certain it was one of the King's bastards. Blythe or Bliss, something of the sort. Spitting image of daddy dearest. Absolutely impeccable condition for five days dead." She released a long sigh. "A horrid shame how her sale went about. Can you believe I wasn't invited? If I could've gotten my hands on a royal corpse for the Vulpine, saints I could've run half of Red Row out of business. But she was already secured four hands down within the hour." Rose sucked her teeth. "Vultures."

"Oh, how ever will your kitten house recover?" Nathaniel bemoaned with a frown. "Now your patrons will have to contend with measly runaways and honey eaters to satisfy them. Pity."

Rose snapped her fan shut.

"Don't you find it rather odd one of the King's bastards is on a surgical table a region away from her manor?"

"Royals die all the time," Nathaniel replied, slipping into his suit jacket. "It's hardly news."

"Be as it may, it's curious that her half-siblings also happen to have disappeared."

"Disappeared?" Nathaniel said with a raised brow.

Rose nodded. "After visiting the good doctor, I decided to see how far the ripples extended. A death of that sort would hardly go unnoticed during the social season. Minor as she may have been, she was still of royal blood. Suffice to say the girl either never kept a full social card or her family was covering for her whereabouts while they looked for the body."

Rose tucked a strand of hair behind her ear. "By all accounts, nothing around her was amidst. 'Good girl' I was told. 'Lovely disposition. A favorite of the Earl of Lindcomb's middle son, I hear.' But when I asked about her three other half siblings, everyone said the same thing: traveling abroad. My sources confirmed the same but found no recent traces of them."

She cut her eyes back to Nathaniel, who had his back to her and one hand on the door handle.

"Someone was keeping an eye on the king's bastards and now they're all gone."

Nathaniel turned to face her. "And you think I did it, then? Whisked them all away?" His expression tittered between amused and annoyed. "People disappear all the time, Rose. How long did it take the City Watch to stop looking for you?"

"Watch yourself," Rose snarled, her unsheathed fangs glinting in warning from behind her canines.

"I'll take it into consideration," Nathaniel replied with a bemused smirk.

Rose lifted her chin, her eyes locking with his. "I need to know you still remember what's important. What you *promised* me."

"And I need to know *you* won't crumble when the time comes."

Rose studied Nathaniel with an unwavering gaze. A beat of silence passed between them. Finally, Rose offered a tight smile. "Give my best to Claude, will you?"

As she passed him in the doorway, her hand rested on his chest. "And do take care, Nathaniel. The streets have been awfully dangerous since you've been away."

9

NATHANIEL

"The Old Crone never spoke to me once before I caught the blood fever, but something changed when she saw me lingering outside the butcher shop. 'Come child, not here,' she told me. 'The Watch has eyes on this one.' She sent me home with three livers and an ointment for the fangs. Saints bless her." – *Anonymous, St. Dahl confessional box, Lordhaven, Halcyon*

Nathaniel stepped out of the inn and scrunched his nose.

His senses were overtaken by the clambering music, deafening cheers, and stomping feet of passersby rumbled along the cobblestone streets, slipping between the tightly packed shops and inns that cluttered either side. Women in blue and gold gowns adorned with gold swords on their skirts twirled to the music of men in white and blue suits, gold swords painted on their cheeks. It was one thing to view the festivities from the comfort of a luxurious suite, but an entirely different matter to be in the thick of it.

Nathaniel scouted the streets for a carriage to hail, but the few he could see were at the mercy of the tides of festival goers pushing past. He'd be stuck inside one all night. With a huff, he turned and followed the crowd towards the Eddleton Stage, careful to keep close to the walls lest he be pulled into the jovial swell.

The streets were slick with liquor and piss. Nathaniel made a note to send Anders in the morning to fetch a new pair of shoes for him.

I'll be home soon enough, he reassured himself as he dabbed at his brow with a kerchief. The balmy night air was a poor pairing with his hand-tailored three-piece suit and trousers, but one's image was key. He'd rather be trampled by a carriage than arrive at an evening meeting in airy daywear.

Nathaniel sighed with relief when he found a side street. He passed drunkards and their giggling companions without sparing them a glance. But the sweet sourness of their skin clung to the air, rousing his hunger. He swallowed down the urge and kept walking. He was no mere beast of impulse. Claude had made sure of that.

"The only thing that separates the elite from the feral is willpower," Claude had told him during their first meeting all those years ago. "Lose your willpower and you lose everything."

Just as Nathaniel neared the mouth of the alley, a woman wearing a blue and gold mask stepped out from the shadows. The tail of her deep blue gown sashayed behind her as she slipped past him and disappeared into the festival crowd like a siren from a dream.

When Nathaniel finally arrived at the corner of Berkley Street and Port Lane, something shifted in his pocket. Inside he found a folded note that read: *The bell chimes a false song. May Yorin travel with you. – B*

When he looked back, the masked woman was long gone. Nathaniel ripped the paper in two and tossed it into the gutter.

Why is Beza reaching out to me? He tried not to dwell on what he would owe the Dagger of Lordhaven for her unexpected generosity. As sure as the sun rose and set, there would be a time and price for her information. He need only wait.

The Dead Hound was a popular drinking spot amongst the local actors and artists. During the Seven Swords festival it transformed into a haven for stragglers looking for a cheap pint and a chair to rest upon.

Nathaniel crossed the street and ascended the front steps of the pub, ignoring the sly stares his tailored suit and groomed appearance fetched.

Inside, people of all heights, sizes, and shades crowded the bar, while a few opted for the booths along either wall. Drunken chatter and heated arguments ebbed and flowed into a raucous blur as the night wore on. Peanut shells littered the floor, but no one paid the filth any mind.

Animals, Nathaniel thought bitterly, yearning for the quiet drinking parlors of the Garden District.

He weaved through the patrons, rife with ale and sweat, and proceeded to the side hall inaccessible to most other guests. He fetched a brass key from his pocket, unlocking the door and quickly leaving behind the rowdy clamor of the lower floor. Muffled voices and clinking glasses could be heard on the other side of the door at the top of the narrow staircase.

Nathaniel knocked once. Warren Miller, one of Claude's loyalists, opened the door. From his pointed brown moustache to his small beady eyes, he wasn't a man who stood out amongst a crowd, even when speaking. Warren stepped aside as Nathaniel walked past with a nod.

"Good evening, Mr. Miller," Nathaniel said, removing his top hat.

"As to you, Mr. Trevet," Warren nodded sheepishly. "I hope you've been enjoying the festival. I daresay even one of the capital's elite such as yourself may find the events pleasant." His smile was controlled, but his eyes were alight with admiration. It made Nathaniel want to stake his own heart.

"Yes, it's quite the spectacle this year."

"Certainly." Warren motioned towards the back of the room. "Mr. Barrow awaits you, sir."

After slipping out of his jacket, Nathaniel made his way towards the back of the room and took a seat. The sweet smell of melia smoke hung over the table. Across from him was a man with brown hair trimmed low on the sides and a long, angular face neither memorably handsome nor dismissively plain. He was dressed in a fine dark green paisley vest and matching cravat that spoke of his highborn tastes. Although he appeared to be in his early twenties like Nathaniel, no one really knew Claude Barrow's true age or his original whereabouts. Time had eroded whatever accent he may have had, if the rumor he sang the time forgotten Aragor's Dirge to reshape his voice was to be ignored.

"I'm glad you could finally join me," Claude chided, taking a drag of his melia packed pipe. Two glasses of whiskey sat between them. Nathaniel noted the play of control but didn't acknowledge it. "Your company was much missed."

Nathaniel tilted his chin and smiled. "It's been quite a festive evening. I can hardly be blamed for joining the merriment."

Claude raised a brow, breathing out a light stream of hickory scented smoke. "You mean to say you've kept me waiting over a glass and a pretty face?"

"Truly the best companions, don't you agree?"

Claude shook his head with laughter. "Fair is fair."

"I'm curious, were you going to ask about my trip?" Nathaniel poached, watching Claude's face for a reaction. He didn't offer one.

"Not really, no." A feint smile played on Claude's lips. "Why do you ask?"

Don't let him rile you, Nathaniel reminded himself. *Not this early.*

"Well, for starters, you asked me at the height of the social season to drop everything to travel to Darby Town and—"

Claude held up his hand. "You feel I wasted your time." He paused to take a sip of whiskey. "And you wouldn't be wrong."

Nathaniel bit back the question Claude wanted him to ask. Better to divert than be led. He leaned slightly forward, lowering his voice.

"Lord Pembroke will make a fine addition to the Order," Nathaniel said, keeping to the lie should any open ears be listening. "I must admit it didn't take much to convince him, which left me ample time to admire the coasts. But I can't help but wonder if this makeshift holiday of yours was to keep me from the rather interesting view inside Dr. Brennan's theatre."

Claude said nothing. He looked down at his whiskey as if mulling over what he was to have for dinner that evening. When he looked up again, the light shifted the brown of his eyes to something dark and muddled.

"Rest assured I did nothing of the sort." A shadow of annoyance passed across Claude's face. "I also heard Miss Wharton met with a most unfortunate fate, but I assure you I had nothing to do with the matter. Or how she came to be at Penrose."

The bell chimes a false song. Was this what Beza wanted to warn him about? No, it didn't seem right. Claude was cautious, but cruel. Rose had said the body was in near perfect condition, which meant Miss Wharton must've died by some internal means. Poison, drowning, maybe even smothering. Claude was far too crude for such a clean disposal.

"I called upon you tonight because I needed to discuss some rather delicate matters with my chief officer. Away from the others." *Away from Badru* went without saying. He was the Malsik's trusted right hand man and second in command, tasked with shadowing Claude while the Malsik traveled. But it was no secret he was the Malsik's eyes and ears.

The air in the room grew heavy. Echoes of the drunks below mixed with the whispers of those scattered about the second-floor hideaway. Each sought to gain something from another, scheming and bartering for their own survival like gamblers with a stolen purse.

"While you were away, I was approached with a rather interesting proposition," Claude began, taking another drag and letting out a slow exhale. "I had no intention of taking it upon myself to decide without your consultation as my second in command, but I'm afraid time was of the essence. Badru agreed, of course."

The urge to run a dagger across Claude's throat crossed Nathaniel's mind, but he tucked the thought away for another day. He forced himself to maintain a mask of coolness that mirrored Claude's own.

"Surely something so important could've been postponed until I returned."

"The Malsik ordered me to proceed."

Nathaniel's head buzzed with alarm. The Malsik was the recognized leader of the remaining nomadic duskborn tribes scattered throughout Halcyon, Waridi, Arcadia, and Khagal, as well as the de facto leader of the Order of the Boar when Claude swore allegiance to him two years previous. A warrior king tethered to no throne or land. Brutality, strength and wits were required of any who wore the dragon teeth necklace that marked the reigning Malsik.

"And what, pray tell, is this proposition?" Nathaniel inquired, reaching for his drink.

"A partnership."

"With whom?"

Claude leaned back in his seat. "I'm afraid I'm not at liberty to say. But you'll know in due time. I shall make the announcement next week at Lord Henley's summer ball, one of your favorites. I trust I'll see you there."

Lord Henley's summer ball was a lavish affair, in part because of an unspoken competition with his brother-in-law, Lord Branston who held his own summer ball during the same week. Neither event was to be missed, and any member of Lordhaven's high society would labor over their schedules to assure they attended both.

"Of course. I wouldn't miss it for the world." Nathaniel's fangs itched to be released. Oh, the throats he would tear into and the hearts he would savor. "I wonder if the Malsik will want to keep such frivolities under his rule. He doesn't strike me as the type who appreciates a good waltz."

A mirthless smirk cut across Claude's face. "Careful, you're embarrassing yourself."

Nathaniel chuckled. "I beg your pardon?"

"The work we've done, and continue to do, is on a scale never seen before. Duskborn won't be recognized as the apex of society lavishing away in a kitten house drunk on blood and booze. A reign of strength and blood is coming." Claude leaned closer, dropping his voice to a caustic whisper. "Wealth and time have softened you. Fix it."

Nathaniel fixed a smile on his face and nodded.

Oh I shall, he thought. *As soon as you and the Malsik do the hard work of disposing the Chases for me.*

Claude raised his glass and smiled, but the warmth didn't reach his eyes. "Cheers are in order then."

Nathaniel picked up his glass. "I'm afraid I'm not certain what we're celebrating."

"To Halcyon's future in the glory of the Malsik's might. A new reign. A new age. A new ruler."

Nathaniel bit down his reproach and raised his glass.

May the Malsik enjoy keeping my throne warm. Long reign indulgence and beauty.

"Cheers," they said in union.

As the whiskey slid down Nathaniel's throat, it took with it the warnings of missing royals and false songs.

10

SYBIL

"Casting is a means to harness the very essence of the world around us. Mastery of magic is futile; it is merely ours to use bearing the right conditions are met."
– *Elowyn Fallbrooke,* An Incomplete History of Arcanists

Sybil Vorn waited with bated breath at her bedroom window.

As the sun burned through the greyish blue of night's past and painted the surrounding trees gold, she braced for the letter that would change her life.

Today is surely the day, Sybil reassured herself. *Today I receive covenship.*

Outside, trees sang with the chirps of morning birds. Squirrels scampered across thatched rooftops, nipping at each other's tails. A day's travel from the Draven Mountains, Sanctis was a settlement hidden far away from the watchful eye of Lordhaven's constables and perilously close to the border of Soliljin, the gelid queendom to the north. But the very distance that granted Sanctinites peace to practice magicks also made correspondence a headache and a half.

Sybil rubbed her eyes. It had been nearly a whole season since she first sent her request to Ephriam of Greyfell, one of the few remaining coven leaders in the Northlands she hadn't queried yet. Surely, he had received her letter.

And yet ...

As the sun climbed higher in the sky, burning away the last traces of yester night, Sybil prepared for another day of silence. And then, as if her mind had willed it, a figure appeared beneath the makeshift archway marking the outskirts of Sanctis.

Sybil pressed against the glass, squinting against the dawn's light. As the figure made its way further down the path, she could make out the hunter green robes and gold trousers worn by the Northland messengers. Sybil tore away from the window and scurried down the stairs. Anticipation and dread had waged war on her emotions since she'd handed a messenger her freshly sealed query beneath the damp Bloom Leaf sky, but today she would finally have an answer.

The messenger approached a cottage two doors down from Sybil's. He pulled a small cloth-wrapped box from his satchel and leaned down to place it in on Mrs. Moorwether's door front. Sybil jostled on the balls of her feet as she watched him, her fingers furling and unfurling as she waited. When he rose, he finally noticed her. She caught the hesitation in his step and an icy stab of dread pierced her stomach. She'd seen that same reluctance in the eyes of the other settlers for some time now, spreading like a disease.

She watched as the messenger approached her family's cottage. His right hand gripped the strap of his satchel tighter, but it was as if his hand were clenching her heart instead.

Today I'll receive covenship from Ephriam, she reminded herself.

"Miss Sybil Vorn?"

She bolted upright when she heard her name.

"Yes?"

The messenger was a twenty something with small brown eyes and a face prickled with the beginnings of a beard. His voice wavered as he spoke.

"If I may speak freely, miss ..."

Today is the day.

"Words are light enough to carry on the wind and blow into the ears of others." He refused to meet her gaze, which irritated her.

I know the proverb, she wanted to scream at him.

"B-But you see," he stammered on, "the wind is faster than any messenger."

Today is ...

Finally, his eyes met hers.

"The wind has blown through Greyfell. Long before any letter of good word could reach it, I'm afraid." The messenger paused, gripping the strap of his satchel tighter. Clenching her heart tighter still. He closed his eyes and swallowed the cruel truths that soured his tongue. "I would perhaps consider working about a shop or sorts here in Sanctis if I were you."

They know what you've done, he may have well said. *They know and they fear you for it. They'll come to hate you like the rest.*

Sybil stared ahead. All she could do was nod. Beyond the gentle, pitiful eyes of the messenger, the sun continued to rise. Another dawn that would come and go in silence.

Always in silence.

"Best of mornings to you," Sybil replied woodenly.

When she turned to leave, the messenger blurted, "Word has it you're quite gifted for someone so young."

Sybil paused at the door. She wanted to laugh and cry all at once. "How fortunate people still say pleasant things about me."

She shut the door behind her, trading one silence for another. The flames in her stomach had all but died away. From their ashes, a white-hot anger bubbled inside her. A scream clawed up her throat, desperate for release, but she held it back with gritted teeth and balled fists.

Life is a game of the gods, my dear, her father's voice called out from memory, tempering her anger for a moment. *Fairness isn't a card in the deck.*

"You're wrong," she muttered beneath her breath, digging her nails into her palms. Anger roiled in her stomach anew. "You're—"

"Here again?"

Sybil's head shot up. Standing on the stairwell was her younger brother, already taller than her despite being a year younger. While they shared the same deep russet complexion, Cal had inherited their mother's straight black hair that now framed his harsh expression.

"Leave me alone, Cal," Sybil grumbled, shifting her gaze to the other side of the room.

"You'll never learn," he snorted, folding his arms across his chest. His gaze bore into her like two pale green suns. "You're just like him. What's done *can't* be undone, Sybil. Why do you insist on embarrassing us even more?"

"Because I can change this!" she snarled in a low whisper lest she wake their mother. "I just need to become a Major, all right? Then I can access the archives. I know the High Council missed something. They had to. I didn't … I would *never* hurt my coven. Ever."

Cal's jaw clenched. "You'll be our ruin." He stalked off back upstairs and shut his door. A swell of gratification bloomed in Sybil's chest watching him leave, but just as quickly it fled from her, leaving her alone to linger in the silence.

Always in silence.

Sybil found her mind too restless to return to the reverie of sleep.

She slipped out of bed and lowered herself until she was eye level with the unending darkness beneath. She reached her hand into the shadows until her fingers touched the cracked leathery spine of a book. The corners of her mouth pulled into a smile as she brought the journal into the morning light. She opened the cover and there, in the top left corner, were the words *Property of Edward Vorn* written in her father's precise hand. She flipped to one of the dog-eared pages in the middle of the journal. The entry was dated shortly after her ninth birthday.

> *"I received word from messenger this morning. Mr. Timsh has been nothing short of a miracle worker, and I count his friendship as a blessing from the Goddess of Fortune herself. My patience and his good word within local ranks have finally bore fruit from Lordhaven. We've received an invitation to speak with the king's own personal council, the good men of the Sentry, on the 25th of Sproutfall.*

> *We are strides closer to receiving royal allowance to sell our wares and elixirs in Lordhaven's markets without risk of arrest or seizure from the City Watch. The taxation shall be hefty to start, and we'd be limited to certain times and locations, but by the gods... Imagine such a victory for our standing! Fateshifters selling at the king's stalls! I could do little to contain my own elation upon reading this news, but at such a dim hour I must refrain lest I risk waking Joan and the children. We have twelve moons time before the meeting is to commence. I can only hope Byrill's scales stay tipped in our favor."*

Sybil closed the journal and held it close, drowning in the memory of her father's green eyes brimming with hopefulness the day before he left for Lordhaven, his rounded chin, so much like hers, pointed proudly towards the sky.

"Da, must you go to the capital?"

"Fret not, poppet. A grand adventure awaits, and one must never turn their back on such marvelous timings."

His smile had been like sunlight upon her face. She'd come to treasure that smile, to carry it with her as a reminder of what still needed to be done. What *she* still had to do in his absence.

"I'll find the truth of what happened to my coven, Da," she whispered to the journal, pressing it close to her chest. "I'll fix everything so your dream can go on. I promise. I'll fix this."

Sybil tucked the journal beneath her bed and pulled her knees to her chest. She closed her eyes and let out a deep breath.

Some would say she had no right to think of her coven, but their memory was a bittersweet comfort. She committed each of their voices and whims to heart, etching them all into the walls of her mind.

Ginny, who never ran out of stories to tell.

Meredith, who wrote the loveliest poetry Sybil had ever read.

Jane, who loved to chart the stars.

Major Quinn, who was the best card player this side of the Silver Sea.

Even three months later, the pain was still a gaping chasm inside her. Sybil hugged her knees closer to her chest. Tears prickled her eyes as the other memories flooded in too, as they always did.

Ginny, whose neck was bent at the wrong angle.

Meredith, whose blood spatter had stained Sybil's travel dress.

Jane, whose blonde hair had been matted with blood from her gaping throat.

Major Quinn, whose charred body was only identified because the others were recognizable.

Sweat prickled her brow. Her heart raced in her chest as a mounting anger warmed her skin. But just as quickly her father's words trickled in from memory like a gentle rain, reminding her of all the times his hands gently held her shoulders and his slow, even speech ebbed away her temper.

"Stay here, poppet. Focus on your breath. You're not going to let anger best you now, are you?"

"For I have become the shepherd of souls," Sybil quietly recited, grounding herself, "and keeper of—"

A knock rattled across her door and Sybil snapped to attention.

"Not now, Cal." She quickly wiped her eyes with the back of her hand.

After a pause, another knock followed. Sybil got to her feet, a snarl curling her lips as she swung open the door.

"I said piss off, Ca—" but her words died on her tongue.

Staring back at her was a shadow slightly taller than herself. Its appearance mirrored that of a teenage boy who lived on the other side of Sanctis except for the claw-like fingertips and fanged-toothed smile. The shade's golden eyes brightened when it saw her.

"Best of mornings to you, Miss Vorn," it greeted in a low, menacing voice. Its purplish black body bent forward in a mock bow. "I do say, you look rather *malicious* today." It peered up and flashed a wicked grin of sharpened yellow teeth. "It suits you well."

Sybil leaned into the hall, looking both ways before turning her attention back to the shadow.

"What are you doing here, Cain?" she said in a frenzy. "Did anyone see you?" The last thing she needed was Cal or her mother seeing her speaking with an illegally conjured shade, even if it did belong to a classmate.

"Ah, you must give me more credit than that, my dear," Cain chided. "Secrecy is my very nature. You needn't worry about us being overheard."

Sybil's heart dropped, but Cain waived away her concern. "They're fine, I assure you. Just a bit of very persuasive whispering to keep them bound to their beds and lingering in their dreams."

"Thank the gods," Sybil let out a sigh of relief, raking a hand through her short black hair. "So why did Heath send you? This wasn't what we agreed to."

Cain leaned in as if to whisper a secret. "Perhaps I've slipped from his grasp and came here of my own choosing. What would you do then, Miss Vorn?"

Sybil didn't answer.

"You fateshifters are an awfully arrogant bunch. So confident in magicks not your own and yet your understanding is no better than that of a toddler. It's all rather amusing."

Sybil was familiar with Cain's sharp tongue, but it still somehow bristled her every time.

"You're quite the confident one to speak so boldly of history not *your* own," she countered. "You know nothing of the magicks the old scholars studied."

"Darkness, my dear," Cain replied, his voice suddenly the deep, rippling echo of a thousand beating insect wings, "has been here long before you and shall remain long after you're gone. Do not speak to me of history and magicks."

He leaned back, his tone suddenly airy. "But such is a tale for another time. There's been a change of plans, I'm afraid. Heath will meet you two days hence at the large oak husk. I trust you know of it."

"Yes," Sybil mumbled, eager to be done with the conversation.

Cain leaned in close. "Tread carefully, Miss Vorn. I'm not the only one following Heath." He winked and melted into the shadows of the hall. A faint snickering echoed from the darkened corners and then was gone. Sybil heard rustling from either side of the hall. Cal and her mum must've been released.

Sybil glanced back at her bed, wishing to hold her father's journal once more.

We're not traitors, Da, she reminded herself. *I'll make Sanctis see.*

11

JULIA

"If an Iver dove's coo is warbled and high pitched, a storm is soon to follow." – *An Iver's call, old wives' tale*

The following morning brought a smattering of damp greyness over Temmings.

Julia awoke with a splitting headache and even less desire to attend class. The drinks that had tasted so pleasant in the shadowed halls of Gafton Manor left her mouth feeling sticky and sour. She rubbed her eyes and yawned wide.

"Really, Julia, do try to temper yourself. Any wider and your soul will flutter out." Agatha set down a basket of folded laundry on George's made bed. Julia snapped her mouth shut, startled by her aunt's sudden appearance.

"Well? Are you going to lay about in bed all day then?"

"What time is it?" A sudden panic ran through her. Had she overslept?

Her aunt snorted. "If you have to ask, then you're already late."

"But Da didn't wake me!"

Her aunt tutted. "I hardly see why he should when you clearly consider yourself a mature adult."

If there was ever a time for a sudden sinkhole to appear and swallow her whole, it was then. She didn't remember making that much noise or seeing anyone on her way back from the party, but thanks to the wine anything after her meeting with Daniel appeared in her mind more like half smudged sketches than living, breathing memories.

Julia slid out of bed and kept her gaze glued to the floor.

Today was certainly going to be one of *those* days. And she hadn't even made it to class yet.

Mrs. Prinn, the head instructor at Elmwood Preparatory School, was standing at her usual post at the top of the stairs when Julia rounded the corner. At just 5'1, she was on eye level with many of the younger students yet none dared to cross her. Mrs. Prinn was nearly as old as the school itself and had the sharpest memory in town. Her mouth flattened when Julia rushed up the walkway.

"Ah, Miss Sheffield. Still working on our punctuality, I see."

"Yes, sorry Mrs. Prinn." Julia hurried past the head instructor's withering gaze and down the hall. She passed the teacher's meeting quarters, the supply room and the Youth Room where anyone under thirteen studied. Yellow and white hand cut flowers bordered the door. Julia paused, her hand frozen on the handle of the Elder Room as she took in the sight of the paper flowers cut haphazardly. The shriek of childish chatter spilled into the hall, warbling in Julia's ears to become the distorted howls of wolves and skittering tree roots.

Julia jerked open the door to the Elder Room just as Mrs. Morwald finished roll call.

"Wonderful of you to join us, Miss Sheffield" she quipped. She motioned towards the empty seat in the front row. "Please do have a seat. Quickly now."

Julia smoothed over her features and held her arms close to hide the goosebumps. Martha wiggled her fingers in hello as Julia passed her, but Dorothy and Emily kept their heads bent low in hushed conversation. A stab of rejection pricked Julia like a thorn. As she slid into her seat, irritation festered in the pit of her stomach for even caring about it at all.

Behind her, Charity Greerson and her two devotees, Mina Appleton and Tilda Roth, snickered.

Julia ignored them and reached inside the desk to retrieve her worn arithmetic study guide.

"Now, before we begin," Mrs. Morwald said, "as you all know, we've had a terribly tragic passing in our community. Little Billie Moore's absence will be felt by not just his classmates across the hall, but all of us here at Elmwood. As Father O'Malley so aptly described yesterday, we must let an honest heart guide us through these difficult times."

Charity cleared her throat. "Excuse me, Mrs. Morwald. May I share a word with the class?"

Mrs. Morwald nodded. "You may, Miss Greerson. Do hurry it along please."

Charity nodded and stood to address her peers, a queen in her court. "A tragedy in Temmings is a tragedy for us all. My father, Deputy Sergeant Greerson has graciously volunteered to hold an open forum with himself and Governor Longworth in hopes of strengthening the community during this time. Refreshments will be provided, of course."

Charity's offer was met with applause, most noticeably from Mina and Tilda.

Before Charity could sit back down, Julia was on her feet. The utter shock on Charity's face was enough to spur her on. Emily, Dorothy and Martha all looked at her, but Julia no longer cared about their attention. The dark satisfaction from Charity's shock was reward enough.

"On behalf of us all, thank you, Charity for your family's generosity," Julia said with a sticky sweet smile. "Considering the horrible events, though, I do hope your father will take this time to more strictly enforce measures against bullying, particularly amongst the younger kids. Perhaps one day it can save others like Billie from such an awful fate."

Charity paused for a beat before gathering herself. "Everyone knows Billie disappeared, Julia. No one said he was bullied."

"Ladies, please take—" Mrs. Morwald interjected, but Julia spoke over her.

"Well, I don't suppose he was taken by wolves, now was he? Seems more likely he was led to them by those looking for a laugh." Julia lowered her tone so only those closest could hear. "You know, just like you used to."

Charity's face flushed with anger. "How *dare*—"

Julia cut her off. "Mrs. Morwald, I'm suddenly not feeling well. I think it's my flow. May I have a lie down in the nurse's office?"

Mrs. Morwald huffed and pointed to the door. "Out. *Now*, Miss Sheffield."

Julia smiled and gathered her bag, not bothering to return her arithmetic book. When she stepped out into the hall, she went straight past the nurse's office and down the stone steps to the bench across from the school.

The sun was hidden behind a thicket of clouds, but Julia didn't mind the sullenness. She rested her elbows on her knees and rubbed her temples, silently urging her hangover to cease and willing her corset to loosen if only for a moment to ease her building headache. At least she was out of that saints awful classroom.

"I think you missed the nurse's office."

Julia looked up to see Harrison standing over her, the hint of a bemused smile tugging at his lips.

"Oh, I hadn't noticed." The shadow of her earlier irritability still lingered, but if Harrison picked up on it, he didn't let on.

"Mind if I sit with you?"

Julia shrugged and scooted over. Her heart skipped a beat as the smell of pine and cinnamon wafted across her nose. She loved his smell, woodsy yet sweet, and wanted nothing more than to snuggle beneath his arm and envelop herself in his warmth. A strange boldness suddenly overcame her. It was enough to urge her on if she wanted, to close the gap between them and finally make her feelings known, but when Harrison cleared his throat, the illusion was broken.

"I'm glad to see you're all right. I was a bit worried that you might've, I dunno, maybe went 'round to the wrong residence or something." He rubbed the back of his neck, unable to meet her eyes. "You were quite a sight."

"A sight not worth accompanying?" Saints, she was a thorn today. But something unnamed and uncertain scratched at the door of her consciousness. She couldn't remember it exactly but the feeling of it lingered. Bitterness, brittle and black. An urge to make Harrison suffer, a slow bleed she could savor the taste of later at her whim.

Julia hadn't been the only sight at the party. That much she remembered, even if her heart wanted to forget it all and enjoy the rare moment alone with Harrison now.

"I meant no offense, I swear. I should've, you're right, but I wasn't well off either. I just—saints, I'm sorry."

"Sorry? For what?"

"It wasn't a great party. I mean it was but, y'know, a bit lethal. Martin and his lot are all big headed poshers. I guess I was too nervous to ask you for a dance but um, maybe next time I suppose? And less drink."

Julia flushed. She bit the inside of her lip to avoid her smile growing too wide. "I'd like that. And absolutely less drink."

Harrison beamed. "You should come then. To the summoning tonight."

"The summoning?"

"It's a bit silly really, but some of the upper years were going to have this mock ritual or something. For a laugh and all. I figured maybe I could see you there?"

Was Harrison asking after her company? Was this truly happening? Julia was fit to burst, but composure was everything. She'd come this far. She couldn't spoil it now. She was a Grace, after all.

"Sure. I'm holding you to that dance, though."

Harrison's cheeks dimpled when he smiled. "Aces. Count on it."

A moment of silence lingered between them. Julia let herself soak in Harrison's presence, his soft brown gaze and the shape of his mouth. When the scratching returned, that pesky, unnamed bitterness, Julia ignored it. Because Harrison had asked after her. Perhaps not *her*, not the darkly minded and sharp edged her, but the sweet-faced mask that she wore so well. But Harrison didn't know that, and she didn't care, and all that was left was for hope, however misguided, to bloom. Julia reflected Harrison's nervous smile because she could. Because she wanted to.

Because Harrison Goldwell, in that quiet moment, was worth suffering the slow bleed.

"Did you see her face?"

"Oh saints, it was absolutely brilliant!"

Dorothy and Martha tossed their heads back in laughter beneath a towering oak tree. Emily stood, chest puffed out, parroting Charity with Lake Promise as her gleaming backdrop.

"Oh, but dearest Papa will open a new shelter for the homeless! We shall eat biscuit jammies while trading missing children stories! Won't that be splendid? Aren't we such an upright family?"

"You even got her annoying pitch down!" Julia blurted between laughter.

Emily smirked. "Only the best for my audience that dared skip class for my performance. Thank you, thank you."

"I swear you and Charity were about to have a row in the middle of class," Martha said to Julia, wiping tears from her eyes and chuckling. "Mrs. Morwald aged five years, saints honest."

"Serves the croon right the way she sucks up to the Greersons and all that." Dorothy reached into Emily's satchel and popped a salted cashew into her mouth. "It's maddening. She wasn't even elected class lead and yet she acts like she runs the whole bloody school. I can't stand her."

"Not like any of it matters anyway," Julia replied, grabbing a cashew for herself and basking in the shaded grass. "Charity and her lot will be off to finishing school after graduation and the rest of us will be spud wives at the market. No shame in going with the tide."

Dorothy paled. "That literally sounds like the most depressing thing ever when you say it out loud like that."

"That's because it is." Julia tucked one arm under her head and stared up at the blanket of puffy white clouds. The meadow fell silent save for the chirping of the finches above. Emily raised her arms in a cat stretch.

"My parents insist I marry and stay here in Temmings, but it's all bollocks. We can do anything we want." Emily's gaze found Julia's, and in that deep sea of blue was a promise. A secret. Their little group was young, beautiful, and dangerous. Temmings could never hope to diminish their radiance. No one could ever hope to do that. Not to them.

Not to the Graces.

Martha twirled a finger around a blonde strand. "So, what's everyone bringing to the summoning?"

"Wait, we have to bring something?" Julia asked.

Emily's eyes narrowed. "You know about the summoning?"

Julia's breath caught in her throat. Beneath the innocent question Julia caught the edge in Emily's voice. A blade hidden beneath the lace of geniality.

"Oh, Harrison asked me about after—"

"Jules!" Martha squealed, face beaming. "Did he have a chat with you? Oh, he did, didn't he?"

"He excused himself right after you left," Dorothy piped in, saddling up beside Martha. They exchanged glances and giggled. "Everyone knew it was to chat with you and of course Charity was absolutely pissed, the hag. Tell us *everything*."

"Yes, tell us everything." Emily smiled, but her gaze was too hungry.

Julia swallowed down the unease burning in her throat. "He asked me if I was going to go to the summoning, and if we could chat."

"If you could *chat*?" Dorothy snorted. "What is he, my grandda? Shall I fetch you two a governess to supervise your stroll?"

Martha playfully smacked Dorothy on her arm. "Don't be a cow. Oi, that's sweet Jules. He's clearly soft on you." Her pink mouth curled into a smile. "Careful Em, you might not be his favorite anymore."

Julia's blood hardened to ice. She didn't dare look at Emily or Dorothy. It was like being in the Gafton Manor all over again, tipsy and untethered, searching for her way down an impossibly endless hall. And then that breathy, familiar voice whispering from the dark.

"Emily."

When Julia finally managed to look at Emily, it was as if she hadn't heard the accusation at all. Or if Emily had, cared so little as to not even bother acknowledging it. Dorothy's gaze shifted between the two of them but she played it off with her silence. Martha stole glances at Emily but said nothing.

When Emily finally looked at Julia—because they would always find each other—there was only warmth in her smile. "As if Harrison ever mattered to us."

It was a declaration if Julia had ever heard one. Neither Temmings nor teachers nor bullies nor lovers could ever hope to invade their inner circle. It would always be them, the four of them, forever and always, trapped in their beautiful garden behind a wall of thorns.

The air shifted and the topic pivoted to class gossip as it always did. As it always would. Julia fell back into the silence of proximity while Dorothy, Martha, and Emily chattered on. But as she laid there, the inkling of unease crept back in like blood seeping from beneath the edges of a bandaged wound.

There had been a warning in that declaration, even if Julia hadn't acknowledged it. The message had been received and they all knew it.

Harrison was out.

The Graces reunited shortly after midnight.

The night air was still, as if holding its breath for the events to come. Julia slipped out as she always had from her bedroom window, except this time George wasn't waiting up to bid her off or plead for her not to go. He had kept his back to her, feigning sleep.

He'll be okay, she reminded herself. *I'll sort it out with him in the morning.*

But the excitement that had lightened her footsteps on her way to see the Graces grew heavy when the forest loomed before them. The branches seemed to twist in ways they never had in the daylight.

Memories of Billie's hollow eyes lingered on the edge of her mind.

If he never left, are the others still out there too?

"Jules, hello?" Martha said, waving her hand in front of Julia's face. Julia shook her head.

"What was that again, sorry?"

"I said," Martha repeated with hands on her hips, "are you ready to be a naughty heathen tonight?"

"It's not like we're going to actually summon anything." Dorothy tucked a stray curl behind her ear. "It's just fun and games and all that."

"I dunno, maybe we could summon something. Or someone," Emily added, wiggling her fingers.

Dorothy rolled her eyes. "As if the White Raven would manifest before a bunch of Elmwood students. Surely the King of Demons has more important matters to attend to."

Woodsmoke and earthen rot hung heavy in the air. Julia's stomach coiled as she crossed the threshold. She'd done this before. Nothing was different. She'd be with the Graces. They wouldn't even be far in.

You're fine. You're fine.

The girls emerged from the dark path and into a small clearing. At least ten others were gathered around a crackling fire, murmuring to each other. One of the figures hissed, "Who's there?" All chatter ceased and ten pair of eyes locked onto the Graces.

Emily stepped forward and lowered her hood.

"Emily here. Also, Martha, Dorothy, and Julia."

The accusing voice lowered their own hood. Long dark hair fell around a sharp, angled face. "So the children decided to come out and play." The bonfire illuminated Charity's wicked smirk. "What a pleasure."

"Can the White Raven smote her first?" Martha grumbled low enough for only their group to hear. Julia and Dorothy chuckled. The Graces joined the others around the fire, but Julia didn't see Harrison among the group. Disappointment soon gave way to unease when a low rustling caught her attention. Julia flinched and twisted to look behind her.

Emily squeezed her hand. "Don't stare too long. Something might stare back."

"As long as it's handsome," Julia teased, slowly turning back around. But behind her coy smile were thousands of needles prickling her skin. Her eyes flickered every few moments from the halo of firelight to the collar of darkness wrapped around them. The whispers of the old wives rang in her ears like the crackling of firewood, breathy and urgent.

Never trust the forest.

"Now, everyone," Charity announced. "Join hands so we can begin."

The group joined hands as silence fell over the clearing.

"Oh dark night, full of stars and terrors, we ask for you to listen to our pleas," Charity began in a low voice. "We ask in your name to bring forth a creature born from your shadow, the demon king of a thousand faces, the White Raven." Charity raised her head. "Mina, fetch the box."

Mina, a short, pretty plump girl to Charity's right walked over to a nearby tree and returned with a small box in her hands. She took off the lid and Charity reached in with both hands. A gasp released from the group. More than a few looked away.

Charity lifted a dead raven above her head and stared into the fire. "Oh dark night, see us. We offer you this raven as price. May the Saint Father forgive our sins and the night release the White Raven before us." Charity placed the carcass into the fire. The flames hissed and crackled with delight as an acrid char filled the air. Julia squeezed Emily's hand until her knuckles ached, unable to look away from the flame-eaten bird.

Several moments passed.

"When is the White Raven supposed to appear?" Emily asked Charity. "Or did you mess up the speech?"

Charity's glare looked all the more menacing beneath the flames. "Piss off, Emily. Everyone, keep your hands locked. The summoning circle can't be—"

A twig snapped somewhere behind them.

Julia's breath caught. She spun around, her heart in her throat. Memories of Billie swam to the surface in her mind. Dorothy left out a small yelp.

"Jules, my hand ..."

"Sorry, Dory." Julia let go and Dorothy cradled her hand to her chest. "I-I thought I heard something. Did you hear something?"

"What? No, I didn't."

"Jules, there's nothing there," Emily whispered beneath her breath.

"Charity, did we miss a step?" Tilda looked around the clearing, her voice shaken.

"Maybe the raven wasn't enough?" Mina ventured with a shrug.

"I *didn't* make a mistake," Charity snapped. "I swear if one of you sabotaged this—Julia, are you mad?"

Julia stepped towards the edge of the clearing. "I think there's something there. Behind the trees." Something had moved in the shadows. Julia was certain of it. Something was watching them, just as Billie had watched her and George.

Martha shifted from foot to foot. "Jules, maybe you should come back."

Emily giggled. "Brilliant, Charity. Looks like you summoned the White Raven in the wrong direction."

And then, as if a dam was broken, a dozen or so figures emerged from the darkness clad in armor and brandishing clubs over their heads. The nearest figure to Charity, his face rimmed in a thick beard, brought down his club across her left shoulder with his full weight. She crumpled to the ground with an agonizing screech. He grabbed her by the hair and looked out into the stunned crowd.

"Grab 'em! All of 'em!" he snarled.

Julia stared at the man barely an arm's reach away. Her legs were locked, her throat closed shut. She couldn't run or scream.

She'd seen that vicious snarl before, those bloodthirsty eyes. But back then it had been only a few mad hunters wandering out of the forest and the townsfolk had dealt with them. Then the fear and panic that ensued when children began disappearing, but again the townsfolk took care of it. As long as they stayed away they would be safe, always safe.

Liars.

Screams tore into the night. The armor-clad figures attacked anyone within arm's reach, beating them to the ground and tying up the rest. Emily grabbed Julia's hand, dragging her away from the fire and towards the dark wilderness.

"Jules, we have to go!" she screamed.

"Where's Martha and Dorothy?" Julia looked around frantically.

"They've probably already fled! Come on!"

"No, we can't leave them!"

As Julia tore her hand away from Emily's, Mina knocked into Julia and sent both of them tumbling to the ground. Mina scrambled to her feet first and fled into the inky blackness with another boy behind her. Julia finally managed to stand just as two large figures closed in on her. She darted around them, but not before one of the figures brought his club down on her shoulder. A yelp tore from Julia's throat as she fell to her knees, face streaked in tears and dirt. White-hot pain bit into her shoulder where the blow had been struck. She winced as she tried to stand against the pain, but a hand pressed down on the base of her neck and began binding her arms.

She kicked her legs and squirmed with all her might against her attacker.

"Get off me! Let me go!"

The man tying her hands leaned down and snarled in her ear, "Hold your tongue, demon, before I cut it off."

His breath reeked of alcohol and kellweed. Julia kept silent as he dragged her to her feet. The other Graces were nowhere to be seen. The clearing was empty except for three bodies strewn on the ground, motionless. When Julia glimpsed long, wavy blonde hair, she screamed Martha's name into the night.

The man, now flanked by another, dragged her away from the clearing.

"You monsters!" she shouted. "Why are you doing this? Why?"

The back of the second man's hand connected with her cheek. A sharp pain burned across her face.

"'Nuff of yer questions," he growled.

Tears continued to pour down Julia's face. How had this happened? How had such a silly night gone so terribly wrong?

The men led her to a lantern lit carriage drawn by a single horse as black as the night around it. The carriage bore no markings and had only two small, barred windows.

"This is the last of 'em," the bearded man called up to the driver, whose face was obscured by a half mask over his mouth and a thick overcoat despite the warm night. One of the men removed the heavy bolt on the back of the carriage. Julia could just make out the writhing shapes of other captives inside before one of the guards shoved a sponge under her nose. A sickly-sweet aroma clouded her senses, her mind, and finally her will.

A heavy tiredness followed, pulling her into its depths and stifling the cry trapped in her throat.

12

JULIA

"The Saint Father, Saint of Industry, gave us a means of inspiration with the discovery of snake oil. Proof that anyone, common or wealthy, can change their station and push society forward for the collective good so long as they work hard. And yet the temptation of unearned gains and demonic promises—of magic—remains a blight over this land." – *Barrister Levi H. Langston, final trial notes from the Kingdom of Halcyon v. Marianne and Richard Crosgrove, Lordhaven High Court, Halcyon*

When Julia finally came to, a sweet bitterness coated her tongue.

Her eyes were open, but she saw nothing. Darkness smothered her like a hot breath. No, she realized, that was her own breath. A sack or bag of some sort was over her face. She struggled to right herself, her breath hitching with each movement, but iron shackles bit into her skin. Suddenly, someone shifted beside her.

"Hello?" Julia whispered. "Who's there?"

The carriage slowed to a crawl. When it came to a stop, the silence broke.

"Are w-we stopped?" a shrill voice asked.

"Did they say where?" a second piped in nervously.

"Shh!" a third hissed. "They're coming!"

Several voices could be heard on the other side of the door. The group inside held their collective breath. Julia's heart pounded in her ears.

"... followed you?" a gruff voice asked.

"No ..." a younger, shakier voice replied. "Got the sterling, then?"

"... will have a look first ..."

The carriage doors swung open. Muffled cries rippled through the group. Julia curled inward as tears streamed down her face unseen. This was all wrong. This wasn't supposed to happen. How would she get back home?

"These two," a surly voice ordered someone. "Two hundred for the pair."

Panicked screams ripped through the carriage but the men continued talking over them.

"We agreed to five!"

"Well, plans changed. You're more than welcome to take it up with Mama Kilburn and her pistol when you get to Lordhaven, but the Green Coats' word is final on this."

The Green Coats? Lordhaven? No, this was only a horrid dream.

Please, Saint Father… Julia silently prayed. *Please let me wake soon.*

A scream cut through the carriage.

"Please, don't kill me! Please!" Another piercing cry followed as a second captive was unshackled and taken from the carriage.

"Names!" a gruff voice boomed.

"D-Deidra Culpepper."

"Clem Mwangi."

A moment's pause, the moving of paper. "Neither match our girl. Sleep 'em." A pause. "There's your bloody two hundred then."

Grunting and the clanking of coins being exchanged was drowned out by the muffled wailing of Deidra and Clem. The doors slammed shut and a lock bolted back into place. The carriage pitched forward. Julia stared ahead, unblinking until her eyes burned.

When the carriage came to a second stop, Julia's mind snapped back to attention. She tried to inch further away from the door opening, but a pair of thickly gloved hands grabbed her legs and dragged her forward. She screamed, thrashing against her captor the best she could. When the bag was ripped off, momentarily blinding her to the midday sun, a sticky sweet cloth pressed against her nose and mouth, silencing her once more.

Julia was jostled awake by a tickle against her cheek.

At first her barely woken mind dismissed the sensation as nothing more than a dream. But when the mouse squeaked, Julia screamed and shot up with enough fervor to startle the intruder, who quickly scuttled between the bars and disappeared. Julia clutched her knees to her chest.

"Bloody vermin." She wiped her cheek with the back of her hand. That's when her eyes caught the glint of oil light off the iron shackles around her wrists. Noticed the itchiness of the damp straw beneath her. Smelled the foulness of the chamber pot beside her.

Where in the seven hells am I?

"Oh, you're finally awake."

Julia's head snapped up. "Tilda?"

Curled at Tilda's feet was Emily. A crescent moon of dried blood clung to her bottom lip. Julia rushed to her best friend's side.

"Em, wake up! Wake up, it's me!"

"Jules?" Emily slurred, rubbing her eyes. "W-Where are we?"

"I-I don't know. But somewhere safe, I think."

"Where's Martha and Dorothy?"

"I dunno, I—"

The memory of Martha lying on the ground stole her breath. She had been so still, so impossibly still amongst the chaos. Dorothy ... had she made it out? Or was she in her own cell somewhere just as confused and scared?

"Don't be daft. We're in a prison cell," Tilda scoffed. Her arms clutched her knees tighter to her chest. "We're never getting out. It's over."

"You don't know that," Julia fired back.

"She's right, Jules." Emily pushed herself upright and leaned against the stone wall. "The woman who grabbed me, she called me a fateshifter. They meant us harm."

Julia's eyes widened. *Fateshifter.* No one in Temmings ever said it aloud as if the very word itself were a curse. Julia remembered being five and playing with George outside the kitchen when she called him a fateshifter in the sing-song innocence of children repeating what they heard adults say. It was the only time her mum had ever slapped her. From then on, Julia knew it to be far more than just a word or name—it was a weapon.

Emily said, "I bet they think we worship the moon and dance naked for Azavith. Well, I for one would much prefer loose infernal silks to these stuffy old corsets. Wouldn't that be grand?"

Julia's chest tightened. How easily Emily's tongue twisted around words others would only dare whisper behind raised fans, even if only in jest. The hint of a smile tugged at the corner of Emily's mouth, playful and sinister all at once.

If only I hadn't followed that smile into the dark.

"Stop it, Em. I'm serious." Julia raked her fingers through her tangled hair. "This can't be right. Clearly they made some sort of mistake." Suddenly, Julia caught a glimpse of someone's shadow on the hallway wall. "Hold on, I think I see someone. Hello, is someone there? Excuse me!"

"Don't, Julia!" Tilda snapped. "The guards aren't—" but the sound of jangling keys and heavy footsteps cut her off.

"Oi, what's all this racket then?"

A guard about Julia's height came up to the cell, hands on his wide hips. Wiry black hair flecked with grey curled over his protruding ears and fell over narrowed, brown eyes.

Julia stepped forward and wrapped her fingers around the bars. The guard immediately took a step back, but kept his eyes trained on her.

"Sir, there's been a mistake. My friends and I were out past hours and this strange group came upon and attacked us. I think they took us to be fateshifters, but I swear to you we're absolutely not. We were just out for a bit of fun is all."

"Is that right? Saints, I'm terribly sorry about this then. We'll get this all sorted out, don't you girls worry. Avonshire was it?"

"Temmings, actually."

"Ah, yes, right then. Let me just round up the other lads and we'll be off."

"Oh, thank you so much," Julia gushed. She turned and smiled triumphantly. "See? Just had to ask—"

"Jules, look out!"

But the pain was already shooting from her hand and snaking up her arm. Julia pressed her struck fingers against her chest and recoiled into a howling ball of agony. She forced her teary eyes open. The guard looked down at her with a snarl to match her own, a metal baton held at his side.

"I hope they sink you heathens to the bottom of the Dorne," he hissed through gritted teeth. "The good your demon god has done for you. Serves your lazy lot right. Think power should come easy then, do you? Think yourselves better than the rest of us?"

His eyes smoldered with a kind of hatred Julia had never seen before. Her mind struggled to make sense of what had happened, but the pain in her fingers was too great to focus on anything else. He spat at her feet and left.

Tilda shook her head. Tears streamed down her pinched face. "I told you! I told you not to call upon them. They're horrible! Utter bloody fiends!" She curled inward, sobbing into her drawn knees.

"We're gonna die here. We're gonna die."

"Pay her no mind," Emily whispered into Julia's ear. "I'm right here, okay? I won't leave you. Lay down, I got you." Julia laid her head on Emily's lap like they used to in the glen when it was just the four of them, laughing and gossiping like their youthful days would never end. Julia cradled her hand in her chest, Emily's lap already damp with tears and snot.

"I'll never leave you, Jules. I promise."

The next time Julia woke, pain was waiting to greet her.

"Easy now." Emily helped Julia upright. "There you go. Careful, careful." Julia winced. Her fingers felt more like flame than flesh.

"Give me your bad hand."

"Why?"

"Stop being so dodgy. Just let me see it."

Julia frowned and lifted her injured hand. Her index and middle finger were swollen purplish blue from nail to knuckle and twice the size they should be. Sleep had helped her ignore the pain, but now that she was awake it coursed through her hand with renewed vigor.

Emily pulled out a thimble sized jar tucked in her skirts. She unscrewed the top and gingerly rubbed a cool salve on Julia's swollen fingers. Within seconds her fingers numbed and the pain ceased to a whimper of its former intensity. Julia stared wide-eyed at her hand as she wiggled her fingers.

"Em, where did you get this? It's wonderful!"

Emily smiled coolly. "Just keep it hidden, okay?"

Julia threw her arms around Emily, careful to keep her injured hand raised. Tears prickled the corners of her eyes. "I'm so glad to have you here with me. I'd much rather be back home, truthfully, but you know."

Emily laughed. "You're awful at this, you know that?"

"Shut up, you know what I mean."

Emily hugged her tighter. "I do."

That's when Julia caught Tilda looking back at her with a mixture of pity and disgust. She pulled away from Emily and scowled. "Something you need to say, Tilda?"

Tilda scoffed and closed her eyes. She burrowed deeper into her arms feigning indifference, but Julia knew whatever words she'd swallowed down for civility when they first arrived had long burned a hole in her throat.

"You know, I didn't think the rumors were true about you, Emily," Tilda replied, ignoring Julia completely. "But it looks like you really will bed anyone."

Emily was on her feet before Julia could say anything.

"Oh, did Charity tell you that one, Tilda? Saving it for a rainy day? Or were you actually able to form a thought of your own for once?"

"He bashed her damn fingers in and you take him for some ointment?"

"And what else was I to do?" Emily barked back. "Give you in my place instead?" She laughed mirthlessly. "I'd be lying if I said it didn't cross my mind, but I couldn't trust a sniveler like you to get the job done properly."

Tilda shook her head, lips pursed. "They were right about you. Nothing but a cursed child of the forest leading your merry little band of Graces to do your bidding. You ruin everything."

Julia's breath caught in her throat as she tried to push out the words crowding her tongue. Everything was moving too fast. "Em, is that true? Did you do something with that guard? For me?"

"I only did it to help," she replied, her voice barely above a whisper. "Your fingers … I couldn't let you suffer like that. You're my best friend."

Tilda let out a wicked laugh. "Best friend? Are you joking? Everyone knows you bed Har—"

Emily had Tilda pinned to the ground with her hands wrapped around Tilda's throat in the blink of an eye.

Julia sprang to her feet to pull Emily off, but she pushed Julia away. For the brief moment when they locked eyes, Julia saw it again. That dark gleefulness hidden beneath the blue of Emily's eyes.

She enjoyed the violence. She *believed* in it.

Bile burned the back of Julia's throat. "Emily, get off her! You're hurting her!"

Emily looked back down at Tilda, who was kicking and flailing trying to buck her off.

"And why shouldn't I make her suffer?" Emily replied. "What has she done but make everyone's life utterly miserable because they don't cower to Charity, or Temming ideals, or their precious Saint Father?"

"Because she's not the villain here!"

Emily went perfectly still. She let go of Tilda's throat and slowly stood. Tilda scrambled back to the corner holding her throat and wheezing between breaths. She never took her eyes off Emily, staring her down like a feral cat ready to strike.

Emily's expression hardened, but her eyes remained soft with hurt. "How can you say that?"

"Did you really bed Harrison?" The words rushed out of Julia in a torrent. Something inside her had broken open and refused to stay contained.

"Yes." Emily met Julia's gaze, sincere and unflinching. She smiled and tilted her head. "For you."

"What?"

"I told you," Tilda wheezed. "She's not your friend."

Emily ignored her. "I didn't want to hurt you, Jules, really. You have to know that. I'm so sorry if I did, but I knew it'd hurt you more if I let your feelings lull you into a courtship with him. I did it to save you from that. From him. He's bad, Jules." Emily took a step closer to Julia, who took a step back. "You said so yourself remember? You want to travel and see the world. All he wants is a wife who will give him kids and stay pretty and quiet. I figured if I could protect you and take his heart instead, then maybe you—"

"What?" Julia cut in. "Run off with you, Martha, and Dorothy and shirk off everything? Just abandon Temmings and our families to go be young and poor in some Lordhaven gutter? Bloody hell, Emily! How could you do that to me?"

But Emily didn't need to answer. Julia already knew. Emily was charming and lovely and beautiful. Of course Harrison would fall in love with her. It would be so easy. But his moral compass would never let his heart cave into such a fantasy. He'd feel foolish and hurt for believing he could ever be with her, the cursed child from the forest, an orphan abandoned in the wickedest of places. How easy it would be for him to fall for the scathing rumors that grew from the seeds of heartbreak she left scattered in her wake. How easy it would be to blame her when he found himself drawn to her best friend, the closest he could be to the real thing, but knowing loving her would never fill the void Emily had intentionally left behind to ruin him. How easy it would be then to fall right into Emily's hands at Gafton Manor, drunk and hurt and wanting, when she offered to let him back in one last time. Not for love, but to destroy him in the eyes of the Graces and further close off their garden with a thorn wall of blood and heartbreak.

How easy.

Julia sank to her knees. She stared into nothing as everything overtook her. Hurt, rage, gratitude, embarrassment, sadness.

Emily had filled her empty spaces, held the keys to her locked doors and named the shadows in her mind, so familiar they were with each other. Emily was her best friend, her first friend, and that had always placed her closer in her heart than even Martha or Dorothy. She always assumed Emily felt the same. But now she wondered if she had been just as foolish as Harrison.

Had it all meant nothing? Was our friendship just another game to her? Julia wondered in horror.

"But you knew ... you knew I ..." Julia swallowed her words and let them fall away into the dark pit growing inside of her. "How many of them did you ruin?"

"Jules, I—"

"How many?"

Emily stilled. "You deserved better than them."

"You don't get to decide what I deserve!"

"I was only trying to help ..."

You made me feel worthless, Julia wanted to say, to scream, to cry out. Her mind crumpled inward into the familiar bed of lies and daydreams that had always comforted her. But her heart was too heavy to hold and instead she tumbled through, further and further down the rabbit hole of her own darkness.

Another crack in the mask.

Emily closed the distance between them. When her hand reached out to hold Julia's cheek, Julia rose to meet it. It would always be this way for them; intrinsically tied like the moon and tides, locked into a cycle of pushing and pulling, but never letting go.

"Did you enjoy it?" Julia said in a whisper colored by grief and anger. "Were you even ready?"

"That doesn't matter."

"It *does* matter, Emily. You matter. Your safety matters. Your well-being fucking matters."

"I did this for you!" Emily cried, mouth twisted into a scowl. "Why do you always make it about them or me? It was for you. It's always been for you! I do everything for you! Can't you see that?"

Julia looked up and met Emily's gaze, unguarded and glassy. The weight of unspoken apologies and broken promises hung in the air between them.

Hot tears pressed behind Julia's eyes.

I know, she wanted to say. *I forgive you.*

"Tilda's right," Julia said instead. "You ruin everything."

Behind them, a door groaned on its hinges. The heavy footfalls of approaching guards echoed down the halls. The guard who had injured Julia's hand approached the cell flanked by four other guards. A satisfied grin warped his face.

"Round up, heathens. Time to face your sins."

Tilda let out a shriek as the guards dragged her to her feet. Emily and Julia went wordlessly behind her. Neither struggled this time. When a bag was shoved over Julia's head, she was grateful for the darkness. She couldn't bear to see Emily's face.

The guards led the girls down several corridors that snaked and curved in various directions. At some point the sunlight warmed Julia's skin and the air changed, only for it to fade back into the balminess and smooth stone floor of a narrow hall. Finally, a pair of doors opened, and they were led inside a room thick with heat and the cloying smell of sweat and perfume. The girls were deposited at the center of the room and shoved down on their knees. Julia let out a small yelp as her knees hit the hardwood floor beneath.

When the bags were removed, Julia winced against the brightness of the sunlight streaming in. When her vision finally adjusted, the towering pulpit of the magistrate caught her attention first. To her right, a grim-faced jury watched them in silence. Each of the twelve looked freshly powdered and rosy cheeked, fashioned more for a ball than a trial.

A constable dressed in the royal dark red and gold livery stood at the base of the magistrate's tower holding a polished glaive. He knocked the bottom of the glaive's pole three times against the floor.

"All arise for The Honorable Chief Magistrate William Sedley."

The room stood in unison while the girls watched, from their knees, as Chief Magistrate Sedley took his seat at the head of the court. He was a rail of a man with a long, gaunt face and a white, powdered wig that made his skin appear sickly pale. His lips were pursed as if he'd just bitten into something sour. Julia didn't much care for anything about him.

Sedley sighed and waived his hand. "Take your seats." Everyone hastily sat back down. He motioned for another man sitting at one of the two tables in front of the girls to come forward.

"The charges, Mr. Ludthorpe."

Thomas Ludthorpe gave a small nod and rose from the table to Julia's left. He was a short, mustached man clad in a stately dark green vest and slicked back blond hair. He strode to the front of the room, hands clasped behind his back.

"Your Honor, I present to you today three young women—Miss Emily Colby, Miss Julia Sheffield and Miss Tilda Conroy— accused of making an unlawful covenant with the Demon King Azavith and the illegal practice of spellcraft."

A collective gasp rang sharp behind Julia, followed by fervent mutterings and prayers. Sedley pounded the gavel.

"Silence! Silence!"

When the room was quiet once again, he motioned to Ludthorpe to continue.

"We have collected evidence of these crimes, Your Honor and the court wishes to present them."

Sedley nodded. "You may proceed."

A young man that had been standing near the jury handed Ludthorpe a sealed envelope. Julia watched with bated breath as he opened the envelope and read aloud the letter inside.

"I present to the jury signed testimonials from one Mr. Harrison Goldwell and one Father Giles O'Malley." He cleared his throat and began to read. "Mr. Harrison, a childhood acquaintance, testifies, under the urging of his parents, to witnessing Miss Colby, Miss Sheffield, and Miss Conroy—the accused—making frequent, unchaperoned trips to the nearby forest for an hour or more leading up to the event of their capture two nights ago during a ritual summoning. Mr. Goldwell testifies he was among several others who were forced to attend this illegal gathering against their will as potential vessels for Azavith."

Julia's hand throbbed and her heart began to beat against her chest. *No no no no no no.* Harrison wouldn't testify against them. He hated lying above all else. And he was her friend. He wouldn't betray her like that ... would he?

Emily had, a small voice reminded her.

Ludthrope barreled ahead like a well-timed train, swift and assured. He read aloud Father O'Malley's testimony next. Father O'Malley, who had known them since they were children, called their whisperings suspicious and that their disinterest during his sermons was concerning.

"Furthermore," Ludthorpe continued, "we found no one willing to come forth to speak to their good character, which was quite troubling indeed." He cast a pitiful glance at the girls as he returned to his seat.

"What of our parents?" Julia blurted. "Our relatives and friends? Did anyone speak with them?"

The deafening knock of Sedley's gavel drowned out her pleas. "I demand silence from the accused!"

Julia trembled with fury. Everything was falling too fast for her bound hands to catch. Emily's ointment was also beginning to wear off and the pain in her hand was rekindling with each passing second.

Sedley gestured to the petite brunette sitting beside Mr. Ludthorpe. "Mrs. Parnell, please proceed to the examinations."

Margaretta Parnell, Ludthorpe's head legal understudy, rose and briskly walked to the front of the room. While pleasant faced, she emanated the efficiency of a hunter closing in on its prey.

"Thank you, Your Honor. I shall now demonstrate to the court and its honorable witnesses a brief mental and physical examination of the accused. It is our hope this examination may clear any doubts our respected jury may still carry." She trained her focus on Tilda.

Parnell opened a copy of the *True Word* to a random page.

"Miss Conroy, please recite Saint James's speech to his son, Samuel, when he discovers a raven has spoken to him." Her gaze flickered to the jury. "For reference, this is page 203, verse four. A very well-known passage Father O'Malley testified to having recited many times in his sermons of which the accused was present."

"Um, he … he says …" but the more Tilda fumbled for the words the more restless the crowd became behind her. Despite her contempt for Tilda, Julia couldn't help but will the memory to surface for the poor girl. Parnell frowned.

"Let the record show Miss Conroy failed to recite a well-known verse from the *True Word*, which is a sign of her pact with Azavith. Scripture can be notoriously difficult to call upon for his followers once a deal has been forged."

She flipped to another, earlier page and looked down at Emily.

"Miss Colby, please recite Saint Andrew's speech upon the Blood Grounds."

Emily's gaze rose to meet Parnell's. She never wavered. "O, brothers and sisters, I beseech thee; eat not from the rotting life tree of this world, for it is poisoned with the blood of spellcasters. Raise your spade in commitment to nurture a garden of your own, fed by the sweat of your brow and the sunlight above."

Parnell nodded, tempering a frown. "Yes, that is correct. However, let the jury note Miss Colby's blood sacrifice to Azavith." She pulled Emily to her feet and jerked her around for the jury to see the ladder of faint pink scars rising from her wrist to the middle of her forearm. Emily tried to break free of Parnell, but the woman's grasp was too tight.

"Get your hands off me!" Emily snarled.

A guard appeared by Parnell's side and quickly shoved Emily back down on her knees. She winced, but Julia knew it was her pride that was truly wounded. She had only ever shown the Graces those scars when they were thirteen. They were easy enough to hide beneath gloves and dress sleeves, easy to ignore the growing number of them behind smiles and laughter.

When Parnell reached Julia, she looked pleased, smug even. Julia's face was flush with rage. "How dare you. You don't know anything about us! None of you do!"

Parnell's gaze narrowed. "Civility, Miss Sheffield. Now, please recite—"

"No, I won't," Julia cut in. "Fuck you, actually."

A collective gasp reverberated through the crowd. An older woman in the jury box fanned herself as if she may faint.

"Excuse me?" Parnell snapped.

"This is a sham, Your Honor," Julia said, ignoring Parnell. "Tilda is clearly too stressed to recall the passage. Her family attends readings nearly every day. And Emily's scars aren't from blood sacrifices. They're from a scared girl too ashamed to tell anyone awful things can sometimes feel too big to control. I promise if you'd just speak to our parents—"

The bang of Sedley's gavel silenced her.

"Miss Sheffield, the court has presented signed testimonials. Your accomplices have proven their heresy when given the chance to demonstrate otherwise. No one in Temmings came forward to speak in your defense and unfortunately your parents couldn't be reached. Now, I urge you to remain silent or risk further incriminating yourself with such outlandish behavior."

Julia sank further into herself. The eyes of the court, the finality of the gavel's ring, Tilda's trembling lip and Emily's empty gaze fell away. Tears ran hot down her cheeks. She could feel herself coming undone. The mask was slipping. She closed her eyes and waited in the darkness.

Somewhere a woman ceased talking and slammed a holy book closed.

Somewhere a jury called three girls fateshifters in a voice loud and certain.

And somewhere else those girls were told they were not girls, they were heretics, and they were to be hung at dawn.

13

TOBIAS

"Day 14: Patient's appetite is normal. Reports persistent migraines, most commonly in the morning. Prescribed a tinct of hypnum. Day 32: Appetite remains normal. Migraines have eased, but dreams persist. Recalls wolves, specifically. Will continue to monitor." – *Dr. Albertson Moraine, Patient Log #42 (R. Taylor), New Castle Medical College, Lordhaven, Halcyon*

Tobias arrived at 134 Dalton Street shortly before mid-morning.

The swell of clouds had all but emptied the Garden District of open roofed social carriages, strolling couples and picnickers on their way to Trolley Green. A stray breeze thick with chill and the promise of rain rustled the trees. Pip fidgeted in her carrier.

"Easy there, girl," Tobias cooed. "I promise to have you back before the thunder kicks in."

Pip pressed her small pink nose to the front of the carrier. She was on the smaller side for a North Sable ferret, but what she lacked in size she more than made up for in chasing out rats. Olly let out a small bark. Tobias shook his head and patted the terrier on the head.

"You getting jealous, huh? Or just eager to snare some rats?"

Olly looked up with wide brown eyes, his short tail wagging eagerly.

"All right you two, let's get on with it then."

Tobias put on fingerless leather gloves to hide his hand tattoo, then opened the waist high gate and walked down the brick pathway to the rear service door. Olly shuffled along beside him. Tobias knocked twice and an older woman opened the door. She was dressed in a crisp black dress and white apron. Her dark brown hair, marbled with grey streaks, was tied back in a bun.

"Good morning, ma'am," Tobias said with a slight bow. "I'm here to respond to the rat removal request."

The woman raised a brow.

"Hmph. A bit on the young side, aren't you?"

"I promise my work is good, ma'am."

She eyed him over, then looked down at Pip and Olly. "Well, can't be any worse than that charlatan the week prior." She opened the door wider and peered over his shoulder at the other manors. "Come in, quickly now."

Tobias hurried in before she could change her mind. Olly trotted in after him.

"You can call me Mrs. Pennison. You'll be inspecting the basement right over here. The pesky beasts have gotten into the food storage and I'm afraid at this rate our pantry will be bare before the leaves turn."

Mrs. Pennison removed a thick set of keys from her apron pocket and unlocked the basement. A musty smell crawled up the stairs.

"Mr. Weatherby will pay at the agreed rate offered—three sterling a head. Do you accept?"

Tobias smiled, already heading down the creaky wooden steps into half-darkness below, an empty rutsack at the ready. Olly yipped with excitement, bolting ahead of him.

"Tell Mr. Weatherby to ready his purse."

Tobias emerged an hour or so later to see a young girl around his age washing plates. She stopped mid-wash when she spotted him in the doorway.

"Done already?"

Tobias's voice caught in his throat as an awkward smile broke across his face. As he grasped for something to say to the pretty housemaid, he didn't notice Olly skirting around him to explore the rest of the kitchen.

The girl's gaze traveled down to the little terrier sniffing a porcelain water dish. "Oh, aren't you the cutest!"

She quickly dried her hands and kneeled down to scratch Olly behind his ears.

"Does he have a name?"

"Oh, uh, Olly. And this here's Pip." Tobias held up the carrier. "She's a bit on the shy side."

"So you use them to catch the rats?"

"Aye. Trained 'em myself."

"Funny, I didn't take rat catchers to be the handsome sort." The girl snuck a scrap of hardened biscuit from her apron and gave it to Olly. "Wait here, I'll be right back."

"R-Right then," Tobias replied, a clumsy grin on his face.

Not a moment later, Mrs. Pennison appeared in the doorway. The young maid trailed behind her, a demure smile on her face.

Tobias tried to catch her eye but caught himself and opened the sack for Mrs. Pennison instead. "Five in all, ma'am. I can pull them out if you'd like."

"Yes, please do," Mrs. Pennison said with a raised nose, turning her clasped hands inward.

Tobias laid out the small corpses in a row. Olly sat nearby, tail wagging with pride. Mrs. Pennison motioned to the rats.

"Yes, yes that'll do." She nodded to the girl. "Amelia, take this to Weston. He'll handle the disposal."

"Yes, ma'am." She gave Tobias a wink as she took the sack from him and disappeared down a nearby hall.

Tobias hid a smile as Mrs. Pennison's narrowed gaze found him. She pulled out a burgundy coin purse and removed a handful of coins.

"Fifteen sterlings, as agreed."

Tobias pocketed the money eagerly. "Thank you, ma'am. I'll be around if the household should be in need again. Come on, Olly."

The wind picked up as Tobias headed down Dalton Street to Arndale Crossing, the main street that ran through the Theatre District. The quiet of the Garden District gave way to the clamor of street peddlers, clomping hooves and pedestrian chatter. Grand, glass domed theatres nestled beside small pill box venues, every arched window, velveteen rich painted exterior, and snake oil powered signage more garish than the last. Cramped, one rider Ellington cabs darted between glossy carriages and daytime show patrons brave enough to venture across the roadway. Painters lined the streets proudly displaying their colorful prints finished just that morning while actors from various tropes staged snippet shows to sell tickets to the evening's full production. Tobias wove his way through the crowded walkway and stopped by a vendor to purchase a meat pie. Pip and Olly both stirred, eager for a bite.

"Oi, give me a minute, you two."

Tobias settled down on the nearby steps of a closed dress shop, its windows glossed over with old playbills and tonic adverts.

He broke off a small piece of the pie for Olly, who was already perched with both paws on Tobias's knee.

"There you go, boy."

Next, he broke off a smaller piece for Pip and fed her through the carrier bars. She eagerly nibbled at the buttery crust.

Tobias smiled. "There's a good girl."

Finally, he tore the remaining pie in half and wrapped one half for Lucy and kept the other out for himself. He took a small bite, knowing better than to rush through a good meal. He closed his eyes as he savored the flaky crust and spiced meat.

These times were his favorite. The quiet moments between jobs when the world paused long enough to let him catch his breath.

But these times were never long enough.

He gave Olly a scratch behind the ear. "All right, time for the next house."

Olly gave a quick bark as Tobias grabbed Pip's carrier. His next stop was at the end of Arndale Crossing and a stone's throw from the Eddleton Stage, the most popular outdoor theatre in the area. Remnants of the Seven Swords Festival still lingered—one man on a ladder untied blue and gold ribbons from a shoe shop awning while another man snored loudly beneath, a smudged blue sword on his cheek and a flask tucked in his breast pocket. A young woman in a blue and yellow dress sat on the corner opposite, calling out for sterling to get a train ride home.

Tobias passed by a boy selling leftover penny papers when he spotted a crowd gathering up ahead. A trio of constables managed to keep the swell of people nearest them at bay, but onlookers were growing around them at a worrisome rate. A woman near the front stumbled backwards, her hand covering her mouth.

"By the Father's mercy!" she wailed, pale as a sheet. "What has become of this city?"

A chill ran up the back of Tobias neck. His grip tightened around Pip's carrier handle. *Walk away,* he urged himself. *Whatever this is doesn't concern you.*

He quickened his pace and kept his head down. All he had to do was walk past this crowd and not look up. It wasn't his business.

"... damn those bloody Market Street thugs," a nearby man swore.

Tobias froze.

Market Street thugs?

He looked to his right. Plain as day, in big, bloody letters along the alley wall read: *FRESH FROM MARKET STREET.* Tobias barely had time to turn around before the meat pie surged from his throat in one burning torrent and into the gutter.

The image was seared into his mind, etched in the darkness behind his eyes—male, young, Seadevil, swaying on the bloody end of his own hook like a caught fish. Beneath him, slumped against the wall, was a second young man with hair white as snow and his throat rimmed in a waterfall of red.

Run.

His body heaved out the last of the meat pie as heat rushed to his face. Breaths came out in fiery, ragged gasps, drowning out Olly's fervent barking.

Run.

More City Watch constables were coming now, pouring in from all sides, shoving the crowd back and shouting for order. Someone knocked into Tobias, their elbow jabbing into his side and jerking him from his nauseated stupor.

RUN.

Tobias grabbed Olly and Pip and ran as fast as his legs could carry him to the Market Street headquarters, bile thick on his tongue and fear fresh in his veins. Overhead, the first rumbles of thunder echoed across the Theatre District.

A storm was coming.

When Tobias burst through the doors of the old distillery, no less than four pistols levelled at his head within seconds.

It was Olly's yelp that brought all the Market Streeters to their senses. The terrier tore from Tobias's grasp and darted beneath a table.

"Bloody hell, mate. Nearly blew your top off." A stocky man with a patchwork of scars across his dark tan face lowered his pistol first. "Oi, lower your arms lads. Just the runt." The man walked to the front as the others resumed their card games and drinking. Yet everyone kept an eye on Tobias, who was doubled over and gulping for air.

"What's all this then?" the man asked, his breath thick with gin and his bottom lip lined with melia chew. "The coppers on you?"

"No," Tobias managed to wheeze. "Mar-Marcellus. Where is he?"

"No go, lad. Boss is with—Oi! I said he's busy!"

Tobias was halfway to Marcellus's office, Pip's carrier still in hand, when he someone grabbed his arm.

"Oi, mate, got a minute?"

Tobias turned and came face to face with his old crewmate, Charley Baxter. Despite being a couple years older, Charley still ran with the graveyard shift, the gang's lowest rung. Tobias lost count of how many times he and Ezra tried to get Charley to join them on the better paying snatcher marks for the colleges and surgical theatres, but Charley always refused.

"Sorry, Charley I really need to see Marcellus and—"

Charley shook his head as Pip squirmed in her carrier. "That mess up there near Brunswick. You saw it, didn't you?"

Tobias nodded. "Aye. It was...bad."

Charley ran his hand over his tight black coils.

"Seven hells. Wes was right then ... I ran into him on my way back here and ... saints, he was rattled like I've never seen. Utterly mad. Said it was absolutely brutal."

"Wes? From the Green Co—"

Charley silenced him with a glare. Tobias let the words die on his tongue and nodded. "Right. His word's good. Just tell him to be careful."

"How can I do that? The Theatre District will be locked down after this. Ain't no place'll be safe. For any of us." Charley lowered his voice to a harsh whisper. "Every gang banner will be out for blood, coin and territory."

Tobias gripped Charley's shoulder. "He'll be fine, Charley. The clovers keep to themselves. Mama Kilburn makes sure of it. They don't dabble in shark and market business. You'll both be back to candlelit dinners soon."

A smile tugged at the corner of Charley's mouth.

"Thanks, mate. I hope so."

Tobias headed down the hall to Marcellus's office. He threw open the door. Inside, three pairs of eyes all directed their attention to him.

"Toby?"

A girl around Tobias's age with deep brown eyes and a tawny beige hue was sitting across from Marcellus. Her dark curly hair was tied back in a hastily done bun. She raised a thick brow in surprise.

Before he could respond, a brawny, blond-haired man permanently tanned by years of pirating under the summer sun, affixed Tobias with a glare as sharp as the dagger sheathed at his waist. He pushed off the far wall and blocked Tobias from further entry.

"No one summoned you, Flemming," the man snarled, twisting Tobias's surname like a slur. "Get back outside."

"Let 'im be, Roderick." Marcellus waived Tobias over. "Have a seat, lad."

Tobias exchanged glares with Roderick as he took a seat beside the girl. Marcellus gestured towards the door.

"Let's pick this up later, Tavia."

"But the—"

"*Later*, Octavia." Marcellus's tone was enough to make Tavia swallow whatever protest she had planned. The chair screeched against the wood floor as she stood to leave. Tobias shot her a quick look but she ignored him. Roderick shut the door behind her with more force than necessary.

Marcellus leaned back in his chair, bridging his fingers over his taunt middle. He was a large man, with a wise, disquieting look trapped behind dark grey eyes and faint scars crossing over his rosy brown arms.

"I take it you have something weighing you down?"

"Aye. I—" Tobias hesitated, pushing down the nausea building in his stomach. "I was in the Theatre District runnin' some rat catching jobs and this crowd started forming and a bunch of coppers swarmed in. I only got a glimpse but—"

Marcellus held up his hand.

"I know of it. No need to do that to yourself." He lifted a letter from his desk. "I received word shortly before you came in." He chuckled, tossing the letter aside. "Looks like I should have you on carrier duty instead. Nearly beat the pigeon here."

"But it's not true, is it? We didn't kill a Seadevil, right?"

"We're already looking into it. In the meantime, I recommend staying here or find a safe place to ride this out at least for a few days. You're at a flat above Higdin's, right? With your sister?"

Tobias didn't bother correcting him. "Aye."

"Well that's as good a place as any. Hilda's a right boar on the worse of days."

"Or the best," Tobias mumbled.

"In any case, I'll be sharing the news with the others soon. For now, lay low and stay vigilant." He nodded towards Pip. "And no more jobs until this matter is settled. I know the boards in every nook and cranny of this city. Kill a rat, sweep a chimney or turn in as much as a fingernail to a college or surgical theatre and I'll hang you under Corvin Bridge myself."

Tobias shot to his feet. "I'm not some kid. I can handle myself. How am I supposed to eat if I can't earn?"

Roderick took a step closer. "Do we have ourselves a problem here?"

Tobias didn't answer.

"I'm not going to let you and your sister starve, Tobias," Marcellus said in a low tone. "Trust that I realize what I'm asking of you and everyone else here."

Tobias clenched his fist. "You didn't ... you didn't see him hanging there. They gutted him. Drove his own hook through his neck. Deadeye will want blood for this."

Marcellus's expression remained unchanged. "He always wants blood. It wouldn't surprise me if he hung the poor bastard there himself." Marcellus rubbed his beard. Flecks of grey dotted it more and more these days.

"Go home, lad. You'll have what you need soon."

Tobias kicked back the chair as he stood and grabbed Pip's carrier. *Like hell I will.* He ignored Roderick's glower as he left Marcellus's office.

Outside, Tavia was seated in the corner of the bar. Olly sat in her lap, tongue lolling to the side.

Tobias took the seat next to hers and set Pip's carrier on top of the bar. Without a word, Shani, the resident bartender and reigning Market Street arm wrestling champ, slid over a glass of sour jack cider.

"Quite the state you're in today," she said as she began polishing a glass.

Tobias finished off his cider in one gulp. Lemon juice, barrel water, and apple cider never tasted so refreshing.

"Spare me," he bemoaned. Did she know the sharks were circling, hungry for revenge? Could she feel the ripples in Lordhaven's waters? Tobias set down his empty glass. Even now he could still taste bile on his tongue.

Tavia cleared her throat. "What happened out there?"

"Do you know where Ezra is?"

"Passed out upstairs, why?"

"Good." Tobias slumped forward. "The Seadevils will be swarming soon. One of 'em was killed with a pedestrian and we were made to look like the ones who did it."

"Bloody hell." Tavia's light brown eyes hardened. "Who did it?"

"Dunno. Seadevils won't care either way. They'll want a Market Streeter or two for sure."

"Wanna bet I find them first?" A wicked grin spread across her face. "Cut my teeth on 'em. No one pushes the Market Streeters into a corner."

"You really need more friends."

Tavia snorted. "I have you and Princess Ezra asleep in his castle upstairs. Also, Charley. And of course, Ollykins and Piplette too!" Tavia squealed, pressing her nose against Olly's and wiggling her finger for Pip to sniff. "The less friends the better. Not so messy when it all goes mad."

Tobias shot her a dark look. "We're not doing this right now."

Tavia stopped petting Olly. "You know I'm right." Her eyes flickered to Tobias's ropeburn. She waited for Shani to be out of earshot before continuing. "The wolf blood is in us. It's not something we can stop," she said in a lowered voice. "You need to get your hands dirty. Feed the violent urges. It'll help ease the nightmares, trust me. I never have to tie my wrists. And I heard from a soothsayer a new moon will bring out the nightmares strongest while a full moon is our highest clarity. She said depending on the phase our violence can heighten or lessen, so mind the phases."

Tobias folded his arms, hiding his wrists. Moon phases, dreams, mad blood. Saints, he didn't need any of this. He wasn't going to become a killer to get a better night's rest.

"You trustin' soothsayer rubbish now, eh?"

"Better to try and tame the beast than fight it. If you change your mind, you know where to find me." Tavia stood and left Olly on her seat. A certain darkness flickered behind her eyes as a crooked smile etched itself across her face.

"Just follow the blood."

14

NATHANIEL

"Similar to snakes, duskborn fangs are hollow. When bitten, a clear, venom-like substance is ejected into the bloodstream through a minute hole at the end of the fangs. Incapacitation will vary based on volume injected." – *Dr. Lillian Loveney,* Characteristics of Reported Duskborn Encounters in Lordhaven, 1852 - 1855

Following his meeting with Claude, Nathaniel reassured himself a battle may have been lost, but the war was far from over.

He mulled over each morsel of information as the Trevet carriage crawled along Chapel Street at a laughably slow pace. Claude was set to reveal the next stage of his plan—some sort of partnership—at Lord Henley's summer ball, but with whom? The Order of the Boar was the strongest organized league of duskborn outside of the Shujaa, the legion of tribes pledged to the Malsik. It would have to be someone not only powerful but well-connected and terribly ambitious.

Sweat pooled beneath Nathaniel's shirt collar. The leather seats and drawn velvet curtains stood little chance against the encroaching Skyfire heat. Nathaniel briskly tapped on the driver's window. An older gentleman with soft blue eyes marked by crow's feet and a snow grey moustache slid back the partition.

"Yes, Master Trevet?"

"Anders, what in the saints is taking so long?"

Anders bowed his head. "I do apologize, sir. It appears to be some sort of roadblock up ahead."

"Roadblock?"

"Yes, sir. There are several constables blocking off Arndale Crossing. I'd wager some sort of gang activity."

"Of course it is." Nathaniel sighed. Lordhaven's four most notable gangs—the Market Streeters, the Seadevils, the Green Coats, and the Barrel Boys—were nuisances on most days, but when their street squabbles spilled over the whole of Lordhaven suffered.

Nathaniel reached beneath his carriage seat and pulled out a sheet of blank parchment and a travel quill set on a lap-sized writing board. He hastily penned two letters, both identical in wording, and slipped each into an envelope. He didn't have a means to seal them, but it was just as well. The source of delivery would be enough.

"Anders, I need you to deliver these letters for me. One to Rose and the other to Samir. Tell them to speak of its contents to no one." He grabbed his top hat. "When you're done, wait for me at the Heritage House Tearoom. It'll be easier to reach my appointment at Brunswick Theatre on foot."

"Of course, sir." Anders peered over his shoulder. "And do be careful."

Nathaniel smirked. "Aren't I always?"

He exited the carriage and weaved through the crowd packed onto Chapel Street. Craned necks and whispered chatter intermingled with the barking orders from constables to disperse in an orderly fashion.

"Nothing to see here, ladies and gentlemen," one pot-bellied constable in red and black uniform called. A black patch with "CITY WATCH" threaded in silver letters adorned his jacket. "Please exit the area at once. Come, move along now."

"Was it a murder?" a woman called.

"Utter monsters!" another man shouted from behind Nathaniel. "When will this city be rid of those criminals? The monarchy needs to *do* something!"

The rich copper tang of blood hung on the heat. Nathaniel's head swiveled in the direction of the scent to find a heavily guarded alleyway. Two men in overalls and boots stood on a scaffold high above the City Watch constables. They scrubbed away at a painted message, but not fast enough to stop onlookers from deducing the Market Streeters were somehow involved in a crime in Green Coats territory.

Ah, petty squabbles of street royalty, Nathaniel mused and moved on. *Let the rats eat each other.*

The swell of people thinned the closer he got to the theatre's main side door entrance. The Brunswick Theatre's famous glass dome top and carved stone ribbon of famous playwrights and figures gave it a dramatic flair Nathaniel never ceased to admire. He skirted past the closed entrance and instead took a discreet set of stairs down to an unmarked basement door. He produced a key from his pocket and unlocked it.

The hall was sparsely lit. Boxes of old costumes, ropes and overhead lights lay scattered about. Posters for bygone shows were plastered along the walls, some overlapping each other, and the oldest of them were yellowed by kellweed smoke. Nathaniel hurried down the hall and into what used to be the theatre's original dressing room. Two beds lined either wall and a makeshift dresser had been made from an old powder vanity. A single crate stood in the center of the room, adorned with a gas lamp, knife and a note with some numbers scrawled across it. By all accounts, the room looked to be no more than a squatter's den.

Just then, Nathaniel's eyes cut to a shadow that had not been there before.

A hooded figure slightly taller than his own six-foot frame emerged from the darkness. They were clad in a slim black hunting vest and pants ribbed in hidden whalebone. The figure watched Nathaniel through a white owl mask that covered the upper half of their face. A second black covering concealed the bottom half.

The owl mask marked the figure as a Watcher, the talons of Lordhaven. Assassins who only acted for the highest bidder of their choosing. Nathaniel didn't waver. A hunter never backed down from another. Anything less would indicate weakness and a swift death.

"Nathaniel," said the figure, his voice surly but tempered. "Here to seek the services of the Watchers, eh?"

"Perhaps." Nathaniel clasped his hands behind him. "It came to my attention that while I was away on a recent business trip, Claude had a meeting with the Malsik. He wouldn't share the finer details of course, but I'm hoping the Watchers can help fill in the blanks."

The Watcher tilted his head. "Sounds like an Order issue. Perhaps you should ask one of your lackeys."

Nathaniel smirked. "It's on my list. But whatever Claude is hiding, Beza sent me a warning last night not to trust it. She must have a reason for reaching out. And as her top *lackey* surely you must know about it too."

The Watcher grunted. "I warned her not to get involved. Let the chips fall where they may." He took a step forward. "I advise you do the same."

"You know I can't do that, Renzo."

Renzo laughed mirthlessly. "Bastards of the same barrel, you and Beza. Aye, nothing but a godsdamn death wish. If the Malsik wants King Leonard's crown so badly let him take the bloody thing. What good has it ever done anyone anyway?"

"Are the Watchers bowing a knee to the future duskborn king now? Careful, Yorin might get jealous."

"Do not speak again of the Lady Goddess," Renzo hissed.

"I meant no offense, of course," Nathaniel added, lifting his hands. "Besides, it's Beza I was looking for. Do you know where she is?"

Renzo folded his arms across his broad chest. "Not around. She has other matters more important to contend with than your schoolyard squabbles."

"That is quite unfortunate. Although it's rather odd the leader of the Watchers would leave when Lordhaven is in such a state. Escalated gang fighting, Claude's secret meeting, a certain royal suddenly appearing in a surgical theatre. Seems...*risky* to leave her post right now."

Renzo closed the gap between them in an instant, hovering close enough for Nathaniel to see the yellow centers of his eyes floating in a sea of reflective black. Unblinking, like an owl.

"You need to leave, Nathaniel. Run along to your mansion now and leave these matters to rest."

Rumors had always alluded to the terrible and cruel ways Yorin, the Goddess of Nature had shaped those chosen few duskborn that renounced the Malsik and Archonix, the God of War, and worshipped her instead. But only now, inches from one of Yorin's devoted, did Nathaniel understand how different the Watchers were from other duskborn. Fanged owls neither the Malsik nor Claude could ever hope to tame in their pursuit for political glory.

Shaped by wicked hands, Nathaniel thought, a somber reminder of his own encounter all those years ago with another goddess. But even the divine wanted something; their devotees were no different.

Nathaniel leaned forward until he was close enough to smell the coal smoke and iron tinge of blood on Renzo's skin. He reeked of the city.

"The fifteenth day of Frostfall."

Renzo stiffened.

"You should be happy, Renzo. You'll no longer owe me a favor. Isn't that what you've always wanted?"

Renzo said nothing, but his hands were balled into knuckle white fists. A smug smile broke across Nathaniel's face.

"I'm not asking for much, really. Just tell me what you've seen. Where has Claude been going and with whom?"

"Beza asked me to keep an eye on him," Renzo said through gritted teeth. "She didn't explain why. I tracked him to a mansion last week in the Garden District. Kendleston Manor, Tyson Hoyt's residence. He exited a carriage with two others. Both were in travel cloaks, but they removed them once inside. One was a young girl, seventeen or eighteen, a proper lady by her hair ornaments, and the other her handmaid by the simple dress. She was around the same age with long, light blonde hair."

"Was Badru there?"

"The Waridian bodyguard? No. Claude was alone."

Nathaniel paced from one side of the room to the other, mulling over Renzo's information.

Hoyt must be the missing piece, he surmised. *The Hoyt's are the second most powerful of the Sacred Seven. They'd never turn down a chance to take down the Chases, especially if Claude volunteered to do the dirty work in exchange for financial backing. But why the girl and her attendant? Who are they?* The thought nagged at him almost as much as the King's missing unofficial heirs. Some parts were too neat while others made no sense at all.

"Consider my debt repaid, Nathaniel." Renzo motioned towards the door. "Don't come here again unless you've got a name to offer to the knife."

Nathaniel opened his pocket watch. "Very well. I appreciate your cooperation, Renzo." He snapped the watch shut and slipped it back inside his jacket. "Do tell Beza to call upon me when she's around again. I'll be returning to Thornwood this evening." As he walked towards the door, he peered over his shoulder, tipping his hat. "I have a feeling we'll be seeing each other again soon."

"May Yorin watch over you." Renzo slipped back into the shadows and vanished from the room as if he'd never been there at all.

Leaving Brunswick Theatre left Nathaniel with more questions than answers. What could Claude be planning to make the Watchers wary enough Beza would divert one of her higher ups to tailing him? And who was the young girl Renzo said Claude was with at Kendleston Manor?

As Nathaniel wrestled with these questions, Anders opened the driver partition and announced they'd be arriving at Thornwood Manor in a moment. Nathaniel paid him no mind. Thornwood dredged up its own questions he hadn't quite brought himself to answer yet.

The carriage came to a stop in front of a towering, wrought iron gate. Nathaniel parted the curtain and looked upon the high stone wall that bordered Thornwood's rose garden and wrapped around the back veranda and greenhouse. In the center loomed the sprawling three story manor outfitted in the ornate trim work of a royal wedding cake. If his father had given him anything at all, it was the appreciation of beautiful craftsmanship and an eye for the finer details. And in Thornwood, his father's eye had not failed.

Anders stepped down to unlock the massive gate. Unlike most residents in the Garden District, Nathaniel didn't have a gatekeep. His staff consisted of only three individuals whom he trusted more than anyone. They were the last of his familial house staff from Greybriar and Nathaniel couldn't bring himself to expand. Money could never buy enough trust.

As the carriage pulled up to the entrance, a woman and young man stood on the top step to greet them. Both were outfitted in dark grey and white staff uniforms and wore reserved expressions.

When Nathaniel stepped out, both the woman and young man offered tempered smiles. "Welcome back, Master Trevet," they greeted in unison.

The young boy, tall, pale and flaxen-haired, assisted Anders with Nathaniel's luggage. The woman, petite, olive-skinned and dark-haired, trailed behind the sole Trevet heir.

"I've prepared your room, Master Trevet," she said, her words still carrying the languid flow of an Arcadian southerner.

"Thank you, Carina. Though I'm quite famished."

"Of course. I'll arrange for lunch. It'll be but a moment, sir." Carina disappeared down a darkened hall to the kitchens while Nathaniel continued to the dining room. Portraits from de Vostoni and Grenwald adorned the room's gilded halls, their artistry illuminated by the soft lighting of the overhead chandelier.

Nathaniel took his place at the head of the table that comfortably sat sixteen. As if on cue, Carina walked into the room with a single domed plate, wine glass, and bottle of red wine. She set down the tray and poured Nathaniel a glass. As she stepped away, Nathaniel said, "Spare a moment, won't you?"

Carina's bright green eyes widened in surprise, but she nodded and took her seat adjacent to him.

"And how has Eribus been?" Nathaniel asked, snapping his napkin and laying it on his lap.

"Fine, sir. A bit fussy this morning, but I imagine he didn't expect you to be away as long as you were." She added in a lower whisper, "None of us did."

"Yes, it was a rather eventful outcome. I'm happy to be back."

He uncovered his plate to reveal a beating human heart, a thin cutlet of pickled liver and a fresh tossed salad to cleanse the palette. He carefully cut into the heart and took a bite. His mouth watered in delight by the subtle rawness. He cleared his throat and looked back at Carina, who watched him silently.

"Vigilance will be key in the upcoming weeks, Carina. I fear a storm is brewing in Lordhaven."

If Carina was troubled by this news, she didn't show it. "Shall I make preparations tonight?"

"Perhaps. And possibly a few of your nonna's concoctions."

Carina's brows furrowed together. "But Master Trevet, those are—"

"I know," Nathaniel replied. *"Not to be trifled with lightly."* He smirked, but he had never ventured into her workspace. Despite wondering what magicks she tinkered with in the estate's greenhouse, what vile whisperings she cast to conjure swirling shadows most hours of the day, blotting out sunlight and leaving occasional scratch marks in the glass, he learned long ago from Anders it was in one's best interest not to see the artist while at work. The process could be such a messy thing.

Nathaniel sipped his wine. "The full picture hasn't revealed itself yet, but when it does I don't want to be ill-prepared."

Carina folded her hands in front of her. Years of working and baking in the Trevet households had weathered them beyond her thirty-something years. "My nonna Marta's magic helped bring down that bastard king Raphaelo and his men and liberate Arcadia for a time. The best resistance fighter this side of the Silver Sea. But it changed her inside. Only a heart of pure vengeance and a knife sharp mind could cause a grimoire to give her the spells it did. I believe she made peace with her darkness. For her country and her family."

She looked up at Nathaniel with renewed determination "You mustn't hesitate, Master Trevet. Make your peace and go forward if that is what you believe best for the good of this kingdom."

Nathaniel took another sip of wine. *For the good of this kingdom and for me. A gift, really, for ages to come. They'll see.*

"What became of your nonna? After the Regent War?"

"She was labeled a war criminal and quartered before the new king and his court."

Nathaniel nodded and took another bite of heart. "That'll be all, Carina, thank you. And do let me know what wisdom you find among your nonna's notes."

About two hours later, Rose and Samir arrived. Anders opened the door to the Drawing Room and set down three cups.

"Your tea, Miss Blakely, Mister Mishra."

Nathaniel waved his hand. "That will be all, thank you Anders."

"Of course, Master Trevet."

Nathaniel took a sip of his tea as Anders slipped out of the room, closing the double doors behind him.

"I appreciate both of you seeing me on such short notice. Let us begin."

Rose spoke up first. She sat straight as a rod, her hands delicately folded in her lap, but her eyes gleamed with a particular viciousness more akin to a huntress than a proper lady.

"Yes, let's discuss why you arrived back in Lordhaven with little more than a hello, and now you call upon Samir and I during the height of social season to have tea in your..." Rose's eyes swept the room, "*empty* salon. It's all rather puzzling, Nathaniel. Perhaps some would say troubling even."

Nathaniel chuckled, as if his easy smile alone could waive away the accusation in Rose's voice or the truth to her words.

"I assure you nothing so dire occurred during my travels. I merely handled a few of the Order's affairs in Darby Town while on my way to Emismore for a bit of seaside air. It was all rather dull if I'm to be honest."

Sitting beside Rose was a young man whose honey brown face barely looked past twenty. His amber brown eyes brimmed with feigned apathy. As the youngest son set to inherit Khagal's largest silk empire, Samir Mishra was responsible for overseeing his father's many factories in southern Halcyon and was no stranger to the area.

"Darby Town? That filthy haunt?" Samir scrunched his nose. "Whatever were you doing there?"

"Claude desired an alliance with Myron Finch. In exchange for a cut of the Finch family's hollium and whiskey sales, he offered Finch and his men the Order's protection at their horse tracks and port entries for the next two years. I was sent to broker the deal."

"Are we rubbing elbows with gangs now?" Rose scoffed.

"Well, while your travels sound positively riveting Thaniel," Samir interjected, brushing a strand of glossy black hair back into place, "I'm afraid Rose is right. Claude has been dodgy, sure, but he's always slinking around Lordhaven like some highborn crypt keeper. It's what he *does*. You, on the other hand, vanish one day without any notice to, what, becoming drinking mates with some half penny peddler." His full lips puckered into a pout. "No offense, love."

Nathaniel cleared his throat.

"I'll get straight to the point then." Nathaniel set down his teacup and clasped his palms together. "Claude forged a partnership with the Finches, but as Rose said, it doesn't quite fit right in the grand scheme of things. The Order was created as a means for duskborn in Halcyon to get a foothold in the aristocracy and influence the Sacred Seven from the inside. So why then would the Malsik care about minor shipping privileges in Finch territory? Something larger is at play here and I need to know if either of you heard or saw anything while I was away."

Samir and Rose exchanged glances.

"Weren't you going to recruit a new Order member?" Rose piped in.

"Yes, but Claude was nervous about the deal so he wanted to keep it hushed until the ink was dry. The Green Coats have been trying to partner with the Finches for years."

"How convenient." Rose took another sip of tea.

"Claude was practically a phantom in your absence," Samir added airily. "Rumor had it he and Badru were in every crook and cranny of Lordhaven drinking with Dukes and whispering with Viceroys. I mean it's no mystery he's courting the aristocracy's favor to sway the Sacred Seven towards supporting the Malsik and his merry band of bone warriors. Perhaps he wants more money in the Order's coffers."

"Not likely. The Order is plenty comfortable from its members and affiliates." Nathaniel turned to Rose. "Well?"

Rose set down her cup. "You already know where I stand. And from here, dare I say you look a bit nervous, Nathaniel."

Samir perked up, his widened gaze shifting between the two. "Hold on, you two saw each other already?" He leaned back in his chair, his lips puckering into a pout. "Unbelievable."

"It wasn't by choice," Nathaniel replied tersely.

Rose rolled her eyes. "Don't be a child, Samir."

"I thought we were friends, Rose," Samir shot back, flashing a look of feigned hurt at Nathaniel. "We always do things together."

"Rose came by *unannounced* to share her concern there may be someone targeting the King's bastard children."

A silence fell across the room. Samir's expression darkened, his brows pinched into a taut, bushy line. "What? How do you—?" Samir shook his head. "That can't be right. Wouldn't the Chases notice something like that? I mean who would even know them all?"

"Easy enough," Nathaniel replied. "Bastards are messy business. They leave money trails in their wake. It's not entirely impossible to find them, especially with Lordhaven's rumor mill churning every minute of the day. One need only be patient enough."

"Even still, it seems ludicrous, really," Rose mused aloud as if to herself. "I can't imagine what someone would gain killing heirs that would never sit on the throne. Why not go after the ones that would?"

Nathaniel stood and walked over to the mantle. What he was about to say next would hasten his plans to reign control away from Claude, but Beza's warning couldn't be ignored. *The bell chimes a false song.* No, he had to get in front of whatever was coming next. It was his only chance to gain the upper hand over Claude and the Malsik to claim the throne for himself.

"A trusted source spotted Claude—without Badru—in the company of two others outside Kendleston Manor while I was in Darby Town. One was a proper young woman and the other her handmaid."

Nathaniel was met by Rose's puzzled stare and Samir's blank face.

"Who was she?" Rose inquired. "Do you think she was related to the Hoyts?"

Nathaniel shook his head. "I don't know, but I plan on finding out. I need you both to look into this further with utmost discretion. If Claude catches even a hint of this, it's over for all of us."

"All of us?" Rose said with an arched brow. "Or you?"

"Do you think he wouldn't hesitate to end either of you?" Nathaniel bit back a laugh. "Trust me, he's hiding something. From *all* of us. And you know as good as anyone else the royal family are just as likely to kill each other for sport as they are to take their tea in the afternoon. The important thing here is that Claude and now the Sacred Seven are somehow involved, and if we can find out whom Claude brought to Kendleston manor and why then we stand a chance at getting ahead of him for once. One step closer to claiming Halcyon for ourselves."

"Are you implying the Sacred Seven are working with Claude to take out one of their own?"

The Sacred Seven—Halcyon's seven oldest and most powerful families—had held power over the kingdom since anyone could remember. It was long believed by historians the Chases had formed the Sacred Seven with the help of the Hoyts and the Foxes to unite the local territories under one banner. The story went Alfred Chase was then bestowed monarchy by the Vicar Antony and the Chase family had ruled ever since. But what if the Sacred Seven wanted to wrestle back power after 500 years in the Chase's shadow?

Samir stood, a bemused smirk on his face.

"Well, I suppose I should prowl the Bathes then. There's plenty of loose tongues there."

Rose frowned. "Honestly, Samir that garish perfumed pit again?"

"Don't be so drab, Rosie dear. I seem to recall you rather enjoyed our stays there once upon a time. Drunk on bloody pomegranate wine, dancing beneath a sunless sky..."

"Yes, but after forty years it grows tiresome," she replied with a dismissive wave of her hand. "You can keep your playthings and glasses of blood wine."

"Ah yes, how positively *alluring* the Vulpine's depravity is in comparison."

"I merely satisfy my clients' appetites. I couldn't care less what they crave. It's all just the same in the end, isn't it? Hunger has many names. Why not profit off them all?"

Samir's dark eyes gleamed with mischief and admiration. Who but they, cursed with gluttonous blood and prolonged lives, would know hunger best?

"You're a vile beast, Rose Blakely."

Her red lips curled into a smile. "I know."

"Rose, you and I shall keep to the—" but Rose snapped open her fan and cut Nathaniel off.

"I'll be doing my own work, thank you." She stood to leave. "I'll send word once I have an update. Good day, gentlemen."

As soon as she left, Samir shrugged and headed for the door. "What're you to do? I'll be at the Baths, Thaniel." He winked. "Do drop in when you've grown tired of investigating Lordhaven's downfall."

15

SYBIL

"The boy's father said his son wanted to see the goddess Yorin's earthly keep. Thought he could find it by using the old stories as a map and his woodsight magic. He found something, but gods know what it was. Not even the Council can parse sense from his grimoire. It now reads in no known language. His vocal cords have also calcified, yet he seems to speak in pulses of magic. Fungal code, perhaps?" – *Major Orin Mallerson, archived journal entry*

Beneath the shadows of a new dawn, Sybil prepared to meet Heath.

She leaned down and tightened the laces of her leather boots, mumbling a quick prayer beneath her breath to her family's patron goddess, Yorin, for safety and guidance. She pulled at her necklace and squeezed the leather wrapped carnelian. A warm rush tinged her fingers as a hint of confidence and ease swirled through her. She tucked the reddish orange gemstone beneath her shirt, grateful for the arcanic aide.

The path leading to the rotted oak was well-trekked. It snaked around the rim of the Outskirts and past Herschel McCreer's small vegetable garden.

As she followed the well-worn path, her mind drifted to stories of the great heart that was said to beat at the center of the forest. It could taste the truth in the blood its tree roots absorbed, watch the happenings of its realm through the eyes of the beasts it sheltered. And on quiet nights, when bonfires burned bright, tales would emerge of Willowfangs from moons past that wielded similar, albeit weakened, forms of the wood's sight. It was said they often blinded themselves because of what they'd seen. It had always made Sybil grateful she was a Dawnslayer. Somatic magicks seemed like far less trouble than elemental magicks.

She pressed onward until a massive, rotted husk of a fallen oak came into view.

"Heath?" Sybil called. "Cain?"

No reply.

Sybil approached the husk. A rich, wet waft of rotting leaves and damp earth emitted from its cavernous maw. She peered inside.

"Hello?"

Empty.

Sybil crossed her arms and sighed. "Of course. Why would Heath *actually* do anything he says he will?"

"A bit harsh, even for you."

Sybil snapped into a blocking stance, her grimoire already materialized.

"Woah, there." Heath raised both hands in surrender. "Gods, it's just me."

Sybil dropped her hands and frowned. "Really, Heath?"

Heath nodded at her grimoire. "You just gonna keep that out here or...?"

"Nervous?"

Heath Ashford let out a hollow chuckle. "Not a fair fight, love." He nodded towards the tree behind her. Sybil looked up to see Cain lounging on a tree branch, his hands resting behind his head. Beneath his mask of indifference Sybil could've sworn she caught a gleam of pleasure in his yellow eyes.

Sybil's lips pressed into a thin line.

Cocky bastard.

As her grimoire dematerialized, a small bit of her pride went with it.

"I guess we can't all be so lucky to have shades do our work for us."

Heath smirked. "Jealous?"

"Not a chance."

"She's not lying," Cain interjected from above.

Sybil swallowed hard. Heath titled his head, regarding her. After a moment's pause, he said, "I could show you the spell if you want. I'm sure your grimoire would—"

"No." It came out faster and sharper than she had intended. "Sorry, I mean I don't want to influence my grimoire like that."

Heath folded his arms. "Shades or corpses, it's all the same in the end isn't it? I'm still a necromancer at heart, just twisted the recipe a bit, you know? You'd still be one, too."

"It's too dangerous. Those kind of spells, they can taint your grimoire. Completely change it from the inside. What if it never goes back to the way it was?"

"You're way too paranoid. Grimoires are arcanically malleable, right? Shaped by the fateshifter they're bound to and all that? Then as long as you maintain your desired casting style, you'll be fine. A rogue spell or two won't hurt it."

Sybil frowned. "Grimoires have *intelligence*, Heath. Limitless magicks to give. Eventually something malicious will slip through if you keep courting it." In a lower voice she added, "I mean, what if it changes you? Or you it? Permanently?"

Heath's expression hardened. "It's complete rubbish the Council only allows us to train using known magicks. Where's the fun in that? Where's the potential?" He looked up at the canopy of green above, his blond bangs falling away from his eyes. "Magic can be so much more. *Is* so much more. Bloody cowards."

Her eyes flickered to his jacket. How many vials of blood did he have on him? Five? Ten? Did animals still make up for what he couldn't give? Or had the cost grown too great? She looked up at Cain, but he was already watching her. Waiting, perhaps, to see if she finally asked him the questions that had been burning inside her for the past month.

How much does it cost to give life to one's shadow? How much does Heath still sacrifice to bind you to him? What happens if he fails his blood debt?

"Sure, cowards," she said after a pause. "Anyway, do you have it?"

"Aye. You have the sterling?"

Sybil took a small pouch from her waistband and tossed it to him. He caught it with one hand and pocketed it.

"Aren't you going to check it?" Sybil asked.

Heath chuckled. "I know you're good for it." He took out a smaller pouch and tossed it to her. "Top students always are."

She caught the pouch. "What is that supposed to mean?"

"Well, for starters, you only ever ask for as much frost as it takes to get through two days, or one week if you're disciplined which I take the Head Girl of her class to be. And you've never missed a meeting, even now when I changed the date and asked you to come all the way here instead of the usual place." He flashed her a wistful smile. "Rather risky of you."

"It's none of your business," she snapped, turning away.

He gave a short wave and watched her leave. "See you again soon, Sybil."

After the morning's events, Sybil wasn't in the mood to sit down to breakfast with her mother or Cal. In fact, she wasn't in the mood to do much at all but sulk in a corner until her mind stopped reminding her of her own guilt.

The frost was supposed to be temporary. A short fix. She'd heard rumors of it after the first week at Lycoris Academy. A wonder pill that sharpened focus and heightened concentration. Back then she was rising so fast, her magic shining so bright, those rumors couldn't touch her. Nothing could.

Until something did.

It's just until the Trials, she reminded herself, fidgeting with her necklace. *Just to make it through the Trials.*

When she reached her home, her hand hovered over the doorknob. She closed her eyes and let out a small sigh. She could quit at any time. And she would, after she passed the Trials and made Major. No one would ever have to know.

She opened the door to find her mother sitting at the kitchen table. Her deep olive skin was almost golden in the morning light. When their eyes met, Joan Vorn set down her cup of tea. The crisp ring of porcelain sliced through the air.

"Mum, uh, good morning." Sybil quickly slipped inside and closed the door, pressing her feet closer together as if it would minimize her presence.

"Good morning," Joan replied coolly.

The Outskirts had done little to tarnish her mother. Even in her simple dress and neat bun, she was as out of place as a hawk among hens. There were no pies baking in the oven or familial chatter or half knitted quilt tucked away in a basket. There was only her mother, sitting alone with a cup of black tea and her polished boots beside the door, the Sentinel's white ouroboros insignia threaded on the side. Even a whole season later, Joan Vorn was ready to leave at a moment's notice. Ready to go back to her old life, if only it would have her.

"Where have you been?" she demanded, her calm exterior unnerving.

Sybil looked off to the side. "The library. I needed to exchange notes with a classmate."

Joan raised a perfectly manicured brow. "Exchange notes? Are you so ahead in your studies you can afford to help the failing now?"

Sybil looked down at her feet. "No, Mum."

"Then don't do it again. You have enough to worry about."

"Yes, Mum."

"Have you eaten?"

"No, but I'm not hungry."

Her mother sighed. "You'll be ravished before mid-period. I'll ready you some toast and jam. Go on, grab your things and change. Cal already left."

Sybil did as she was told. She headed upstairs and grabbed her canvas bag and switched out of her clothes into her school uniform; ox hide jerkin over a white tunic, fitted pants and knee length leather boots. She fastened her red armband, identifying her as a wielder of Dawnslayer magic, and beneath it pinned her silver Second Year Head Girl cuff.

As she slid her bag strap over her shoulders, she glanced down the hall. Cal's door was open. His room was sparse—bed made with not a pillow or blanket out of place, a small desk along the wall, and a handful of books shelved overhead.

She stared at his empty room, her shoulders suddenly heavy with the stillness in the air. In their old home, Cal's room had books crammed along the shelves their father had built. Nautical charts and paintings of sea creatures crowded his desk and floor. A whole life left behind because of her.

You shouldn't have come back.

Tears pulled at the back of her eyes.

You're just like him! You only think of yourself!

Sybil took two frost pills and hid the rest in a small hole beneath her mattress. She grabbed her bag and didn't look at Cal's room again.

Her mother was waiting for her by the door. A moment of silence passed between the two of them. How easily her father had fit into this space in her mornings. There was no break in his laughter or hesitation in his smile. He was at home in his roost.

But a hawk is no hen. The skin of it too tight, the contours all wrong. Her mother cleared her throat and offered a tight smile.

"Do your best today." She handed Sybil two slices of wrapped toast and jam.

"Thanks, Mum."

Only outside did Sybil feel like she could breathe. She made her way past the other neighboring cottages, sunken and bound in vines, until she came upon the stone archway of the Outskirts.

The unspoken divide between the shunned and the welcomed in Sanctis.

Carved into the stone was the story of Felnor the Betrayer. He who was a beacon of his village hundreds of moons before Sanctis. He who was loved and respected above all others for his courage and kindness as his village's protector. He who fell in love with Cephonia, Goddess of Song and Marriage, Protector of Mothers, and left his world behind to be with her in the realm of the gods. He who abandoned his village selfishly for his own desires. He who let his village fall to ruin at the hand of a powerful duskborn tribe.

Sybil kept her eyes down. She hated looking at those carved stones and passed beneath the archway as quickly as she could.

Standing on the other side was a girl about Sybil's age with sun-kissed brown skin. A brilliant blue and gold muslin scarf draped around her shoulders and left arm. Her silky black hair was plaited in two rows that weaved into a bun at the base of her neck.

"Morning, Priya," Sybil called.

Priya looked up from her daydreaming and beamed, the gold earrings lining the edges of her ears swaying with each movement. "Morning, Sybil!" she called back. "So? Any news? Did you hear back from Ephriam yet?"

Sybil shook her head.

"Not yet," she lied. "I'm sure word will come around soon though."

"You're absolutely brilliant, of course he can't help but take you on. Besides, how could he resist such an elegantly worded letter?" Both girls looked at each other and broke into a fit of laughter.

"Thank the gods, Anjali took pity on me. My first draft was absolutely horrendous. She's a literal savior."

Priya rolled her eyes. "Bah, it was all spellwork anyway. If she had to *actually* write something it'd probably turn into a curse."

Sybil chuckled. "Come off it, you know she's good. She just knows how to bring words to *life*. It's brilliant work really."

"She can barely walk into a room these days with that ego of hers," Priya grumbled. "All she talks about is receiving covenship from *the* Mara Rowen. Mum parades her around like she's a living saint. Gods, I hate it. Papa says to pay her no mind and let her enjoy her moment, but it feels like Surjan and I are just servants in Anjali's temple, you know?"

Sybil understood Priya's frustrations. Not that long ago her parents used to speak of her high marks and casting proficiency to anyone who would listen. It became normal, almost numbingly so, to be at the top of her class. She had cast such a long shadow she didn't notice when Cal had stopped standing in it.

"Well, I'm grateful for you both." Sybil gently elbowed Priya's side, which forfeited a smile from her. "But gods know I'll need Byrill's favor for the Trials."

The Trials of Six, an ever-changing six-part exam fateshifters had to pass to be promoted to Majors and form their own covens, was only a season away and was in addition to the end of year exams she already had to study for. No mercy was given to students who wished to participate in the Trials and anyone who was daft enough to ask for leniency on their coursework to train for it was swiftly barred from participating for that given year.

"You're still going to go through with it?" Priya asked. "I mean, the official exams won't begin until Fourth Year. You have time you know. Besides, if another coven takes you on you won't need to test for it."

It was true. Sybil was only a Second Year, but Third Year was around the corner. With her chances of gaining covenship dwindling by the day, testing for and passing the Trials was her only option to regain favor in Sanctis. If she passed the preliminary testing offered to Third Years, then she would only need to take the written portion again in her Fourth Year. If she failed, she still had one more chance to retake the Trials in her Fourth Year. Only those who scored in the top ten percent were promoted to Major. Students who didn't pass in their Fourth Year had to get a signed letter of recommendation from a professor or Major to participate again. But if the Council didn't honor the letter, it was all for naught.

Sybil wasn't foolish enough to think anyone on the Council would honor her letter, even if she did manage to secure one. No, her Third Year had to be the year she passed the Trials. She couldn't risk leaving everything up to her Fourth Year. This was her final chance at redemption. Her final chance to find the truth of what happened to her coven and clear her name.

"Covenship isn't guaranteed," Sybil replied, her voice almost a whisper. "If I can become a Major, I can gain security access to the Hightower archive records, be allowed to leave Sanctis, review my case files, anything I wanted. Start my own coven, even in Lordhaven. Like my da wanted."

Priya grabbed her hand and squeezed it. "You'll be the best Major, I know it."

Sybil squeezed back, silently thanking Byrill for granting her the great fortune of still having Priya Majumdar as a friend.

Halfway into Professor Pearl Fielding's lecture on Kingdom History, Sybil's pen ran dry.

"… and in Phoenix Year 1817," Professor Fielding droned on, the clattering of chalk punctuating each word she spoke, "Bronwen officially joined the Avalon Pact. From then on, the citizens of Bronwen fell under the jurisdiction and leadership of Halcyon's monarchy, making Halcyon the leader of the Avalon Isles...."

Sybil leaned down to grab another from her bag, angling her within earshot of Almira Shaw, who sat in the row behind her.

"Wasn't Eiriana Quinn from Bronwen?" Almira whispered to Daisy Morrison, who sat beside her.

Sybil stiffened.

Major Quinn. Her old coven's Major.

"I think so," Daisy replied. "I still can't believe what happened to her."

"It's so sad. How *that one* still shows her face here is sick."

"Do you think she did it? Actually killed her coven?"

"I think she went mad. All that pressure being the youngest head girl and studying so much. It definitely cracked her."

Sybil grabbed her pen and buried herself in her notes. Anything to push Almira's words from her mind. Her stomach tightened as she gritted her teeth together. She closed her eyes and steadied her breathing, willing the anger to subside.

She wasn't mad. She didn't crack. She didn't—

"Miss Harker?"

Sybil opened her eyes and peered over at the petite girl beside her, who was gently snoring.

"Miss Har-*ker*," Professor Fielding repeated, drawing out each syllable. Her mulberry lips twisted into a dissatisfied frown.

"Tianna," Sybil hissed, nudging her. "Tianna, wake up!"

"Sanctis is the twelfth known fateshifter settlement in the Northlands," Tianna said with a yawn, stretching her arms above her head with a grunt. "And the forty-eighth in Halcyon according to the High Council of Mages."

"So wonderful of you to partake in today's lesson with us." Professor Fielding's lingering gaze silenced the room. She turned to the next page in her lesson book and resumed writing with her free hand. "Now, can you tell me the names of three settlements outside the mainland?"

Tianna snorted. "Settlements in Bronwen are just sissy lass rumors. King Leonard would sooner prance naked in the streets then let fateshifters spread beyond the mainland's borders."

The class erupted into laughter.

Professor Fielding slammed her palm down on her podium.

"Enough!" she bellowed, her face flushed a bright crimson. "Miss Harker, perhaps the class would greatly benefit from your study of Sanctis's founding. A speech of your findings in two moon's time should suffice."

Tianna shrugged and slumped down in her seat.

Sybil stole a glance a few minutes later to see Tianna doodling in the margins of her notebook. She recognized the sunburst centers of the flowers right away. Forget-me-nots.

The same flowers Sybil put on her coven's makeshift grave.

After class, Sybil filed out of the classroom until a tug at her elbow stopped her in the hall.

"You all right?" Tianna asked. Her smoky grey eyes, which rarely seemed to focus on anything, narrowed. "You seem off."

Sybil shook her head. "I'm fine." She hated how the words sounded hollower each time she said them. "Are you? I've never seen Professor Fielding so pissed."

Tianna scoffed. "She's a hag. It's bloody kingdom histories. Not like it's going to change." She popped a toffee square into her mouth, pulling a stray coppery curl from her mouth. "She can bother me when I stop having the highest marks in her class."

Multicolored banners decorated the ivy-strewn ceilings, symbolizing the three arcane classes that made up Lycoris Academy: red for Dawnslayers with affinity for somatic magic, green for Willowfang with affinity for elemental magic and blue for Skybreakers with affinity for both.

Sybil stared at the blue banner, a replica of the armband Tianna wore. The coil inside her tightened again. Would she have been forgiven if she'd been born a Skybreaker instead? Would the Council have come to her defense back then if she'd been more valuable to them? Almira's words rang in her ears like a cruel whisper.

How that one *still shows her face here is sick.*

"Wait, is that ... Heath Tanner?"

Sybil shifted her attention to the window. Heath walked across the courtyard to the library next door. His jerkin wasn't fastened properly and his shirt was untucked, but somehow it suited him far better.

"I thought he was still suspended."

"Me too," Sybil murmured. She watched the shadow trailing behind him and a shiver ran down her spine. Cain hid his presence well.

"I heard there's still a few students who have a copy of that shadow spell he created."

"But the Headmistress purged everyone's grimoires."

"They didn't write it in their grimoires," Tianna said with a sly smirk. "Wrote it beneath their skin. Blood magic and all that. Shifty, innit? Guessing they sold it, the idiots. Rumor has it a few Dawnslayers wrote it in their grimoires and were then able to bind ghouls to themselves."

Sybil shivered. "And risk causing a possession? No thank you."

Tianna shrugged. "Risk and reward I suppose. Harder to control but they're far stronger than your average human soul."

There was no denying Heath's brilliance. He was able to summon and maintain Cain's binding after all. But would he know when to stop? Would others? How far was too far with magic?

Tianna turned back to the window, her frizzy, coppery golden hair gleaming beneath the sunlight. "Burnout or not, I'd love his company."

"You can't be serious!"

Tianna giggled. "Oh, come off it. You know he's the best catch of the Second Years."

Sybil rolled her eyes. "If you say so."

As she was about to leave, Priya and two other girls—May Fitzharris and Adriana Russo—were coming down the hall. Priya and May were laughing at something Adriana had said.

Sybil didn't mean to make eye contact. But Adriana spotted her and a look of disgust passed over her face. May stopped laughing and averted her gaze. Only Priya gave her a small wave.

I miss you, Sybil wanted to tell them. *We were best friends once, remember?*

Without saying goodbye, Sybil parted ways with Tianna and continued down the hall and up the stone steps. As she went, she noticed a strange carving in one of the stones. She stopped to look at it but didn't touch it. Past and present students could never agree on what the strange carvings meant that periodically appeared inside Lycoris, but they never remained for more than a day or two. Sybil had seen symbols appear before, but not this one. It reminded her of an unraveling spire. She made a mental note to tell Tianna about it in case she hadn't sketched it.

She passed a stained-glass window, one of several on the third floor, and crossed to Professor Cooper's classroom. A sign was posted on the door that read "MEET ON THE GREEN."

"For the love of the gods." Sybil sighed, readjusting her bag strap. Suddenly, a hand reached out and shoved her into the room.

Sybil stumbled backward, startled. She whirled around just as the door latched shut.

Randall Bancrest blocked the door. His massive shoulders nearly fit across the doorframe.

Standing just off to the side was Dean Carlyle, the Head Boy of First Year and Captain of the Sparring Team. Beside him, perched atop the nearest desk were his two lackeys, Felicity Greenwell and Sabine Wellington. Each wore a green arm cuff over their uniform.

"You know, you have some nerve pretending like you still belong here," Dean scoffed.

"I just want to go to class, Dean," Sybil said through gritted teeth.

"I bet you do," Sabine sneered. Felicity giggled. "Have to maintain those precious marks."

"And do you know what we want?" Dean added. "A safe space. The Council laid down those protective cornerstones when they converted this place to Lycoris, but see the problem with that is it doesn't keep out the filth already inside."

He took a seat in one of the front rows and kicked up his feet.

"Look, Cal's one of my best mates. And Lycoris is set to take the Solstice Tourney this year from Malerson. That means covens looking at us. *Big* ones. But there's talk the Tourney bigwigs are going to disqualify us because we have the brother of a murderer on our roaster."

Sybil wanted to punch Dean in the face, but instead she clutched her bag strap until her knuckles hurt. "This isn't Cal's fault, all right? Leave him out of it, Dean or I swear to Yorin I'll come for you myself."

An icy jet of water shot out from Sabine's hand and pushed Sybil back. "Watch out, Dean. She might kill you next."

"Of course, why would the Second Year Head Girl care?" Felicity quipped. "You already had a coven recruit you early. Who cares about the rest of us, right?"

Sabine's grimoire hovered in front of her. *Stupid*, Sybil cursed herself. She'd been so preoccupied getting out of the classroom she hadn't noticed when Sabine had summoned it.

"It's not about Cal participating in the tourney, Sybil," Dean continued, spitting her name back at her like a curse. "It's forcing to sideline him because of *your* actions. The rest of us get to suffer because you went bloodbath mad. So do us all a favor and leave already. Lycoris doesn't need you."

"Don't say we didn't ask nicely," Felicity added with a smirk.

Sybil glanced at the door. Randall was planted there like a boulder. As if reading her mind, Dean gestured to the window. "Didn't want to be late to class, right?"

"We're on the third floor you arsehole!"

Dean shrugged. "You won't die. Probably."

Sybil's grimoire materialized in the next blink, it's mana flowing through her. It was a part of her just as she was a part of it. Her arms shot out in front of her, palms open to complete her survey of the room.

There.

She focused her will to her left where the foul presence of death lingered strongest. She began focusing all her strength into stitching a soul into the unseen remains. Sabine shot another jet of water at her, but Sybil leapt to the right just as the stream shot through a desk, snapping it in two. Felicity conjured wind to grow the fireball churning in Dean's palm. He gave her a pitying look.

"This didn't have to be difficult, you know."

The soul was nearly bound. A sharp rasp echoed from behind the wall. Two, no three more. She grabbed for them too, stitching the souls to the skeletal remains. When the souls were fully stitched, Sybil released three tethers linking her soul to theirs. Sweat beaded along her brow as lifeforce leeched out of her and into the undead.

The rasp continued until it intensified into a full pounding roar. But beneath her death magic, something white hot bubbled beneath the surface. An anger, palpable and true, driven by a tunnel-like focus on Dean. Unlike her necromancy that pulled on mana from the natural world around her, this power drew inward, deep in her core, if only she would reach for it. Dark thoughts churned through her head, spurred on by the rage burning through her.

Make him eat his words.

Sybil lunged forward, an unbridled fury in her eyes. Sabine screamed and dodged. Dean faltered long enough for Sybil's fist to connect with his face, searing his skin where hers touched his. He spun back and knocked into Randall, who looked just as startled as Dean did.

"I'm out, I'm out!" Randall cried, shoving Dean off him and scrambling out of the room. Felicity quickly followed behind him, her face pale. Sabine grabbed Dean's arm and hauled him to his feet. She shot Sybil a reproachful glare.

"We're not done here," she spat and the pair slipped out of the room. When they were gone, Sybil let out a shaky breath and released the souls from her command. The pounding stopped. She recalled her grimoire and slid to the ground.

Hot tears burned her eyes. She covered her face with her palms and wept until her body shook.

She heard someone open the door and then quickly slam it closed, but she didn't care. Let them see. Let them see her shatter and weep. It didn't matter. None of it mattered.

After a few minutes, she wiped her eyes with the back of her hands and smoothed down her hair. She was itching for some frost to clear her head. Maybe Heath had more. With each step she took, she pushed down the incident further and further in mind. It did her no good to worry over it or ask questions. It'd only drag her down.

By the time she reached the hallway, she could swallow the lie nothing had happened at all.

16

JULIA

"In times of war, sacrifices are expected to be made to achieve peace. But it is during times of peace that many forget sacrifices must also be made to maintain that peace." – *Carmilla Morsley,* An Exploration of Ancient and Modern Halcyon, Vol. I

The end was nearing.

Julia heard it in Tilda's sobs. She saw it in Emily's glassy stare. No one said anything as the hands of an imaginary clock ticked closer to a new day. Their last day.

What was left to say except goodbye? Panic fled Julia in the moments following the sham trial. All that remained was untethered calmness.

How can death be terrifyingly real and absurdly meaningless? Julia wondered.

The balm was gone. Pain thrummed through Julia's hand in ebbs and flows. When sleep opened its arms to her, she fell into them without question, eager to slip beneath the surface of her nightmarish reality.

"He liked you, you know."

Julia's eyes flickered open. She stared at the ground but Emily's gaze prickled her skin. Even in the dark, they always knew how to find each other.

"He told me once. When it was just us. He said you were pretty."

Julia said nothing.

"When he said I was beautiful," Emily continued, "that's when I decided I would ruin him."

"Ruin him?" Julia lifted her head.

Emily was tracing circles with her finger on the ground. "To love someone is to see their whole self. Because you're not pretty and I'm not beautiful. We're Kaia. We're Sulmara. We're Ineva. We're without divide."

Emily went back to tracing her circles. In the corner, Tilda's sobs had finally quieted.

"I saw a fawn corpse once when I was little," Emily went on. "Right near Lake Promise. Its flesh had partially fallen from its face and maggots were wriggling in its eye sockets. It was awful, just absolutely disgusting, but I couldn't stop staring at it. It was so...honest. So wholly itself when undone. It was all I wanted to be."

A fresh wave of pain crashed against Julia's hand, but this time she bore it. The pain kept her anchored. Sleep would be so easy, so simple. But Emily pulled her in with her words, her watchful eyes, and her never-ending circles.

"Harrison would never look at your rotten parts."

Julia let out a shaky breath. "Would you?"

Emily stopped tracing. The moment hung between them like a held breath, charged and delicate all at once. The corner of her mouth pulled into a smirk.

"I guess we'll see at dawn."

"Get up!" a voice barked.

Julia's eyes fluttered open, but her mind, thick with the fog of sleep, was slow to catch on to the commotion around her. "What's happening?"

"I said get up!" A bolt of pain spread through her stomach as a foot drove into her side. Julia yelped and staggered to her feet. Her hair was tangled around her face and her mouth tasted of bile, but the guards standing in the doorway didn't give her a chance to right herself. She caught a glimpse of two hooded figures standing in the hallway before a bag was put over her head.

"Move it."

Julia said nothing. She was seeing through eyes that were not her own. This was happening to someone else. This was their nightmare she was watching unfold like some twisted play. Legs that were not her legs shuffled forward. Pain that was not her pain shot through a hand that was not her hand. She sunk deeper and deeper until her ears buzzed with muffled silence.

A familiar sweetness overcame her senses and then she was falling, falling into a numbing silence neither the baying horses nor jostling carriage ride could lift.

Sometime later, when the sticky sweetness dissipated and her senses awakened, a heavy door groaned open. Suddenly warmth flooded Julia's skin from above and the darkness of the bag over her head became speckled with light. A low growl like a pack of wild dogs echoed in the distance. Julia's stomach tightened.

"Watch your step," a voice in front of her called. Julia had half a mind to pitch herself forward but didn't know if Emily or Tilda were in front of or behind her.

The orchestra of cries swelled to a fever pitch the further they descended the stairs. Bile burned Julia's throat. Seven hells, she was going to be sick.

"I-I can't," she sputtered, but the guard behind her tightened his grip on her already sore shoulder.

"You don't have a choice, shifter."

The yelping of dogs morphed into the howl of humans. Hundreds, perhaps thousands of them. Shouts of heresy mixed with cries of "Hang the fateshifters! Hang them all!"

I'm not a fateshifter! You're wrong! Julia wanted to shout back, but fear bound her jaw shut.

She was led up a set of wooden stairs and told to wait. Her head buzzed amidst the undulating cries around her. She would've done anything to hold Emily's hand in that moment, but there was no one there to comfort her. She was alone on a platform facing torrents of anger from people she didn't know.

A deep voice cut through the shouts.

"Here upon this day, the 12th day of Skyfire, we bring forth the accused fateshifters to hang for their crimes of making an unlawful covenant with the Demon King Azavith and the illegal practice of spellcraft as determined by the High Court of Lordhaven."

The crowd roared as Julia bit back a sob. Tears burned hot against her cheeks.

This wasn't happening. This *wasn't* happening.

The deep voice continued, getting closer now. "As Overseer of the Knights of the Royal Order, I officially proclaim the hanging to proceed." A thick corded rope was fastened to Julia's neck.

"No, please!" Julia wailed, her heart racing. "I'm not a fateshifter! I swear it! Please, I'm not!"

"May the blight of magic and its promise of power at the safety and expense of others rest with you," the Overseer continued, his voice booming over Julia's.

"Please!"

The floor beneath her gave way. The fall was sudden and absolute, but for just the tiniest moment there was freedom in her descent.

Weightlessness. An untethering of all that had been.

Then the rope caught Julia's throat in its vice grip and she lurched upward. Her legs kicked desperately for purchase, but there was only air beneath her. Her body writhed like a fish on a line as vibrant colors danced across her vision, blurring and melting in the darkness.

A warm stream raced down her leg. She tried to cry out, but the rope cut off her words. Her mind filled with memories of her family in better times, smiling and together. Her mum home, George clinging to her skirts, her father's cheeks rosy, Aunt Agatha baking in the kitchen, Uncle Arden and Frederick playing jacks.

I'm sorry. I'm sorry. I'm—

Pressure burned behind her eyes.

I'm not ready. But then her thoughts fell away as the walls separating her mind and body crumbled. There was only silence in the dark.

Her last breath passed her lips.

She let go.

17

JULIA

"Suspect reported entering the forest after spotting his daughter (6yrs). She had disappeared three days prior. Suspect found with multiple injuries to his back and upper neck, possibly an animal of some sort. Claims a tree creature attacked him. Daughter has not been located. Psych eval pending." – *City Watch Asst. Chief Addison Gromm, excerpt from official arrest report dated Harvestgrain 1819, Temmings, Halcyon*

The sun was warm on Julia's face.

Brilliant reds and yellows danced behind her eyes. Water filled her ears and the world was blissfully silent. When she stretched her arms and legs, she was met with nothing but water. A small sigh of relief slipped from her as she floated across Lake Promise, her hair fanning out behind her in an auburn crown. The future and past were absent from her mind. She was only here and now, free of all else.

How perfect, she thought.

"Jules, I've just read the best story," Emily gushed. "Do you want to hear it?"

Julia slipped upright and glided towards her best friend. She rested her arms on the shoreline so only her freckled shoulders were exposed.

"Funny, I feel like I had the most awful dream," Julia said with only a tinge of concern.

Emily sat beneath a tree just a short way off, a book open on her lap. Her cotton spun dress, a deep pomegranate red, was splayed out in front of her and a single black choker was tied around her neck.

"Did you fall asleep floating again? You're lucky I'm here so you don't get another awful sunburn."

Julia laughed. "Don't remind me, I still hurt thinking about it."

"Saints your aunt was furious, wasn't she?"

"Murderous!" Julia giggled. "And can you believe I still had to do chores? While trapped in the house so, in her words, I wouldn't *embarrass* myself? It was criminal!"

They broke into a fit of laughter that drifted through the glen like music. Julia wiped tears from her eyes and nodded towards the book in Emily's hands.

"What're you reading?"

"*The Little Sun Princess.*"

A sudden chill carried on the wind. Julia's skin prickled. "*The Little Sun Princess?* What's it about?"

"It's about a girl known as the Little Sun Princess," Emily replied. "She lives in a magical kingdom with her siblings and wants for nothing. One day, she wakes up and sees a raven at her window. The raven asks the Little Sun Princess what her name is, and being ever so polite, she tells the raven. It then thanks her and flies away. The next day, her sister, the Big Sun Princess, falls into a deep sleep and nobody can wake her. The Little Sun Princess must take over, but she wishes to learn more to be a great queen, so she locks herself in the kingdom's biggest library and reads and reads and reads.

"But one day, while the Little Sun Princess is reading, she hears someone call her name. She looks up and sees the raven. When she looks into the raven's eyes, it steals her soul. The Little Sun Princess and the raven become one and, no longer forced to take over the throne, they fly away to see worlds far beyond the kingdom."

Emily closed the book. "Isn't it lovely? The Little Sun Princess gained such freedom."

Julia looked up. The sun was now hidden behind the clouds, its warmth out of reach. When she turned back, she noticed a white bird perched on the lowest branch right above Emily. She took it to be a large dove at first, but the angles were all wrong. The beak was too sharp, the claws too long.

It was a raven. A white raven.

"Careful now," Emily warned. "Don't want your soul stolen, do you?"

But Julia didn't hear her. She was transfixed by the raven's deep violet eyes. There existed whole worlds in them, violent and beautiful and ever changing.

Freedom.

A hundred hands grabbed Julia at once—arms, legs, hands, mouth, neck. She couldn't see or hear or speak. All she could feel was herself being dragged under the surface and into the frigid depths of darkness.

Julia opened her eyes.

The world was a blur of whites and yellows. Suddenly, a sharp pain seared through her chest. Julia doubled over, hand clutched over her heart as if it were on fire. When the burning sensation finally subsided a few minutes later, Julia pulled her knees up to rest her cheek against them and took large, slow breaths.

In, out. In, out. In, out.

As she lowered her knees, she caught herself staring intently at her left hand. There were no visible cuts and her fingers all moved normally. She flipped her hand over and over as a feeling she couldn't quite place gnawed at her. What was wrong? What was she missing? Just then, something dark beneath her nails caught her attention.

Using her thumb nail, she dug beneath her middle finger's nail and flecks of dark red came away. Her breath caught in her throat. She spread out her trembling hands and gasped. Blood was beneath every nail.

What did I...?

Just then, the door opened. An older, bald man with light blue eyes and a white moustache peered in. He was dressed in a pressed white doctor's coat and black pants.

"Ah, you're awake. Splendid." He stepped inside and gently closed the door behind him.

Where am I? she started to say, but it was too painful to continue past the first couple of syllables. What's more, her voice sounded like stones grating against each other. Her hand went to her throat and found it was tightly secured with a bandage. She looked up at the bald man in sudden alarm. He raised a hand to calm her as he grabbed a chair with his other hand.

"I'm sure you have many questions, Miss Sheffield. Rest assured all will be answered in due time." He took a seat at her bedside, prompting Julia to move further away. "I believe introductions are in order first, hmm? My name is Dr. Cornelius Ward. I'm the head physician here."

"Here?" Julia croaked, but Dr. Ward held up his hand again and gave a small shake of his head.

"A question for a later time. For now, let's focus on your health, shall we? You've been through a great ordeal. Why not have some tea? The nurse left some for you on her last visit."

Her mind returned to the bandage around her throat and the dried blood beneath her nails. Her heart began to quicken, but the mellow earthy flavor of the tea eased some of her panic.

"With a few days bedrest and light broth, you should be back on your feet again within the week." Dr. Ward stood to leave, but Julia forced herself upright to delay him.

"Wait," she pleaded, setting down her cup. "My family."

A look Julia didn't recognize flitted across Dr. Ward's face. It was quickly replaced with feigned joviality.

"They've been informed of your condition and await your recovery. Until then, do save your strength for the days ahead." He tucked the chair beneath a nearby writing desk and stood in the doorway. "A nurse will see to your daily needs, but I'll be back again tomorrow. Take care and get some rest, Miss Sheffield."

He closed the door. In his absence, Julia took a proper look around her. She was in by far the nicest room she'd ever seen. Pressed curtains were drawn in front of ceiling-high windows. A fine wooden writing desk was against the wall. On the other side was a hand-carved cabinet fit for highborn gowns.

Julia tried to remember how she'd got here, but her memories were hazy. The start of a headache was beginning to build behind her eyes. She curled in on herself and retreated beneath the covers. When her throat healed, she'd be sure to ask Dr. Ward more questions.

While she laid in bed, a restlessness began to stir in her. Her body craved sleep, but the gnawing thought returned again.

Something isn't right.

After tossing and turning for several minutes, she finally gave up on sleep and rose from bed. She stumbled towards the door, gritting her teeth against the strangeness of her own body. She tried the handle, but it was locked. She pounded on the door.

"Hello? Excuse me?"

Silence.

She frowned. *Why would they lock a patient's door?*

Her focus next went to the window across from her. She parted the curtain and gasped.

A storybook garden sprawled out before her. Bushels of red and white roses thick with their radiant perfume nestled beneath her window and traveled outward along a winding stone pathway shaded by wisteria laden arches. Finely manicured hedges trimmed in towering spires lined the pathway leading to a large domed portico framed by bundles of pink and yellow wildflowers in the center of the garden.

A young woman with long coppery hair adorned by a yellow bow sat on one of the portico's benches. Her head was bent over as if reading something. Was she another patient?

A dull ache pulsed behind Julia's eyes. How had her lids gotten so heavy? She let the curtain fall and made her way back to bed. Sleep pulled her down in minutes, and soon all thoughts of her left hand, the garden and the other patient were long forgotten.

Dr. Ward continued to visit Julia as promised.

Unlike the nurses who only changed out her meals or bandages and never spoke to her, he was a break in the monotonous cycle of naps and hazy-headed boredom, even if their conversations were kept to only pleasantries and her condition.

Julia was careful not to mention the other patient she'd seen outside her window. She didn't suspect Dr. Ward meant any ill-will towards her, but she couldn't bring herself to trust him. He refused to give her any details as to which hospital she was in or let her out for any walks, supervised or not. The only question he did fully answer was why her door was kept locked.

"For your own safety, my dear. It would be unwise for you to be roaming the halls in your condition."

Did anyone truly know where she was? And why hadn't her family visited yet?

On the third day of her stay, her voice was back to normal. Even her body, although slightly sluggish, was finally back to feeling like her own again.

It's time.

Before Dr. Ward's late morning visit, a nurse was scheduled to bring her breakfast. On cue, the nurse arrived and set down the silver breakfast tray just after sunrise. Julia normally feigned being asleep, but today she had her voice.

She grabbed the nurse's wrist as soon as she set down the breakfast tray and pulled her close. The nurse's dark brown eyes sprung wide. She let out a small yelp, but Julia quickly covered her mouth.

"I'm not going to hurt you," Julia said slowly, careful not to strain her throat. "I just want answers."

The nurse hesitated.

"Please. I won't tell Dr. Ward about this, I swear it."

After a few seconds, the nurse finally relented and nodded. Julia dropped her hand and the nurse backed away.

"It's not my place to tell you what Dr. Ward hasn't, miss. It's best left to him."

"He won't tell me anything. I don't know where I am or why. Please, can you tell me?"

The nurse sighed. "You're safe here. Dr. Ward is a brilliant man, he is. I don't know what happened, but you were in quite a state when I first saw you."

"What happened? My memory of it is all hazy."

The nurse kneeled closer and lowered her voice. "Keep to the toast and eggs. The tea has a lull in it. Keeps your head dull."

She leaned back and resumed taking last night's supper tray. "Good day to you, miss. Blessed be."

Julia recalled the blood that was beneath her nails that first day. She touched the bandage at her neck. What was Dr. Ward trying to prevent her from remembering? No matter, she told herself. She would find out on her own. She downed her breakfast and poured some of the tea in a corner of her blanket. When a new nurse came to retrieve her breakfast tray, Julia said she needed to have her blanket changed with an embarrassed murmur as if she'd sullied herself.

As the day crept into night, Julia grew nervous. Dr. Ward hadn't come by to check in on her. He had never missed a day before. Had the breakfast nurse said something to him? Did he know she was onto the lull they'd been giving her?

When Julia tried to fish out his whereabouts from the supper nurse, she said he had been called away for another patient but would return in the morning.

As Julia laid down to sleep, the troubles of the day carried into the night. Her mind was free of lull and full of shadows. In her dream, she found herself in a crowd of faceless strangers. She pushed herself to the front and saw three people standing on a platform with cloth bags over their heads.

Her chest tightened. The crowd roared around her, spittle flying from their mouths and anger burning in their eyes.

Death to the heathens! Death to the heathens!

Her eyes widened. She knew them. The heretics. No, not heretics—the girls. Tilda. Emily. *Her.*

She opened her mouth to scream but someone covered it before she had the chance.

"They deserve this," whispered a familiar voice in her ear. "They were bad people."

Julia couldn't move her head to look back, but she would recognize that voice anywhere. *Emily.* She watched in horror as the floor beneath the three hooded figures gave way. Julia tried to scream for it to stop, but Emily kept her hand over Julia's mouth.

"They deserve this." Emily pressed harder until her nails dug into Julia's cheeks, drawing small half-moons of blood. "We deserve this, you deserve this, you deserve—"

Julia's eyes flew open. She pitched forward in bed, her body racked with sobs. She clutched her knees and drew them close, burying her face between her legs to steady her breathing.

"It was just a dream, it was just dream," she whispered like a mantra. "It was just a dream ..."

But even she couldn't swallow her own lie.

Her fingers shook as they slowly touched her neck. Memories came back in brief, broken fragments. The darkness of the hood. The rope biting into her neck. The air leaving her. The dark tide. The final silence.

Tears spilled down Julia's cheeks as she tore off the bandage from her neck. With shaking fingers, she traced over the scabbing scratch marks. She remembered. She'd been stolen from death. Torn from her end and made to begin again. But a broken mind had to be lulled into stillness to take to the body properly.

Julia's mouth opened in a silent scream.

She remembered it all.

18

TOBIAS

Saints, this is bad.

Tobias looked over his fresh draw. It was a complete toss—two of clubs, three of hearts, four of hearts, and ten of spades—but Ezra's beaming smile alluded to the rotten hand he too was hiding.

"It's really happening, innit?" Charley said this more to himself than to anyone else, but Tobias caught the waver in his voice. Heard the fear beneath the feigned indifference.

Tavia, who was cradled on the windowsill with a notebook nestled on her knee, tilted her head.

"You mean a gang war?" She shrugged. "Maybe. Saints knows for sure."

Charley hugged his knees closer to his chest. He hadn't moved from the top bunk all morning. The corn muffin Tavia had grabbed for him in the Distillery's mess hall downstairs sat untouched.

"I just ... I dunno ... somethin' bad about all this."

"Well, obviously," Tavia scoffed. "Two blokes are dead."

Tobias didn't say anything. He focused on his cards instead, staring so hard the numbers began bleeding together with the suits. He didn't need to say it aloud. He'd already seen the answer laid out in the alleyway a few days prior. The Seadevils had been practically handed an invitation into the Ironworks District. And given the crime happened in Green

Coat territory, it would be only a matter of time before Mama Kilburn and her hollium pushers would be knocking on Marcellus's door for an owed favor.

"Toby, you got sterlings on you? I like being paid in full." Ezra double tapped the deck between them signaling he was passing his last remaining draw.

"Fat chance of that," Tobias countered, double tapping the deck too.

Ezra raised a brow. "Well, well, Toby's gone bold, ladies and gents."

Tavia went back to jotting down in her notebook. "Don't worry yourself, Charley. Marcellus will get it all sorted. He always does." She scribbled a note in the margin and smirked. "Oi, did any of you hear about the hanging in Iron Square the other day? Quincy said the rumor was true about the crest. One of the prisoners lit up like a star when they died. That means they were bloody royal!"

"Quincy's full of gas," Ezra scoffed. "Said he was the nephew of a duke once just to avoid paying his tab at the Hidden Pearl."

"No, I think he's good on this." Tavia sat straighter. "Rory heard the same thing. Said they ended the hanging right after that. She even snuck back that night and said only one body was loaded on the constable's reaper barge. They kept the other two. It's off. Why keep them?"

"You really need to lay off those gossip papers. Saints honest." Ezra signaled to Charley. "Oi, Char, you gonna eat that muffin, mate?"

"I know I'm being paranoid," Charley said, ignoring Ezra's question, "but can we all agree it wasn't a simple hit and split?" Ezra and Tavia rolled their eyes, but Charley pressed on. "Those blokes in the alleyway, they were put out for everyone to see. Whoever killed them wanted the Seadevils to know it was us." Charley shifted his pleading gaze to Tobias, who clutched his cards even tighter. "Right, Tobias?"

Tobias didn't mention it was *all* he'd been seeing at night when he finally managed to fall asleep.

"We dunno if it was a Market Streeter who did it," Tobias said without looking up. "Might've been the Seadevils staging it and all that like Marcellus said. Or could be the Barrel Boys looking for a laugh."

"Bloody twats," Ezra spat. "If anyone is a menace to Lordhaven, it's them. Our parents tossed all of us too and you don't see us being brats about it."

Tavia chuckled. "You still mad about that one nicking your love letter?"

"It was not a *love letter*. It was a private correspondence between me and Miss Rosenfeld. She'd went through a great deal of trouble to send it private post."

"Probably on account she already had an engagement set with Brenton Northmoor," Tobias added flatly, laying down his hand. "It'd been in the papers, mate."

"Wait, when have you ever read the papers?" Ezra ventured. "Only Tavia reads those."

"Just lay down your hand and lose already."

"But I'm serious—"

Suddenly, the door to Charley's room swung open. Every head swiveled to see Rum Petey, Charley's roommate, taking up nearly the whole doorway. At nearly six foot five, Rum Petey was able to command a room by presence alone.

"Uh, Marcellus wants everyone down at Mess now." Rum Petey turned to Tavia, his voice as deep as the night was dark. "And uh, word is Viv is back. Thought you'd wanna know."

Tavia perked up. "Viv? She's here?"

Ezra laid his hand facedown. "Well, you heard him. Boss man's got a word. We're off then."

"You still owe me, Ez!" Tobias called out, but Ezra and Tavia had already darted past Rum Petey. Charley jumped down like a lithe cat. Up close the shadows beneath his eyes rivaled Tobias's.

"That'll be the war call then, I guess."

The Mess Hall was the largest part of the Distillery—the Market Street gang's longtime base—having served as the main factory floor when Seltwood Whiskey was in operation over three decades ago.

Ezra waived Tobias and Charley over. He secured a spot near the rusted balcony railing with a perfect view of the makeshift stage.

"They're really back." Tavia leaned against the railing, her gaze trained on a trio of Market Streeters standing off to the side of the stage. "Saints, I wish I could be a runner too."

"So you can lick their boots up clos—ow!" Ezra cried as Tavia's elbow jabbed into his side.

"Don't think I won't throw you off this balcony right now Ezra Molyns."

"Fine, ow, fine I'm sorry!"

A hush suddenly fell over the room. Marcellus, a mask of calmness clouding his features, and Roderick, surly faced as ever, exited from a side door. Behind them was a giant of a man sleeved in Highgate prison tattoos and a petite woman with a mask covering the lower half of her face. The tattooed man stood off to the side while the petite woman squatted beside him, perched on the balls of her feet like a bird.

Tobias's nose scrunched. "Who let Elspeth out?"

"Bloody feral, that one," Ezra added.

As if on cue, Elspeth's head swiveled, and her large glassy eyes fixated on them. An icy jolt shot through Tobias. As her eyes slowly narrowed into crescents, he realized with a sickening lurch that she was smiling beneath her mask. He tore his gaze away, his heart hammering in his ears.

"Thank you all for joining us on such short notice," Marcellus began. "I'll cut straight to the meat of it. A few days ago, word reached us a Seadevil and a civilian were murdered in the Theatre District. A message was left behind tying us to the crime."

A collective howl of swears and booing rumbled through the Mess Hall. Marcellus held up his hand.

"Now, we Market Streeters have plenty to be guilty for and I wouldn't blame any one of you for taking out a Seadevil if the matter came to it. But what happened in that alleyway was not how we handle things." Marcellus held his hands behind his back, his gaze sweeping over every face.

"So I'll ask this one time, and this one time only. If someone in this room is responsible, step forward now."

Murmurs rippled through the crowd as the Market Street gang waited for their confessor. When no one stepped forward, Marcellus gave a curt nod. "If someone knows of anyone in this room who is responsible, step forward now."

Again, silence followed. As people looked from one neighbor to another, low whispers and pinched tones darting between them, Marcellus watched from the stage with a stony, almost placid, resolve. A sinking feeling nagged at Tobias. Something was being broken that couldn't be mended. A hairline crack in the glass of the Market Street mirror.

Marcellus cleared his throat. "All right then. From this point forward, if I find anyone in this room killed those two, I'll be handing you over to Deadeye myself *after* I'm through with you."

Ezra let out a low whistle. "Saints, we're in it now then, aren't we? Wonder if someone here really did do it."

Tobias and Tavia exchanged a look. She raised an inquisitive brow as if looking for a rogue Market Streeter was a new game.

He looked away, jaw clenched. No, that wasn't who they were. It wasn't how they handled business. Sure, they knocked people out, but they didn't kill them. That was the theatre surgeons. Not them.

His hands were dirty. Not red.

Marcellus motioned for the trio of Market Streeters standing off to the side to come forward. A young woman in her early twenties stepped forward first, followed by twin brothers around the same age. She lowered her hood to reveal shorn coils framing a dark heart-shaped face and deep brown eyes.

"Vivian and her team have surveyed near Port Vale." Marcellus nodded toward the crowd. "Fill them in."

"The Seadevils are eager for blood, but Deadeye is holding them back." Vivian folded her arms, thrumming her dark, pointed nails. "Word is Deadeye wants to play this one smart. Churn up a coordinated frenzy. We think they may try to strike soon and bleed us out slowly over the coming weeks. Silence from the Green Coats, but they usually operate on business tact so no surprise if they ask to meet when the time suits them."

"But a little fishy told us there's a group in the Seadevils that wants blood now." One of the twins slunk his tanned arm around Vivian's shoulders. A swatch of slicked back blonde hair brushed his ear as he unclasped his lighter and flicked its wheel in one fluid motion. Golden snakelight danced in his olive green eyes. He flashed a crooked smile to the crowd.

"They're quite talkative under a little heat, wouldn't you say Edwin?"

Edwin chuckled. "Quite. Not so confident without their hooks, either."

"Elwin, Edwin." Vivian narrowed her eyes. "Focus."

The twins frowned. Elwin shoved his hands into his pockets. "The rogues are set to meet two days hence somewhere near the Bowery. Our little fishy said they often frequent the Drunken Jester, so bets are it'll be there."

"Excellent." Marcellus looked out at the crowd. "A group of runners and brawlers will be positioned to take on this rogue group. We'll be questioning them from there. Once we have the info we need, the rest of you will be free to roam the streets again and resume your marks, collections, and raids."

Cheers erupted throughout the Mess Hall. A few "For Market Street!" and "Drown the Devils!" echoed amongst the crowd.

Tobias's stomach sank. He would be expected to defend the Ironworks District. Maybe even take out a Seadevil or two if it meant defanging Deadeye and taking Seadevil territory in the process. This wasn't just a war—this was an *opportunity*.

As the realization hit him, a hand touched his shoulder.

"You okay, mate?" Ezra asked.

Clean hands earn no coin.

Tobias stormed away without a word to any of his friends. How could he face them when he couldn't even face what he'd always known? Being a Market Streeter was more than marks and theft. When the war siren blared, all were called to duty. For loyalty. For coin. For power. And this time there was no running from it.

In the end, his hands would be red.

The sun was high in the sky when Tobias left the Distillery. By the time he reached Higdin's his brow was slick with sweat. He knocked on the back door in three short raps, then one pound of his fist. A moment passed. Then a second. Silence.

"Come on, Ari," he said beneath his breath, shifting from foot to foot.

Finally, two locks were undone and the door creaked open. Ari Mutu, Higdin's cook, poked her head out, her bright orange head scarf, bouquet of locs, and chestnut brown eyes catching the sun's rays.

"What are you doing here?" She peered over her shoulder. "Roy will be back any minute."

"I'll be quick, I promise." Tobias took a deep breath. "There's been some gang business between the Seadevils and Market Streeters. Maybe even the Green Coats, I dunno. Marcellus thinks it might get bad, so I need you and Lucy to lie low for a while. Stay here if possible."

Ari opened the door wider. "Ack, Tobias, slow down. What're you on about now?"

"Just stay off the streets. Hilda will get word eventually, but I wanted you to hear it from me first. I won't be round for a bit."

Ari pressed him into a hug. "Don't do anything stupid, all right? And look after yourself. I've got Lucy."

Tobias let out a small sigh. "Thanks, Ari. I owe you big time."

"Oh, I won't forget." Her downcast eyes didn't match her easy smile. "She's been asking about you. She still needs her big brother."

"I know."

Ari gave him a short nod. "I expect you back here soon. Pip and Olly do, too." She stepped aside to let him through but he shook his head.

"Better not to risk the ol' wench seeing me. She'd be right pissed I'm sure."

Ari's laugh was high and bright. "Love you, Toby. Be good out there."

She ruffled his hair and closed the door. Tobias lingered for a few seconds before circling around the side. He climbed up on a trashcan and reached for the hanging fire escape. It hissed under his weight as he made the climb to the third-floor landing. He did two quick rasps against the window and then two full knocks.

Lucy was at the window before Tobias could even pull his hand away.

"Toby!" she squealed, beaming from ear to ear. "You're back, you're back!"

For a moment, he lost himself in her shine and all the dangers below fell away.

"Hey there, Luce." He climbed inside and found the once dreaded flat almost comfortable. Sleeping streetside the past few nights had been a sobering experience. If what Tavia had mentioned before about the moon phases, he had little less than a month to try and find new lodging or risk another episode without ropes to bind him.

"Listen, I can't stay long but how've you been? Everything all right?"

"Ari took me to the market yesterday and bought me a pack of marbles. Oh Toby, they're so pretty! Look, look this one is my favorite."

She pulled out a blueish green marble from her dress pocket. In the light, brilliant aqua blue and seafoam green flecks danced against her face.

"It's lovely, Luce. And is Mrs. Hilda and everyone treating you well? Feeding you and all?"

Lucy nodded. "Yes. They've all been really nice. Francesca had a tea party with me the other day."

"That's good. And have you been minding your manners? Studying your letters?"

Lucy nodded again.

He rubbed the top of her head. "Good. Listen, I'm going to have to be gone a little while longer, okay?"

She pouted. "But why?"

"There's some bad people in the city. I need to help Ezra and Tavia fight them off. But don't worry, I'll be back as soon as I'm done. So I need you," he said, kneeling down and pointing at her, "to be good and stay here where it's safe. Can you do that for me?"

Lucy frowned and looked down at her feet. "Promise you'll be back?"

"I promise."

"Pinky swear?"

Tobias held up his little finger. "Pinky swear."

Lucy locked her pinky finger with his, smiling from ear to ear. Tobias stood up and gave her a long hug. "I'll see you soon. Love you, Luce."

"Love you, Toby!"

As he traveled down the ladder, Lucy waved at him from overhead.

I will be back, Tobias promised himself. *I will.*

But as he made his way over to Decker Street, about fifteen minutes at a leisure pace, he wondered just how messy this whole affair could get if Deadeye was serious about retaliating. If too much blood was shed the City Watch would be forced to act. Constables would swarm the docks of Port Vale to the coin parlors of the North Rim for weeks. The Garden District would be all but a fortress. No rats, no bodies, no grave digs, no coin.

Just as Tobias crossed over onto Decker Street, he noticed Lee Drole standing in the doorway of the Oleander, a ramshackle, wayward house that had more fleas than people. A young man around Tobias's age or a little older cowered on his knees in the street.

"This ain't no charity," Drole bellowed loud enough for the entire street to hear. "You either pay in full or nothing at all. I don't haggle with beggars."

"Please sir," the young man pleaded, a lilt to his Halic. Arcadian or Khagalese perhaps. "I can pay some now. I promise I will get the rest later."

Drole's lower lip curled into a sneer. "Promises don't fill me belly, lad. Come back when your coin matches your promises."

"Please, sir, I haven't anywhere else to go."

"Nonsense! You've got all of Lordhaven." Drole spread his arms wide. "Plenty of streets and back alleyways. Take your pick."

Drole turned and slammed the inn's door in the young man's face.

Tobias put his head down and continued walking. When he reached the end of Decker Street, a small, out of sight ladder led down to the walkway beneath Cloverton Bridge. Just as he and Ezra had done countless times all those years before, he jumped down the few rungs to the narrow stone pathway beneath. Home away from home.

The cloying smell of sewer wafted up from the Plithe River. As Tobias neared the underside of the bridge, he spotted a small figure near his makeshift camp.

He froze.

Someone was waiting for him.

19

NATHANIEL

"Medicine has taught us our mind is hidden behind our eyes. History has taught us this is for a reason." – *T. Brendle, excerpt from* Musings of a Drifter, *The Davenport Post*

When Nathaniel opened the penny paper to read with breakfast, the last thing he expected to see was news that Princess Angelina Chase may have been found.

The story was printed on page 7, so it could only be taken as gossip at best, but the kernels of truth Nathaniel did pick up on were hard to ignore. There had been a prisoner tried and hung in Iron Square. Upon her death, a phoenix sigil unique to the Chase bloodline radiated above her like the sun itself. It was well known when one of the Sacred Seven died, their familial crest would radiate above them. The sigil represented a mythical beast that was said to grant each bloodline power not seen outside of fateshifter magicks. Power gifted by the Saint Father himself to his disciples, to be passed on to their descendants, in his final living act—the Last Miracle—as opposed to the blasphemous power fateshifters supposedly bargained their souls away for with Azavith the Demon King.

Nathaniel reread the article. The author noted the phoenix sigil radiated over the prisoner with such clarity only seen in direct descendants of the ruling line. After years' worth of imposters and hacks claiming to be the missing princess, Nathaniel stared awe struck that the real one may have been found. But if this girl was the true princess, the same one who'd been snatched from her crib sixteen years ago and presumed dead, how had she escaped the fate of her step siblings?

"Hmph. Perhaps Rose *was* onto something," Nathaniel murmured.

"Excuse me, Master Trevet?" a feeble voice called from the other side of the dining room doors.

Nathaniel didn't look up from the penny paper.

"Come in, Ivan."

A young man stepped into the room dressed in a dark grey suit jacket and knee-length shorts. His flaxen hair, polished and parted to the side, barely skirted above his pitch-black eyes void of any white.

"Pardon my disturbance, Master Trevet," Ivan apologized. His face, still clinging to baby fat and not quite grown into his outward eighteen years, always remained calm when he spoke, as if waking from a deep, peaceful sleep. "You have a visitor who insists it is of utmost urgency that he speak with you at once."

"You know very well I don't accept visitors at this hour, Ivan," Nathaniel chided. "Or have you forgotten?"

Ivan adverted his eyes and nodded. "Apologies again, sir, but he insisted it was an urgent matter."

"Who is this guest?"

"Mr. Spencer Crane, sir."

Nathaniel's eyes cut back to Ivan.

"Crane? Are you sure?"

"Yes, sir."

"Did he state the reason for his visit?"

"No, sir." Ivan's voice deflated. "I pressed, but he offered no further details. I'm afraid I'm not as direct as grandfather."

"Think nothing more of it. Anders is away and you did what you could." Nathaniel set down the penny paper and rose from his seat. "Tell Crane I'll meet him in the drawing room in ten minutes."

Spencer Crane was pacing in front of the room's unlit fireplace when Nathaniel entered. The tea Ivan prepared for Crane sat untouched on the side table.

"Good day, Spencer."

The cloud of worry that had darkened Crane's mousy features only moments before suddenly lifted.

"Oh, Nathaniel, I do apologize for visiting unannounced. It was the only time I could spare, I'm afraid. I'm to board the seven o'clock train to Dempsey. I received word just the evening prior Gemma had fallen ill. If it's believed to be the same illness that took her sister just last season ..." His eyes glassed over. "I just can't bear to think Lionel or Ann may follow suit. I don't trust the housemaids to care for them long. I must return at once."

Nathaniel patted Crane's arm.

"My deepest regrets, Spencer. Your wife has a strong will so try not to think much of it. She'll pull through, I'm sure."

Crane's bloodshot eyes remained downcast for some time. "They tell me scarlet lung spreads rather hastily. Not even three days previous Gemma wrote saying how well the house was fairing. I just don't understand how things could change so rapidly."

Because humans are weaker than us.

"Yes, life is quite fickle," Nathaniel mused.

"And the children are so young. They wouldn't be able to stand being without their mother. I can't imagine how we'd make do without her."

"Truly. On another note," Nathaniel convened with a polite, but tight smile, "You requested a private word?"

Crane, as if suddenly remembering why he was there, nodded and frantically searched his trouser pockets. He paused for a moment, a blank look on his face, before reaching into his jacket with a sheepish smile.

"This is for you," Crane said, handing Nathaniel a sealed envelope. The front was blank, but the back was sealed with a wax crest Nathaniel didn't recognize. The crest itself was a deep violet with the image of an eye in the center. It bore no other initials or coat of arms.

"What is this? An unaddressed correspondence?"

Crane shifted his weight from one foot to another. Beads of sweat clustered near his receding hairline and his ashen cheeks flushed red.

"I understand how this may appear suspect, but I assure you of its legitimacy." Crane cast a weary glance in Ivan's direction. "Trust me when I say this letter was meant only for you."

"I should say you seem rather *frightened* by this whole affair, Spencer," Nathaniel said coolly. "Which leads me to believe you've not arrived on my doorstep of your own accord."

Crane chuckled. "Come now, Nathaniel. Surely you don't believe I—"

"Who sent you?" Nathaniel snapped, revealing his unsheathed upper fangs. They gleamed like two razor thin knives behind his outermost incisors.

Crane reeled back as if burned. "Nathaniel, be reasonable. I would never dare cross you, I swear it." His muddy brown eyes found Nathaniel's dark blue ones. Fear shaped them into something pitiful, even for Crane.

"Someone outside the Order knows about us. About the Mayfair plot, about all of it."

The Mayfair plot. Only those in his conspirator circle of Rose, Samir, and Spencer knew of it. Nathaniel had dreamt the whole thing in all its utter simplicity. Freedom from the shackles that bound him to kings and gods and all those who would deny him of his visions for this kingdom. Halcyon was broken, rotten and ugly.

But he saw its potential. He imagined it as the paradise of eternal pleasure and beauty and art it could be for duskborn. Halcyon only needed a well guided hand to make it so. Not Claude's or the Malsik's, but his.

And so it would be.

"Nathaniel? Nathaniel, did you hear me? Someone knows we mean to kill Clau—"

Nathaniel gave a small shake of his head and retracted his fangs. "Listen to yourself. How could anyone know of the plot unless someone betrayed us?"

Crane winced beneath Nathaniel's reproachful glare.

"I said nothing of it, I swear it!" Crane blubbered. "B-But someone approached me at the theatre the night before last. A-A woman. Young I think, but I didn't see her. She sat behind me and said I must give this letter to you. T-That if I didn't the Malsik and Claude would know of the Mayfair plot. She said the name of it, Nathaniel! She knew!"

Nathaniel looked down at the envelope again. Its unfamiliar violet eye stared back at him. A young woman? Could it be Claude's mysterious guest or her handmaiden? Coincidence seemed unlikely. But the woman in the theatre had called the plot by name. If she knew of it, and if it was one of the women Claude had met with at Kendleston Manor, there was a chance Claude now knew as well and Spencer's visit was for naught. No, he couldn't take that chance. He had to get ahead this.

"Have you told anyone about this mystery woman?"

Crane shook his head. "No, not a soul. I did exactly as she instructed." He took a large step towards Nathaniel, who instinctively stepped back. "Oh, Nathaniel what are we to do?" He paced where he stood, running his fingers through his thinning hair. "If we're found out, Claude will kill us! Or worse, the Malsik and his brutish lot will hunt us down and wear our bones as trophies."

Crane's lip quivered. "Do you think they'd harm my Gemma?"

Worse. Death would be a gift, Nathaniel wanted to say, almost said, but held his tongue. He needed Crane halfway sane if he was to cope with the idea someone was following him. Nathaniel couldn't risk the attention Crane would bring upon them, not with Claude lurking in every shadow and watching from every perch.

"Hurry along to Dempsey, Spencer. Speak not a word of this to anyone, not even the others. I shall sort out who the mole is and call upon you when I know more." Nathaniel's voice grew sterner. "Do nothing and say nothing."

"Y-Yes, of course. Thank you, Nathaniel, thank you. I knew you would know what to do."

"Ivan will see you out."

Crane nodded hurriedly and disappeared into the hall. Ivan returned a moment later with a pearl-handled letter opener. Nathaniel took it and in one swift motion opened the envelope. The letter itself was short, but it hit like a punch to the stomach. All thoughts of a betrayer in his conspirator circle immediately fell away.

Nathaniel slumped into the nearest chair. His eyes hovered over the signature at the bottom of the letter. How long had it been since he'd seen that name? His eyes roved over the languid scrawl. How his mother had loved watching him practice perfecting the same pattern each morning before his grammar lessons.

He scrutinized the flow and turn of each letter for several minutes. Ivan hovered an arm's length away studying Nathaniel's features.

"Sir?"

Nathaniel dropped the note on a side table and strode to the nearest window. He stared out onto Thornwood's well-trimmed lawn but all he could see was the letter's message imprinted over the greenery.

Come to the Under City, my dearest. I shall be waiting to answer a forgotten prayer.

It beckoned him like a siren song. But why had the letter been given to Crane? Why not Nathaniel himself?

He closed his eyes and allowed himself the rare indulgence to think of her. The woman who had shaped everything. The hand that had guided him when he was broken, rotten and ugly.

"Master Trevet?"

Anders stood in the doorway. Nearly as silent as his grandson, Ivan, Anders studied Nathaniel, a mixture of curiosity and concern in his eyes. His hands remained clasped behind his back. Ivan stood in stone silence at the door, glancing between Nathaniel and his grandfather.

"It's her, Anders," Nathaniel said quietly.

"Whom, sir?"

"My mother."

He could feel the weight behind the silence bearing down on him. The memory of a cold, rainy morning long past prickled his skin. Looking up at his father, who stood stoically beside him. His father, whose eyes were trained ahead, always looking towards the future. His father, whose duty for the Trevet legacy would always rise above his duty as a father. So Nathaniel took his father's hand and looked down at his mother's casket for them. He, the outcast son who had taken the tonic. He, the handsome son who radiated with beauty all but he could see. He, the sole heir who stared at death, adorned in a crown of lilies and forget-me-nots.

Anders approached the window, and Nathaniel handed the letter to him.

"If I may speak freely sir," Anders said when he was finished reading. "I do believe I have information you may find useful regarding this letter."

Nathaniel raised a brow. "Is that so? I didn't take you as one to dabble in rumors, Anders."

"And I shall not begin today, sir." A ghost of a smile lingered behind his bushy white moustache. He cast a brief glance in Ivan's direction. The young boy immediately redirected his attention to a rather uninteresting corner of the room.

"The Under City was run aground after the Dorne flooded it. This was before even your time. I dare say nothing remains there but thieves and vagrants, but the letter mentions a prayer being answered. I believe it may be in reference to St. Evangeline's cathedral. I used to frequent there when I was a boy."

"Very well, we'll start there."

"Whomever is forging the Mistress' hand has used a most foul means to lure you to them, Master Trevet. And I fear ..." Anders's voice dropped to a soft, almost sorrowful whisper. "I fear it may work."

Nathaniel's gaze slid to the portrait hanging just above the mantel. It was one of the few items he had moved from his family manor, Greybriar. He gazed up at the tall, stern-faced man with sharp eyes. His hand rested on the shoulder of a young woman with a soft, pleasant face. Both were dressed in garments fit for a ball. Nathaniel looked at the oily blue eyes of his mother.

But what is death to a wish everlong?

"Crane has an incurable weakness for dice," said Nathaniel. "He's currently in debt to four parlors and word is a fifth is watching his name in their books."

He turned away from his family's portrait and faced Anders. "This isn't one of Crane's debtors. It's too intimate. And I don't believe it's one of my fellow conspirators. They know only what I've told them of myself. This is the work of someone far older and wickeder than that."

Who, after all, would seek out the seeker? Who would know of the outcast heir Nathaniel had so carefully buried beneath time?

Someone who knew cruelty and its beauty.

Someone who knew of Lordhaven's hidden places.

Someone Nathaniel intended to find.

The Ironworks District roared to life with the new dawn.

Thick clouds of smoke billowed from the stacks above as the thunderous bellow of machinery drowned out all below. Factories crowded the cobbled streets and lorded over the bleary-eyed workers passing to and fro, water cannisters for most and lunch pails for the lucky ones.

As the Trevet family carriage crawled down Camden Street, Nathaniel poured over the letter in his hands for the umpteenth time. He had read it enough now to know it by heart, but he hoped the morning light might reveal some clue he may have missed.

After several more minutes, he finally tossed the letter on the seat beside him. An utter waste. He sighed, pinching the bridge of his nose.

"Idiot."

There was no one alive except himself and Anders that understood what really happened to him at Greybriar. They, who bore witness to what human hearts were truly capable of when no one was looking.

And only one of them wasn't bound by blood to silence.

No, whomever it had been—Claude, the Malsik, a no-name scribe paid for his mimicking hand—must have only meant to squander his time. Perhaps they knew him better than he'd given them credit for, and that was the most irritating thought of all.

But what if it really was her...

A flicker of light caught Nathaniel's eye, pulling him back to Lordhaven. He peered out the carriage window to see flames consuming an old factory. Black smoke twisted and twirled from its glassless windows and licked at its tin roof. The light of the inferno lit up the faces of passerby watching and pointing at the spectacle from afar. A few were even shaking their heads. Up ahead, two young men with large fishhooks on their belts sprinted around the corner, the light of the flames glinting off their hooks before they disappeared into the labyrinthine alleyways.

Nathaniel sat back in his seat. The gangs of Lordhaven were generally of no particular concern to the Order so long as they kept to their territories, but the Seadevils had started their retaliation for the theatre debacle.

Maybe this time they'll finally end each other, Nathaniel mused half-heartedly.

The carriage descended the curved slope of Weller's Low until the pinkish gold sky was blocked out by the overarching spine of the Elder Bridge.

Anders brought the carriage to a halt and opened the door.

"We've arrived, Master Trevet." A tinge of worry coated his voice, but his face remained stoic. Nathaniel stepped out of the carriage and was immediately hit by a sharp foulness emanating from the forgotten port town below.

"Do call upon Holt tomorrow morning," Nathaniel said with a scrunched nose. "Even Carina's magic won't be able to save this suit after a turn down there."

"Of course, sir. But I'm afraid I can go no further than here." Anders nodded toward the barricades a few feet ahead. Yellowed penny papers and discarded rags littered the area. Crows sat along the barricades, pecking at the debris in hopes of a meal. "It would seem the Crown has the awful sense of trying to dissuade people from venturing into areas better left forgotten."

"All the better to keep this jaunt brief then."

Orbs of gaslight flickered in the Under City's makeshift corridors, illuminating the half-shadowed faces regarding Nathaniel and Anders.

"Master Trevet, I ask you again to reconsider this venture. The Under City is home to dead things better left drowned at the bottom of the Dorne. There's a reason the Crown tried to bury it under Lordhaven."

"I appreciate your concern, but this is something I must see through."

A shadow passed over Anders' face, faster than Nathaniel could perceive. He lowered his voice to just above a whisper. "It's not her, sir."

"Well, I'd be concerned if it was. Mother would look rather dreadful by now, don't you think?" He ran a hand through his dark hair. "Now, how best to get to this cathedral of yours?"

Anders frowned. "If it must be done, then you'll want to speak to Mr. Samuel Lockley. His grandfather used to run a tinker shop before the flood, and he carried on the trade in stubborn hopes of the city returning. I hear addiction has gotten the better of him, but he knows all who enter and leave the Under City. They call him the Caretaker. He'll be your best chance finding St. Evangeline's. For a price of course."

"Lovely." Nathaniel looked past Anders to a few men lingering near the bank of the Dorne pretending to fish.

"You may wait at the bridge while I'm gone. Not worth troubling yourself over some port filth."

Anders flashed a haunted smile.

"I shall be fine here, sir."

Nathaniel watched in silence as Anders began removing his white gloves. A faint tightness pulled at his chest. Even now, all these years later, he hadn't forgotten what he saw that day beyond the barely cracked cellar door at Greybriar. A stable boy caught stealing. Anders looming over him, his left hand firmly planted over the boy's face so only his wild, pleading eyes were visible. A strange light snaking through the veins of Anders's hand like black fire.

"You would do best to turn away now, young Master Trevet."

Nathaniel snapped open his pocket watch. "As you wish but do try not to cause too much harm. I shouldn't be longer than half past."

The shrill cry of the local fire siren blared in the distance. The factory was surely ashes by now. Nathaniel tucked the letter into his jacket and took out a cane from a hidden compartment under the carriage's passenger seat. The less he had to rely on his fangs the better.

Anders tipped his hat and Nathaniel flashed a smug smile as he descended the grimy stone steps. A parade of broken bottles, newsprint and mottled clothing clung to the sides of the Dorne's brownish black surface. Along the old harbor, half caved buildings lined the road of what was once the busiest port in Halcyon. Bricks sat in heaps at the base of the exposed floors, the furniture long ago taken for coin or kindling. Squatters peered down at him from open windows, fleeting in and out of his periphery like shadows.

Why anyone would choose to live in a dead city buried beneath Lordhaven's shadow was beyond him. No one had even cared to remember its original name.

As Nathaniel continued along the main pathway, he noticed a shop with a thin stream of smoke snaking out of its chimney. An unkindness of ravens lined the shop's slanted tin roof, their large, beady eyes watching his every move.

Slumped in a chair beneath the shop's weathered kettle sign was a thin man with a pipe tucked between his lips. A wiry grey beard hung like moss from his sunken face.

"Pardon me, but do you run this shop?" Nathaniel inquired.

The man exhaled a cloud of grey smoke. His bloodshot eyes narrowed as he looked Nathaniel over.

"Aye," he grunted with a voice thick as tar. "What be it to you?"

"Ah, a man of business. That shall do nicely." Nathaniel reached into his jacket and pulled out his gold watch. The Caretaker's eyes immediately drew to it. "I haven't got long, but I wish to make a trade."

"For what?"

"Information. Do you know where I can find St. Evangeline's?"

The Caretaker tensed. "Ain't never heard of it."

"Odd. You are the Caretaker, are you not? Or have I been speaking to a liar this whole time?" His fangs slid down for the old man to see. "Well?"

The smoking pipe fell from between the Caretaker's lips. He shot to his feet and raised his hands in front of him. "No, not at all. By the Saints, I swear it! I do!"

"Good." Nathaniel's fangs slid back as quickly as they'd appeared. "Now that we better understand each other, I wish to make that trade."

Suddenly, the door to the tinker shop burst open and a young woman rushed out onto the landing. She wore a grease streaked apron and a thin spun green dress beneath. She held a parry knife in her hand but made no move to threaten Nathaniel with it.

"I can take you to St. Evangeline's. Just leave him alone."

"You get back in that shop, Penny!"

When she didn't move, the Caretaker went to grab her arm but she side stepped out of his reach.

"He's duskborn, Grandda. Just let it be." Her gaze flickered to the ravens perched on the rooftop. "They'll know it was us that told him anyway. No point trying to stop it now."

"I said," the Caretaker drawled, pointing to the doorway, "get back in that shop. I don't care if it's the bloody Saint Father himself, you hear me?"

Nathaniel was behind the Caretaker before either he or Penny noticed. He leaned down and whispered in the old man's ear, "Why don't you head inside and I'll take the young miss with me instead."

He slipped a few sterlings in the man's pocket as Penny watched in silent horror. She gripped the knife in her trembling fist.

"There now," he said, squeezing the Caretaker's shoulder firmer than necessary. "I'd say that's fair."

He stepped back and motioned for Penny to join him. "After you, miss."

Penny looked back at the Caretaker, who waved her off. "Go on then. You heard the man."

She hurried down the steps and joined Nathaniel. He held out his arm to her, but she shirked away and clasped her wrist tightly.

"This way."

She never looked back to see if he was following, but his long strides easily kept pace with her shorter ones. When they were out of earshot of the Caretaker, she finally spoke. "You're right mad to go there, you know."

"And why is that?"

"You can't fool them. They'll know what you're looking for even if you don't say. They *always* know." She cut her eyes at him, adding in a whisper, "Because the White Raven does."

Nathaniel narrowed his eyes. "Who is 'they'? And what do mean about the White Raven?"

But the girl said no more. She quickened her pace, slipping between half lit streets slick with stagnant puddles and soiled debris. Nathaniel spotted ravens along some of the rooftops and exposed beams.

Are they following us?

"Those people you spoke of earlier, do they have anything to do with those ravens there?"

Penny stopped so suddenly Nathaniel nearly collided with her. She spun around, dark eyes narrowed.

"I get it, all right? My grandda's a proper bastard, but you needn't insult me with this bloody dull act."

"Interesting." Nathaniel slid his hands into his pockets. "Is that what you think this is then? An act?"

Penny scoffed. "You're just like every other posh bastard from the high slats that comes down here thinking if one god doesn't answer you another will." She folded her arms tightly across her chest. "But you're all just cheats and liars, the lot of you. Empty, retched things. You'll never believe in anything you can't buy."

Nathaniel held up his hands. "I assure you, miss, my presence here is far from baseless. If you'll allow me to be so bold, can you read correspondence?"

"Yes," Penny snapped. "I can even count my numbers if you can believe it."

Nathaniel reached into his jacket and removed the letter.

"This letter was given to me last evening. I believe it's a summons to St. Evangeline's. It was signed in my mother's hand, but she's been dead for ... quite some time."

Penny sucked in a sharp breath.

"Blessed be the sight which falls upon us," she whispered, running her trembling fingers over the wax seal.

She lifted her eyes towards the west. Nathaniel followed her gaze and caught the outline of a cathedral lingering in the darkened corners of the Under City, easily missed by the untrained eye. Fear flickered across her young face as the ravens screeched and took flight.

"I'm truly sorry," she murmured. "Follow me."

20

NATHANIEL

Penny led Nathaniel across a city square. A barrel fire illuminated a nearby carriage riddled with rust and missing all four wheels. A torn dress hung limply across its moldy seat.

Two children were playing on the other end of the square. They stopped when Penny and Nathaniel approached. A woman clad in rags from head to toe opened the door and ushered them inside.

"Divert your eyes, lads," she hissed at them before slamming the door closed. "Get in now. Go! Away from the windows."

The air grew damp as the pair continued down the abandoned street.

"Are there others who live here?"

Penny nodded but offered nothing further.

At the end of the street loomed the hollowed ruins of St. Evangeline's. Its stained-glass windows had been painted black and a single snake oil lamp burned outside its door.

"St. Evangeline's became a hedge shrine for the White Raven many years ago. Some say even before the flood." Penny sucked in a sharp breath. "But only madness resides there now."

Shrines dedicated to the hedge gods of old were tucked away in the darkest corners of Halcyon, away from the unforgiving eyes of the City Watch who would sooner shoot someone dead than arrest them for it. But Nathaniel had the feeling this was far more than a simple altar.

"You were called, and so you came." She shook her head, her voice wrought with sympathy. "The White Raven is a messenger. A harbinger of the end to come. And truth will always demand to be heard."

"The White Raven is a children's tale to ward off bad behavior," Nathaniel corrected. "Or, if the True Word is to be believed, another face of Azavith, the big bad demon king."

"They will show you otherwise," Penny warned.

"They?"

"The Ravenhood. Worshippers of the White Raven." Her jaw clenched as if she wished to say more. "This cathedral is their altar."

"And you're one of them?"

"No!" she snarled. "Never. The principles they live by ... an eye for an eye, blood for blood ... it's ...it's all for the sight and ..." She shook her head. "It's awful. No one's meant to see those kinds of things."

Penny approached the cathedral. A tall wrought iron gate hung askew on its hinge. She slipped through with ease, but Nathaniel's tall frame forced him to shove the rusted metal as much as it would budge to worm his way through. A robed statue lay forgotten in the courtyard, beheaded.

Penny cast a wary eye at the front doors.

"It's true the Saint Father has no home here in the Under City," she went on. "Hope left with the flood and many prayed to the White Raven for strength. But we are *not* the Ravenhood."

She trailed off, and Nathaniel didn't press. He could hear faint movement on the other side of the doors, two, maybe three pairs of feet.

"I'll speak first," she continued. "Wait for them to present themselves. It'll be better that way."

The doors creaked open with protest. Stagnant air thick with damp and wick smoke clogged their noses. Rows of lit, dripping white candles lined the walls, revealing the crudely drawn eyes covering the room floor to ceiling and carved into the pews like childish scrawls.

"We come on invitation," Penny called out into the darkened belly of the cathedral. "I guide the invited into this sacred space."

Silence.

"He has been called by the Unsacred One."

Again, Penny was met with silence.

"This is absurd," Nathaniel growled. "I have other affairs to—"

A robed figure detached themselves from the shadows of the pulpit. They were short, barely above Penny's height.

"Who summoned you?" the figure demanded, her words hoarse yet sharp. A white veil covered the upper half of her face, leaving only her mouth and chin exposed. Long, dark hair snaked across her arms and brushed her thighs.

Before Penny could respond, Nathaniel stepped forward. "The dead."

He could feel the hooded woman's eyes on him now. Her black lips twisted into a scowl.

"He has been called here, High Priestess," Penny repeated. "He has been tasked to witness the true vision."

The High Priestess ignored her.

"Blessed be the sight which falls upon us, for it is true and everlong." The High Priestess held up her hand. Carved into her palm was the same eye that was drawn on every surface of the cathedral. "What would you ask of it?"

Nathaniel moved a notch on his cane.

"An eye for an eye." In a motion too quick to catch, he unsheathed his cane's hidden blade and swept it across Penny's throat. She gurgled a surprised cry and collapsed onto the ground. He watched the stream of blood slip between her fingers and run down her hands, staining her dress.

He gave a shallow bow. "My thanks and apologies, Penny."

Nathaniel took out a handkerchief and wiped the blade clean. He slid it back into his cane and looked up at the High Priestess with a mask of calmness. He stepped forward and offered a deep bow.

"Dearest Holy Maiden, I have made my offer. Now tell me, why has the White Raven summoned me here?"

The High Priestess lifted her staff and slammed it back down on the ground.

"What is owed for an unseer slayed? What you ask is too great for the price paid."

Nathaniel swallowed his disappointment. "I see. Very well then. Tell me this, Holy Maiden. Does the White Raven walk among us?"

The High Priestess's shrill laugh rang through the broken ceiling of the cathedral. She raised her arms high above her head in praise.

"Does the sun not rise and the moon not wane? The Unsacred One has been here long before us and shall be here long after us."

"Then why praise one so grand here in the shadows of a dead city?" Nathaniel pressed. "Should there not be shrines for the White Raven alongside those erected for the saints by the vicaress and her holy legion?"

The High Priestess let out a low, guttural moan.

"Bold be the Saint Father and his Sacred Seven, slayers of beasts and eaters of magicks. Thieves of the Unsacred One's eternal heart," she snarled. "They turned the world against the Unsacred One, tore their great name from history and trapped them in fables. The vicaress is their liar and the True Word is their spectacle. But we," she crooned, looking up at the ceiling beams towering above her, "we were blessed by the Unsacred One's true sight and it shall guide us towards their truth. Our undoing shall set us free."

Nathaniel removed the letter from his jacket and placed it on the floor. "I've traveled far and offered blood as price. I have an unanswered prayer."

The High Priestess studied him for a moment, then tapped her staff in a rapid succession.

"You have paid an eye for an eye and acknowledged the Unsacred One. Now, tell me, are you prepared to bear witness to their vision?"

Nathaniel swallowed back his refusal. "It would be an honor."

The High Priestess broke into a grin of blackened teeth. She slammed her staff twice. Nathaniel could hear something scampering behind him, but he refused to take his eyes off the High Priestess.

"Can you see it now?" she whispered.

Nausea slithered through Nathaniel. He took a step back and shook his head, but the light-headiness refused to leave him. When he looked back up, the High Priestess was gone.

And so was Penny's body.

Laughter echoed through the cathedral as the shadows deepened around him.

"Is this it then? Children's games? Do you think me a fool?"

Silence followed. Nathaniel looked around him but there was no sign of anyone. Even the puddle of blood was gone. He bit back panic. No, he was fine, just hallucinating. Mold spores or toxic vapors.

Curse this bloody damp.

Suddenly, the shadows near the pulpit shifted.

"Who's there?" Nathaniel called, releasing his fangs. "Priestess? Show yourself!"

The shadow lingered, almost swaying in a nonexistent breeze. It was small, almost child-like.

"I say, who goes there?"

Laughter echoed from the rafters. He glanced upwards but saw nothing beyond the candlelight.

When Nathaniel looked back, the figure had moved. It was now in front of the pulpit swaying ever slightly. The faint glow of a nearby candle illuminated the figure's left arm.

It appeared too small for the figure's size and hung close to its chest in a horrid bend. A drunken fuzziness clouded Nathaniel's head the longer he stared at the peevish, bent arm. Something old and familiar gnawed at him.

The figure twitched and heaved, struggling for breath.

A dull ringing filled Nathaniel's ears. The sound of a thousand flapping wings, the screeching caw of laughter buried in a thousand truths.

"A deal is a deal," Nathaniel bellowed against the noise, his hands pressed against his ears. "If you have nothing to tell me, then I shall see myself ou—"

"Nathaniel."

Nathaniel's eyes widened. That voice. *Her* voice. Just behind him. Just—

He dropped his hands and spun around.

"Mother?"

No one.

When he turned around, the cathedral was gone. He was standing in his childhood bedroom at Greybriar. Outside, rain lashed against the windows. Lightning split the sky in two and a low, rumble of thunderous laughter followed.

Nathaniel was rooted in place, the weight of a thousand eyes bearing down on him.

"Why did you bring me here?" he whispered, voice cracking.

"Nathaniel."

Nathaniel's head snapped up toward the portrait of his mother and father—the same portrait he had taken from Greybriar and hung in Thornwood. But where his parents' eyes should've been were the crudely drawn eyes from St. Evangeline's.

Nathaniel backed against the wall. His head was swimming. He tried shaking their gaze, but those eyes saw everything.

Knew everything.

The ringing in his ears grew louder. He had to get out. He ran to the door. Locked. He tried the knob but it held steadfast.

"Open this door, now!" He slammed his fist against the wood until it was sure to crack. "Let me out!"

"Nathaniel, dear, please. Do settle down now, won't you?"

Nathaniel's fist hovered in midair. His whole body iced over, and suddenly the confidence his ill-gotten years afforded him stripped away until he was reduced to a defenseless six year old boy again.

Mother.

He slowly turned and there, standing with her back to the window was Priscilla Trevet, as stunning and golden-haired as she'd always been in life. She was draped in a blush pink day dress and matching slippers. Delicate gold earrings adorned her ears and only the slightest hint of color dotted her cheeks.

Standing beside her was a hunched waif of a child dressed in a tailored dark blazer and shorts. Charcoal grey socks came to his knobby, buckled knees. The boy's head hung low, hiding his face as he grappled for breath.

"Now look what you've done," Priscilla chided. "You've excited him. You know he hasn't the lungs for it."

She knelt and held the boy's face between her gloved hands.

"Now, there, there," she whispered, patting his cheek. "One breath, two breath. Easy now. That does it. There we go."

When the boy's wheezing finally soothed, she stood and looked back at Nathaniel.

"The world is so very uncaring. Only the strong survive. And he ..." She looked at the boy with downcast eyes, a mixture of pity and resolve wading beneath their blue surface. "He's so very weak. And weakness simply won't do, you understand? Not in this world. He deserves everything. And what mother would I be if I didn't give him everything?"

Nathaniel watched in silence as the boy reflexively held his crooked arm close.

"You ..." The words were lodged in his throat. It had been too long and they were buried too deep, but still he tried to claw them out. "Are you proud? Proud of any of it?" Nathaniel's voice fell to a harsh whisper. "Proud of me?"

Priscilla smiled softly. "You're strong now, Nathaniel. But you still must keep going. To stop is to settle. To stop is to be weak." She clutched the boy's shoulder, ignoring his wince of pain. "And my precious son is not weak. Not the heir to the Trevet name."

The ringing in Nathaniel's ears rose to a deafening buzz as the boy finally raised his head. A white veil with a crudely drawn violet eye on its front was draped over his face.

His lips parted into a crooked smile, revealing jagged, yellow teeth crowding his mouth like gravestones.

"Make me perfect," the boy said in a gravelly voice. "You can. You must. One more deal. Just one more."

A flash of lightning split the sky, illuminating them both in a brilliant halo.

"Find the eternal heart," the boy urged. "Find it. Make the deal. *Make us perfect.*"

The floor fell away. Nathaniel landed on his back with a hard thud. He rolled onto his side, sputtering for breath. Seconds, maybe minutes passed in the sweet bliss of the damp darkness. Finally, Nathaniel managed to stand.

The candles had gone out. He was trapped, alone, in the foul, dark maw of St. Evangeline's. Only the shards of sunrise from the open roof above guided him to the entrance.

A storm brewed inside him. His hands clutched the door handles, but he couldn't bring himself to open them. Was this where he belonged?

Steeped in darkness, rotten things grow anew. He had changed, shaped himself into something new. Something better. He was not the filth his mother had known in life. He was better, couldn't she see? Did she see? Did she? Did she?

Make us perfect. You can. You must.

Fangs barred, Nathaniel shoved the cathedral doors open and never looked back.

21

SYBIL

"Plain garments are best for long travels. Always be sure to remove any jewelry or indication of certain gemstones from your person. Constabulary are aware of their affiliation to magicks. Best practice is to hide in the soles of a shoe or lining of a purse when at City Watch checkpoints." *–Edgar B. Hawkins,* The Arcanic Traveler's Guide, 7th Edition

Sweat dripped down Sybil's brow. "Again!"

Priya arched her arms in a half circle and a small golem formed from fallen tree limbs and vines in front of her.

"Give it a weapon!" Sybil shouted from the other end of the clearing.

"Come on, Sybil. It's just practice."

"Do it!"

Priya let out an audible sigh. She referenced her conjured grimoire and after several hand gestures a tangle of vines snaked around a nearby rock from the creek. A rotted tree root tore itself away and latched onto the rock to form a mallet's handle.

The golem charged forward. Sybil took a deep breath and extended her arms. The icy grip of death slithered over her left hand first. She wiggled her fingers, shifting mana around the bones to gauge the body's size. Priya leaned forward and the golem picked up speed.

It was nearly on her now. Sybil's eyes flew open. She arched her left arm toward the golem and a half-rotted fox corpse burst from the softened ground. She made a tearing motion near her mouth and elongated fangs of concentrated mana formed over the fox's existing teeth. Just as Priya and the golem lifted both of their arms in attack, the fox leapt to the side, dodging the attack, and tore through the golem's exposed vine throat. The surrounding leaves and twigs burned away as if touched by acid.

The golem crumpled to the forest floor in a thudding heap.

"How did you manage to do *that*?" Priya squealed. "You didn't tell me you formed a new attack!"

Sybil recalled the fox to her side. She grabbed her water canister and took a long gulp.

"I can't reveal all my new tricks," she said with a triumphant smile. "That one I'm saving for the Trials."

Priya put a hand on her hip. "So you really want to be a Major, huh?" Sybil was silent for a moment.

"It's hard getting covenship when you've already had it once." She instinctively reached for the area just above her sternum where her coven's oath seal used to be emblazoned. Now all that remained was a barely perceptible scar.

"But that was ... different." Priya's brow furrowed as the sun dipped behind the clouds, casting the forest in shadow. "Your coven was officially disbanded. You weren't cast out or left by choice. That's not fair."

"Doesn't matter much when everyone thinks I killed them." Sybil shook her head. "I'm going to pass the Trials and become a Major. Then I won't need to grovel to anyone anymore."

"Sybil ..."

Sybil set down her canister and summoned her grimoire.

"Another go then?"

Priya nodded and arched her arms again. This time, two golems formed in front of her. Priya crouched and slammed her hands together. Their eyes glowed a brilliant blue. They curled into stone balls of ivy and vine and slingshot forward in alternating paths towards Sybil.

Looks like she has new tricks too.

Sybil bent her knees and took a deep breath. Two against one wasn't great odds, but she had no other choice. She siphoned more of her lifeforce through the tether, strengthening the fox corpse. Its eyes burned a miasmic green.

The fox barreled towards the golems, but with a wave of her hand Priya had one of the golem's change its formation. Instead of both coming toward Sybil at once, one diverted behind her and the other unfurled in front of her for a charge attack.

Sybil's heart skipped a beat.

If she didn't act, she'd be crushed beneath the golem's stone fist.

A seething rage boiled inside of her, just as it had at Lycoris. She swept her right arm to the side, diverting her undead fox to handle the golem behind her, and formed a second tether between herself and the golem charging towards her.

She summoned a second soul with her free hand and forced it inside the golem. The golem broke its attack and stumbled as the soul fought against being stitched to a stone doll of ivy and roots.

"NOT HUMAN! NOT HUMAN!" the soul screeched. Sybil wrestled against it with gritted teeth. She tried to clasp her hands together to seal the binding, but invisible fingers fought to pry her hands apart.

On the other side, Priya struggled as Sybil's tether choked off her control. The small amount of mana siphoned into vines and bramble was no match against the concentrated lifeforce of a human soul.

The golem's eyes flickered between green and blue.

"You're *mine!*" Sybil snarled. She slammed her hands together as a thin stream of blood poured from the corner of her mouth.

The golem bellowed as its eyes went dark then reignited a fiery green. Priya fell to one knee, her breath hoarse.

Sybil refused to buckle. A human soul demanded far more lifeforce than an animal one, but having two souls bound and actively fighting was pushing her limit. The thick taste of copper coated her mouth as she struggled for air, but she ignored it. Death was hers to wield.

And wield it she would.

With barred teeth, she flung her golem's arm at the one behind her. It was not enough to destroy it, but it knocked Priya's golem off balance long enough for the fox to tear open its throat and finish it off.

Sybil fell to her knees, panting. She spit out a gob of blood and wiped the back of her mouth with her arm. She released her tethers and sighed in sweet relief as her lifeforce returned to her.

Priya walked over, sweaty and out of breath, and extended her hand. "If that's not Major material, I don't know what is."

Sybil laughed and took Priya's hand. Her head spun when she got to her feet, but the rush of battle left her grinning.

"But you really shouldn't overdo it like that," Priya added.

"I swear, you really worry too mu—"

Priya's scream cut her off. Sybil whirled around to see Cain leaning against a tree, arms folded and an amused smirk on his face.

"Well done, Miss Vorn. I must say I'm rather impressed," he said.

Sybil tensed. Priya looked between Cain and Sybil with wide eyes.

"Sybil, what is that thing?"

Sybil ignored her. "Where's Heath?" she snapped. Unease wound her stomach in knots. This was *not* good.

"Tsk. You're not the only one who needs frost, Miss Vorn. But this was far more interesting to watch."

Sybil swallowed hard. She could feel Priya's accusing glare, but she'd have to worry about smoothing that over later.

She grabbed Priya's hand. "Come on, we're leaving."

But before she could take a step, Cain slipped between them. One hand covered Priya's mouth, gripping her cheeks between shadowy clawed fingers. The other clasped around Sybil's throat.

"The fun is just about to start," he cooed. Sybil followed his gaze and saw the beast first.

It was a great hulking thing, twice as large as any wolf ought to be, with matted black fur and rounded shoulders like that of a hunched man. Its movements were jittery and uncertain as if it were fighting with itself. Sybil had seen glimpses of blood wolves before, but never one so close and so very much alive.

Cain's gripped tightened around Sybil's throat, stifling her cries of panic. Priya shook her head violently, wide eyes darting between the blood wolf and Sybil.

"I've seen it in you. Go on, Miss Vorn. Tap into it. That dark reverie. Let's see what you can *really* do." Cain released Sybil and Priya, then melted into the shadows.

Sybil clutched her throat, sputtering for breath.

"Sybil, over there!"

Sybil looked up to see Cain standing halfway between them and the blood wolf. A wispy, crooked grin carved into his shadowy face. Sybil's eyes widened.

No ...

And then in the blink of an eye, Cain was thrice his height, his wispy edges now jagged and writhing. His head leaned back until it rested between his shoulder blades. A banshee's howl tore from his throat and clawed at the sky. The girls covered their ears, but it did little against Cain's piercing howl.

When all fell silent, Sybil opened her eyes to see the blood wolf barreling towards them. Cain had disappeared.

She stared at the beast's face as it rushed forward at a pace she could never hope to outrun. Her fingers reached out for something, anything to summon, but her focus was shattered by the snarling mess of teeth and foam-soaked jaws heading straight for them. Madness clouded its eyes like two dark moons, blocking out any rays of sanity still left on the other side.

Time slowed. Priya's cries fell away to a muffled hum and the fog in Sybil's mind partially lifted.

Major Quinn had the same maddening look when she slayed the tradesmen on the road the day everything went wrong.

Two dark moons over her eyes.

A pulse reverberated deep inside her. It echoed in her chest and rang in her ears. Something on an unseen shore pulled back.

The blood wolf was only a few feet from them now. Priya was frozen in shock, her mouth agape. A guttural snarl tore from the beast's throat, fervent and desperate. The ringing in Sybil's ears grew louder as her head gave way to a horrid sense of vertigo.

"Tear those moons from its eyes." The thought was as clear as if someone had spoken it in her ear. *"Find the truth beneath."*

Her body went rigid as the blood wolf raised its forearm to slice her and Priya to ribbons.

"Your death shall be your own!"

As Sybil's consciousness slipped beneath the surface, a powerful torrent rushed from the unseen shore and out through her hands, igniting everything with furious absolution.

A voice called her.

Low and hopeful, but Sybil ignored it. The figure standing at the sea's edge captivated her. How desperately she wanted him to turn around, to look at her with that same beaming smile he had when he first brought her to the seashore all those years ago.

I promise I won't fail you, Da.

The voice called louder.

Sybil quickened her pace. She had so much to tell him. He'd been away so long, missed so much—

The dark sea beneath them began to stir. Like a beast waking from its slumber, its blackish blue surface shifted and broke the closer she got to the edge. She was nearly upon him, just an arm's reach away. Tears streamed down her cheeks.

"Da, please come back," she pleaded, her voice hoarse. "I need you."

The voice was screaming now. A deep growl emanated from the sea in response. White capped waves shattered against the shore, pelting Sybil and her father in fine mist.

She reached out her hand but stopped halfway. Her mind finally caught on to the screaming. She knew that voice. Stern, unforgiving, desperate.

"Mum?"

"Sybil," her father finally said.

He kept his back to her, but his voice was sunshine against the raging sea and screaming sky. A lighthouse to guide her through the storm.

"For you have become the shepherd of souls and keeper of sin," he said. "Bear their names, poppet. Find the truth beneath."

The crackling blaze of a hearth filled Sybil's vision.

Her thoughts trickled in one by one like droplets, nagging but too delicate to catch. Ignoring the ache in her muscles, she noticed a sweet, calming scent. *Lavendar? In the forest?* She tried to focus on her thoughts, but her mind was too jumbled. As she moved to sit upright, a hand gently pushed her back down.

"Easy there, dear. Not so fast."

"Lady Ilva?"

"Yes, I'm right here." Lady Ilva pulled her stool closer to the bed. The light of the flames danced off the purple bellflowers intertwined in her waist long grey locs. Her dark grey eyes softened. "I know you're none too good at being still for long, mia tempesta, but I insist you rest. You need it."

Sybil's eyes drifted up to the cottage's ceiling, where dried lavender bundles hung from the wooden rafters. Tinctures in various glass bottles lined the back walls of the cottage, and bundles of herbs crowded her drying rack.

"How do you feel?"

"Tired. And my ..." Sybil's voice tapered off. She squinted, turning her hands over several times.

"Something wrong, dear?"

"My hands, they ... hurt. Before. Like they were ..." Fragments of the encounter rushed to the surface.

A mad beast. Two dark moons. An unseen shore. Her father.

"Da..." Sybil's voice fell to a whisper. "Lady Ilva, did I ...were my hands burned?"

"No. A little irritated but not burned."

"B-But they were so hot ... and my face ..."

Lady Ilva wrapped her arm gently around Sybil's shoulders. "You're still in shock, dear, that's all. Confusion is normal. The body is much better at healing than the mind. All that matters is you're safe now."

Sybil leaned away. "I'm not confused."

She wanted to believe in the reassurance of Lady Ilva's words, in the gentleness of her smile and the wisdom afforded to one old enough to earn their crow's feet. She wanted to believe her instincts were wrong.

Why would she lie to me?

"I meant no offense, mia tempesta," Lady Ilva continued. "You've been out for most of the day. You need time to let your mind settle. But it's getting on in hours, so you'll stay the night here. Thank the gods you only suffered a bit of shock."

Ilva rose to her full five foot four height, which was only a hair taller than Sybil herself. "Now, the time is upon us to rest. Your mother has asked this much of me."

Mum.

Sybil remembered a voice, her mother's she swore, that had pulled her back from the shore. But how could she have known? Had she sensed her fall to that place?

And what even was that place?

"Miss Ilva, where's Priya? Is she okay?"

"Yes, dear. Miss Majumdar is fine. She's resting at home. Rattled, but otherwise un-harmed. Ah, a tipping of Byrill's scales that Mr. Tanner was there to help." Ilva bent down and coaxed the logs in the hearth. The flames jumped and hissed. Sybil's head began to spin again. She closed her eyes to steady herself.

Cain. Anger roiled fresh and hot inside her.

"Heath saved me?" Sybil said slowly, more for her own understanding.

"Carried you here on his back. Miss Majumdar followed behind him." Ilva shook her head. "To imagine a mother wolf venturing so close. Mr. Tanner said she was rather vicious. I imagine a cub must've been nearby to lash out as she did on you and Miss Majumdar. You're very lucky to have such kind friends."

He's not my friend, Sybil almost said, but held her tongue. Instead, she sank deeper into the bed, her body suddenly leaden. None of it made any sense. Why had he lied about the blood wolf to Lady Ilva? And why were her palms uninjured if she had felt a roiling heat over them before she passed out?

Roiling heat. Sybil turned to her side and stared at her right hand. Perfectly healed. But the body remembers pain, even if the mind is slow to follow. Her breath quickened. She held it in, fearful Lady Ilva would notice the terrible truth written on her face. Read the guilt in her wide, teary eyes.

Something was terribly wrong with her.

22

JULIA

"How are you feeling today, Julia?"

Julia looked up from her book. Dr. Ward stood in the doorway. He had on the same starched white coat she'd come to believe he slept in.

"Good. Although ..." She shook her head. "Ah, never mind. It's silly really."

Dr. Ward closed the door. "No such thing. What's troubling you?"

Julia set aside her book, careful not to meet his gaze. She only had one shot to get this right.

"I truly hate to waste your time like this, Dr. Ward but it's my dreams. Something is rather ... off about them."

"Off you say? How so?"

Julia fidgeted with the button on her dress pocket. "Just the other night, I dreamed I was trapped in this strange place. There was a large crowd and they were saying terrible things. I think they were angry with me." Julia offered a weary smile. "I'm really sorry to trouble you. It just gave me an awful fright."

Dr. Ward shook his head. "Nothing to worry yourself over, I assure you. A simple nightmare is all. It's to be expected in your delicate state."

Julia brightened. "Oh, what a relief. I was afraid I was going mad. It all felt so real."

Dr. Ward pressed his glasses up the bridge of his nose. "As long as you don't dream of wolves, of course."

An incredulous laugh escaped her lips. "Wolves? Of course not." Stories of people who believed themselves to be turning into beasts, murderous and mad blood wolves, floated through Temmings from time to time, but most talk of blood wolves were dismissed as the delirium of living in large, cramped cities.

"Only hollium addicts and perverse scoundrels would say they're becoming wolves," Julia added. "Everyone knows that's impossible."

"I see. And have you been resting?" Dr. Ward probed, changing the subject. "I hear you haven't been finishing your meals. Is the tea not to your liking?"

"I haven't been very hungry," Julia lied.

Dr. Ward frowned. "Well, you must do your best to have all your meals and plenty of rest. I'll see what I can do to—"

"You know, I think a bit of fresh air would do me good. I was so often outdoors before."

"Julia, we already talked about this." His normally soft voice revealed its edges, but Julia remained undeterred. He still believed she was a docile patient under the tea's lull.

She was out of bed and to the window before Dr. Ward could protest. She threw open the curtains and sunlight flooded into the room, prompting Dr. Ward to raise his hand to shield his face.

"By the looks of that garden, this must be quite the posh hospital. And my family can't afford any such thing. I haven't seen them in days and they would never abandon me." Julia folded her arms, her smugness nearly as brilliant as the sunlight pouring in behind her. "So tell me, where am I really Dr. Ward?"

She wanted to see the fury on his face, delighted in the idea of him underestimating her.

But when Dr. Ward lowered his arm, his cool, placid mask remained. Only his eyes darkened with an unbridled anger. Julia's bravado faltered. Her gaze flickered to the door, suddenly wishing for one of the nurses to come by and relieve her of being alone with him.

"I understand you must have many questions, Julia," Dr. Ward said calmly. "But as I've said before, every action my staff and I have taken has been for your benefit. You're in such a fragile state."

Julia swallowed hard. Just as she was about to respond, a noise at the front door pulled her attention away.

Standing in the doorway was a portly man a bit shorter than Dr. Ward with legs that looked far too thin to hold him up. He was clad in a garish blue and gold tailcoat with a matching gold trimmed cape that brought out his golden amber eyes.

"My, my," the man exclaimed. "You must be Julia Sheffield, I presume?"

Julia's mouth parted but no words came out. All she could manage was a feeble nod. The man clapped his hands together.

"Brilliant. I was worried you'd be whisked away again." The man's face soured when he noticed Dr. Ward. "Cornelius. A pleasure as always."

Dr. Ward's jaw tightened. "Piers. I don't recall summoning you."

"Oh, you didn't. I came to clean up your mess." Piers looked from the storybook garden back to Dr. Ward with a raised brow. "Saints forbid this got any worse. You may leave."

Before Dr. Ward could retort, Piers leveled an icy glare at him. "And if you have any misgivings, Cornelius, you're more than welcome to speak to Philomena about them."

Dr. Ward and Piers silently regarded each other. Finally, Dr. Ward cleared his throat and nodded towards Julia. "Do take care. May your health stay well."

Julia didn't say anything. When he was gone, she sighed in relief.

"Pay him no mind," Piers replied. "Cornelius is hardly the worst beast in the forest. Moving on then, introductions are in order." He held out his cape and dipped into a deep courtesy. "*The* Piers Astley. A pleasure to make your acquaintance."

He held out his hand to Julia and her eyes widened. Every finger was lined with a different jeweled ring. Even his nails were painted a shimmering gold. Julia reasoned he carried more sterlings worth on his hand than her family could ever hope to see in their lifetimes.

She took his hand in hers and offered a limp shake. "Julia Sheffield. Um, a pleasure, sir."

Piers closed the door and motioned for Julia to sit. "We have a lot to discuss so do get comfortable, Miss Sheffield."

Julia took a seat on the bed and Piers sat at the desk chair near the window. His slicked-back chestnut brown hair glinted in the sunlight.

"Now before we get into the heart of the matter, let me begin by saying what I'm about to tell you is not something you have to believe or even trust, but you do have to agree to it."

Julia's stomach tightened. Beneath the theatrics and niceties, she realized too late Piers was just another adult who wanted to control her. Her face grew hot.

"Says you," she snapped. "I don't have to agree to anything."

She hated the pitiful look in Piers's eyes.

"I know you've stopped taking the lull they've been giving you. I take it you're not sleeping very well?"

"I'm sleeping fine."

"Is that so?" His lips quirked into a mocking smile. "Tell me, have you had any strange dreams? Do you remember what happened after your trial?"

Julia's hand reflexively went to her neck. Thinking about her trial made her breath catch, tumbling over itself in short pants. *No, not here. No no no.* She dug her nails into her palm until they were tight, bloody fists.

She closed her eyes. The mask would hold, pretty and proper. Free of troubles. And yet … there were cracks. So many cracks. In the mask. In her. She could feel them splitting her into a thousand tiny, nameless pieces.

"Breathe, Julia. Just breathe."

She slowly opened her eyes and finally reined her breathing back in. Her eyes prickled with tears as she unfurled her fingers.

"I'm sorry to upset you," he said, quieter this time. "Please know that I only mean to be honest. I can only imagine how difficult this must be for you, but the stakes are too high for sugar spun tales and we haven't the time to dawdle. We must press on, I'm afraid."

Piers folded his leg over the other. "Do you recall the story of Princess Angelina?"

"She was taken from the castle as a baby and never found." Julia had heard the story many times as a child. It was tradition in Temmings to offer prayers and flowers in her honor on Children's Day every Bloomfall.

When they were younger, Emily had taken some of the flowers from the prayer altar when Father O'Malley wasn't looking and wove herself a crown. Julia had wanted it so badly she snatched it off Emily's head when she wasn't looking. But instead of being mad, Emily had only laughed.

"Go on, have it."

"Rumors have persisted for years the princess survived her kidnapping," Piers continued. "Of course, as time wore on they were dismissed as gossip and wishful thinking, but there are girls—and older women if you can believe it—who come forth year after year with claims they're Angelina."

Piers's tone grew grave. "Something marvelous and terrible happened the day you and your companions were brought to Iron Square."

Julia recoiled. The memories she had tried to shudder, the same horrible nightmares that only the lull was able to suppress, lingered on her mind's edge, waiting to consume her. Her heart began to race.

"Please, I don't want to talk about that again."

"We made a horrible mistake."

Julia locked eyes with Piers. The sorrow she saw there released her own unshed tears for Emily and Tilda.

"You wronged us," Julia said through sobs, wiping her eyes. "The judge didn't even try to listen. We weren't fateshifters. We told them. We told all of them ... and no one believed us. No one even listened."

Piers nodded but didn't say anything. He stared out the window while Julia quietly wept.

"I know. But the judgement still holds for two of you."

"What?" Julia's head snapped up. "I-I don't understand."

Piers let out a deep breath. "The girl you knew as Emily Colby was Princess Angelina Chase."

A deafening buzz rang in Julia's ears. She stared dumbstruck at Piers, unable to take her eyes off him. His mouth was moving but she heard nothing.

"You're wrong," she finally managed to say. "That's impossible. She can't—couldn't be. Emily was from Temmings. S-She ..." but then there had been the rumors. Whispers that Emily didn't look quite like her parents, that the Colbys had bought her because Mrs. Colby had trouble conceiving, that she had come from an orphanage far away.

And then there were the hushed whispers, the cruelest of all, that she was found abandoned in the forest as a baby, half dead with hunger and cold. A cursed child, ruining all she touched.

Julia stood and pressed her forehead against the window, desperate to steady herself. This wasn't happening. How was this happening?

"I understand it's a lot to take in," Piers continued, "but evidence suggests that she was the princess."

"What evidence?"

Piers didn't answer.

Julia's mouth curled into a snarl. "*What evidence?*"

"It's not for you to know at this time," Piers replied evenly. "But suffice to say it's compelling enough for His Majesty to allow you stay here in Dutchenson Castle."

Julia gasped. "What did you—hold on, I'm in Dutchenson *Castle*?" Her eyes brushed over the room as if seeing it for the first time. The expensive linens. The storybook garden. Piers himself.

Seven bloody saints.

Her whole body trembled.

"N-No, this isn't right. This can't be right. Why are you telling me this? How did I even get here? I—" But she couldn't bring herself to say it. To admit the impossible.

I died.

Piers held up his hand. "Listen to me. Emily and Tilda are gone. You're all we have left. Thank the saints you're not far off passing as a Chase. And it's in everyone's mutual interest—including your own—that Princess Angelina be alive."

They held each other's gaze. Only then did Julia notice the shadows beneath his eyes. The weariness beneath the golden sheen and parlor powders.

"Why?" Julia stammered.

"As I said at the start, you don't have to believe a word I say, but you do have to agree to it," Piers replied, ignoring her question. "In return for your service and absolute discretion, your family will be well-cared for and the Colbys won't be tried for kidnapping and treason."

Julia wanted to scream. Emily had been happy. She had been loved. Mr. and Mrs. Colby treasonous kidnappers? Liars? No, Piers was wrong. But the words wouldn't come out, so Julia was left trembling and seething instead.

Piers closed the distance between them. "You're a bright girl. I strongly advise you not to squander this opportunity. It won't come around again. Play along and you and those you love will never want for a thing. It's far better than they deserve."

Julia's hands were fists at her sides. Emily and Tilda were dead. Her own family probably assumed the same for her. All the while Emily had been a princess and her family—maybe even the whole of Temmings—hid it for years. And now she was supposed to swallow all that and go on lying for the Crown's mistake? For the adults she had trusted?

"I'm not Princess Angelina," Julia spat. "I'm not even supposed to be here. I ... I died."

"A true phoenix then," Piers said through a tight smile.

"Liar, liar."

Julia whirled around, certain Emily was just behind her, whispering in her ear. But no one was there.

"Did you hear that?"

"No, nothing at all." Piers moved towards the door. "As I said, it's in everyone's best interest, including your own to cooperate. Now, I advise you get some rest while you can. You'll need to stay sharp in the days ahead." He lingered in the doorway, a pensive look passing over his features.

"Our futures depend on it."

23

Julia

"And ne'ermore would the Maiden move from her chair, flame alit at her feet, for her beloved knew only of her at his home dearest. And there she would wait for his lost soul to return home, a crown of ash about her head, bound to her faith, to her love, and all she held dear." – *Emma Haley, "The Maiden", Lovers from Myth and Legend: Poems & Essays*

In the silence of the small hours, Julia found herself arrested by impossibilities.

Emily was a princess. Martha is dead. Tilda is dead. Emily is too. I'm alive again. Mr. and Mrs. Colby kept a stolen child and lied to everyone …

Sweat dampened her skin and neck. She sat perfectly still, curled in on herself against her bed, cloaked in shadow. The polished floor chilled her bare feet but its sturdiness offered a margin of comfort. She buried her face in her knees. Tears sprang from her eyes, fast and heavy. She dug her fingers into the crooks of her arms until her nails bit into flesh.

How had everything gone so wrong? How had the lies become so tangled it became their noose?

"I'm sorry," she whispered into the darkness. "I'm so sorry."

Julia stayed in her cocoon for hours. When she finally opened her eyes, the desk and writing chair were outlined in dawn light. She sniffled, wishing she could have another cup of tea to lull her back to sleep. Only nightmares awaited her otherwise.

She laid down on the floor as the sun burned away the last traces of night. A new day was upon her whether she was ready to face it or not.

Piers arrived just as Julia was wading into the waters of sleep.

"Best of mornings, Your—" He stopped when he saw her puffy eyes and disheveled hair. He cleared his throat.

"Troubles, Your Highness?"

Julia shot him a withering look. "My name is Julia."

"Need I remind you, *Your Highness*, of our agreement yesterday. From this morning forth, you shall be addressed per your station as custom dictates."

"Because of your secret evidence," Julia scoffed. "Right."

"Ah, so you were listening."

Julia cut her eyes at him. His amused expression only made her more annoyed. He clasped his hands behind his back as he approached her.

"Perhaps I was not clear during our initial meeting." He lowered his voice so the guards posted outside couldn't overhear. "Princess Angelina is alive. The moment she isn't, neither are you, *Julia*."

"You never told me why. Is it because they killed Emily?"

Piers pulled back and studied her.

"All you need to know is that you now have a role, and as long as you play it well, you'll be safe. Do you understand?"

Julia nodded.

"Brilliant." He smiled. "Now, you will be meeting with His and Her Majesties this afternoon. The chambermaids shall tend to your bathing and dress arrangements after breakfast. There are two guards stationed outside your door; you can have them call upon me if you need anything."

As Piers swept out of the room, a young girl not much older than Julia outfitted in the crimson and gold uniform dress of the castle chambermaids entered with a covered tray. A matching gold bun clasp adorned with the phoenix crest completed her ensemble. She set the tray on the corner table and bowed. She dared a curious glance at Julia. "Good morning, Your Highness."

Julia said nothing as she bit away on her thumb nail. Her mind was too busy trying to wrap itself around the idea of meeting the King and Queen of Halcyon. What would she even say? Was she even allowed to speak to them?

"Excuse me, um, Your Highness?"

Julia looked up. "Yes—wait, who are you?"

"Ramali Dresdi, ma'am. I've brought you your breakfast tray."

"Oh, um, thank you."

"My pleasure, ma'am. Please do enjoy the biscuits. They're a favorite of Princess Madelyn." Ramali bowed and quickly exited the room.

Julia rose from bed and lifted the tray. Her mouth fell open. Before her was a feast the likes of which she'd never seen. Fluffy eggs, toasted biscuits with sweet almond jam, smoked fish fillets, quartered strawberries dipped in edible gold, and hot earl grey tea.

Everything looked out of a dream, and Julia wasn't certain which to try first. How could this all be for her? Was this what it would be like every morning?

Taking Ramali's advice she reached for a biscuit. She often admired ones just like them in the window of the Sugary, her favorite pastry shop in Temmings.

"Sweets are dreadful for a young lady," Aunt Agatha would tell her with a frown. *"You don't want to mess up your teeth and waistline now do you?"*

"Why, I think I do," Julia said with a satisfied smirk, popping a toasted biscuit into her mouth. The sweet almond paste and rich, buttery crumble melted on her tongue. It was only when she reached for her third biscuit did she notice the light blue envelope peeking out from beneath the other biscuits. It was unaddressed on the outside, but who would've known she was here to send it? When she opened it, a hairpin fell out. Julia picked it up and studied it before setting it down on the desk and reading the note inside.

There is a door beneath the rug in your room. Use the enclosed pin to unlock it when night falls and follow the tunnel until its end. Tell no one. Saints be with you.

Julia looked down at the large ornate rug beneath her feet. She stepped off and tried to pull it back, but proving too heavy, rolled it back instead. And there, in the middle of the room was a square metal door set into the floor roughly large enough for one adult to fit through. It was unadorned save for a single gold lock flush against its surface.

Suddenly, a knock rattled across the front door.

"Your Highness? We're here for your dressing."

It was a woman's voice Julia didn't recognize. She scrambled to roll the rug back into place.

"Just one minute!"

She shoved the hair pin and the note in the desk drawer just as four chambermaids entered. Each one wore matching crimson and gold dresses, the same as Ramali's. The oldest of the four stepped forward first. A few years younger than Aunt Agatha, she had a smattering of grey in her blonde hair and was only slightly taller than Julia. Behind her, the other three twenty-somethings waited in silence.

"Good day to you, Your Highness," said the woman with a smile that met her light green eyes. All four women curtsied to Julia, who looked away, unable to stop fidgeting with her hands.

Can they see this is all a lie?

"My name is Beatrice Adams," the older woman introduced. "And these girls here are Clara Burkes, Hannah Merton, and Hester Fairchild." The trio smiled politely, but their curious stares and muffled whispers were unnerving. Julia smiled back uncomfortably. "We're here to prepare you for your lunch with His and Her Majesties."

"But I've not yet finished breakfast. And there's still so much left." Julia looked back at the tray she'd only barely touched. Her stomach growled in protest.

"Oh, dear you needn't worry about that. You'll be off to lunch in no time at all. And the kitchens will worry about the waste. Think nothing more of it."

The three chambermaids stifled their snickers. Julia swallowed down her pride and guilt, determined to find the mask best suited for Angelina Chase. She could do this.

She *had* to do this.

Beatrice gestured to the door. "Now let's get you to the bathing parlor, shall we?"

Beatrice and her chambermaids were a whirlwind team.

They stripped Julia of her sweaty night slip and put her in a claw footed ivory tub. A barrage of oils and spice bags were poured into the hot water and within moments, the air was rich with lavender, chamomile, and rosemary. Fingers worked through Julia's tangled hair while every bit of excess hair was removed from her body with swift mercilessness. Afterwards, her skin was rubbed down in a thick cold cream that made her body smoother than it ever had before. The entire washing and prepping had taken longer than expected, but when she saw herself in her bedroom mirror, she was stunned. Beatrice and her chambermaids had indeed performed a miraculous feat.

The afternoon sun reached its zenith when the chambermaids finally left. Golden flecks of light danced along her freshly pressed white dress. A sense of airiness lifted her spirits. No longer did the filth of the prison cell or the dampness of the restless night before cling to her.

Julia opened the desk drawer and stared down at the hairpin and note she received at breakfast. Piers had warned her to stay the course and all would be well enough. But could she trust him? Could she trust whoever sent her this note?

"Poor little princess."

"Emily?"

But no one was behind her.

It's just grief, she reminded herself. Yet there was no mistaking the gooseflesh on her arms or the racing of her heart.

A knock on the door and the turn of a key interrupted her thoughts. Piers stepped in and beamed with pride.

"Oh, what a sight you are, Your Highness! Far better than your state this morning. I do believe you're ready for your gown now."

In his arms he held the most elegant gown Julia had ever laid eyes upon. It was a light cream color with a modest neckline rimmed in pearls. A wave of delicate ruffles flowed down from the waistline to the dress's skirts. Julia couldn't take her eyes away.

"It's lovely ..." Her fingers drew closer to the dress but stopped. "I can't."

Piers shook his head. "This is who you are now, my dear. A princess. It's time you dress like one, too. Cotton spun dresses and night slips simply won't do, I'm afraid."

Her fingers reached out and stroked the dress. The silk was water beneath her fingertips. Behind Piers, Julia caught a glimpse of more chambermaids waiting patiently outside the door.

"This is a dress fitting for Princess Angelina."

Julia froze. Beneath the encouragement, the warning lingered: *Become the princess or else.*

"A royal dress indeed," she replied, challenging his gaze.

A smirk pulled at the corner of his lips. He ushered the chambermaids in and handed off the gown before departing. As they dressed her, Julia's gaze slid to the ground, wondering all the while about the secret door beneath their feet.

Piers returned to fetch Julia nearly an hour later.

Give me another day, she desperately wanted to tell him. She wasn't ready to face the king and queen. This should be Emily, not her. She was nobody, just some girl from Temmings. She was no princess, no lost heir stolen from her crib. She was a liar stolen from death.

Piers held out his arm. "Ready, then?"

"Yes," she lied. In a lower voice, she added, "Will you be there, too?"

Piers regarded her curiously. "Yes. And I do find silence to be the best policy in these formal meetings."

Five guards were waiting outside Julia's room, each clad in garnet red uniforms trimmed in black. One of them, a tall man with a curtain of black hair and a permanent grimace stepped forward first. He nodded to Piers. "Lord Astley, sir."

"Good day to you, Sir Edmund. We're ready to go."

Edmund extended his hand to Julia, but she clasped hers to her chest on instinct. A tingle of phantom pain ran through her fingers.

"I'm sorry, I-I can't," she stammered.

Edmund dropped his hand and exchanged an annoyed look with Piers. Piers waived him off and placed his hands on Julia's shoulders. "Your Highness, it's all right. I promise."

"You can't promise that."

He lowered his voice so only she could hear his next words. "They could hurt Julia Sheffield. They can't touch Angelina Chase." He turned back to the guards and smiled. "Please do lead the way, gentlemen."

The guards led Julia and Piers through the corridor and into a sprawling hallway. Julia kept close to Piers while staring, mouth agape at the wonders of the castle. Crimson and gold tapestries embellished with the phoenix crest adorned each arched window. As they walked, Julia craned her neck to see the ribbed vault ceiling, its piped masonry carved in patterns too small for her eyes to see completely.

Portraits of the past rulers hung on each wall. Julia recognized a few from her studies: King Arthur, the Sun King and first ruler of Halcyon. Queen Minerva, the Blood Queen who's said to have gone mad. Queen Ottalie, the Sword Queen who led her knights into battle against invading pirates. King Walter, the Silent King who stopped the Raven Revolt.

The doors at the end of the corridor were hidden in shadow. A shiver of foreboding prickled Julia's skin. She was about to face the rulers of Halcyon. Emily's birth parents. She bit her lip and instead focused her attention on a large oil painting hovering over the doorway. It depicted a man, his lean body clad in a long white robe. But it was the open wound on his exposed chest that made Julia uneasy. In his bloody hand was a human heart—his heart—presented to the golden skies above as a gift.

Or something to take back.

Edmund opened the double doors at the end of the corridor and motioned Julia and Piers to follow. She didn't hesitate.

The royal hall was a massive chamber that rose as tall as any cathedral. A marble stairway led to an open chamber outfitted with several stone columns collared in gold and arched windows. Crimson and gold banners embellished with the phoenix crest lined either side of the hall between the columns. Gleaming chandeliers hung from the ribbed ceiling, ending at the crimson and gold tapestry woven over the royal dais. Julia stared with wide eyes, devouring each new sight with an insatiable appetite. How colorless Temmings seemed next to the haunting, gilded halls of the monarchy.

When the doors closed behind her, the echo reverberated like a gavel through the hall. There was no turning back now.

Two different sets of knights stood on either side of the column. On the left side—where the king sat on the dais—were four knights clad in crimson and silver armor and open-faced winged helmets. Swords were clad to each of their sides. On the other side, aligned with the queen's throne, were another four knights glad in gold and silver armor, each with matching winged helmets and swords. All eight pairs of eyes were trained on the approaching party.

But it was the king's gaze that unmoored Julia.

Dressed in a navy brocade tunic and breeches, his grey eyes were stern and unblinking. His broad build and thick beard leant him a daunting, almost frightening, presence far more intimidating than his portrait in Elmwood offered. Julia's gaze fell to her feet, weighed down by the gravitas of King Leonard.

The group paused just short of the dais. Edmund stepped forward first and dropped to one knee, resting his forearm on his kneecap. His fine hair swept in front of his face.

"Your Majesty, we present Lord Astley and his charge."

"You may rise, Lord Astley."

"Thank you, Your Majesty." Piers stepped forward. "As requested, I present Miss Julia Sheffield from Temmings, sir."

"Very well." The king's voice was deep like her da's but lacked his warmth and jolliness. She swallowed down the memory and focused instead on counting her breaths. She couldn't afford to unravel now.

"Come forth, child." This time it was Queen Catherine who spoke. Although her voice lacked the loudness and strength of the king's, a certain assuredness strengthened her words all the same.

Bile burned the back of Julia's throat. She gritted her teeth and forced herself to raise her gaze.

A wave of light auburn curls spiraled down Queen Catherine's back. Her emerald green dress swept across her shoulders and flowed into a dark green corset. She sat perfectly poised in her seat beside the King, haughty and infallible. Her blue eyes glided over Julia as if assessing her worth.

Just as Emily had done when they first met all those years ago.

Silence roiled through the great hall like a thick fog. Trapped between the guards at her back and the monarchy at her front, Julia was rooted in place. She kept her mouth shut, afraid to speak lest what may come out.

Queen Catherine rose from her seat and approached. Panic rippled through Julia. Should she bow? Should she curtsy? Why was *the queen* approaching *her*? Everything Piers had instructed fled her mind in an instant. But before she realized it, the queen embraced her in a hug.

Julia shot Piers a look, but even he looked at a rare loss for words.

"Be brave," the queen whispered in her ear, barely loud enough for Julia to hear. She pulled back and stared down at the young girl before her with a tearful smile. "My Angelina, returned to us at last. Bless the Saint Father and his miracles. He has brought us our daughter back."

King Leonard was silent for several seconds. And there, in the shifting afternoon light, Julia caught a glimpse of Emily in the king's features and it stole her breath. She quickly averted her eyes. She couldn't do this, she couldn't—

"My Angelina, welcome home."

King Leonard was on his feet, arms spread wide. Tears pricked Julia's eyes. How she wished to see her own father with arms spread wide to sweep her into them. Emily should be here, not her. But Emily was dead, robbed of the second chance Julia was given.

This wasn't right. This wasn't for her. But then Piers cleared his throat and her mind snapped back to attention.

They could hurt Julia Sheffield. They can't touch Angelina Chase.

As if on cue, the lie slid off her lips. Her mask, cracked but still pretty and free of troubles, slid into place.

"I'm so grateful to be here with my true family. I hope to not disappoint either of you."

The king nodded and took his seat. "Lord Astley has reported your health has drastically improved. I trust your accommodations have suited your needs?"

"Yes, Your Majesty."

"Very good. You'll need to be well for your crowning ceremony. It shall commence five days hence, following a grand ball. Halcyon shall welcome home their princess."

Julia paled. Her crowning? Five days from now? "But with all due respect, that's rather—"

Edmund shot her a piercing glare.

Piers stepped forward, cutting off Edmund's line of sight. "I believe it's all rather sudden for Her Highness, but I will see all preparations are looked after, of course."

The queen's eyes softened. "Yes, please do coordinate with Philomena. She was ever so pleased to hear of the coming festivities."

"Oh, I'm sure she was delighted by the news, Your Majesty," Piers replied with a mock smile.

The queen turned back to Julia and clutched her hands between her own. They were incredibly soft. "You will be standing on the great pillars of history. Your phoenix blood defied death itself, and now you will stand as the Chase you were always meant to be."

Julia dipped into a curtsy. Let them have their fun and spin their tales, she decided. She could swallow her words and play along for now.

They had just given her five days to plot her escape.

24

TOBIAS

"The bones foretell battle and transformation. The Harbinger of Ruin has taken flight and shall land in Halcyon. We advise you warn King Leonard and Queen Catherine the end is coming." – *Unknown, private correspondence to Queen Ragna Scarthsen, Svaberg, Soliljin*

Two things crossed Tobias's mind in the span of blink: *There is a stranger on my bed,* and *he has to die.*

Tobias didn't lower his knife. "Who are you? And what're you doing on my bedroll?"

The young man blinked several times. The dreariness of deep sleep gradually gave way to the dawning of realization. "Oh, I-I'm sorry. I didn't know."

"You didn't answer my question." Tobias took a step forward. If this squatter was a Seadevil spy—and a shoddy one so far at that—then his hiding spot had been compromised and he'd have to find a new place to sleep for the night. The idea made Tobias surly all over again.

"I meant no harm," the young man sputtered in heavily accented Halic. The hooded cloak he wore shielded most of his pale face, but it did nothing to hide the tremble in his voice. "I lost my way and needed to sleep."

"On a stranger's bedroll? You mad then, or just stupid? What if I had mites?"

The young man's eyes widened. "You have mites?" He looked from the bedroll back to Tobias then back to the bedroll. "Is that true?"

"You callin' me dirty now, mate?"

"Wait, no that's not—"

"Look, it's not proper stealing people's bedrolls like that. Think yourself above street code then?"

The young man shook his head. "I don't know what that is. I swear I meant no harm."

So not a thief, Tobias realized. He flicked his knife closed and slid it back into his pocket. "You from around here?"

The young man lowered his hands. "No. I traveled here from Scarvik."

"Scarvik? That's what, north? Past the mountains?"

"Ja. In Soliljin."

"So, you're *not* with the Seadevils?"

The young man titled his head. "The Sea ... devils?"

Tobias sighed. *Thank the saints.* "Good. Thought I'd have to kill you there for a minute."

The young man's eyes doubled in size and he scrambled to his feet. He was taller than Tobias anticipated and for a second he regretted putting his knife away.

"Woah." Tobias held up his hands. "I was just foolin'." But Tobias recognized the terror in the young man's pale eyes. He'd seen the same look in Lucy's eyes after he'd had his first nightmare. Before he knew to bind his wrists with rope. Lucy wouldn't go near him for two days after that.

Like he was some kind of monster.

"You okay, mate?" Tobias said as calmly as possible.

The young man didn't say anything. His mouth set in a hard line. "Show me your palms."

"What?"

"Show me your palms."

He really is mad, Tobias realized. *A thieving mad bedroll stealer.* He sighed but did as he was asked and raised his hands. The young man let out a sigh of relief. He sunk down to the ground and let his arms drape over his knees. A brittle laugh escaped his lips, echoing in the shadows of the bridge like warbled birdsong.

"I thought you were hunting me." He raised his head. Unrest flinted behind his eyes. "I wasn't sure if you were with them."

"Them?"

"The Ravenhood."

Tobias let out a low chuckle. "I thought you were gonna kill *me* because you were with the bloody Seadevils."

The young man held out his hand. "I'm Jóhann."

Tobias shot a skeptical look at Jóhann's outstretched hand. "Tobias." As soon as their hands clasped together, fear flickered in Jóhann's milky white eyes. He jerked his hand back and the sudden movement caused the hood of his cloak to fall away, revealing pure white hair.

"You're a—" Jóhann started to say, but Tobias cut him off.

"Your hair. It's just like …" Tobias blinked several times, trying to suppress the nausea threatening to come up.

A collar of red, hair white as snow.

Before Tobias could say anything more, he picked up voices overhead.

"You sure he went this way?"

"Aye, I swear it. Left that piss hole pub and came down here. Gotta be somewhere around here."

Tobia's throat seized. Seadevils. *Seven hells.*

"We gotta go," Tobias whispered. "*Now.*"

Just then, the sound of feet landing hard echoed behind him. Jóhann inhaled sharply as a man outfitted in dark belted pants and a loose spun sailor's top rose to full height. A large fish hook glinted from his belt.

"Well, well, what've we have here." The man flashed a razor sharp smile. "That wouldn't happen to be a Streeter skull on your hand there, would it lad? 'Cause that'd be very bad for you if it were."

"Go drown in the Dorse, boozer," Tobias snapped, making no move to hide his tattoo.

The man's smile grew wide. "Oi, Royce! Merk! Get your arses down here! Found our rat!"

Jóhann looked between Tobias and the man.

"One of your Seadevils?"

"Unfortunately."

Behind them, Royce and Merk came down the ladder from the main street. Merk, the taller of the pair, pointed at Tobias.

"Oi, Amos, that's 'im!" He flashed a yellowed grin. "Let's gut the little fish and let 'im rot in the sun. Knick the other one too."

Tobias reached for the knife in his pocket and snapped it open with the flick of his wrist. He backed closer to Jóhann.

"Can you fight?"

"W-What?"

"*Can you fight or not?*"

"N-No not really."

Amos barked with laughter. "You lads were done the moment you hung Clive on his own hook."

Royce charged forward, but Tobias ducked and drove his full weight into Royce's side, toppling them both and pushing Merk into the Plithe River. Tobias was quicker to recover. He leapt to his feet and grabbed Royce by his hair.

"Gut this, you bastard!" he snarled. He drove his knife into the side of Royce's neck. Hot flecks of blood spattered across Tobias's arm and cheek.

As Royce sank to his knees cradling his neck in vain, Amos was closing in on Jóhann. Tobias's heart was a pounding drum and his blood raced like lightning beneath his skin. Nothing could stop him. Nothing *would* stop him. His vision narrowed in on Amos, who was still grinning.

"Die, street trash!" Amos hollered as he raised his hook.

Tobias was on Amos before the fishhook could implant itself in Jóhann. Satisfaction bloomed in Tobias's chest seeing Amos's face go slack with horror. Even when a sudden sharpness tore into Tobias's left shoulder, all that mattered was the knife's blade driving further into Amos's abdomen. The blood spreading against his grimy white tunic. The dimming gleam in his sandy brown eyes.

Jóhann shouted Tobias's name but Tobias ignored him. All that mattered was this. The *conquest*.

Amos's face twisted into a mask of pain as he stumbled sideways. Tobias pulled out the knife just as the Seadevil tumbled into the river. Tobias shook off the knife and shoved it back into his pocket, ignoring the blood trickling down his shoulder from his own wound.

"You okay?" he asked Jóhann, his breathing labored.

"Behind you!"

A surge of pain shot through Tobias's already injured shoulder. He winced, reaching behind him to tear the hook from his back. It hadn't imbedded itself deep, but enough to wedge into his prior wound.

A few feet down, Merk was halfway out of the river, his face splotched red. "I'll kill you! I'll bloody gut you both!"

"Run!" Tobias shouted, grabbing Jóhann's hand and leading him to the street level ladder.

Pain seared in his shoulder as he hauled himself up and fell over the edge with a cry.

Onlookers were crowded along the bridge trying to peer down at the scuffle underneath. As Jóhann cleared the ladder, Tobias knew the City Watch would be swarming the area any second now. They had to leave but going to Higdin's was too risky and the Distillery was too far.

Seven hells. He had no other choice. Jóhann was being hunted. He was injured. And the Seadevils and Constables would be more than happy to get their hands on a Market Streeter.

"Follow me," Tobias instructed.

Jóhann helped Tobias to his feet. "But you're hurt. You need a doctor."

"There's no time. Just follow me. *Hurry.*"

Tobias could only hope the old flat was still there. If it wasn't, collapsed by age or finally sold off, he wasn't sure he was strong enough to fend off constables or Seadevils and still protect Jóhann. The fear of death pushed his legs forward. He sent a silent begrudging prayer to the Saint Father or whomever was above that cared to listen to a body snatcher's plea.

Jóhann ran after Tobias down Carter Street until they reached a small bend that led to a crowded tenant row. The sign for Abernacky Way was within sight.

Tobias stopped at the fifth flat in, pausing to swallow down the pain he was feeling now and the pain yet to come. He gritted his teeth and pushed on through the narrow alleyway laden with overflowing bins. Jóhann followed behind, a shadow on his heels.

They ran past gossip posters proclaiming Princess Angelina had been found, past an old woman selling tinctures from a traveling suitcase, and a beggar pleading for hollium. Tobias slowed down to a walk as the Portkey came into view. He looked up to the fourth floor of the abandoned tenant building, hollowed windows like gaping maws pulling Tobias further and further in until he was six years old again. A voice like his mum's, wailing and accusing, twisted by his own guilty mind, roared in his ears.

You were supposed to protect him, you didn't watch him, you promised me, you promised me, you—

"Tobias? Is this the place?" Jóhann shuffled from one foot to the other, glancing behind him.

Tobias swallowed hard, biting back the pain in his shoulder and the memories he had so carefully locked away. He wouldn't let the past repeat itself, no matter the cost. *I have to survive this*, he reminded himself. *For Lucy.*

He would not fail again.

25

—◆◇◆—

TOBIAS

"To worship the White Raven is to be undone. To see their truth is to be reborn." – *Anonymous Ravenhood member, final personal correspondence, dated 10th Day of Frostfall, year unknown*

Tobias and Jóhann fled down a cluttered alleyway tucked out of sight behind a half-rotted partition.

Jóhann squeezed under it with as much grace as his injuries would allow, swearing in Solandic under his breath. Tobias followed him, the hook wound on his shoulder protesting with each movement.

A ladder was fastened to the building across from the Portkey. Tobias started climbing and Jóhann trailed behind him until they reached the roof, which was far flatter and easier to traverse than Jóhann expected.

"Do you always get into fights and climb roofs like a stray cat?" Jóhann said with a nervous laugh.

"Well, I had a perfectly good spot until ..." Tobias let the unspoken words hang in the air.

Jóhann held up his cut hands. "I know, I know, until I stole your bedroll. I do apologize for that, you know."

"No, before that. I, um, had a good spot. A room somewhere. But I messed it up." Tobias ran a hand through his disheveled curls. "As per usual, I suppose."

Jóhann looked down at his feet. "So ... is this where we stay then?"

"Saints, we're not damn birds. Right over there. See that ledge?" Tobias pointed to a ledge that protruded from the roof of the Portkey just wide enough to walk on.

"It leads to a flat that should still be blocked off from the inside. But you can get through that window right there easy."

Jóhann looked at the ledge and then back to Tobias. His pale brows pinched together before repeating the process.

"We have to jump, half broken as we are, over there and not fall?"

"Welcome to Lordhaven." Tobias grinned as he stepped back to get his start. "You either risk dying to stay alive or give up and die proper."

He rushed forward, bending his knees at the last moment and sprang forward, landing on the opposite ledge with a teetering thud. He waved over Jóhann.

"Oi, your turn!"

Jóhann peered over the side again and gulped. Not high enough to kill but enough to break almost anything.

"Come on, then!" Tobias called from the other side. Jóhann let out a deep breath, and repeated Tobias's maneuvers. When he almost fell face forward into the Portkey's slanted roof, he nearly wept with joy.

As Tobias approached the window, a paralyzing stillness overcame him. The urge to turn back, to pitch himself off the roof, to cry, to scream, surged through him all at once. His mouth ran thick with saliva at the sight of the partially opened window knowing what lay on the other side. The room where he lost everything. The room that marked his failure as a son and a brother. It was only the distant shouts of Seadevils that pulled him out of his own head.

It's only for a short while. For Jóhann. Until he's safe. Then never again.

The flat was just as Tobias remembered it. A damp, muskiness held in the air. A simple wooden desk was pushed against one wall. On the opposite side was a squat stool with a collection of candle nubs sealed in a pool of wax. Five metal cot frames lined the walls. Three still had mattresses, but the moth-eaten holes and stench of mold offered little comfort.

Tobias ran his fingers over the desk. The yellowed newspaper clippings he had collected proclaiming long gone shows at the Brunswick Theatre still hung on their tacks.

"You and your friends lived here?" Jóhann asked.

"No. It was me and my—" The final word stuck in his throat. "Anyway, you can stay here while you sort yourself out and heal up. Easy in and out access so long as you're not piss drunk."

Jóhann put his hand on Tobias's shoulder. "Thank you, friend."

Tobias shirked off Jóhann's hand. "We're not friends. It's just a place to lie low for a bit. We'd be arrested or dead if we'd stayed back there. Besides, the Seadevils will be on the lookout for a white-eyed, white-haired kid now."

Jóhann twirled a strand of his shaggy white hair. "I see."

"So is that a family trait?" Tobias asked, nodding at Jóhann's hair. Anything to shirk off the shadows of his past seeping through, creeping ever closer.

"No. It's because I'm a voxossa. A bone reader."

"A bone reader? Like those alley hacks claim to be?"

Jóhann tilted his head. "Alley ... hacks?"

"You know, fortune diviners and palm readers. That lot. Don't they have those in Soliljin too?"

"Yes, but the evigni live in grand residences provided by Queen Ragna, not on the streets. I heard Halcyonians don't take kindly to arcanists."

"You could say that." Princess Angelina's hanging surfaced in his mind. If that truly was her, then it meant the Crown would risk killing even their own if they believed them to be a fateshifter. Anything to stamp out threats. Anything to keep up appearances. Anything to keep control of the unknown.

"My companions and I traveled here to have a very important meeting. We were to meet a man named Edgar Porter who agreed to help us pass a message to a powerful duke here in Lordhaven. But he never arrived at the Drunken Jester."

Tobias's pulse quickened. The Drunken Jester was where the Seadevil rogues frequented. Were they connected to Porter's disappearance? But why would the Seadevils risk a gang war over bone readers?

"Diðrik, the oldest of us, said we should leave Halcyon and go to Arcadia. Said Halcyon and Soliljin were no longer safe to travel. But Gunnar, the strongest disagreed and said we'd come too far to give up. The people here had a right to know of the danger here. He said Diðrik was a coward and I agreed with him." Jóhann's eyes became glassy.

"But I was the real coward. We were all so scared, but Gunnar was the noble one, really. He argued only suffering waited for us if we dared return to Soliljin. Leaving the Ossillium is grounds for treason alone." Jóhann rubbed the back of his neck. "We had betrayed Queen Ragna, so we stayed here. Gunnar searched for our contact but never returned. Then Diðrik disappeared a few days ago. He was heading to this area, so if I could find him and apologize, we could find another way to reach the duke."

Tobias's stomach gave way.

A throat rimmed in a waterfall of red.

"Your friend, did he have white hair like you?"

"Ja, but shorter."

Tobia sighed. *Seven bloody hells.* "Your mates, you said they were trying to reach a duke. You a spy or something?"

"No, only voxossa bearing a warning," Jóhann protested. "We wanted to help save Halcyon and her people. We were going to visit Bronwen, Khagal, Waridi, and Arcadia too. But the White Raven is hunting us. I know it."

"The White Raven is hunting you?" Tobias shook his head and chuckled. "You do know the White Raven is bollocks, right? It's a legend in the—"

"You're wrong. They've been here, waiting. Watching. Voxossa have read about it in bones for years, but it wasn't until recently our readings confirmed everything leads back to Halcyon. That's why we came here first, in secret. It's against Soliljin law for anyone, especially voxossa, to reveal what we read in bones to anyone other than the Iron Hand and Queen Ragna. Torture awaits all traitors." Jóhann edged closer. "Listen, I don't know why, but the White Raven is here in Halcyon. I swear it to you. I read it myself, many times. No one here is safe."

"Look, I promise you the White Raven isn't real. You can look it up. It's based off the story of the Demon King Azavith from the *Book of the True Word*. Just a way for the church to peddle protective trinkets and adults to scare their kids into being good."

Jóhann squared his shoulders. "I thank you again for letting me stay here, but I must see this journey through. As soon as I can I'll be on my way."

"Saints, you're truly gonna risk your life for what, a prophecy? That you read in some *skeleton*? Do you know how absolutely mental that sounds?"

"Magic exists in many forms. Some good, others not so good. You should know it's not so simple, ja? The magic in your blood carving your bones into a wolf is far from good or bad, isn't it?"

Tobias stilled his fist from locking onto Jóhann's jaw.

This stupid, stupid kid.

"Fine, go save Halcyon from the big bad monster. See if you don't end up with a slit throat too."

Tobias stormed out onto the ledge and crossed the threshold where Jóhann dared not follow. In the back of his head, he pushed down the inner voice mocking him for leaving Jóhann behind to the dangers of Lordhaven. Failing someone else again.

Just like his little brother.

26

◄—●—►

JULIA

"The Hoyts have wealth; the Vaughns have the markets; the Blackwells have influence; the Donnahues have the courts; the Bancrofts have the Church; the Foxes have the people. But the Chases? They have secrets." – *Confiscated pamphlet, City Watch headquarters, Lordhaven, Halcyon*

Five days.

Five days to run. Five days to stay. Five days before she would be Angelina Chase forever.

Julia bit her thumbnail as she paced back and forth. Outside, the royal gardens were bathed in silvery moonlight. Her gaze fell to the rug, then back to the door. It was time. There were two guards outside, but they would have no reason to check on her as long as she was back before sunup.

What if it's a trap?

She took a deep breath and opened the drawer holding the hairpin. She rolled back the rug and got to work on the lock. After several minutes, it finally gave way. Julia beamed, wiping away the beads of sweat on her brow.

As soon as she opened the latch, a rush of stale, musky air billowed out. She plugged her nose, desperately trying to muffle her coughs.

Her bedroom's snakelight revealed the beginnings of a ladder, but the darkness of the tunnel swallowed up the rest. Tears pricked the corner of her eyes. Mimicking monsters, faceless guards, and stolen children existed in the absolute darkness. What if there was worse still to be found? She caught her reflection in the mirror. The beautiful cream gown she wore glistened like snakeskin. No, she had to shed this dress, this skin, this mask or risk it staying on forever.

Five days.

Julia grabbed the ladder and began her descent. When her feet touched packed soil a few moments later, she looked up to the comforts above with grim longing. It would be so simple to pretend she never received the note.

But maybe whoever reached out to her could help her escape. *If they know about the tunnel, what else do they know?*

Julia took a deep breath and ran her fingers along the cool stone walls, careful to take small, slow steps. Sweat pooled beneath her arms as she traveled further, her heart hammering with every noise she heard, certain the darkness was a breathing, writhing thing watching her, waiting to swallow her whole.

She glanced over her shoulder. The light from her bedroom was a stone's throw behind her, but it felt like miles away. Suddenly, something brushed against her leg. She jumped and barely covered her mouth before a scream slipped out. Her heart thrummed against her chest as she stood stock still, bracing for the shout of the guards overhead.

Something's here. Move. Have to move.

Julia ran. Arms pumping at her sides, she tore through the darkness with reckless abandon, monsters be damned.

A light suddenly flickered to life at the end of the tunnel. A smile broke across Julia's face as she came to a halt near the lantern's illuminated halo.

"Hello? Who's there?"

The figure brought the lantern to their face and pulled back their hood. Julia gasped.

"Princess Madelyn." Julia took a deep breath and tried to start over but the words refused to come. "It's you and you're standing there and I'm here and—"

Madelyn smiled sheepishly. "A bit of a shock, I'm certain."

"Y-yes. A shock. That's what this is." As if just remembering herself, Julia hastily bowed. "I-It's nice to meet you, Your Highness."

"Likewise. And Madelyn is fine. Though I'm terribly sorry for the, um, less than desirable meeting place." Madelyn frowned. "Getting anywhere near the East Wing right now is impossible. This was the best I could do."

"Why did you want to speak with me?"

Madelyn hesitated. A weariness passed over her face. She was only a few years older than Julia but any trace of teenage folly had been stripped away long ago. Her eyes were stern, her slender jaw set.

"I don't know what you've been told or promised but you must leave here at all costs." Madelyn embraced her in a hug. "Please, trust me." She squeezed Julia tighter. "Even if you're my sister, it's not safe here. Dutchenson Castle is a dangerous place."

Julia pulled back. *She doesn't know about Emily*, she realized. A small part of her wanted to tell Madelyn but decided against it. What difference would it make? She would be leaving this world behind soon enough. And yet curiosity had roused her.

"Dangerous how?"

"The less you know the better." Madelyn reached into her robe pocket and passed a slip of paper to Julia. "This is a ticket for the Borealis. It leaves Port Vale two days from now. It'll take you to Durnstad."

"Durnstad? In Soliljin?" Julia shook her head. "Are you mad? What about my family? I can't just leave them and run away to the bloody frostlands."

"They're already dead to you. I'm sorry, but you can't go back to them. Not ever."

"You're wrong." Julia held the ticket out for Madelyn. "I'm sorry, but I can't take this. I won't leave them behind."

Madelyn looked down at the ticket then back at Julia. Her lips pursed as if holding back a retort royal decorum wouldn't allow. "Let me speak plainly then. If you leave this castle, your only chance of surviving is to leave Halcyon. Father won't pursue you to Soliljin. It's enemy territory and far enough away Arcadia would think twice about pressuring for your release to fulfil the Royal Accords. Waridi's twindom will certainly hold you as collateral and Khagal's Golden Court will hand you over to Halcyon by teatime tomorrow to avoid war. But if you stay in Halcyon, you and everyone you love will be hunted down like criminals."

"The good it did them finding me as a baby," Julia replied, feeling cheeky.

Madelyn's voice sharpened. "I'm trying to help you."

"And why is that anyway? If you say I can't trust anyone, how can I trust you? How can I know this isn't all a test and there won't be guards waiting for me on the docks if I try to leave?"

Madelyn was about to respond but then stopped. Weariness fleeted across her features. "You can't, I suppose." She gently pushed the ticket back towards Julia. "I can only hope you do."

After her meeting with Madelyn, Julia emerged from the tunnel drained. She closed the hidden door and rolled the rug back over the top, burying the darkness beneath her once more. She took one last look at the Borealis ticket before shoving it in the desk drawer.

She sunk down on the corner of the bed and ran her hands through her hair. She had five days left to flee Dutchenson Castle. The king and queen surely didn't have her best interests at heart, and although Piers promised to keep her safe, he was loyal to the Crown, not her. She was just an imposter. A puppet. A lie.

Yet how could she live with herself if she fled to Soliljin without her family? She didn't doubt the Crown would retaliate against them if she did, but she didn't have the coin or means to get her family out of Halcyon. The most they could do was flee north to Bronwen, which was still within Halcyon's territory. Fleeing further north to Soliljin meant crossing the Draven Mountains—which none of them were equipped for—let alone the bandits, duskborn and wild beasts along the way. Fleeing south to Khagal was no better because they were on friendly terms politically with Halcyon. And fleeing further south to Waridi was far too expensive. The only option left was Arcadia, Halcyon's largest rival, but Madelyn mentioned something about the Royal Accords. A legally binding treaty.

Stay in Halcyon or flee to Arcadia. Either way we lose. How had she been so naïve? Of course her family wouldn't be safe in Halcyon or Arcadia. They'd be fugitives always looking over their shoulders. Forced to hide no matter which city or town they fled to. Hunted to the ends of either kingdom for political gain.

"Dammit!" Julia cursed, doubling over.

Five days. She only had five days to figure all of this out and act upon it.

Sleep was out of the question. Julia pushed herself up from the bed and drifted to the window, leaning her head against the glass. How she longed to feel the warm night air on her face.

Outside, all was eerily quiet, but not all was still. Near one of the gazebos Julia noticed a tall, broad-shouldered figure walking a large dog. As the figure passed by the spiral hedges and stepped into the clearing, the moonlight glinted off their mask. Four gold jester faces, each looking in a different direction, frozen in gilded laughter.

Dread crawled up Julia's arms. *Look away,* her mind screamed. But she couldn't. Because the dog was no dog at all. What she had taken for a shaggy coat was revealed in the moonlight to be a crimson cloak. Its paws, while large, were too long and narrow to be claws. And while the masked figure held it on a short leash, the way the creature's front and back legs protruded from its body lacked a canine's graceful form. It was closer to a human, broken at all the wrong angles.

A human creature crawling on all fours.

The masked figure stopped. The not dog stood a few paces ahead, uncannily still. As if listening. Julia wanted to scream but didn't want to alert the guards outside her door. Beneath her feet, the darkness of the tunnel writhed, reeking of dirt and rot.

The laughing jester faces and not-dog's cowled head swiveled at breakneck speed to both stare at Julia. She tore from the window and yanked the curtains closed. She forced her shaking hand to stay clamped over her mouth. Air couldn't come fast enough.

Was someone playing a prank on her? Jostling her nerves for a laugh? It had to have been, had to. Julia shook her head, sinking to her knees.

"You saw nothing, you saw nothing, nothing at all." She clutched her sides, taking deeper and slower breaths until finally her heart wasn't hammering against her ribcage.

Her eyes slid down to the tunnel entrance as Madelyn's voice echoed in her ears.

Dutchenson Castle is a dangerous place.

Julia pulled her knees to her chest as a terrible realization hit her. Piers hadn't kept her locked away because he feared she would run away. After all, where was she to run to?

He had warned her. Only Angelina Chase would be safe. But from who or what he hadn't said. Julia's thoughts went back to darkness lurking just beneath her feet and waiting outside her window.

The bellows of a grandfather clock echoed from down the hall. Her nails dug into her legs as she clutched her knees tighter.

Four days remaining.

27

Nathaniel

"*A*lone we are ideals, but together we are a promise." – *King Hayden Chase, from the Royal Address regarding the Halcyon-Khagal Alliance, 1724*

For as long as Nathaniel had known Dolly Theall, the Silver-Tongued Kitten of the North Rim, she had always been a believer in fate, in the language of the stars and the destined course of the soul.

Luck, according to her, had nothing to do with things. If presented with an unfair matter, she would shrug her shoulders and say in her usual languid whisper, "If the stars say it's true, then it shall come to pass."

Nathaniel paused at the mouth of Spade Alley. Behind him, the echoes of lively chatter and laughs rang from the North Rim like a song beckoning him with promise of drink and coin. Comfort. Ease.

Ignorance.

If the White Raven lives, it changes everything.

He was making the right choice. A far-fetched problem needed a far-fetched solution. He crossed through the narrow, piss-stained streets. Rats nibbled on the toes of beggars clustered along the walls, too deep in hollium fueled deliriums to notice. Nathaniel pressed ahead, recalling the single blue door that marked his destination.

As he took his next step, a bald man in stained, tattered clothing stumbled forward from the shadows. He held a flask in his right hand, but his diluted pupils spoke of another, deadlier addiction at play.

"Take everything we have, why don'tcha?" the man garbled, pointing a shaky finger at Nathaniel. "Take all the sallies away from us! All the honey and all the work. Leave us nothin', ya bloody bastards. Liars! All of you nothin' but liars!"

Nathaniel took in the sight of the man, worn gaunt no doubt by a steady diet of hollium and little else. His eyes were glassy things that had trouble focusing.

"Steal everything ..." the man slurred, spittle flinging from his lips. "I shoulda left when the reaper's lung hit. Now all you bloody bastards bark for the king. All you!" He suddenly fell silent and stared somewhere beyond Nathaniel. Then, as if remembering something, the man clumsily lowered himself near a brackish puddle and rolled onto his side. Several fist sized blisters coated in a dark, yellowish crust trailed up the man's ribcage. Nathaniel had seen honey boils before, but never a case of infected injection sites so bad. With a snort, the man began scratching away at the blisters, coating his fingers in the yellowish white ooze that seeped out.

Nathaniel scrunched his nose. "Best to pray your saints take you before the hollium decay."

After visiting the Under City, he assumed the North Rim would be a small feat. But away from the glimmering coin parlors and smoky dining halls, the other side of paradise revealed itself to be little more than an alleyway brimming with addicts and honey dens.

As he ventured further, he passed several crooked pathways that branched off from the main alleyway. Flickering gaslight dotted the corners, revealing glimpses of wanderers with twisted hollium grins and beady-eyed peddlers trying to sell goods siphoned from Port Vale cargo ships.

Finally, Nathaniel saw it: the blue door. The five-story rowhouse it belonged to bore no markings or signs other than a small cat statue perched inside its top window. In another lifetime it had a caring resident, but the abandoned flowerboxes outside the first-floor windows were now glorified bins brimming with kellweed butts, used needles and retch. Only regulars of the Rim knew this to be a kitten house at all, and even fewer still knew it by its actual name—the Blue Rose.

Just before Nathaniel crossed the street, a woman with rheumy eyes stepped in front of him. The same seeping blisters crawled up her arms, but these were far more inflamed.

"Spare some coin?" she croaked in a voice far too coarse for her youthful face. Her spindly fingers unfurled, exposing needle-marked palms. "My baby, sir ... she's so very hungry. Please, some coin sir?"

Nathaniel pushed past her, his eyes trained on the blue door ahead.

"Please, some coin, sir! Some coin!" The woman's pleading cries soon faded into the collective cacophony of Spade Alley. Nathaniel ascended the Blue Rose's stairs only to find the doorknob held steadfast. As he was about to knock, a cloaked figure leaning against the wall made his previously undetected presence known.

"No entry tonight," the guard said.

"I beg your pardon?"

"You heard me," the man replied, folding his arms. "No. Entry. Forsvinn."

"Ah, someone new," Nathaniel lamented, pinching the bridge of his nose. "Wonderful." Before the guard could react, Nathaniel was behind him. In the next breath, he held the man's hands behind his back in an ironclad grip.

"You must be awfully troubled by this turn of events," Nathaniel cooed against the guard's neck, cherishing the erratic pulse reverberating like a stifled scream beneath the man's skin. "But I crave a drink of another sort at this very moment, so let's end this little dance shall we?"

The guard tensed but didn't struggle.

"You ... You're duskni."

"I'm sure there's a key you were instructed to keep safe." Nathaniel's fangs slid across the guard's ear. "But I don't need a key. I'm going to walk right through that door you're going to graciously open for me."

Nathaniel retracted his fangs. He leaned in close enough so that his words weren't overheard by passerby.

The guard went rigid.

"P—Please, sir," he stammered, unable to meet Nathaniel's eyes. "I ask upon your honor. Please don't."

"The door," Nathaniel said flatly.

The guard's hand hovered over his own wrist, wracked by a tremble that hadn't been there before. With a heavy sigh, his body went still, ceasing whatever moral war waged within him. Suddenly, the skin around his wrist began to unravel. There, tied to one of his bones in threads of muscle and blood was a brass key. Once the guard grabbed it with his free hand, the muscle, blood, and skin began to rethread itself until the wound sealed shut. No trace of a scar was left behind and no blood leaked from the temporary wound. No sign at all the guard's wrist had been exposed down to the bone.

He unlocked the door and ushered Nathaniel inside.

"Take me to the matron first," Nathaniel instructed, ignoring the guard's confused look as he stepped away from the door leading to the cellar bar. He led Nathaniel up the rickety stairwell to the fourth floor. Hushed voices and garbled moans drifted through the dark, smoky halls. A hazy-eyed man flush with hollium drifted past him like a phantom. A red-headed kitten watched him leave, slunk against the doorway with a pipe tucked between her fingers and only a shawl draped across her shoulders. She openly eyed Nathaniel, a smile pulling at her wine red lips as she inhaled from the pipe.

Nathaniel scowled. It all was so tasteless, so wasteful.

Lust should be clad in only the finest silks and gems to take its lovers; gluttony was nothing without golden cutlery for which to dine on their hearts afterwards. Where was the beauty? The wonder? This was not art; this was gratification.

Finally, the pair reached the top floor. It was a large and open space decorated with jewel toned silk slips, feathered hats, and wire mannequins sinched in stunning corsets befitting a court lady.

The guard stepped forward and cleared his throat. "Your company is requested, Mistress."

Dolly remained seated in front of a large mirror lined to the brim with perfume bottles in a variety of shades and sizes. She continued to dot her cheeks with powder, although her eyes traveled away from her reflection long enough to catch sight of the guard. Nathaniel had already slipped into a corner of the room, careful to remain out of the mirror's gaze.

"By whom?" she asked with only the slightest interest.

"I think you have an idea," Nathaniel replied, leaning casually against the wall opposite her.

Dolly put down her powder brush with a knowing look. "You may leave us, Pétur."

Pétur hurriedly shut the door behind him.

Dolly looked up at Nathaniel beneath thickly coated lashes. Her hair was pinned to the side in a short bundle of loose blonde curls. "If I didn't know any better, I'd say you didn't come for tea."

"Perhaps if your establishment carried a clean cup, I might consider it."

Dolly smiled. "Everything here is dirty, darling." She resumed dressing her face. "It makes people feel safe."

"And you?"

"It doesn't quite matter what I think," she replied as she painted her lips a bright red, her movements slow to offset the tremble in her hand. "The silver-tongued kitten who speaks of goblin markets and midsummer revels has no place to dream such things."

"And yet you stay."

Dolly gazed at her own reflection, nearly the same age as Nathaniel appeared to be. She tilted her head, curiosity dancing in her eyes. "I wonder ... funny that."

She softly smacked her lips together. Apparently satisfied, she took the shawl from her thin shoulders and draped it over her mirror. Even in just a silk underdress, robe and stockings, Nathaniel marveled at Dolly's timelessness. "Better?"

Nathaniel smirked. "You could say that."

She popped a small chocolate into her mouth. "Here, for a weary traveler." She tossed another chocolate to Nathaniel. He caught it and let the sweetness melt on his tongue.

Her large blue eyes took in his cool gaze. They brimmed with the eagerness of youth and the lull of hollium. Words churned inside of him, but his tongue remained leaden. How easy it would be to purge every dark, twisted thing inside, every infernal desire that spurned him and slip away to a world of ease with her.

A glint of silver caught his eye. A flask sat on Dolly's powder table tucked between brushes and perfumes as if it belonged there. She followed his gaze and smiled.

"Follow the honey road, follow it all the way down," Dolly sang softly. Her melodious laughter filled the room. "Really, what is a bit of drink now and then?"

"It's not just the drink," Nathaniel replied.

Dolly lips puffed into a pout. "It's not all so awful, you know."

"Most addictions aren't."

"Perhaps." Her glassy eyes languished on some faraway spot over Nathaniel's shoulder. "But I've never been closer to Ilrith. It's down the honeyed road, darling. I'm certain of it. Just a little further down. I'll find it." Her voice fell to a whisper. "And then I can dance in those wonderful golden slippers again ..."

Nathaniel took a seat across from her. He knew what it meant to long for a world no one could see, understood how her soul ached for what she had lost as a child. He didn't fault her for running down the honey road, hand-in hand with hope and hollium, seeking the one place where she was happiest. Perhaps if he had made different choices—different deals—he could've been on the path with her.

But time was slipping away. He couldn't outrun the insatiable duskborn blood in his veins forever, couldn't outrun death, no matter how much he fed on blood and hearts.

One day the scales would tip, and it would eat away the last of his human blood, then his organs.

Perhaps another time, my dear. I must outwit death first.

"Tell me," Nathaniel said in a low whisper, "what do you know of the Ravenhood?"

"The Ravenhood?" Dolly put a finger to her chin. "I can't say I've heard of them. But they sound awfully dreadful."

"Do you know what the Ravenhood is?"

"You're trying to be rather clever with your wording, aren't you? Do you really think I'd try to lie to you?"

"I never said that."

"Now who's lying?" Dolly asked with a smirk. She leaned forward, folding herself over her knees. "No one believed me when I told them about Ilrith. The dream of a silly little girl they said. Even when I returned fifty years later not aged a day with a silver tongue that wouldn't let me lie and bloodied feet that trembled to dance." She offered a weak smile. "It's a fate most cruel not to be believed."

The Under City had shown Nathaniel the terrible truths in his heart. Ilrith had given Dolly the delightful lies in hers. Two sides of the same cruel coin. Nathaniel raked his fingers through his thick hair.

"I have reason to believe the White Raven may exist. This cult of worshippers, the Ravenhood, they showed me things no one else could've known. I assumed you might know of them."

Dolly suddenly looked more sober than she had in years. But it wasn't clarity behind her widened eyes. It was fear.

"You mustn't call upon the White Raven. Not ever."

"You're not actually worried, are you?"

"Please, Nathaniel." Dolly wrapped her hands around his. "*Please*. The White Raven is a broken thing who promises broken things."

The image of his younger self surfaced in Nathaniel's mind. The eternal heart. The key to immortality. The answer to the riddle of obtaining the perfect state of being, the loophole to his ravenous duskborn blood and his escape from a deal made long ago with the goddess of dreams and nightmares. Or had the priestess only shown him what he wanted to see? A vision of his own crafting? A lie of his own making?

Nathaniel's voice grew stern. "Do you have proof the White Raven is real?"

Dolly's face fell. She was silent for a long time before answering. "It can take any face or any voice. It hides among us." She pulled back her hands. "That's all I know."

She reached for the flask on her vanity and took a swig. Nathaniel wanted to press her more. Had she seen the fabled monster? Did the Crown know of its whereabouts?

If the White Raven lives, if the eternal heart truly exists, then it changes everything.

"I appreciate the information, Dolly."

Dolly didn't look at him. He'd seen her clamp up before and knew his visit was coming to an end whether he liked it or not.

"Before I go," Nathaniel added, "I have a favor to ask of you."

Dolly tilted her head in the small way of a curious child. "A favor?"

"Yes. I need you to find someone for me."

"Find someone? Oh tell me, whoever are you looking for? The Snow Queen? Bramblebin? Sir Galot the Manx?"

Nathaniel's jaw tightened. She was slipping again. "No, one of the king's bastards. Leander Winslett. Has Bennett mentioned him lately or said anything regarding his whereabouts?"

Dolly's nose scrunched as if she suddenly smelled something foul. "Why must you bring up Bennett on such a pleasant evening?"

Nathaniel tried to hide the desperation in his voice. Dolly was the only one he knew close enough to Reginald Bennett, the Crown's spymaster, to earn some semblance of his trust. If the king had ordered a move against his own or suspected someone of the crime, Bennett would know of it. "You're one of his best spies. He relies on you. Has he mentioned anything at all?"

Dolly took another swig from the flask.

"Follow the honey road, follow it all the way down," she sang again, her cheeks flush pink. *"Trust the Golden Lady, see her gossamer gown. The road ends in the sky and falls into the sea and in Our Lady we trust to keep us safe and free."*

"I don't have time to waste with this foolishness," Nathaniel snapped, turning to leave. "This was clearly a mistake. Enjoy your fables."

Dolly's lips parted as if to say something, then closed without a word. Nathaniel hated the taste of weakness in his outburst, but he loathed the idea of saying so aloud more. It was his own fault. He'd known better. Dolly was but a waking dream of a girl, really. She'd been away too long in that other place. The world of rot and revels, hidden between slants of light and curves of shadows. The prison of the Forsaken.

Ilrith.

"I'll find him if you wish it, Nathaniel. Bennett only says what he must to me, but the king will say more."

Nathaniel paused at the door. "Thank you."

"I'm expecting a visitor soon, darling. You'll have to scuttle." Dolly's frown lifted into a weak smile. "He's awfully delicate around other handsome men."

"How boring," Nathaniel replied with a smirk. But Dolly wasn't looking at him. Her glassy-eyed gaze was looking elsewhere, far beyond Lordhaven. Nathaniel lingered for a moment before closing the door behind him. He let out a sigh before straightening himself and walking down the dimly lit corridor.

Suddenly, a woman with intricately beaded braids and dark, beckoning eyes appeared in one of the doorways. She ran a finger along Nathaniel's jaw.

"Going so soon? The night is young, love. Why not have a lie down?"

"Perhaps anoth—" Nathaniel paused midsentence, realizing what he took for beads were small bones. Garish trophies at initial glance, but Nathaniel knew better. The Malsik's loyalists kept them as signs of strength to anyone who would dare challenge them.

As the syringe's needlepoint drove into Nathaniel's neck, he made a grab for the woman's throat but she shifted out of his reach in a blink. He stumbled forward, darkness clouding the edges of his vision.

"Better luck next time, Nathaniel Trevet."

The woman's fanged smile was the last thing he saw before all went dark.

28

NATHANIEL

"They were taken in the middle of the night to the sea cave beneath Swan Tower and made to hold their breath in the cavern pool. Mad waters, those were. Made you see things. If anyone surfaced before two minutes they were immediately thrown out. Those who stayed under and still had their sanity joined the ranks. First years would sometimes practice in the West Hall pools after hours to be ready if they were chosen. It was an honor." – *Brenden Fairwater, notes on* The Augur Society *initiation ritual, sealed court transcript, Penrose College, Lordhaven, Halcyon*

In darkness there was truth.

Nathaniel knew this, his mind reminded him. He *knew* this. And in the darkness, far beyond his slumbering body, a memory flickered like a dying flame. He struggled to make sense of the vision. It was a moment so removed from him now to be as strange as it was familiar.

He as a young man, still human, so painfully human, kneeling at the edge of a lake, shaking with furious sobs. His right hand curled around a pistol that seemed too heavy for him to lift. Too heavy for him to fire.

Years of being hidden away. Then one day a tonic, followed by years of bones rearranging themselves beneath the skin, one by one, breaking and healing, day and night, until the duck became a swan. But the outcast couldn't be unseen. In every mirror, every metal surface, every puddle and pond, the outcast stared back.

Failure.

But Evelyn had loved him. Not the new him. Not the favorite everyone admired but something beyond—the perfect. How he longed to see the person she did, the shape that kindled so much love in her heart for his humanity, but illness took her because humans aren't enough against nature.

Failure.

The pistol never fired that day near the lake. In the end, he was too selfish to let go of the gift his mother had given him. And so, his tormented mind hid in the labyrinth of sleep while his young body wasted away in his darkened room, far from the society he craved. Then one day, from the shadows of his waking dream a voice, splendid and terrible, spoke with the gentleness of a mother and whispered to him: *"Weep not, little rabbit. For I see that you have the mind of a fox and I shall give you fangs…"* And then he saw her, Moxra, the Goddess of Dreams and Nightmares, and remembered only her eyes, for none had been so violet and deep.

Distant voices trickled in like rain, washing away the memory of the lake. They were muffled at first. Jibberish. Gradually they sharpened as Nathaniel emerged from his stupor.

"Let's be done with this already. He's too weak to wake."

"Oh, this one's a fighter. He'll wake."

A low grunt. "We should've just given him over to the Malsik."

"Ah, but where's the fun in that?"

Nathaniel slowly opened his eyes. As he did, the memories flooded back to him in waves.

The pistol. The girl. The loss. Always the loss— and the deal. Saints, the *deal*. A promise of something greater. Something …

More …

More

More—

Nathaniel's eyes flew open. He inhaled a sharp breath as his mind finally, mercifully, cleared. Moonlight slipped through the shattered glass of an overhead window. A few battered crates and empty bottles littered the ground. Rusted machinery crowded the main floor with only narrow aisles between them. The echo of approaching footsteps rang through the rafters.

"Ah, there he is."

A man in his early thirties stepped into Nathaniel's field of view. He had short blond hair and the arrogant sort of airs that spoke of power taken, not earned. He kneeled down and patted Nathaniel on the cheek.

"Right as rain now, eh?" He smiled, revealing the tips of his fangs.

"The next time you want to flash fangs at me," Nathaniel snapped, "I advise you best be prepared for what that means."

The blond haired man rubbed his chin.

"Oi, got us a cheeky one then." Another young man came into view, closer to his mid-twenties. He was taller with low cropped curls and dark eyes. Unlike his cohort, he wore a bracelet of welded finger bones. A small victory, but one earned. "Tell us about the Ravenhood, Trevet."

Nathaniel parsed the shakiness beneath the curly one's bravado. A smirk slipped onto his face.

Rabbits always tremble before foxes.

"I don't think I will." Nathaniel quietly tested his hand restraints. "Now, where is Claude?"

"Not here to help you," the blond one snorted. He pulled a jack cutter from his pocket and held its blade against the base of Nathaniel's throat. "Now, why don't you behave like a good little prisoner and spare yourself a lot of pain?"

"You always were a bit too confident in yourself, Caleb. Hideously so. And your friend over there—Griff was it?—hasn't shaken his worries, I see. Still as fretful as a field mouse."

Caleb's lips twisted into a scowl.

Griff took a step back. "Wait, how do you—?"

"A cheeky showman then, huh?" Caleb sneered. "From where I sit, parlor tricks won't save you, traitor."

"And where *do* you sit, exactly?"

"In a far better—"

Nathaniel closed the gap between himself and Griff before Caleb could finish his sentence. His hands expertly found their way on either side of Griff's face and twisted. The young man fell to floor, motionless and wide-eyed, his head resting at a horrible angle. Caleb's eyes held Griff's still body for only a moment before his fangs were fully bared, but it was a moment too late. Nathaniel slammed Caleb to the floor, pressing his right foot down on Caleb's throat with just enough pressure to hold him.

He tucked his hands in his pockets, relishing in the panic and anger contorting Caleb's features. Caleb reached for Nathaniel's ankle, but Nathaniel only pressed his foot down harder. "I wouldn't do that again if I were you."

"Piss off!" Caleb shrieked.

"Now, let me tell you where you *actually* sit," Nathaniel growled. "Far beneath me and even further beneath my notice. But I never forget a name and its face, especially anyone pledged to the Malsik. Even lowly fangling filth like you."

"Y-You're nothing," Caleb sputtered between gritted teeth. "You've earned no bones. The Order of the Boar is just a social club for highborn trash. A mockery of duskborns." He grinned, revealing bloody fangs. "The Malsik will end you."

"And he won't mourn you." Nathaniel pressed down and down and down. When all had gone quiet, he stepped away from Caleb and brushed off his shirt sleeves. After pushing back the hair from his eyes, he took in the scene around him. A factory of this size could only be housed in the Ironworks District, which meant he wasn't but a short carriage ride from the Blue Rose. They hadn't taken him far then. Nathaniel reached for his pocket watch but found it was missing.

He looked back at Caleb with newfound annoyance. He kneeled down and ruffled through the man's pant pockets. Finally, the right pocket yielded a gold watch with a black stag head, the Trevet family crest, carved on the front.

"Unbelievable."

He tucked the watch back into his vest pocket and exited through a nearby side entrance. Moonlight filtered through the cloud cover overhead, illuminating the nearby steelwork and snake oil factories churning through their night shift.

Nathaniel straightened his shoulders and moved quickly through the warehouses until he reached a livelier street. The smell of boiling meat slipped out from a rowdy pub across from him, its windows a filmy yellow that clouded the patrons inside. They drifted like puppet theatre shadows, darting in and out of view.

Nathaniel continued on his way. Given the tension simmering between the gangs, the quicker he was back in the Garden District the better. His head already throbbed plenty. Just as he was about to cross Wentworth Parry, a carriage turned the corner and slowed in front of him.

"Looking for a ride, sir?"

Nathaniel paused. A cloth covered the lower half of the driver's face from view, but Nathaniel heard the cracks of youth in the boy's voice.

"Can you even operate such a carriage?"

"Rough night for my da. Mum is busy keepin' an eye on him, but the carriage still needs to be run."

Nathaniel was about to turn the boy down but then considered the lengthy way back to Thornwood and all the undesirable hassles in between. "Very well. Do you know the way to Felden Street?"

The boy smiled beneath his cloth mask. "Not the Blue Rose, sir?"

Nathaniel froze. The tips of his fangs instinctively slid down behind his teeth, ready to strike, just as the boy added: "Lots of highborns heading that way tonight. You, sir?"

Nathaniel retracted his fangs. "No, Felden Street will do."

"Aye. It'll be ten sterlings."

Nathaniel handed the boy the coins and slipped into the carriage. The inside of it was simple, but comfortable—worn red velvet seats and dark wood paneling. But it was a vase of lilacs fastened near the door that caught Nathaniel's eye. The smell was pleasant enough, but as the carriage pulled forward and Nathaniel mulled over the boy's mention of the Blue Rose, he realized he couldn't shake the scent of the lilacs. He stared at the light purple blooms. Sweet and beautiful, much like a girl he once knew, a lifetime ago or maybe more, who saw something beyond ...

Nathaniel shot forward. The carriage had come to a halt. He looked out the window to see Thornwood towering behind its wrought iron gate. His attention returned to the lilacs. For beneath their lulling sweetness lurked a fainter sweetness, staining all it touched even when scrubbed away.

Blood.

The boy opened the carriage door. Dark blond strands of hair poked from beneath his cap. "Good evening to you then, sir."

"You as well."

As the carriage pulled off into the night, his eyes flickered to its retreating figure. A feeling of familiarity lingered. A feeling of being watched.

A feeling of being *seen*.

"Master Trevet? Is that you, sir?" Anders appeared at the gate and unlocked its doors.

"Anders, please have Carina draw a bath. This turned into a rather dreadful evening and I'm in desperate need to wash it off. Also, any word from the Jeweler on those eyes I ordered?"

"Yes, sir, I'll tell her and yes, the Jeweler sent word he'll have them ready for you by tomorrow night, but there's another matter we need to—"

"Also, have Ivan prep Eribus's meal if he hasn't already. And make sure he doesn't use too much draughtwort. Eribus damn near melted the cage bars last time."

"Understood, sir, but I must tell you—"

Nathaniel paused just outside the parlor as the smell of melia smoke wafted through the air. Every muscle in his body went taut.

That bastard.

He swung open the parlor doors and found Claude seated in a winged-back chair staring idly at the unlit fireplace.

"Ah, Nathaniel, home at last. I trust your journey fared well?"

"Anders," Nathaniel growled. "Leave us."

"Yes, Master Trevet," Anders replied, swiftly closing the doors behind him.

"Strange really, I never did quite understand why you insisted on keeping this place," Claude continued, unfazed. "I mean it hardly lacks taste, but most people would've sold off the manor their father gave his mistress at the first chance they got. Quite odd given you have such an exquisite residence in Presdale and yet you choose to spend your time here. But then again, you are a man of many secrets, aren't you?"

"If you wanted to talk, you needn't send the Malsik's fanglings to do so."

"Now, now I'm sure you've had quite the eventful evening, but I assure you it was no mere jest." Claude stood and straightened his tailored navy jacket. "You left me with no choice, Nathaniel. As leader of the Order, it's in poor taste for me to allow such reckless behavior from a high-ranking member to go unpunished. The Order of the Boar and its members, as agreed long before you, shall follow the sacred pledge to the trinity: the God of War, Archonix, our absolute leader the Malsik, and our rightful kingdom, Halcyon."

Claude tilted his head and smiled. "I apologize for calling upon you at such a late hour. This visit was most inconvenient to you I'm sure, but I believe we can both agree quite necessary for our continued future."

Nathaniel remained silent.

"I have a task for you. I confirmed Lord Galbrooke will be attending Lord Henley's summer ball. This will be our last courting of him. Should he pass, you'll approach him with an invite to the Order. His access to the Sentry's inner circle is most tempting indeed."

"Of course," Nathaniel said through clenched teeth.

"And do remember to think on tonight's events." Claude paused in front of Nathaniel, gently running his fingers along Nathaniel's sharp jawline just as the woman from the Blue Rose had done before betraying him.

"You are indeed a favored member of the Order. But much like beauty," Claude continued, curling his fingers and dropping his hand, "favor can fade."

"Is that what the Malsik told you? Might I recommend combing the local graves for some bones to earn back that favor. I promise I won't tell."

"Careful, Nathaniel," Claude replied, his features darkening.

Nathaniel stepped forward. "Well, since you're so close with our dear leader, you can relay the message that where I go and who I meet with is none of his concern. Perhaps he should busy himself getting briefed on your meeting with Tyson Hoyt considering Badru wasn't there to report back to him."

A flicker of surprise flashed across Claude's face.

"Who is she?" Nathaniel pressed. "The young woman you had with you."

A smirk pulled at the corner of Claude's mouth. Nathaniel held firm, but he had the sinking feeling he'd already lost.

"You always were the clever one. Too clever in fact. It's why I recruited you. You never cease the hunt. It's almost maddening, isn't it? The need to turn over *every single* stone so you have an answer for any question at any moment." Claude clasped his hands behind his back and held Nathaniel's gaze. "The Malsik doesn't know you other than your position in my ranks. He doesn't need to know who you are, really. It's not important. On the other hand, the Ravenhood and the royal spy you were speaking to tonight are connected to very important people. People the Malsik doesn't want the attention of at the present moment."

Nathaniel's heart raced.

The White Raven.

Claude fetched his traveling coat from the nearby rack. "The Malsik told me once of an old Waridian proverb. The clever cat hunts the mouse, but the wise dog sleeps at the wharf." Claude opened the door and stepped into the hall. "Have a pleasant evening, Nathaniel."

Nathaniel said nothing as Claude left. A dark mood settled over him like a brewing storm. Sleep was futile, so he retreated to his study instead. If he had any hope of overthrowing Claude and the Malsik to take the throne, he'd need to find out what part this girl served in their play. If she didn't matter, she wouldn't have been in a room with Claude Barrow and Tyson Hoyt.

If the eternal heart is my ace, what if that girl is his? He leaned forward and rested his elbows on his desk. *It's a game of timing, then. Not power.*

When Anders entered the study some moments later Nathaniel gave him a single request: "Find my mother's soothsayer. It's time to reveal this raven."

"Shall I contact Sampson Cowell then, sir?"

"Yes, please do." Nathaniel leaned back in his desk chair. "What better way to find a medium time forgot than a monster that serves it."

29

JULIA

"Blyton Holdings quietly opened a new workhouse near Port Vale about a month ago. Slinging snake oil by the barrel to ship out saints knows where. Hobs left it off our patrols, but he's on Lusky's books. Send one of yours 'round. Those kids deserve to know what they signed up for. Ain't no bloody way they understood a word of whatever contract Lusky cooked up." – *Anonymous note to Hallie Foale, senior editor, Lordhaven Tribune*

"Must it be so tight for breakfast?"

"Aye, Your Highness," Beatrice chided behind her. "Have you never worn one?"

"If I could help it."

"Well you best get used to it sooner than not, I'm afraid. It's standard fashion for Lordhaven and mandatory for a princess."

"But how am I supposed to eat if I can't even feel my stomach?" Julia whined.

"Less eating and more chatter." Beatrice finished tying off the corset and gave Julia's shoulder a small squeeze. "Fret not. I heard the Sun King was rather fond of corsets himself and took most of his meals at midnight."

"*Midnight?* Only? Was he a plant?"

A knock rattled across the door followed by a brief pause.

"Come in."

Piers strode into the room with an air of bergamot and sandalwood about him. A garnet capelet draped over his golden paisley vest, perfectly complementing his curled mustache and rosy cheeks. Julia hesitated if she had misremembered the event. Hadn't he said they were only attending breakfast?

"Good morning, ladies."

"Good morning, Lord Astley," the chambermaids crowed. Beatrice looked up from her lacework.

"You're a bit early to collect our princess, my lord. Lucky for you my girls and I don't dawdle."

At that, Clara picked up her pace putting the last touches on Julia's makeup. Hannah and Hester exchanged glances and scooped up Julia's linens and shuffled out of the room.

"No need to rush on my behalf. Splendor takes time." Piers shifted his attention to Julia, who stood quietly in front of her room's floor-length mirror. When she noticed him looking, she flashed a tight smile.

"Good morning, Lord Astley."

"Good morning, Your Highness. How are you faring today?"

"Fine." In truth, Julia had hardly slept at all since her arrival, even less so the night before. Yet it was in the quiet hours of sleeplessness that her escape plan emerged. King Leonard and Queen Catherine were going to be holding a small, private gala that evening to celebrate her upcoming crowning. While everyone else would be busy drinking and dancing, she would slip past the guards, take the Borealis ticket Madelyn had given her and pawn off her gown, shoes, and jewelry to pay for her family's passage.

It was risky, deadly even, but it was the only chance for her and her family to be together again. All she had to do was survive breakfast with the Chase siblings, sit through etiquette training in preparation for the gala, and be utterly boring and forgettable when nightfall came. No suspicion meant no attention.

Clara stepped back as Piers approached.

"Wonderful job, Miss Burkes. Our dear Angelina will be the gem of the garden." Clara gave a sheepish grin as Julia caught a glimpse of herself in the mirror.

Just one more day as Angelina Chase.

"I hear the Duchess of Rosedale arrived in Lordhaven last night." Beatrice cast a knowing eye at Piers. "Surely Lady Audrey will find Princess Angelina most intriguing."

Julia caught something in the mirror flash across Piers's features. Annoyance? Contempt? But in an instant a practiced smile slid into its place and the moment was gone.

"This morning's gathering is strictly for Her Highness to better acquaint herself with her siblings before tonight's festivities. The Majesties have quite a full evening planned."

Julia's stomach dropped. *Dammit. New plan for tonight then. Migraine? Cramps? Food allergy? No, it can't be food. They don't bloody eat.*

"Ready then, Your Highness?"

He handed Julia a lacey white parasol.

"An umbrella? But it's not raining outside."

"It's a parasol, dear. The sun is a formidable foe this time of year." He turned on his heels, his own white parasol in hand. "Now then, your first official duty as princess awaits."

Pushing back the issue of how she would slip out of the gala, Julia followed Piers down the hall in silence.

Just one silly breakfast, she reminded herself. *I can do this.*

The moment Julia stepped into the sunlight, she tilted her head upwards and beamed. She was a flower drinking in the warmth, a girl drifting along the surface of a lake. If only for a moment every care drained from her at once. She inhaled and let the warmth linger on her face as she slowly spun in place with arms spread wide.

"Ready, Jules?"

Julia leapt back as if burned. But it wasn't Emily standing in front of her. Piers tilted his parasol back, his eyes ever so narrowed.

"Are you all right, Your Highness?"

Julia's smile faltered for only a moment.

"Yes, fine. Thought I heard something." She followed him across the stone pathway leading to the gazebo. But beneath the fragrant floral air of the storybook garden around her and the faint salty undercurrent from the distant Silver Sea, Julia's skin crawled at the memory of the masked figure and the not-dog creature walking the very same path. Those terrible golden faces staring back at her.

Right *through* her.

"She's late."

A girl's voice, sharp and assured, cut through the garden. Julia followed the source of the noise down a checkered stone pathway lined on either side with blooming rose bushes to a small, shaded clearing. A white clothed table longer than Julia was tall had been setup and arranged atop it was a silver tower rimmed in golden brown pastries, ripe fruit slices and colorful glazed tartlets. But it was the three teenagers sitting at the table that gave Julia pause.

Madelyn, Theodore, and Tabitha Chase.

Heirs to Halycon's most influential seats of power. Emily's siblings. And now *her* siblings, at least for today.

A gentle hand touched Julia's back.

"Play nice," Piers muttered beneath his breath. Julia shot him a glare he ignored.

"Good morning, Your Highnesses." Piers approached the table and dipped into a bow. Julia dipped into a hurried curtsy. She cast a furtive glace at Piers as to what she should do next. Should she sit down? Wait for them to invite her to sit down? What if they never acknowledged her? Was she to stand there until she met her demise by heat, hunger or corset?

"Good morning, Lord Astley," Princess Madelyn greeted. Julia's heart hammered when their eyes met.

"Our long lost sister." Madelyn's blue eyes glistened. "You've grown so much!"

Julia smiled sheepishly. Even she almost believed this was their first meeting. The deep shadows and hushed warnings shared in the secret tunnel beneath her room felt worlds away from the Royal Gardens. Here, Madelyn was the Princess Holiant, beaming in her marigold and cream dress, ready to one day become the next vicaress. Here, she was not the conspirator offering Julia escape from Dutchenson Castle.

Tabitha, the youngest Chase at fourteen, cast a sidelong glance in Julia's direction. Her slate brown curls brushed against her shoulders as she reached for a tartlet.

"Mother and Father hate tardiness. Best not form bad habits so soon." Tabitha popped the tartlet into her mouth and Julia silently willed it to lodge in her throat.

"Real classy, Tabs," Theo said a chortled laugh.

"What? I'm not being rude if it's true."

"You do realize she probably hates you already, right?" The sole Chase son and second oldest, Theodore, looked at Julia with the same grey eyes as his father. "Well, long lost sister? Want to throw Tabitha in the bin? I'll take one arm if you take the other."

Two large Dobermans were lying on either side of him, their heads nestled over their paws, but their attention trained on Julia. Piers had assured her previously they were only to protect Theo during his panic manifestations and not to be treated like pets.

"Theo, Tabitha." Madelyn's otherwise gentle voice carried an edge Julia hadn't expected. The pair fell silent. While Tabitha sulked and Theo looked mildly annoyed, Julia considered turning heel and leaving Piers to deal with the Chase siblings. Saints, how could he ever think this would be a good idea?

Madelyn extended her hand to the empty seat across from her. "Please, have a seat. I insist."

Piers put a hand on Julia's shoulder. "I shall return in time for your first lesson."

"Looking forward to it," Julia replied through a forced smile.

Reluctantly, she took a seat across from Madelyn. She could feel Tabitha and Theo staring at her from either end of the table. Birdsong carried on the breeze, ever so gently lifting the mood.

"To be honest, I wasn't sure if you were going to meet us today," Madelyn began. "You must have so many questions. I'd be in utter straights if I were you."

"You mean delight," Tabitha interjected, a slight sneer tinging her words. "How often can one say they've become a princess overnight?"

"You're right, Tabitha it *is* utterly unbelievable," Julia mused, the hint of a smirk on her lips. "How often does a peasant come along and make you the spare?"

Tabitha's face fell and Theo howled with laughter.

"Penniless trash," she spat, storming away as Madelyn called after her.

"Oh, I like her!" Theo beamed, taking a large bite out of his crumpet. The dobermans at his feet lifted their heads at the sound of Tabitha's sudden departure, but very quickly laid back down.

Madelyn sank back into her seat and sighed. "Look, I know this is hard for everyone, but can you please try to be a bit more civil, Angelina?"

"I'll be civil when I receive civility back." Julia reached for a strawberry slice and let it sit on her tongue, savoring the sweet juices. She swallowed and reached for a toasted biscuit.

"Come off it, Mads," Theo interjected. "She's right. Everyone knows Tabitha is an insufferable brat most days, bless her twisted little heart. About time someone in this family tells it to her face besides me." He raised his buttered crumpet to Julia. "Glad to have you back, sis."

"Thank you, Theo."

Madelyn cleared her throat. "I know you've been through a great deal. But this is a lot for all of us, not just you." She took a sip of barley rose tea as her eyes glazed over.

"We lost our sister. Mourned her. Mourned *you*. For years we assumed you were dead. Tabitha grew up only knowing herself as Halcyon's future queen. So imagine after all this time to have your older sister return, a stranger really, and the life you prepared for completely turned upside down because of it."

"I'd be happy to give the crown back if she wants to be queen so badly."

"You think she wants the title if she had a choice? Would you?"

The question hit Julia like a punch to the gut. Madelyn knew the answer, knew Julia wanted nothing more than to leave Dutchenson Castle and return to her family, and yet the weight of her answer—and the implications of Tabitha's future—hung heavy on her shoulders.

"If it meant I needn't worry about being falsely accused and killed for spellcasting, then yes, I think I would," Julia shot back.

Theo grabbed a tartlet as his gaze volleyed between the girls.

"I meant no disrespect," Madelyn quipped. "But you're utterly naïve to the political costs that keep the kingdom stable. All you've ever known is your town, your schooling, your family, your friends. You simply exist. But every child born a Chase has a purpose. We all have a role, and we're expected to fulfill it. We live and die by the Royal Accords. It's everything. I'm sworn to the church. Theo is sworn to Arcadia's eldest. You the throne. Tabitha—"

"Madelyn, stop." Theo reached out his hand to hers. "You're hitting a spiral."

Madelyn paused, her face softening, and she let out a deep breath.

"You're right, thank you. My apologies."

Theo turned to Julia. "Sorry about the rubbish morning. My sisters aren't so bad, I promise. It's all very new for everyone."

Julia frowned. "If you say so." In his own way, Theo's honesty and concern for others reminded her of her own brother. *George.* Her heart broke at the thought of what he must be going through back home.

When Madelyn spoke up next, her voice was quieter, composed.

"Forgive me. Our strife is not your burden to bear. Tabitha will be fine. She's sour now but she'll come around."

Julia said nothing. All she'd seen were lavish dresses, lovely gardens and precious jewels. But what if behind the scenes she wasn't the only one the king and queen were controlling for their own purpose? What if their children were under a similar fate, bound to these Royal Accords as she was bound to live out her lie? Julia recalled her first meeting with Madelyn in the tunnel. *Dutchenson Castle is a dangerous place.* Was this what she was trying to warn her about? Was this the danger she faced if she stayed? The unseen machinations guiding entire lives from the shadows, steering them along on an arranged track from birth until death?

Just then Julia heard a noise behind her. She glanced behind her to see Piers standing at the mouth of the clearing, his gold ensemble dazzling in the sunlight. He tilted his parasol and frowned at Tabitha's empty seat. He looked over to Madelyn whose gaze fell.

"Well, I trust this was a productive outing," Piers said to no one in particular.

"Oh, positively delightful," Theo replied and took another bite of tartlet. "We simply must do it again soon."

When Piers said Julia would be assigned an etiquette instructor, Louisa Heatherford was not who Julia had in mind. She was young for an instructor—barely into twenty-one—but carried all the sternness of an Elmwood instructor with the fashion sensibility of a highborn. She also had the unnerving habit of not blinking when she spoke.

They sat side by side in the sprawling, two-story library down the hall from her room. Twice as large as Julia's home in Temmings and brimming with more books than she could possibly read in a single lifetime, Julia wondered what other marvels remained locked away in the castle.

"When being introduced," Louisa began in a voice as rigid as her posture, "one must greet His and Her Majesties first, then by eldest child—Princess Holiant Madelyn, Prince Accordant Theodore, Crown Princess Angelina, and Princess Regent Tabitha. Once all formal introductions are made, any member of the royal family may be addressed at any given time." Louisa cleared her throat. "Title courtesy also extends to immediate family and the Sacred Seven—"

A knock rapped across the door. Louisa's eyes darted to the source of the interruption with unmasked irritation. Standing in the entrance was a castle messenger flanked by two stony-faced guards.

"Can I help you, Mr. Langford?"

"Yes, terribly sorry to interrupt, Ms. Heatherford but, um, Lord Astley has summoned you for a word."

"Has he now? And pray tell what for? I'm in the middle of lessons."

"He didn't elaborate, ma'am."

Louisa snapped the *Histories of the Isles* shut. "Apologies, Your Highness, but it appears that concludes our lessons for today." She sighed. "Do finish the remaining house chart exercises from earlier and leave your work here. I'll collect it when I've finished business with Lord Astley."

"Yes, ma'am."

After Louisa departed with the messenger and guards, the room fell oddly quiet. Julia looked down at the remaining exercises she hadn't finished during her first hour. With no one watching, she slipped into a slouch and began finetuning her escape plan for the evening. Knowing the title of the Earl of Tonbury's son and when to properly address him wasn't going to help her flee the castle any sooner.

Just then, a sudden prickle crawled up Julia's arm. The air had changed, heavy with another presence. Julia's fidgeting stilled.

Emily?

No, it wasn't her. Couldn't be her. Wouldn't be her ever again. Julia slowly turned in her seat. The door behind her was closed. Her heart quieted. She searched the aisles above her.

Empty.

As she turned back around, she came face to face with a blonde-haired girl leaning halfway across the table, grinning at her. Julia sprang from her seat, sending her chair clattering to the floor.

"Oops, did I give you start, cousin?"

"Bloody hell, you nearly gave me a heart attack."

The girl, a couple years younger than Julia, muffled her giggles behind lacey gloved hands.

"Mum says I'm quieter than a cat sometimes."

"You shouldn't sneak up on people like that." Julia set her chair upright and sat down. "Wait, did you say cousin?"

"Oh yes, last time I checked." She tucked a blonde strand behind her diamond studded ear. "I'm Audrey Amelia Deloris Chase, youngest child thus far of Roger and Maxine Chase and revered enemy of Tabitha Chase."

Julia snorted. "I may have taken your place as revered enemy over breakfast I'm afraid."

Audrey's hazel eyes widened.

"That was fast. Did death make you less likeable?"

Julia blinked. "Excuse me?"

"When I was a child, Mum used to put a bell on me so I couldn't sneak off. I stayed perfectly still for years and years and years. And I heard all sorts of secrets." Audrey rested her head in her hand, a glint of a smile curling her lips. "You seem like someone who likes secrets."

"Um, sure, I guess. I think everyone does."

"I knew you were a fun one!" A broad smile spread across Audrey's face as she clapped. "We must really have tea sometime. Bas would like that too."

"Bas?"

"Yes, Sir Bas." Audrey leaned over and picked up a massive cat with long, silky white fur and altering blue and green eyes. "He loves teatime, don't you, Bas?"

"He's very cute. I've never seen a cat with two different colored eyes before."

"It is curious, isn't it?" Audrey snuggled against his neck. "The whispers said he's seen many things."

"The whispers?"

Audrey nodded, setting Bas back down. "The rats, of course. They whisper about all sorts of things. If you stand perfectly still and listen very closely you can hear them whispering behind the walls."

"I ... see." Julia picked up her pencil and began filling out the house chart with random names. She glanced at the doorway, willing Louisa to appear.

Audrey twirled a strand of hair around her finger. A beat of silence passed between them but Audrey didn't seem bothered by it.

"Is it true then, cousin? That you possess magic? Like a fateshifter?"

Julia felt sick. *Magic. Heretic. Demon.* The words hovered in her mind as if conjured. Julia's fingers were on her neck before she could think better of herself. Although the rope's scar was hidden beneath the high collar of her dress, she could still feel it biting into her skin, squeezing the breath out of her. The noose's grip, the thinning oxygen, the devouring darkness... Without the mercy of the lull all of those memories, the final moments of Julia Sheffield, were there, right there, waiting for her when she closed her eyes. Julia dug her nails into the collar of her dress. Her breathing hitched in her throat.

"Breathe, Jules," Emily whispered into her ear.

Julia dropped her hand. She wanted to cry. *Saints, I'm going mad.*

"I don't think I'm ready to talk about this." Julia offered a shaky smile that barely hid the tremble in her voice.

"Of course," Audrey replied, patting Julia's hand. "I meant no offense. It's just so dull these days, but then *you* appear. It's so very interesting, your come about. You must have a dozen invitations a night!"

Julia shook her head. "Not that I know of at least. Piers handles my coming and goings." Saying it aloud, it was clear just how much she was a prisoner under the guise of a princess. She looked down at her finely tailored dress, at the cousin that wasn't hers, at the exquisite library adorned in rare books, fine art, and even finer furnishings.

All of it, she reminded herself, was a ruse. An agreement. A *lie*. She was to play her role, Piers to play his and the monarchy to play theirs. It was to be a win for everyone. So why didn't it feel that way? *Such a selfish child*, Aunt Agatha's voice crooned in her head. *Just like your mum.*

"Uncle Leo wants to keep you close," Audrey said, cutting through Julia's thoughts. "You're the future queen after all. Tabitha must be terribly sour with you for that."

"Oh, she very much is."

"How dreadful." Audrey rested her chin in her cupped palm as an impish smile flickered across her face.

"But I wonder—a sin or a miracle? A fateshifter or a phoenix?" She clapped her hands together like a delighted child. "Who could say? Oh, such a delight you are, cousin!"

Julia shifted in her seat. A bad idea was brewing just beneath the surface. But the days were slipping away. She had to take a chance.

"Audrey, I have a favor to ask."

Audrey blinked. "A favor?" A sticky sweet smile spread across her face. Julia ignored the alarms sounding in her head.

"Why of course, cousin. What can I do for you?"

"Careful." Emily again. Julia bit down hard on the inside of her lip. For a split second, she considered asking Audrey if she could hear Emily too. No, if she opened that door, spoke of the madness clawing at her mind, she feared she'd never be able to close it.

"I need to leave. Tonight, if possible." Julia held Audrey's gaze. For her part, Audrey never wavered. She tilted her head and looked at Julia with wide, curious eyes.

"You mean to leave the castle? And never return?"

"Yes. Can you help me?"

Audrey frowned. "Do you not like us?"

"What? No, of course I do. Everyone's been ..." She hesitated. The lies, the fear, the secrets. Nothing was what it appeared to be. Even still, she swallowed down her protest and the mask held in place, pretty and free of troubles. "Everyone's been so pleasant, but I need to get back to my other family. Please, Audrey. Surely you must know a way."

Audrey was silent for a moment. "I do, but it's a bit dodgy. And you very well could die. Again."

"Tell me."

"There are hidden pathways behind the walls. Ghost tunnels. I don't know where they all lead or even how far they spread, but rumor has it some lead outside. To bleed out the spirits of the castle."

Several questions sprang to mind, but she had to stay focused. Louisa could return any minute. "Like secret passageways?"

"No, the castle has proper passageways in case of an emergency. And other ones no one talks about. But the ghost tunnels are different. They're not meant for adults, not really. They're more suited for children."

Julia frowned. The ghost tunnels didn't seem too promising, but they stood to be her best chance of making her escape. She pushed down the rising dread cinching her stomach. What if the halls were blocked? It'd be dark and no one would know where she'd gone to rescue her. Should she leave a note? But no, then she'd surely be found out and punished. Her mind raced with questions but she had no other choice. Time was running out. Her crowning was approaching with every minute that passed. If she didn't leave during the gala, she would be trapped in Lordhaven and never see her family again.

"Do you know an entrance?"

"You don't mean to actually traverse the walls?"

The image of the golden masked figure and the not dog creature flashed in her mind.

"I don't want to travel the castle grounds at night. Where's an entrance?"

"The only one I know of is in Tabitha's room."

Julia's heart dropped. "Are you serious? How am I supposed to get in there? I can't just stroll into her room."

Audrey shrugged. "Dunno. I suppose you'll just have to tell her and hope she's supportive."

"This isn't a game, Audrey," Julia snapped.

"I know. You asked for my help and I told you the truth. Oh! Are you upset because Madelyn didn't tell you about the entrance in Tabitha's room? I suppose that was a bit rude of her, but she did give you that passage ticket. Presents are always nice."

Julia's eyes went wide and a chill raced across her skin. "How do you know about that?"

Julia and Madelyn had been alone in that tunnel. Sure, it had been dark, but wouldn't one of them noticed if Audrey had been there? And suddenly it struck her. The scurrying near her feet. The chittering in the shadows.

Rats.

Audrey stifled a snicker. "You're so silly, cousin. I told you, remember? All you have to do is stand perfectly still and listen. But you already do, don't you? They've seen you listening to someone. Someone who frightens you."

"Wait, what do you—"

The door swung open and Louisa reappeared but immediately stepped back with a start.

"Oh, Lady Audrey, I didn't expect to see you here." Louisa dipped into a shallow curtsy. "The countess has been looking all over for you."

"Well, it's been a delight, dear cousin, but Mumsy is waiting." Audrey rose from her seat and scooped up Bas, who obliged without protest. "I did very much enjoy myself, and please do consider what we discussed. I simply don't see any other way for you. See you at tonight's gala!" With a wave of her lacey fingers, she was gone, leaving Julia once again with her unanswered questions and maddening thoughts.

30

SYBIL

"Remember the song / it spun her so / Remember the words / it called her fro / Remember the night / black as pitch / Remember the time / gone but rich."
— *Claris Browning, "Upon the Shores of Darnby," folk song*

The rumble of thunder woke Sybil from her slumber.

She opened her eyes partly, her vision mottled and blurry. Shadows stained her room in soft blues and greys.

Shadows. Shadows ...

"I've seen it in you." Cain's howl echoed in her ears, morphing into Major Quinn's screams.

Sybil pitched forward. She clutched her chest as if to hold back something seething inside of her, ready to strike.

"No, it wasn't me," she growled, slamming her fist. Her shoulders shook as she thought of the fear on Priya's face in the clearing. Frozen, helpless. She closed her eyes and took a deep breath. No, she wouldn't let Cain or her fears get this much power over her.

A roil of thunder snapped her to attention.

What time is it? She looked out her window to see the brewing storm outside. Had she overslept? If it wasn't dawn ...

The messenger! She tossed the covers back and flew out of her room.

"Stupid, stupid, stupid!" she muttered as she rushed down the stairs. Cal was sitting at the kitchen table eating porridge and toast. When their eyes met, he lowered his spoon and glanced at their mother.

"Good morning, dear," Joan Vorn greeted tersely, keeping her back turned as she washed dishes. "How are you feeling?"

"Fine, but I wasn't woken for school." The words came out measured, even quiet, but lacked the accusation a question would imply. It should've been safe. But as Joan set down the bowl she was washing and wiped her hands on her apron, Sybil's shoulders reflexively tensed. A misstep.

"You've not been back from Ilva's cottage but for a night, Sybil. I sent correspondence to the headmistress you wouldn't be attending class today." Joan's mouth pursed. "You need to rest. Cal will look after you."

"I told you she wouldn't listen," Cal grumbled as he resumed eating. Joan shot him a glare.

"Enough, the both of you." She turned back to Sybil. "Lady Ilva expressed concern regarding your mental health and I concur."

"But, Mum—"

"This is not open for discussion, Sybil. You're staying home."

"But I'm fine, really, Mum, I promise. I have to practice my form." Sybil's heart raced beneath her dress. Did she dare it?

"I'm training," she continued, her voice suddenly a small, shaky thing. "I'm going to try out for the Trials."

Cal stopped eating.

"Wait, what? You're going out for the Trials? The Trials of Six?" He burst out laughing and looked between her and their mother with an incredulous smile. "Gods honest?"

Sybil ignored him and only looked at her mother, who remained silent. Doubt began to creep up Sybil's neck as the first drops of rain pattered against the window.

"Mum, did you hear me?"

Something in her mother's face smoothed over. Hardened.

"Yes."

Sybil swallowed hard. Another misstep. *Stupid, stupid, stupid.*

"What do you think?"

Her mother's eyes narrowed. "You want to become a Major. Have your own coven, then?" She folded her arms. "And what exactly do you hope to achieve by doing that?"

Cal set down his spoon, his shoulders tensing but Sybil knew this storm was only intended for her. And she had nowhere to hide.

"If I pass the Trials and become a Major, I can find out what really happened to my coven. We might even be allowed to return to Hillside." She added more quietly, "And the Council might give you your Sentinel position back."

"The standing of our family name is the concern of the High Council and the High Council only," her mother countered, her voice as swift as a blade. "As it were, we've earned our place here in the Outskirts. Redemption is a construct of the guilty."

Her mother's words were a punch to the gut. Cal stared at Joan with a mixture of shock and disbelief.

"Do you really think I killed my coven, mum?" Sybil asked, her heart tearing apart with each word.

Joan inhaled, raising her chin ever so slightly. "Of course not. But only doubt casts a shadow, Sybil. What you're trying to do is a gross misuse of the Major role. It will only make people suspicious of your motives. Do you really want more questioning?"

"Is it so wrong to want to know the truth? Why can't anyone see that? It's just like with Da! No one tried to find out what really happened to him, like he didn't even matter! Like my coven didn't matter because I was right there to blame!" Sybil shot back, tears threatening to release.

"This obsession needs to stop!" Joan turned her back on Sybil and rested her hands on the counter, letting her head fall. After a moment of silence, she added, "You need to let them go. Your coven. Your father. *All* of them. You have to move on and stop letting your emotions get the best of you. They're gone, Sybil."

"Mum—" Cal interjected, but she spoke over him.

"Otherwise," she continued, "the dead will be your undoing."

"I—" The words lingered on Sybil's tongue with no direction. She closed her eyes and inhaled deeply, just like her parents had taught her when her anger became too much to bear. When she reopened them, her mother's gaze was upon her once more, sharp and reproachful.

There were a thousand things Sybil wanted to say, to scream, to confess. But it was the image of her father on the shore, warm as the Skyfire sun that gave her pause. A home, a settlement, a kingdom—all broken by the seed of fear. She couldn't let the cycle continue. Why couldn't her mother see that?

"I just wanted to help," Sybil said finally.

"Help by minding your own future and your classes. It's more than enough to handle I should think." Joan gave a small shake of her head. "I don't want to hear about this Trial business again, is that clear?"

Sybil bit back her tears.

"Yes, ma'am."

Joan took off her apron. "Good." She hung it on the wrung near the door and grabbed her knife holster. "I have a meeting at the Citadel with the Council. I'll return soon." She strapped the knife holster to her thigh and gave Cal a steely glare. "And I expect no trouble when I return."

"Yes, Mum."

She nodded farewell to Sybil and Cal and then she was gone. After a few moments, Cal pushed back his chair and began washing his dishes in silence.

Without turning around, he asked, "How are you really feeling?"

Sybil, still standing in place, snapped from her haze.

"Fine, I guess." She slid into Cal's old seat and stared down at the table. Cal dried his bowl and slumped into the chair across from her. They sat that way for several minutes, the pattering of the rain outside filling the silence between them.

Finally, Sybil said, "It feels strange sitting this way again."

"Aye."

A crackle of thunder.

"It was nice though ... when he was here."

Cal snorted and folded his arms across his chest. Sybil stole a glance at her brother. He was looking off in the distance. Anywhere but at her.

"You miss him too, don't you?"

"Of course I do!" Cal barked, finally looking at her. "But it doesn't change the fact he left us to deal with his mess. Or that he's probably dead like Mum says."

"Da didn't leave us and he isn't dead. He disappeared through the Wandering Wood. His route cut right through the Blood Grounds. Mercer swore it before the High Council. And the Wandering Wood is reported to appear there more often than anywhere else."

"The Wandering Wood is bollocks and you know it. A wood that can shift in and out of time and space and take people with it? Don't be daft. If it really happened, Mercer would've disappeared, too."

"He said Da woke up before him to refill their cannisters. The woods would've already shifted once Da walked through."

Cal shook his head, a mirthless smile on his face. "You're such a blind follower to Da that you can't even see him. He buckled under the pressure of the High Council to drop the whole fateshifter rights business and left when he couldn't handle the backlash here. He ran away, Sybil. He never intended to go to Lordhaven with Mercer. Just admit it! He was scared, so he abandoned us!"

"He was trying to help us! *All* of us. He did more work for fateshifter rights in Halcyon than the High Council has ever bothered to do." She shook her head, her words acid in her mouth. "They sit in the Citadel and do absolutely nothing."

"They keep us safe."

"So we're just supposed to live and die out here in secrecy forever? Hiding away our magicks like criminals? Being told what we can and can't cast? And you're fine with that?"

"Would you prefer being hunted down then? Hmm? Hated by your neighbors and working in rat-infested factories for crumbs? Is that what you want?" Cal motioned towards the door. "Go on, then. Leave. Just like he did. There's a whole kingdom out there ready to hate you."

A clap of thunder tore between them like a gavel silencing a rowdy courtroom. Sybil stared at her brother as if looking at him for the first time. When had his hair grown past his ears? When had his shoulders become so broad?

When had his eyes gone so cold like their mother's?

He's not a little boy anymore, she realized. Something in him had hardened and she hadn't even noticed. Regret and guilt welled up inside her. She leaned forward and extended her hand, palm upward. "I'm sorry. I know I wasn't there when you needed me. I was an awful sister, I know. But I'm here now."

Cal kept his arms folded. He regarded her with a stony expression she couldn't read. The rain began to settle down.

"And where were you when he left? Or when we had to leave everything in Hillside after your trial? Buried in books and shut up in your room. For what? To keep your precious Head Girl title? Salvage your perfect marks? Mum lost her job because of Da's antics and then we lose our home, our *life*, because of you. Do you know how hard it is? Because of you I can't fail at *anything* ever or else Mum scolds me I'll waste my potential like you." Cal stood. "Pretend to be the big sister all you want, but I don't need any more false promises. You don't care about anyone but yourself."

"Cal—"

He headed up the stairs and out of sight. A door slam followed a moment later.

Sybil pressed her lips into a thin line. Cal wasn't the only one who could storm off. She went upstairs, changed into her uniform and swallowed two pills. The frost couldn't kick in soon enough. She grabbed her bag and without a second glance left the house.

The storm had subsided, but stray droplets still dampened her cheeks. Not wanting to run into her mother, she kept to the back ridge of the Outskirts, cutting along the forest near the communal garden. She slipped past the back stand of Sorinia's Soup House, and the waft of potato cream stew made her mouth water.

Several minutes later, she neared Lycoris Academy. A few upper years milled about on the quad, but she hurried past them and cut across to the library.

Sybil ascended the stone stairs and stepped through its large, wooden doors. Sitting at the entrance behind a tall wooden desk was a young girl a few years older than Sybil. Flaming red hair fell down her back in messy, curled waves.

"Morning, Mabel," Sybil greeted with a wave.

Mabel looked up from her book and grinned from ear to ear. "Ah, she walks!" Mabel slipped off her stool and pulled Sybil into a hug.

"I was so worried you would've taken to bed for much longer, but here you are!" she beamed, her mossy green eyes shining. "How you feeling then?"

"Better," Sybil lied. "I have some studying to catch up on, but I wanted to thank you. Lady Ilva said you assisted her when I was first brought in."

Mabel waived her off. "Think nothing more of it. I'm just glad you're okay."

"Lady Ilva does brilliant work. My hands are like new."

Sybil waited with bated breath behind her casualness. A flicker of hesitance passed over Mabel's face, but it was gone in an instant.

"Oh, she's a miracle worker. Thankfully you weren't too bad off."

Before Sybil could press further, Mabel changed course. "Sadly, nothing new has been added to the shelves since you've been at Lady Ilva's, but Barth is waiting to receive word back from one of the book traders in Magside on trade terms. We could be getting a new shelf worth if we're lucky."

"That's wonderful news!" Sybil replied, her disappointment immediately forgotten. "So is it really true their library is underground?"

"Yes!" Mabel gushed. "Oh gods, it's a dream, Sybil. I heard they use an entire cave system as their library and their calcite formations are simply gorgeous. Can you imagine?" Mabel slid back on her stool. "Course, that oaf Barth won't take me along anymore. Says it's 'too dangerous' on the main roads lately." She slumped forward and let her head rest in her palm. "Can you believe that rubbish? I've been here for ages tending this desk, aiding the book keeps and the like since I was a First Year and *still* the Headmistress won't approve me to be a field trader. It's infuriating. I'll graduate next year with not a single trip to speak of. How can I apply to the Citadel's acquisitions team without experience? I'm sure I'll hear the Council's laughter from here."

"You're a brilliant healer and Lady Ilva is lucky to have you as an assistant. I'm sure the Headmistress doesn't want her to lose you."

Mabel snorted. "Yes, because I'm merely my magic and nothing more." She flashed a sympathetic smile. "Sorry, I'm insufferable today. Just anxious to hear word from Magside's messenger, is all. If this goes through, it'd be the first big trade in seasons. I'm *desperate* for a new read."

She squeezed Sybil's hand and broke into a beaming smile. "It's been moons since we had something to look forward to like this!"

Lycoris had three paltry shelves for "leisure reading" near the back of the library. Sybil had read through all the titles numerous times, Mabel even more. A new book would be the perfect distraction.

Mabel glanced towards the steps and then dropped her voice to a whisper.

"But that's not all Barth heard from Magside."

Her face suddenly looked grave. Sybil's stomach twisted. "What is it?"

"His contact said word from the capital is that Princess Angelina is alive."

Sybil's face scrunched. "Princess Angelina?" She shook her head. "That's impossible. It's been so long."

Mabel shrugged. "Dunno, but I overheard Professor Brevig and Professor Sanghvi talking about it this morning when I was restocking the shelves. They said she was hung but came back to life!"

Sybil covered her mouth. "What! How? And why did they hang her?"

"Not sure. Professor Sangvhi said the penny papers reported a large phoenix shadow illuminated the entire area when she died. Barth told me only the Sacred Seven can do that. Something about a miracle mark in their bloodlines. It must be her."

"Something in their blood? Are they cursed? Because that sounds like magic."

Sybil had assumed the aristocracy were all unseers, those without a second nervous system unique to arcanics—the sacral system—and therefore unable to harness mana for casting. But what if that wasn't true? What if there was far more magic hidden throughout Lordhaven?

Mabel lowered her voice as a group of giggling first years passed by. "Listen, you can't say anything. No one here is supposed to know. Barth wasn't even supposed to tell me, but he's horrid at keeping even his own name to himself."

Sybil nodded. "I promise I won't say anything. But how did she come back to life if she's an unseer?"

"Who knows. She could be an arcanic. Maybe a Dawnslayer with death magic like you?"

"Maybe," Sybil said quietly, "but she'd have to be incredibly powerful to do that. I've never heard of any necromancy spell that could bring yourself back to life."

Unless someone brought her back to life, Sybil almost said, but kept the idea to herself. Any practicing arcanic worth their necromancy salt knew it was nearly impossible to summon a particular soul. Umbrin, the God of Souls and Trickery, was known for not letting necromancers have their sway over his charges so easily.

Sybil knew firsthand. Desperation had driven her to seek out her coven when they first died. But the pursuit of answers blinded one to the lies and deceit souls often used for a chance at life, however brief. They grasped at the emotions stained on her own soul, as easily read by the dead as seeing through glass and fed her the words she wanted to hear. Only her quick wit and steely mind severed her tethers before the hungry spirits could overwhelm and break her mind, completing the possession.

Mabel lowered her voice as an older student approached. "I'll find you once those new books come in."

Sybil thanked her friend then shuffled inside the library. As much as the smell of worn pages and leather covers comforted her, the image of the young princess returning to her family only to be taken as a criminal and hung iced her bones. How had her father ever believe he could reason with such barbarians? Perhaps her mum and Cal had been right all along about Lordhaven.

Just then, Sybil caught sight of a dark-haired boy with four large books open in front of him. She recognized him as Fletcher Bronson, a timid Second Year who was only a few marks below her in ranking. She walked over, suddenly aching for a familiar face to wash away her horrid morning. "Morning, Fletcher. May I sit with you?"

Fletcher didn't look up, but he nodded and replied in a timid voice, "Best of mornings to you too, Sybil. Yes, you may."

"Thank you. I appreciate the company."

He didn't look up at her but shifted in his seat, almost twitching. She set down her bag and patiently waited for him to continue.

"You haven't been in class. Are you unwell?" he asked.

"Something like that. Bit of a cold I think. I'm better now though."

He offered a small smile. "Good. That's good."

She opened her bag and opened her copy of *Historical Dawnslayer Magicks and Their Practice.* She looked over her notes scribbled in the margins and let the morning's grievances recede like a wave.

As the frost honed her attention to a needlepoint, Sybil found herself in a blissful bubble. An hour slipped past without notice. As she was busy making a footnote, someone grabbed her arm. Startled, she shot to her feet and came face to face with Heath.

"What are you doing here?" he scolded beneath his breath.

A wave of disgust roiled over her.

"I should ask you the same," she spat, snatching her arm back.

Fletcher watched in stunned horror, his gaze darting between the two.

"S-Sybil?" he stuttered, but her frost-induced focus blocked him out.

"Leave, Heath. Now," she demanded, oblivious to the dozen heads turned their way. "I never want to talk to you again."

Heath's jaw clenched. "They lied to you, didn't they?"

"What?"

"Come with me."

"Hey! Hey, stop it!" Sybil protested, struggling against his iron grip. "Let me *go!*"

Students stood frozen as he led her to an empty classroom near the back of the library. He shoved her forward and stood guard at the door.

Sybil shot him a seething glare, fighting back the pain in her wrist.

"What is your problem?"

Heath's face remained darkly calm. "Do you know what you are?"

"Excuse me?"

"Do you know what you are?" he repeated, enunciating each word in a harsh whisper.

Something in his voice tempered her anger. She narrowed her eyes. "Enlighten me."

"You're a bomb. A very large, dangerous bomb."

Sybil wanted to laugh, laugh at the absurdity of all of it, right down to Heath Ashford even talking to her after the antics Cain pulled. But something in his words struck her as true. As if he'd finally given a name to the coiling snake that seemed to live inside her, ready to strike if she dared not restrain herself.

"What's your problem? Haven't you done enough?" Her anger tightened around her chest, ready to consume her if she let it. "Hasn't everyone already done enough?"

Heath took a step closer, but Sybil held her ground.

"Listen, I'm sorry. I shouldn't have let Cain out of my sight. It was bad. Really bad, I know."

"Bad? He could've *killed* us, you idiot! We almost died!"

Without thinking, she searched for signs of Cain, but any trace of Heath's shadow was lost in the darkened room. A chill crawled up her spine. "Where is he?"

"Sybil that's not—"

"Where *is* he, Heath?"

"Not here, okay?" Heath ran a hand through his shaggy hair. "I ... I need to lay low for a while. The shadow binding, the frost—all of it. I can't deal to you anymore. Not right now. Cain stirred up a lot of attention and so did you."

Sybil's brows scrunched together. Was that why her mother had to go to the Citadel? Had the High Council finally caught wind of Cain's existence? "Look, I don't care what you and Cain are involved in. You brought it on yourself messing with illegal magic."

"Don't act like you're not involved in this. The whole lot of us haven't been the same since you came back. That's the thick of it. You, the brilliant star of Lycoris, came back all bloody and mute and your coven didn't. How were we not supposed to be scared? We live in this constant fear. We're in a damn sea of it, Sybil and everyone is drowning!"

Sybil's jaw tightened. "So that's it, then? If I left, then everyone could breathe easier? Is that what you wanted Cain to do? Kill me so you could feel better?"

"What? No! Gods, no, of course not."

"Then what?" she snarled. "Tell me!"

Heath looked down at the floor. "When I found you, the blood wolf was already dead. Scorched until there nothing was left. And your hands, the palms were blistered. Burned."

Sybil tasted ash in her mouth. "You're lying. I don't have fire magic. I'm a Dawnslayer. And Dawnslayers can only use somatic magic and I'm not a Skybreaker because I was tested when I was a kid and I failed and that would also mean Lady Ilva lied to me which she would never do, ever." When she finally took a breath and met Heath's gaze, only pity stared back.

"I'm sorry. I know it's a lot to take in," Heath continued. "But I remember something about the air was strange. Like the mana was … different." He took a deep breath. "Listen, Cain told me once about this cursed magic that manifests in fateshifters sometimes. He said there was a legend about it, something about the curse coming from the four rivers in the realm of the dead and passed onto souls. But the magic is cast using emotions instead of mana, so it's wicked bad to use."

"Really, Heath? You honestly believe some legend Cain told you about cursed magic is real?" Sybil scoffed. "Unbelievable."

"Not like the Council would ever tell us if it were true. They control what we read, what we learn, what jobs we can take. What kind of life is that, truly? What if the fire you have—"

Sybil had heard enough. It was easier to forget, to move on, to swallow all the fear and doubt until it disappeared into the dark recesses of her mind where it belonged. "I have to go."

"You know this will come out, one way or another. If you're really a late blooming Skybreaker, the Council will never let you leave. They'll force you to become a Sentinel and work for them."

"I'm not a Skybreaker, okay? And I don't care what the Council wants! Let them choke on their secrets."

She shoved past Heath and gathered her books. Fletcher watched her and said in a shaky whisper, "S-Sybil, are you all right? You and Heath looked upset."

"I'm fine, Fletcher," Sybil said with a tight smile. "Thank you for the company earlier. It was very pleasant."

"Yes, very pleasant. I do agree with that."

Sybil grabbed her bag and left the library. Mabel wasn't at her desk, but it was just as well. With class nearly done and no coin on her, she reluctantly made her way back to the Outskirts.

On her way, she caught sight of the foreboding stone tower at the western edge of Sanctis. Standing just over the tree line, the Citadel was the ever-present shadow of the High Council and the training quarters for the Sentinels and graduated Skybreakers. But after her run in with Heath, it now came across as an imposing warden rather than an amiable protector.

She continued across the quad and considered passing through Merchant Row, maybe seeing if Donna Basi had returned with any new charms from Arcadia, but that would risk running into old Hillside friends like May and Adriana.

She turned away from Merchant Row and instead ventured through the main square rimmed with eateries and stall cooks and past cottages to the quietness of the forest edge.

Ada Dresden, a middle-aged woman who lived with her mute daughter, gave her a rare wave.

"You're by early," she said in her usual dry tone. She continued her sweeping as she spoke. "Was Mallory on her way then?"

"I don't believe so, Mrs. Dresden."

"Hmph. Professors these days don't engage you children enough. Dulled to bits you all are." She stopped sweeping and leaned on her broom. "Back when I was a professor—not that long ago mind you—I drove discipline into my students. Not a one was without high marks. It's no wonder the other settlements have been knocking Lycoris out of the Tourney in the first bouts. Bloody shame it is."

Eager to leave, Sybil nodded. "Certainly."

"Mr. Dresden believes so, too, but of course once you're marked for trouble, the High Council wants nothing to do with you. I've no blame in my heart towards my Joseph, mind you. People make mistakes. So do children."

Sybil gritted her teeth. "Of course."

"Do mind yourself and your brother now."

"Yes, ma'am."

Sybil hurried home. To her surprise, the house was quiet.

"Mum?" No one answered. She considered stealing away to train, but the memory of the wandering blood wolf made her hesitate.

A sudden tiredness overcame her. She went upstairs and laid down. Sleep pulled at her and she easily succumbed to the quietness it offered. But her dreams were filled with terrors.

Beneath a steel grey sky, animals ambushed Sanctis. But something was wrong. Wolves with rotting flesh, bears with inky black eyes and foxes with exposed ribs where flesh should've been converged on the settlement, attacking villagers with a fervent viciousness known to no mortal beast. Their movements were the crude and unnatural puppetry of creatures long since dead. Sybil stood on the steps of Lycoris, watching in silence. Several tethers pulled on her—five, ten, maybe more—all gnawing at her life force.

In her hands was a coiled black snake with bone white eyes. Someone was pressed against her back, but she couldn't see who it was. As a wolf tore out a woman's throat, the stranger behind her began reciting the story of Felnor the Betrayer.

"Awash with light was he," the stranger recited, their voice barely above a whisper but husky and deep. "The golden son. The protector of Priory."

The snake hissed in her hands. But she wasn't afraid. She continued to watch as the fallen beasts tore through Sanctis, attacking anyone who crossed their path.

"But his love for the goddess Cephonia far outshined his promise, blinding him to any future other than one with her. A fire burned inside of him, a love so strong it burned all else to ash."

Suddenly, a bright orange flame erupted from Sybil's hands, engulfing the snake in a fiery orb. It wriggled and hissed as its body burned to ash in her hands.

She felt no pain. She continued staring ahead, watching the fall of Santcis unfold before her eyes.

By her hand.

31

TOBIAS

"Galway is the fourth one this week. Get your men in line down there, Monty. Any more talk of striking gets back to the foremen and this place will be crawling with High Hampton goons before week's end. Better an accident or two than a picket line of miners." – *Unsigned telegram to Monty Kiprono, Brackworth Mine Supervisor, Low Hampton, Halcyon*

In the back corner of Finn & Fough, an old shack of a tavern with yellowed walls and dim gaslight, Tobias and Tavia sat around a table better suited for one person than two. Tobias took a swig of his sour jack cider and frowned.

"So, you gonna tell me what's this all about or should I start guessing?" Tavia lifted her own glass to her lips.

"I need a quick job."

"You heard Marcellus. No work until the Devils are sorted."

"I know, but just something small. Just to get a bit more coin. I want to send Lucy off for a bit."

Tavia's brows drew together. "What do you mean 'send her off'? Send her where?"

Tobia's clutched his glass but it did little to steady him. The glint of the bloody fishhook flashed in his mind.

"I have an aunt in Debney. My da's sister. She hated him, but Mum told me once to go to her if I was ever in big trouble. She could look after Lucy while this gang business blows over." His leg bounced with renewed vigor beneath the table. He hated lying to Tavia, but he couldn't risk telling her he intended to go with Lucy. Marcellus would have his head for defection. Even still, his mum's warning the day she fell ill reminded him it was a worthwhile risk if it meant Lucy was kept safe.

"Only go to Aunt Nettie if you absolutely must," his mum had cautioned. *"She has a good heart, but her moods are fickle, and her bad ones are terrors."*

"Those Seadevil rogues Vivian and the twins are hunting," Tobias pressed on, "I think they might be in some nasty business. And if the Streeters truly get involved I don't know how safe she'll be here." Tavia's hand shot out to steady Tobia's leg.

"You have a hunch. Tell me."

"It's stupid."

Tavia lowered her voice so only Tobias could hear.

"Wolves know better."

Tobias snorted but let her have this one.

"The Seadevils might be in deeper business than we thought. Lucy will be safer out of Lordhaven, at least for a little bit."

"What other business? Tobias, if you know something you have to tell Marcellus—"

"It's nothing, all right?" Tobias snapped, cutting her off. "Just a bloody hunch like you said."

Tavia crossed her arms.

"You asked me here, remember? If you need my help, say so. If you're afraid of something, tell me."

"Look, the less you know the better."

"I'll follow the blood trail all the way to Deadeye himself. You don't get to take that choice away from me to make yourself feel better. I don't need your protection."

"Knives can't solve everything, Tavia."

Tavia smirked. "Says you. I'm far less hungry nowadays."

Tobias hunched over his cider. The hunger in those early years out of Chapman's House haunted them like an old wound that never quite healed properly. In those days, there was little else to do but steal or die. No one wanted to apprentice street orphans and soup kitchens only had so much to pass around. And so they took up brooms and scurried up chimneys to stave off the hunger. When they grew too wide for the chimneys, Market Street called. Marcellus took their brooms and gave them knives and batons.

But it wasn't knives or brooms that kept hunger at bay. It was the primal urge beneath the stubbornness. It was the hot-blooded selfishness to take from others without apology. It was seeing everything in black and white to justify the red.

Tavia peered around before speaking. "So this job I have, you might not like it."

"Doesn't matter."

"It's off book."

"*You* have an *off book* job?" Tobias barked with laughter. "Ez, I get, but you? What, not enough scraps under Marcellus's boot this week?"

"Don't be a twat. You want in or not?"

"Who's the mark?"

"A raven-eyed."

Tobias's throat tightened. He'd never seen someone with the tell-tale violet eyes that marked them as raven-eyed. They were a rare bunch, rumored to be descendants of Azavith himself and stronger than any fateshifter, duskborn or blood wolf. Warnings ran through the streets they stole souls just by looking at someone and lived forever. But that couldn't be true, could it? He pushed his glass aside and leaned closer so Tavia was only a breath away.

"You serious?"

Tavia's eyes gleamed. "You scared of monsters, Toby?"

"Hardly." Tobias leaned back and took another sip of cider. He would face whatever monsters he had to for Lucy. He would protect her just as he always had when the warm winds of Skyfire simpered out and the orange gold of Harvestgrain rolled through the trees and chilled the air. But each year grew harder. How long would his mind still be sharp? Still be his?

"Where's the job?"

"High Hampton. The front cut will be enough to cover our train tickets. We'll get our mark and take the last car back to Lordhaven. Marcellus and the high ups will be too busy preparing for the Bowery raid. They won't even notice we left."

Tobias let out a low whistle. "We going by rail now? Might nick a suit for the occasion."

"Just meet me at the station tonight at seven. And *don't* tell Ezra."

By the time the train station clock chimed seven, Tobias was caught between Tavia's glowering stare and an irritated porter.

"Honestly, I'm not even mad I wasn't invited," Ezra lamented. "But have you both forgotten one very not so small detail of our house contracts? *A thief is owed nothing but death*? Hmm? If we cross Marcellus and take the house cut of this job then they'll be bloody hell to pay."

"I *told* you not to bring him," Tavia growled.

Tobias held up his hands. "I didn't, I swear! He made his own way!"

"So, just curious why, you know, I wasn't invited …?"

"Not now, Ez!" Tavia and Tobias barked in unison. Ezra nodded, backing up slowly. The porter, who had been glancing at his pocket watch several times, finally snapped it shut and cleared his throat. "Are you all boarding or not? I have to close the doors now."

Ezra and Tobias looked at Tavia, who rolled her eyes.

"For the record, you both are absolutely insufferable." She reached into her bag and handed the porter ten sterlings. "This is for my friend here. He'll be sure to have a ticket by the time you come around to check them. If not, please do feel free to toss him off the train while traveling at the highest possible speed."

Tavia slung her bag back onto her shoulder and boarded the train without so much as a glance behind her.

Ezra let out a low whistle. "Oi, she's right pissed at you now, Toby. Save you a seat but I get window!"

As Ezra bounded onto the train, Tobias could only shake his head and wonder if he really had bit off more than he could chew.

Tobias ran his fingers over the sterling in his pocket as he watched Low Hampton come into view from the train car window. The evening sky painted the city in brilliant pinks and golds. Snakelamps glowed like fireflies along the streets beneath the rosy windows of kitten houses crowded around the approaching station. For a moment, Tobias lost himself in the magic of dreaming, believing for a moment he could be any young man traveling to a warm home filled with delicious food. And there his family would be waiting to greet him; a mother alive and well, a father brimming with pride and free of drink, a sister dressed in the most fashionable petticoat and a—

Tavia reached across the aisle and nudged his foot. It was the first she'd spoken to him since they'd left Lordhaven.

"You ready?"

Tobias looked over, careful not to stir Ezra awake. In the dusklight, her dark eyes shone as sharp and clear as a jackal's.

"The hunt is on."

"I guess so."

Tobias turned back to the window. Deep swaths of indigo swallowed most of the dusklight when he hadn't been looking.

Nightfall was upon them.

Low Hampton was a township at the base of Blackridge Hill. Tobias had heard stories of the Brothers of Industry—John and Daniel Ward—building a sprawling empire of iron named High Hamtpon atop it, but to witness the weight of wealth living atop the backs of the residents of Low Hampton spoke to the aristocracy's cruel honesty. When they rose to their manors in the sky, they constructed the ladders with iron to remain there.

A lattice work of thin walkways ran like a web above nearly every street and rooftop, blocking out the sun. Constables prowled the walkways like cats, peering down at the passerby below, some shouting, a couple catcalling, but most silently watching beneath brimmed caps with holstered pistols at the ready. Tobias couldn't help but stare.

"Toby, you hear me? Oi, Toby!" Tavia smacked his arm.

"Ow, I hear you." He rubbed his arm but glanced back at the constables above. "Who orders their watch?"

Tavia gestured towards the glimmering upper side of Blackridge Hill. "The Iron Barons of High Hampton. They make sure the poor bastards down here keep the mines running day in and day out." She lowered her voice as a constable walked overhead. "I got a tip most of the City Watch here is on their payroll. They'd sooner shoot the king himself than turn on the Ward brothers."

"And who told you that?" Tobias pressed, but Tavia ignored him.

"Let's run through this one more time. Ezra?"

"Right, so the mark is holed up in one of the upper rooms of the Rochester. Not far off, but there are eyes in the sky so slow and steady."

Tavia nodded. "Good. Now—"

"So what's this mark look like?" Tobias interrupted.

Tavia frowned. "I'll handle the mark. You both keep watch and get us in and back out alive."

Tobias crossed his arms. "Ez and I aren't going in blind."

"You won't be. You have me, remember?" Tavia gripped her bag strap tighter. "Now let's go before one of those vultures decides to shoot at us for sport."

32

TOBIAS

"Lot 107—Ashton Leet, *Power*, 1512. Complete blood wolf skeleton, articulated, coated in gold leaf. Estimate 750,000 – 800,000 sterling. Anonymous sale; the 8th of Goldrise, 1845." – *Closed auction listing, Wolston's, Lordhaven, Halcyon*

The Rochester was a grand dame of a building.

Framed in towering white pillars wrapped in ivy and surrounded by two sprawling fountains, it sat alone at the very ridge separating Low Hampton from the gated entrance leading up to High Hampton. Porters bustled to and fro tending to incoming guests and their luggage as carriages lined up beneath the staffed flags jutting out from the entrance. The middle, most prominent flag flew the royal crest of the crimson phoenix in front of a pair of crossed golden swords. To the left of it was a flag with a white rose against a pale green background representing the province of Rosedale. But the flag to the right of the royal crest caught Tobias's eye in particular—a black flag with the crest of a silver, multi-headed serpentine creature.

He elbowed Ezra. "You know that one?"

"What? The black flag?" Ezra shook his head. "Never seen it before."

"House crest of the Vaughns," Tavia added, her mouth twisted into a scowl. "The hydra."

"One of the Sacred Seven." Tobias spit on the ground. "Figures the only nice thing in Low Hampton belongs to them."

"One of the Iron Barons more like," Tavia corrected. "John Ward's eldest son, Thaddeus married into the Vaughn family a few years back. With his iron and the Vaughn fortune, he owns the Rochester, half of Low Hampton, and the train rail we came in on."

Ezra low whistled. "Bloody hell. Must be nice to be the Saint Father's favorite."

"More like Tavia's favorite," Tobias teased. "She's a walking catalogue of Sacred Seven gossip."

Tavia rolled her eyes. "Their wedding was in the papers if either of you ever bothered to read them."

"It doesn't take a degree from Penrose to know they wouldn't want us in their posh establishment," Tobias huffed.

Tavia gestured to the other end of the street, where the snakelight illuminated four hanging figures turning slowly beneath the iron walkway. Crudely painted signs hung around their necks declaring their crime: thievery.

Tobias's breath caught in his throat. What sunset had cast as magical from the train car was nothing but despair beneath the scaffolding.

"Right then. Don't get caught." Ezra let out a deep breath. "Scaling the building is out, and there's too many guests at the entrance. Service entrance?"

"Lift some uniforms?"

Tavia beamed. "Brilliant. I knew you two weren't completely hopeless." She swung her bag around and reached inside. "Now, masks at the ready and no names once we're inside."

"Yes, mum."

The trio split up and carefully made their way to the back alley of the Rochester. Once the constables overhead had left the walkway, Tavia pulled her black half mask over her mouth and nose. She knocked on the service entrance door then hugged the wall and waited. As soon as a cook opened the door and stepped out, Tavia ambushed him and shut the door. A few minutes later, she reopened it and signaled for Tobias and Ezra to join her.

When Tobias stepped into the Rochester's kitchen, its crew were frozen at their stations with backs turned and arms raised in surrender. The poor bloke that had stepped out lay sprawled on the floor.

"Don't worry, he's fine," Tavia reassured Ezra and Tobias. "Just napping."

"I swear, every single time—"

Tavia cut her eyes at Ezra. One of her daggers spun in her fingers faster than Tobias could follow and in a breath its blade was pointing at Ezra's throat like a compass needle.

"What was that?"

Ezra's hands shot up. "Just having some fun with your mates, no?" He chuckled. "Right?"

"And who said we were mates?"

"Since we were tykes," Ezra replied. "We got lice together. That's a bond right there."

Tobias rolled his eyes. "Can we please get a move on?"

"Fine." Tavia lowered her dagger and nodded at Tobias. "You come with me. Grab a uniform off one of them. And you," she said, looking at Ezra, "keep watch here. Anyone runs, kill 'em."

"Wait, what? You both can't just—wait! We're still mates, right? Right?"

But Tavia and Tobias were already making their way down the hall in their stolen porter and maid uniforms with an empty tray and fresh towel in hand. Ezra groaned and ducked back into the kitchen.

It was easier than expected to reach the top floor. No one batted a second glance at the pair. The help was to be seen, never heard. They took the stairs until they reached the top floor. To their relief no one was posted outside the grand suite's door.

It's just another job. Nothing to worry about, Tobias reassured himself.

He looked at Tavia, but she was already halfway down the hall. It still bothered him she had been so dodgy about the job. Was it because the mark was a raven-eyed?

Tavia approached the door and put her ear to it. She paused, then gestured to Tobias.

"What's the play here?" he whispered.

"We knock, they answer, we go in. No answer, we go in anyway."

"And the mark?"

Tavia knocked but didn't say anything.

Silence. The pair waited for several tense minutes. Just as Tobias was about to reach for the pick sown into the waist of his trousers beneath the stolen uniform, Tavia grabbed his hand.

They exchanged a look. "What're—"

Tavia suddenly dropped her hand and raised her smile as footsteps approached the door.

A heavyset man with a full red beard and stony expression stood in the doorway. He crossed his arms, which accentuated the thick scar snaking down his neck and beneath the collar of his open tunic.

"Good evening, sir," Tavia greeted, dipping into a courtesy. All trace of her gutter wall accent was gone and replaced with a flat, cheerful one that mimicked a proper Lordhaven housemaid.

"Service wasn't requested," the man grumbled.

"A courtesy visit is provided for all the Rochester's honored guests. Can I get the master of the suite tea, perhaps?"

"He's out."

Before he could refuse her, Tavia quickly added, "Then can I offer *you* a cup of tea? One of the Rochester's special nightcaps perhaps?" She looked up at him from beneath thick lashes, a demure smile on her lips.

"Well then," the man replied, a sly grin spreading across his face, "I do believe that's just what I need."

"Excellent choice, sir. Our porter will fetch the tea at once for you. In the meantime, it would be best if I prepare the suite for the serving plates."

She gave Tobias a small nod. Taking her cue, he left without another word. As soon as he heard the door shut behind him, he immediately spun around and reached for the handle. The bearded man dropped his hands from Tavia's shoulders in surprise just long enough for her to run both of her hidden daggers across his neck. He grabbed at the wounds but the blood was already gushing between his fingers. He staggered backwards, his eyes wild and defiant. An animal caught in a death trap. He knocked into an armchair and released his hold on his neck to break his fall, but the light had already faded from his eyes before he hit the floor.

Tavia wiped her blades clean on his tunic and pushed up her dress sleeves where her hidden arm sheaths were strapped.

"Is this what you didn't want Ezra seeing?"

Tavia laughed. "Hardly."

"Then what is it you're not telling me about this job? Why didn't you want Ezra coming with us?"

"Follow me."

She crept past the study and into the first bedroom. It was dark and empty. She opened the second door and found two men inside. The first was draped over a chair, a hand of cards resting on his stomach and the second had his chin to his chest, snoring. Both had three empty wine bottles between them.

"Slow night."

Tavia nodded. "Lucky for us their boss is a social one."

They continued to the second wing on the other side of the room and found the master suite. The door was locked.

Tobias made quick work of it with his lockpick and pushed opened the door. The sharp spice of cigar smoke hung in the air. Tavia scrunched her nose as she entered. She pointed to a door leading to a second inner chamber not accessible by the other rooms.

"Should be in there."

A sinking feeling pulled at Tobias' stomach as he approached the door.

I can face this, Tobias silently willed himself. *For the coin. For Lucy.*

He picked the lock and steeling himself, opened the door. On the other side, curled up in a ball asleep was a young boy no more than seven or eight.

"Hullo?" the boy asked groggily. He wore a black blindfold and cuffs around his hands and legs, although in his condition Tobias figured he barely knew how to spell his own name.

"Hello, there," Tobias replied, kneeling down. "What's yo—"

"Don't talk to him," Tavia snapped. She stepped in between Tobias and the boy, one of her knives at the ready.

"What are you doing? He clearly has enough in his blood to put down a horse."

"Good, all the better for us." She turned back to the boy, who was hovering between a half sitting, half laying position. Her expression steeled over as she said, "The mark isn't him. It's his eyes."

Tobias froze. He willed himself to speak, to stop this madness, but his voice refused to work. Finally, he managed to say in a coarse whisper, "He's why then."

Tavia said nothing, but her silence was answer enough.

Tobias ran a hand over his mouth and shook his head slowly. "No, no we can't do this. He's just a kid. We can't do that to him."

"As long as the eyes are unharmed, his condition is irrelevant." She reached inside the front of her dress and took out a small vial of a dark purple liquid as deep as the shadows that had crawled along the pink and gold sky over High Hampton.

Nightfall was indeed upon them.

"This is a mercy. He hasn't much hope otherwise."

"He could if we only take one."

Tavia frowned. "And who would that help exactly? We'd lose our cut for half work and the boy would die from a slow infection if he isn't sold for parts first. The Jeweler wouldn't have use for him if he doesn't have a perfect pair."

"The Jeweler?"

"He's a monster that collects rare colored eyes and occasionally sells them off at private auctions. My contact warned me the Jeweler might be involved. He runs in the same circles as the Ward brothers."

Her gaze shifted to the young raven-eyed boy.

"We don't have much time." She handed him the vial. "Three drops should do the trick. He won't feel a thing."

Tobias looked down at the vial in his hand, still warm from Tavia's skin. He wrapped his hand around it and shook his head. "We can't do this. This isn't who we are." "You came to me, remember? Any chance of getting Lucy out before a gang war is lost if you don't do this."

Tavia had made good on her word. She'd let him in on a quick job. But he'd been a fool. The cost was too great. It had always been too great.

You should've left me in that alleyway, Ez.

Tobias looked up from the vial and met Tavia's steadfast gaze.

You should've left Tavia and I to die back then. We're no good. The wolfbite made us worse than monsters.

"Fine." He outstretched his hand and Tavia handed him one of her daggers. Something stirred in him then, something familiar, bestial. He knew this release. He savored it once, in his dreams, where he ran through his mind's shadows as a wolf, restless with violence. He looked down at the vial in one hand and the dagger in the other.

"You asked me what I didn't want Ezra to see." Tavia was at his back now, whispering into his ear. "It was this. The wolf."

Tobias jerked away as if stung.

"Don't—"

"It helps," she cut in. "For down the line. When the urges grow stronger."

"That won't happen."

"We're sick, Toby." Tavia's gaze fell to her hands. Her voice cracked in the darkness. "And there's no changing that. It's only a matter of time before we turn into blood wolves."

Tobias was silent for several seconds. "No using names, remember?" He shoved past her and knelt beside the boy.

"Hullo?" the boy said again, his voice heavy with sleep.

Tobias kept his voice far steadier than his hand. "There, now, how about a sip of some tea and a tale before bed?"

The final train ride for the night was known as the ghost line. Bandits most often robbed passengers under the cloak of darkness when knives and pistol could be easily concealed, so few ever traveled in the late hours. But seeing the ring of red he had missed beneath his thumbnail reminded Tobias of another reason for the nickname.

It was beneath a pitch-black sky that ghosts roamed, searching for a way out from what haunted them.

Ezra stretched his arms over his head and yawned.

"So any plans for spending your sterlings? Fine dining on Cutler Row? Getting a tailored suit?"

"We all know you're going to spend it on the first girl you see," Tavia said smugly. "Who's it gonna be this week?"

"Perhaps you can read about it in your beloved penny papers," Ezra said with a mocking smile.

Tavia rolled her eyes but the shadows hid her bemused smile. Ezra turned to Tobias who had already closed his eyes feigning sleep.

"Oi, what about you, Toby?"

"Leave it, Ez," Tobias replied tersely.

"Touchy, aren't we?"

"Lay off him." Tavia leaned against the window. "It's been a long night."

"Ah yes, quite a long night I had in the *kitchens*. Lovely time, in case anyone was wondering. So glad I could be a part of a swell adventure I wasn't invited to by my *best friends*."

Tavia sighed. "Don't be cross. Someone needed to watch the entry point and if one of us had to talk their way out of something, you're the best choice."

Ezra shrugged, a cheeky smile curling his lips. "Guilty." He rested his chin in his hand. "Then what fine skills did you need Toby for?"

Tobias's skin prickled.

"He's the better lock picker," Tavia replied with no hesitation. "No offense."

Tobias sighed inwardly. *Another bullet dodged.*

Yet the blood remained, hidden from view beneath a tucked thumb. How long could he keep hiding his soiled hands?

33

NATHANIEL

"She doesn't trust me, H. Not after the Emissary Ball. I'm sorry but we're out of time. She must not reach the Brunswick Theatre tomorrow night. Saints be with you." – *Unknown castle hand, confiscated note regarding the failed assassination attempt on Queen Minerva Chase, the Royal Library Vault, Dutchenson Castle*

Nathaniel glanced again at his pocket watch.

It was already half past ten. If Rose was to keep this on, they'd be lucky to make it into Lord Henley's foyer before the last guest emptied out.

When Rose finally emerged from the ladies sitting room twenty minutes later, she was a sight to behold. Her lacy black gown was sinched with a silver and black corset and rimmed in a high lace collar. A pearl broch buckled at her throat and diamond and pearl pins held her thick black hair in place.

"Cheer up, Nathaniel," she purred, her dark red lips curling into a smile. "We're at a ball."

"Well, waiting nearly two hours outside a lady's sitting room at one of the biggest events of the season isn't as grand as you may think it is."

Rose slid her arms into the crook of his. "Oh, come now, no need to be sour. Besides, gossip is like wine—the best ones take time to procure."

The air hummed with the delicate beginnings of the Sinclair Quadrille Band. The dances had started without them.

"Well? What's the good word then?"

"Two of the Sacred Seven are here: Darian Carlyle and Lucas Taft. I assumed they were bored, but word is there's a very private gala happening right now at Dutchenson Castle, so my bet is their families sent them here to see who else received an invite. Insufferable trites, I swear. A few noble families are also attending, but Darian would be quite a prize for the Order. Shall tonight be his turn?"

Nathaniel scoffed. "I'm afraid Darian isn't the target tonight but do have a dance with him. He could use a little nudge towards the Order."

Rose raised a carefully crafted brow. "Pray tell, who does our fearless leader have you chasing after this time?"

"Abrom Galbrooke."

Rose rolled her eyes. "How utterly boring. Let's go dance instead."

"Are you suggesting lazing off? How wicked of you, Miss Blakely."

Rose batted at his arm playfully. "I don't recall Claude being my date. Besides, it's only fair we enjoy ourselves a little. I promise you Galbrooke will be holed up in one of the veil rooms upstairs high off his arse on dewdrops and pretty girls. Fetch me a program, will you?"

The pair exited the sitting room hall and walked into one of the largest ballrooms in Lordhaven. A sea of intricately tailored gowns and patterned suits mingled and swept across the ballroom floor, their steps carefully partnered to each note of the band. For those not dancing, crystal flutes were quietly filled with sweet, bubbly Canterford wine at every turn, ensuring no cheek went uncolored and no dance card unfilled.

Nathaniel made his way through to the programmer, an inconspicuous older woman who gave a slight bow and handed Nathaniel two programs. He thanked her and slipped back into the crowd. He gave the room a quick once over but didn't see Sampson anywhere. Thanks to Rose, they were hopelessly past their scheduled meet-up time.

Rose took a sip of wine as Nathaniel approached. "Wonderful." She set down her flute. "My dance card is simply far too—"

A tall, brutish man with a swirled moustache and dark brown hair cut low suddenly emerged from the crowd and patted Nathaniel on the back. His eyes were the greyish black of wet stone. "Ah, there you are, Nathaniel! I was worried you wouldn't make it tonight."

"Ah, Sampson." Nathaniel shook the man's hand. "You know I wouldn't miss it for the world. Rose, you remember Sampson Cowell, don't you?"

Rose gripped her flute harder. Vora, stone beasts that typically posed as long forgotten rooftop statues, largely avoided hunting duskborn, but their presence was no less unnerving. Devouring wandering spirits was one thing. To do so in the name of Tycaldra, the Goddess of Fates was another. Her doctrine of balance amongst mortals had turned the vora into cruel lovers, stealing the appearance of the souls they devoured to pray on the living using love as bait. Once the victims were killed, their souls would be chained to the realm because of their devotion, primed to then be hunted and eaten by the vora.

"Pleasure making your acquaintance again, Mr. Cowell," Rose replied with a slight bow. "It's not common to see you enjoying yourself. Finally taking a day off then?"

"Work and pleasure are one in the same for me, particularly in Lordhaven." A trace of his true features flickered across his face—battish ears, curved horns, tusked mouth crowded with horribly sharp teeth—but all too quickly receded back beneath the surface of his stolen human face. "But that's the fun, isn't it? The hunt. The *chase*."

"I wouldn't know," Rose replied. "Hunting isn't my preferred sport."

"Ah, yes, I've heard about certain dining establishments for the posh of you. I suppose the surgical theatres don't need to keep everything after their little demonstrations." Sampson rested on his heels, standing taller. His gaze slid to Nathaniel. "A rather curious way to honor the god of war, wouldn't you say?"

"Not all supernaturals choose to be bound to servitude," Rose quipped. "Some of us are just here for the party."

Nathaniel cleared his throat. "Sampson, have you any good dances tonight?"

"Yes, but I'm afraid none quite as memorable as the shimmering stars out tonight."

He found Mother's soothsayer.

"Unfortunate," Nathaniel replied with mock sadness. "But as they say, the best dance shall be at the last hour."

"As is tradition."

Nathaniel excused himself and led Rose out to the dance floor. As a new song began, she leaned in and whispered, "Out with it, Nathaniel."

"I beg your pardon?"

Any couple nearby would've heard Rose laugh airily, but Nathaniel alone deciphered the venomous curve in her mirth. "Do you think me simple?"

He chuckled and arched his arms for Rose to slip under and pivot.

"I would never dare."

"What is it that you're up to? I know a child's code when I hear it."

Nathaniel tilted his chin upward, an amused smirk playing across his face as they rejoined for the bridge.

"It's quite a dangerous venture," he challenged. "Certainly not suitable for a proper lady who is trying to curry the favor of the Order for her own promotion."

Her gaze flickered to his face. Her eyes took him in like she hadn't in years.

"You're hiding something." Her lips brushed the side of his neck. "And here I thought we were friends. A pity."

"Rose ..."

She smiled demurely. "I believe this conversation is done."

The song was ending. Soon the dance would be over and Rose would be lost to a sea of suitors biting at the chance to have a coveted spot on her dance card. If he were to go down this crooked path, he needed her. And they both knew it.

Nathaniel leaned in closer, as if to whisper sweet nothings to his lady of the night. "I've secured an invite to meet with my late mother's soothsayer. Sampson was my means of finding her."

Rose's face didn't betray her. Instead, she whispered, "Your *mother's* soothsayer? She's still alive? She'd have to be well into her hundreds by now."

"She's eluded death by her own means and isn't fond of being found."

"But a vora of all things?" Rose chided. "Honestly, have you ever seen one devour a spirit? It's barbaric. Get too cozy and they'll follow you like a vulture waiting for you to die and claim it was your fate all along."

The quartet finished off its sonata. Nathaniel and Rose took a step back to face each other. That's when Nathaniel spied the Malsik's Emissary heading to the second-floor balcony alone.

Well, well, that's odd.

As Rose dipped into a curtsey and Nathaniel bowed, he murmured so only she could hear, "I've discovered our source of power. If we can secure it, then everything will be ours. The Order, the Malsik, Claude, everyone."

When they faced each other again, Rose replied, "I shall keep your secret for now. I do hope to see you again, Mr. Trevet."

"As do I, Miss Blakely. A good evening to you."

Nathaniel excused himself from the next dance and instead slipped away to the second floor. It didn't take long to find the Emissary.

Badru Abdi was around Nathaniel's height with a low faded cut, dark umber skin and eyes the color of molten bronze. His arms rested on the balcony's rails, a glass of deep red wine tucked between his long, slim fingers. His tailored black suit and vest only heightened his stoic presence.

"You're not downstairs," he said as Nathaniel approached. His voice was as deep as it was monotone, lifted only by his rhythmic Waridian accent. "Shouldn't you be courting Lord Galbrooke?"

"Good evening to you as well, Badru." Nathaniel glanced at his pocket watch. "And I do believe I still have roughly three hours or so until the party is expected to unwind, which means the night is ripe with possibility. I find its best not to show others how hungry you are."

Badru swirled the wine in his glass with measured control. He stared at the garden below, his features as unreadable as Claude's.

"Careful not to starve then."

"That was never a concern."

Badru sighed and took a sip of wine. "My friend, listen. The way you are going isn't good. Tonight is not the time to show yourself off your leash."

"Is it not Halcyon's social season? Honestly, Badru, do try not to make it so obvious you live underground most of the year."

"You should refer to the holy city when you speak of it, even if you're unworthy to enter it at this moment. Claude may tolerate your childishness but the Malsik won't, trust you me."

Nathaniel shrugged. "Unworthy, uninterested. Who's to say, really? Between you and I, an ancient underground city of bones seems a bit vulgar for my tastes. But of course, to each their own."

Badru grunted and took another sip of wine.

"You may look young, but see I know you're old enough to know Claude has taken a bite too big for his mouth. He's leaving a blood trail other predators will surely follow. It's only a matter time, trust."

Nathaniel raised a brow. Even in the darkness, he could see the rigidness in the Emissary's jaw.

"Trouble in the happy marriage?"

Badru huffed. "The Malsik trusts his judgement."

"Do you?"

Badru said nothing.

What is Claude planning that could rile this boulder so much? As Nathaniel mulled over the meeting he was required to attend later that evening, the feeling of someone watching him prickled the hairs on his neck. He glanced at the doorway, but no one was there.

An unease he'd shaken off in the Under City crept back beneath his skin.

"If you'll excuse me," he said to Badru and returned to the hall. A group of men with grey hair were clustered at the top of the stairs, a glow of drunkenness to their ashen cheeks. To the right of them, tucked away in a corner, a young couple exchanged hushed laughter.

A moment later, Nathaniel spotted Samir at the foot of the stairs, arm in arm with the Norwood twins, Ella and Layla.

Just the refreshment he needed.

Nathaniel made his way down the stairs. Samir turned and beamed. The sisters smiled up at him, batting their lashes with invitation.

"Well, well, our dear Nathaniel makes an appearance at last." Samir nodded towards the dance floor. "We can't let Rose have all the fun now, can we?"

"I humbly agree."

Soon Nathaniel found himself swept into a whirlwind of waltzes and wine. Ella and Layla slipped between him and Samir like sprites, their laughter giddy and their amber eyes bright. When Nathaniel and Samir retired upstairs to one of the many veil rooms, the sisters followed.

Behind closed doors, spicy Waridian wine flowed freely and tinctures of mind-numbing dewdrops passed between neighbors. Nathaniel didn't see Lord Galbrooke, but no matter. As Rose said, he was there to enjoy himself. What harm would a few dewdrops do before he had to get to work? He leaned back and let the icy drops hit his eyes. The tingling effect was nearly immediate. As Ella dotted his neck with kisses, he watched stars dance upon the ceiling, his lips tasting of cinnamon and elderberries and his eyes delightfully numb. Samir's rich laughter filled the air. Nathaniel smiled. His mother's letter, the Ravenhood, the eternal heart, the soothsayer—all were forgotten to the bliss of the moment.

The quartet started up again, signaling the last dance of the evening. Samir patted Nathaniel's cheek.

"Time to go, love. Duty calls downstairs."

Nathaniel sighed and untangled himself from Ella, who flashed a red lipped pout.

"Do save me a spot on your next dance card," Nathaniel said with a wink. He left with Samir to the main hall and down a flight of stairs to a smaller hallway off the ballroom floor.

With each step he took, Nathaniel's duskborn blood ate away at the effects of the dewdrops, returning his clarity far sooner than he would've liked. The attendant at the end of the hall nodded to Nathaniel and Samir but waited for the given coded phrase.

"Good evening, sir," Samir greeted. "It's a nice evening for a gathering in the east."

"I agree," the attendant replied, opening the door for the pair.

Nathaniel and Samir entered a large gathering room basked in the warm glow of snakelight. Ten high-backed seating chairs occupied by Order members fanned across an ornately woven rug in the room's center. Rose, who was already seated near the front, watched as Nathaniel and Samir took the last remaining seats near the back.

At the head of the group was Claude and to his left stood Badru. His face was more relaxed, but his eyes remained sharp. Nathaniel didn't notice either of them. He was staring at the girl standing on Claude's other side, chin held high, as if the room belonged to her alone. A human girl no older than seventeen or eighteen with long dark hair, fair skin and piercing blue eyes.

Victoria Whitmont, the youngest of King Leonard's children born out of wedlock.

Nathaniel and Rose exchanged confused looks. Based on her sources, all the King's bastards had disappeared or been presumed dead. So how was Victoria alive? And why did she match the description of the young lady seen with Claude and Tyson Hoyt at Kendleston Manor?

Nathaniel's mind reeled. This was Claude's ace. *What in the seven hells has he done?*

"Isn't that Victoria Whitmont?" Samir whispered, the sharp edge of his voice cutting through his wine-thick breath. "Please tell me you know what's going on."

Before Nathaniel could respond, Claude took a step forward and held up his hand for silence.

"Thank you all for coming tonight," he began. "I do hope you continue to enjoy the evening festivities that are to come. Lord Henley has assured me they are not to be missed."

He turned to his guest of honor. "But first, I would like to introduce you to the lovely Lady Victoria Whitmont, Countess of Bristin."

A soft applause followed, peppered with a few murmurs. Nathaniel didn't move.

"Lady Victoria understands our desire to extend the Malsik's influence across the kingdom and beyond, to unify the Order and the Shujaa, our warrior brethren, under one banner and combine our might as the will of Lord Archonix dictates. Lady Victoria will be working closely with us to ensure it's our collective, not the Sacred Seven, who holds the throne."

Nathaniel stood, ignoring Badru's glare and Claude's annoyance. "If I may, how is it that Miss Whitmont, a mere human, stands before us, members of the Order, when her fellow siblings can't do the same?"

The room fell quiet, and all eyes found Victoria. Claude cleared his throat, but Victoria stepped forward and spoke first.

"A pleasure meeting you as well, Mr. Trevet. I've heard much about you." Victoria gave a small nod but didn't curtsey. "To answer your question, I orchestrated their demises before they could think of doing the same to me. I may not be pledged to your god of war or bear your duskborn blood, but I pledge to do everything I can to help the Order succeed. The power and knowledge duskborn longevity can offer the kingdom is...tremendous. My father and grandfather may have feared the power of supernaturals, but science and industrialization can only protect Halcyon for so long. Magic will try to rise again, and it's our duty to keep its wielders in their place." She smirked. "Anything else you'd like to know?"

Ah, so this one has teeth, Nathaniel mused.

"I don't know what fanciful tale Claude has spun you, Miss Whitmont," Nathaniel continued, "but I assure you this isn't a game."

"Well, when I take the crown off my father's head, it would be your loss not to find me in favor." Victoria tilted her head and softened her gaze, but her confidence remained. "I'd much rather be friends than enemies, Mr. Trevet."

In her eyes reflected his own desire for perfection. A need to devour all others, cursed with an insatiable ambition for the absolute self.

Take my throne for now, bastard daughter, but I will end you like all the rest. No one is hungrier than I.

Outside, the quartet finished its set. The night had grown late and the shadows stretched long over Lordhaven.

34

JULIA

"Dutchenson Castle is less a historical landmark than a tragic spectacle. While it has housed the royal family through countless generations, I must remind the honorable members of the Sentry that the castle invites questions that no proper family should be forced to speak upon. To leave it standing would be a stain upon Lordhaven."
– *Lord Collin Merriwether, excerpt from Proposal #46 to the Sentry, denied the 23rd of Stormfall, 1846*

The East Wing ballroom had come alive for the evening's gala.

A full orchestra was stationed in the back of the grand room, inspiring those of all ages to find a waltz partner and lose themselves in the crowded center. Despite her nerves, even Julia found herself smiling. How easy it was to lose herself in the heady sweetness of wine, the savory char of roasted meats and the rich promise of chocolate confections. How simple it was to watch couples dance from afar, mesmerized by the sashaying gowns and jacket tails of seasoned dancers.

Memories of her family back in Temmings cleaved her heart in two. This life as Angelina Chase, these riches, these nights of carefree dances and morning tea parties—it could be hers if she wore the right mask and said the right lies. But she could never have both.

She bit the inside of her lip until she tasted blood.

But if I stay, they would never want for anything ever again. They wouldn't be criminals. And I'll ... be queen one day.

Julia pushed down the ugly thought. No, she wanted to be with her family even if it meant they could never return to their old lives. At least they would have each other. It was the right thing to do. The *responsible* thing to do. Aunt Agatha was wrong. She wasn't selfish. She wouldn't leave them behind for her own ambitions.

She wasn't like her mother.

As the next song was about to begin, Julia slipped between the aristocracy of Lordhaven—people she never would've met in her lifetime had her decisions been different—and made her way to the exit. She needed to leave and find the ghost tunnel in Tabitha's room that would lead her back to her family. The longer she stayed the more the royal dream of Dutchenson Castle was becoming a tangible reality.

This isn't your life. This isn't your life.

She ducked past a member of the Sentry and his wife just as they entered the ballroom. Outside, the parlor and surrounding halls were clear. As she approached the foot of the stairs opposite the ballroom, she caught movement in the corner of her eye. She turned.

A young woman in her early twenties neared the ballroom doors. She wore a lovely off-shoulder dress embellished with silver roses and ivy and a black lace veil that covered her eyes. The soft blue of the dress reminded Julia of those rare spring mornings in Temmings when the air carried a gentle warmth. As Julia was about to turn away, the young woman walked through the closed doors and disappeared into the ballroom.

Julia stood frozen at the foot of the stairs. She could feel her brain scrambling to make sense of what she had just witnessed.

A young woman had walked towards the doors.

She never opened them.

Now she was gone.

It was a mistake to leave the stairwell. Julia knew every second counted in the hunt for Tabitha's room and the entrance to the ghost tunnel. But here and now the only conscious thought running through her mind was the fact someone had walked *through a closed door.* Julia pressed her hands against the doors and felt the solid wood beneath her fingers.

"What? No, that can't be." She ran her hands along the doors.

There must've been some kind of apparatus involved, she thought.

"Good evening, Your Highness."

Julia whirled around. Standing before her was a tall, narrow-shouldered man with deep brown skin. He had a pleasing face framed by fine black hair tied at the nape of his neck with a satin ribbon and eyes the greyish brown of cedar trees. But it was his extended fangs that stilled her heart, even if they were capped by a gold-plated brace that stretched across his top teeth.

"You seem troubled." His words carried the fluctuating pitch of a Khagalese accent. "Have you lost something?"

Just my mind is all, thanks, she wanted to say as she tried to keep her face neutral. She had never met a duskborn—at least that she knew of—but had heard enough horror stories of cultish blood draining and cannibalism to know never to approach one, even if they were only victims of a rare and deadly blood fever as her mum once pointed out.

What is he doing in Dutchenson Castle? And why is he roaming free and unguarded?

"Angelina, there you are." Madelyn appeared behind the man, her face a perfect mask of feigned ignorance.

"Oh, Farhan, good evening. Such a surprise to see you." Madelyn subtly slipped between Farhan and herself. "I take it you'll be joining in the festivities this evening?"

"Just popping in for a moment, I'm afraid. Dr. Loveney and I still have a good deal of work left before the evening retires, but given this was a special occasion ..." As he said this, his gaze flickered to Julia. Something in his eyes unsettled her.

No, her own inner voice assured her. *I've always wanted to talk to Farhan.*

"I wouldn't dare miss the return of our beloved princess," he continued, returning his attention to Madelyn.

"That's very kind of you. If you'll excuse us, I must be returning our guest of honor." Just as Madelyn grabbed Julia's hand harder than she needed to, Farhan shortened the distance between himself and the Princess Holiant. "No need to trouble yourself, Your Highness. Allow me to escort the young miss back."

"Yes," Julia heard herself saying. "I'd like that."

"*Expelle Farhan, Magos,*" Madelyn said with calm focus. Something in Julia shifted and the world lost its veneer of softness. All at once the deepness of the hallway shadows, the sharpness in Madelyn's eyes, and the pain in her squeezed hand flooded back. Farhan clenched his jaw against whatever pain he was suddenly feeling. He shot Madelyn a murderous glare before realigning his features into a smile that didn't meet his eyes.

"My apologies, Your Highness. Please forgive my assumptions." He dipped into a half bow. "Enjoy your evening."

Madelyn and Julia stepped aside as Farhan entered the ballroom.

When he was out of sight, Julia fumed, "What in the saints name happ—" but stopped when Madelyn started shaking violently.

Julia threw her arms around the Princess Holiant and squeezed tight, just as her mother used to when she was little and thunder frightened her.

"Madelyn, here, here I have you. It's okay. It's okay."

They stood this way for several minutes until Madelyn finally regained herself. Julia let her arms fall and took a cautious step back. "You all right?"

Madelyn nodded. "I'm fine. Sorry, I—" She shook her head and her face hardened. "Never mind. You shouldn't be out here. I told you it was dangerous to roam the castle, especially alone."

Julia ignored her jab and instead released the torrent of questions racing through her mind. "Who was that? Is he actually a duskborn? A full, *unguarded* duskborn, about in the castle? And what was that thing you said?"

"Julia, stop!" Madelyn said curtly, dispelling any hope Julia had of getting answers. "You need to return to the party right now. Before Mother or Father notices you're missing."

Madelyn reached for Julia's arm, but Julia pulled away. "No, I'm leaving."

"Right now? But—oh, Mother."

Julia bolted upright at the sight of Queen Catherine stepping out of the ballroom in a perfectly tailored olive green dress. With the flick of her hand, both queen's attendants dismissed themselves and shut the ballroom doors behind them. The thin golden tassels laced through Catherine's crown of auburn curls shimmered as she turned her attention to her eldest daughter.

"Madelyn, is everything all right? The vicaress was asking after you and I was terribly embarrassed to find you nowhere at all."

"I'm sorry, Mother. Angelina wasn't feeling well so I stepped out to assist her getting some air."

The queen looked at Julia as if just noticing her. Julia's blood chilled under her piercing blue gaze.

"Is that right? Well, we can't have her feeling faint. Madelyn, dear, do return to the gala. I shall attend to Angelina myself."

Madelyn opened her mouth to protest but one raised brow from the queen and she quickly shut it, offering a nod instead. "Yes, Mother."

Julia watched Madelyn go with a heavy heart. As the door shut behind her, Queen Catherine walked toward the courtyard down the hall from the main stairwell. Julia knew better than to not follow.

The night air was cloying on Julia's skin. Already she could feel the base of her purple high collar dress beginning to dampen. Overhead, the moon loomed, round and jaundiced. The queen stood with her back to Julia, overlooking the courtyard below.

"Tell me, how has your time at Dutchenson been so far?"

"Pleasant, Your Majesty."

The queen nodded knowingly, smiling to herself. "Ah yes, to be young in a beautiful, strange castle. It's terribly frightening, isn't it?"

"I-I suppose so, yes." Sweat beaded at her brow. She squeezed her hands together in hopes of steadying her nerves, but to no avail.

"You know, as a new queen I had countless responsibilities placed on me. I was expected to carry myself and the Chase name with utmost honor and poise. Any less would be shameful to myself and my family. I had our people to think of, after all. I couldn't let Halcyon down."

Queen Catherine tilted her chin, a portrait of beauty and control. "You will be taught to be a queen as I was and all those before me. But I've come to find there is something even the finest instructors Halcyon has to offer can't teach you."

"Your Majesty?"

"Come here."

Julia hesitated but soon joined Queen Catherine at the railing.

"What do you see below?" the queen asked.

Julia looked out onto the castle grounds. From here she could see part of the Royal Gardens and some of the outer courtyard near the castle's entrance. The long swatch of forestry surrounding the back of the castle curved around like a fanned collar, blocking out the seaside cliffs beyond. But under the moon's glow she could make out a figure traversing through one of the courtyards. A figure in a golden multifaced mask holding the leash of a not-dog creature. Even from this distance, the leashed beast paused and swiveled its cloaked head towards the balcony.

Julia's fingers curled around the railing until her knuckles were white. The same fear looking into Billie's deadpan eyes once again rooted her in place. The queen tilted Julia's face towards hers and away from the thing staring at them. "Do you understand now why I didn't bother to lock you in your room tonight? Because there was never going to be a chance of you boarding the Borealis. The howlers would notice you the moment you stepped outside. They're bred to smell mana remnants, among other things. And I can promise you they run faster than you think."

"Mana remnants?"

"The unseen traces left behind when magic has been used," Queen Catherine clarified. "Some magical-imbued objects, like the heart beating in your chest right now, also emit it naturally."

This close to the queen, Julia could see Madelyn in her features. The same gentle eyes and upturned mouth. But where Madelyn's traces of doubt flickered like a flame across her face, her mother harbored no such hesitancy. Her assuredness had been polished to a fine glint, seamless in its craftmanship.

"What did you people do to me?" Julia croaked, tears pricking her eyes.

When the queen didn't answer, Julia realized any hope or nerves or bravery she had harbored these past few days had been in vain. The game had ended before it'd ever begun.

"To rule as queen is to use the wield the four oldest tactics—beauty, wits, patience and fear. Do you understand?"

"Why are you doing this?" Julia murmured. Hot tears streamed down her face. "Why are you keeping me here? I'm not *her*."

Queen Catherine's gaze softened and she dropped her hand. "I wanted Piers to lie to you. I fought for it, but Leo disagreed, of course. He feared you seek out answers just like..." Queen Catherine's eyes glassed over as the words died on her lips. "Grief and fear changes people. It was a terrible thing that happened to you, and I wish my daughter were —" She closed her eyes and let her head bow, her voice falling to a whisper. "I'm sorry, Julia. But the line must be protected. The Chases must never fall."

"I swear I won't tell anyone what happened. Please, Your Majesty. Please, just let me go home."

"I can't let you leave," the queen lamented. "I wish it could be different, truly I do, but if you remain inside Dutchenson Castle, no harm will come to you. You're protected here."

"Protected from what?" Julia pressed.

"Not what, dear. Who." The queen lowered her voice. "The White Raven knows you're here."

A reassuring smile replaced the concern present there only a moment before.

"Now, let us put these dark matters to rest, shall we? Staring into the shadows only invites something to stare back." She put a guiding hand on Julia's shoulder, steering her back towards the hall. "Best we return to the gala. It would be a shame to let a good party go to waste."

This time, Julia didn't argue.

The night was a flurry of greetings, cheek kisses, and dances.

Julia was numb to it all. Her lips smiled, her head nodded, and her feet shuffled from one dancing partner to another, but her mind was a storm uncontained.

The queen spoke as if the White Raven—one of Azavith's thousand faces—was real and not only knew of her but meant her harm. That because of this, Dutchenson Castle was to forever be her cage and her new heart the lock that kept her there. The assuredness of her words, the panic swimming in those darkened blue pools all spoke of true fear.

And Julia knew lies. Knew their lilt on the tongue. Knew the comfort when they wrapped around the mind or when they were meant to spur the heart.

Queen Catherine hadn't been lying. And if the White Raven was real, then the rotting thing roaming the forest that took Billie, the impossible heart beating in her chest, the ever-present voice of her dead best friend were—

"Tell me, has the swan twirl reached the banquet halls where you're from?" Sir Eustace asked, her first dance partner. "You have a most interesting style, Your Highness."

The White Raven knows you're here.

"How delighted you must be to be reunited with your true family," said Lord Hammond, her next partner.

The White Raven knows you're here. Hunting you, hunting you.

"I'm curious, did you ever know you were Princess Angelina?" Lady Iyer, her third dance partner, whispered with a raised brow. "I promise I shan't tell a soul."

Hunting, hunting, HUNTINGHUNTINGHUN—

The familiar scent of bergamot and sandalwood caught Julia's attention halfway through the night. Piers approached just as the dance ended.

"Good evening, Sir Helmond. I'm afraid Her Highness is requested elsewhere at the moment."

"That's quite all right," Sir Helmond replied, quickly dropping his hands. He nodded to Julia. "It was a pleasure, Your Highness."

Julia forced a half smile before Piers ushered her out of the room. When they were in the hall alone, Piers let out a small chuckle.

"I'd say with steps like those you're all but guaranteed to bruise half the gentry."

When Julia said nothing, Piers motioned for her to follow him. "I heard the Queen spoke with you."

"How did—?"

Piers held up his hand. "If it had been the King, you and I would be having this conversation in your room with several guards present to relay back our every word." Piers stopped in front of a set of double doors. "After you, Your Highness."

The room was bathed in shadow, hiding its true size. The sweetness of kellweed smoke and woodiness of old books permeated the air. Julia ran her fingers over the velvet chair closest to her.

"Queen Catherine knew everything," Julia said with a brittle laugh. "She knew I was trying to escape tonight and even how I'd bloody do it. It was all a game to her. I must've looked like the biggest idiot." Julia dug her fingers into the chair. "You said all I had to do was play my part, *not* that I would be trapped here forever."

"You misunderstand, Your Highness. You're free to leave at any time. But if you do, I can't guarantee your safety."

"From what, the White Raven?" Julia snapped mockingly.

Piers didn't answer, but his stricken features spoke to the horrid truth Queen Catherine had alluded to on the balcony. Saliva flooded Julia's mouth as if she were to be sick. She steadied herself against the chair, swallowing over and over as Emily's tittering laughter filled her ears.

"The Majesties won't let you leave," a familiar voice said, "because you're too precious a test subject to lose." Farhan emerged from the hall and leaned against the doorway, arms folded. "And of course, the little spectacle your friend's phoenix sigil caused at the hanging. 'A Chase always rises' as they say. And what better miracle than the beloved missing princess?"

Julia's breath caught in her throat. "You ..."

"Nice to see you again, Your Highness." Farhan's gaze slid to Piers. "This has been a rather exciting experiment wouldn't you say, Lord Astley? But even so, I think we can agree your method was never destined for success. Fear may motivate her into silence, but cooperation was never an equally measured variable."

"I'm a bit disappointed, Farhan. As a man of the sciences, I assumed you would understand it best to try all possibilities. Or am I misquoting your mentor?"

Farhan frowned, annoyed. "Thanks to your dalliances, I was forced to test Her Highness's suggestibility in front of the Princess Holiant. We could've lost everything because of you."

"Ah, what's life without a bit of drama?" Piers mused, a smirk playing across his face.

"I strongly urge you do not get between Dr. Loveney and her data again. We won't have another chance at this. Too much emotion has led this experiment."

Farhan lowered his voice until it was but a murmured warning.

"Don't let the princess share Elizabeth's fate."

Julia backed away until she was in front of the window. Moonlight enshrined her, illuminating her wide eyes. This was all wrong. She was a test subject? In an experiment Piers knew about?

So he knew about my new heart ... and let it happen?

"I want to go back to the party," Julia stammered, hot tears pressing against her eyes. "Right now. Take me right now."

Piers slowly turned to face her. In the silvery glow, she could see a mixture of resolve and regret in his glassy eyes and downturned mouth. "I'm sorry, Your Highness. Please know I did this to keep you safe."

"What ar—"

Before she could finish, Farhan was across the room in the blink of an eye. He gently gripped her chin between his long fingers, forcing her to look up at him. As she stared into his grey eyes, the icy grip of fear began to melt away.

"There now, Princess. You are, and always were, Angelina Chase. Let Julia Sheffield sleep now. She is oh so very tired."

"So very tired," Julia parroted. "And ... scared. Scared the White Raven is real, scared the *Book of the True Word* is real, scared the monster that took Billie is real, scared the rumors about Emily are real, scared, so scar—"

Farhan placed his hand on her cheek. "My, my, how much Julia tries to carry. But you're not her." His eyes narrowed ever so slightly in his effort to quiet a fracturing mind.

"You're Angelina Chase, the Crown Princess. And Princess Angelina is happy. She is happy to be in Dutchenson Castle. She only wants to be in the castle where it is warm and safe."

"Warm and safe." Julia smiled dreamily. "It's so pleasant here ..."

Farhan let his hand fall. "How are you feeling, Your Highness?"

"Fine, of course," she replied with a polite, but confused smile. "Piers, can we go back to the party already? I'd hate to miss another dance." She looped her arm through his and looked up at him curiously. "Why do you look so dreary? Something wrong?"

Piers cleared his throat. "It's nothing, Your Highness. Farhan, thank you for your time. Good evening to you."

"You as well, Lord Astley." Farhan smirked as he straightened his jacket. "Do try to enjoy the party."

35

ANGELINA

"Hang my picture on the walls. Carve my name in every tree. Speak of me, dearest, in tongues known and new so that my memory may live on and always comfort you." – *Madame Patrizia,* La Stagione del Desiderio

The sun was warm on Angelina's face.

Reddish gold light danced behind her eyes. Water slipped over her body like a second skin, encasing her in its protection.

"Ange, I've just read the best story," Emily gushed. "Do you want to hear it?"

Angelina's brows knitted together. *Ange ... no, that's not my ...*

"Once upon a time," Emily began, "there was a princess who told a white raven her name."

Angelina pushed off the grassy edge and floated on her back. She closed her eyes and let her mind wander. "I've already heard that story. Tell me another."

Silence.

"Em?"

Angelina opened her eyes. The reddish gold light had slipped away. How hadn't she noticed? She righted herself as a chill blew over her exposed shoulders. The moon was hidden behind clouds, veiling the glen in shadows. She spun around but Emily was gone. Lake Promise had been transformed into a pool of black water, a mirror darkest.

"Emily?"

The loud croak of a raven pierced the silence.

Angelina's eyes flew open. She was staring at the ceiling of her room. No, not her room. A princess's room. *No,* she corrected herself, fighting off the strangeness weighing her down. *This* is *my room.*

Angelina sat up. Pinkish gold light streamed through the windows. Emily sat across from her with a book open in her lap. She wore a dress the deep red of a pomegranate and a velvet black choker tied right where …

Something …

Something … broken …

Angelina's head began to throb. Emily looked up from reading and smiled. "You really shouldn't dwell on such silly thoughts."

Angelina closed her eyes and rested her head between her legs. When the throbbing finally subsided, she noticed a white raven with piercing violet eyes perched on Emily's shoulder.

"I have a story for you," Emily said. "It's called the 'Tale of Ember and Frost.' "

The moment Angelina looked into the raven's eyes pain fluttered in her chest. She tore her gaze away, clutching the place over her heart.

"Once upon a time," Emily began, ignoring Angelina's labored breathing and sweat laden brow, "in a land faraway, there lived twin siblings named Ember and Frost."

Angelina could feel the raven's eyes on her.

Don't look don't look don't look don't—

"One day, a powerful god gave each twin a quest and one rule: complete the quest or perish."

"What were their quests?" Angelina asked.

A wicked gleam shone in Emily's eyes that set Angelina on edge.

"Why don't you find out?" She gestured to Angelina's dress cabinet in the corner of the room. Angelina's breath caught in her throat. The cabinet was open, but instead of dresses there were rows upon rows of masks. Angelina slipped out of bed and crossed the room. A particularly pretty mask caught her eye. But when she reached for it, her fingers came away sticky and red.

A scream tore from her throat.

Emily closed the book in her lap. She leaned forward, resting her chin in her hand as a thin ribbon of blood slid down from the corner of her mouth.

"They all look so lovely on you. Say, don't you think this one fits me well?" Emily gestured to her own face. "But you can have it if you want. I know you'll take it any way." Her voice twisted into an ancient croak.

"You always do."

The cabinet began to rattle. Bloody faces fell to the floor as the raven spread its massive white wings and landed on Angelina's shoulder. She screamed, trying to knock the bird away, but it sank its talons into her shoulders, anchoring itself in place. As she twisted to hit it, she glimpsed an uncanny creature her mind could only grasp in pieces: mottled grey flesh, spindly long fingers tipped in sharp, black nails and three pairs of piercing violent eyes staring back at her. Its voice was the echo of a thousand songs, the words twisting and reverberating back to her in languages lost to time until her ears finally picked out familiar word shaped sounds.

"Open the Twilight Gate to kill the dreaming gods."

Angelina fled from the room, but instead of entering the castle hallway, she found herself in a forest. A worn pathway laced with gnarled roots led to a dead end blocked by a thick wall of trees Angelina couldn't see past. Portraits hung from the trunks on either side of her. Vines clutched at their gilded edges and dug into the frames. She recognized the face of the nearest portrait: Arthur Chase, the Sun King and first ruler of Halcyon.

Angelina stepped back. She knew this place. The hall of portraits outside of the Royal Hall. But when had she been there?

At the end of the row of trees was a portrait far larger than the others. As she walked towards it, her skin itched with the feeling of being watched.

Don't look don't look don't look don't—

Where the portrait of Walter Chase, the Silent King and Emily's grandfather, should've been instead was an ornate black mirror edged in burnished filigree. Three jagged cracks split its glass face.

Suddenly, the faint reflection of a young woman appeared on the other side. A black lace veil obscured her eyes and she wore a blue dress that seemed familiar, yet not. But it was her voice, haunting and worlds away, that seized Angelina.

"The White Raven is coming for you."

Minutes, hours, days blurred together in a blissful haze.

Angelina spoke to no one. She drifted through the halls wearing a pleasant smile and a faraway, dreamy look in her eyes. None of the chambermaids spoke to her, which suited her just fine. She was perfectly content looking out at the gardens from her window and attending her lessons. She was fulfilled. Above all, she was happy.

Sometimes she would catch Beatrice looking at her, her lips pursed as if to say something. In those moments, Angelina would hold her breath, waiting, but for what she didn't know. Yet far beneath the surface a tiny part of her knew she was missing something. Knew something was beyond her reach, locked away within a coffin of frosted glass deep in the dark, twisted forest of her mind.

Tell me, she would silently urge Beatrice. *Tell me.*

But then Beatrice would avert her gaze and Angelina would breathe again. Their roles resumed and her mind softened her worries until she no longer cared about secrets or lost things.

Piers hardly visited anymore. Beatrice assured her he was very busy with her approaching Crowning.

"And what of Madelyn, Theo, and Tabitha? Are they busy too?"

"Yes dear, I'm afraid so."

Angelina shrugged. What was a little more time? They would always be together at Dutchenson Castle.

Always and forever.

The following day, the air was rife with excitement.

Chambermaids fluttered about with tablecloths and curtains tucked beneath their arms, tittering about everything from the visiting Chases to the crowds already assembled in Saint Square.

"Have you seen the queen's gown?"

"I heard the Duchess of Mayfield nearly wore the same color!"

Hushed gasping.

"Aye, but have you seen St. Dahls? I heard the vicaress agreed to open the courtyard because the cathedral was so full!"

More gasps.

"They say people came from as far north as Swallow Hill and Belton End. They must've traveled through the night to get here!"

Tsk tsks. "More like for days! I heard all the stations were brimming with people. My cousin thankfully got a train ticket, but it nearly cost him a month's salary. Can you believe it?"

"Aye, but have you seen the checkpoints? A bloody nightmare to get through. And I heard they have those horrid dogs there standing watch."

Collective sighs.

"Oh, you must mean the howlers. Awful things. But saints forbid any fateshifters make an appearance and sour everything. At least those things will protect us."

"Is it true then? Can they really smell magic? How does Dr. Loveney make them like that, you think?"

The kitchens were a hive of activity. The aroma of sticky caramel apple bakes, roasted vegetables, and spiced racks of lamb filled the castle halls. Orders for more linens and wine were being shouted alongside demands for more guards to patrol the outer rim of the city, fears of brawls at the gates lingering behind their words.

The number of guards also doubled overnight. No hallway or quarter in the castle was without at least three standing post, present but unacknowledged. Their hands clutched their sabers and rifles as they stood at attention, lips pursed and eyes alert, waiting for the worst. Crownings were a dangerous time for any kingdom. It was when members of the royal family and nobility were closest together and most vulnerable to an attack. And the Chase family was in no short supply of enemies.

But none of these matters crossed Angelina's mind sitting before her mirror. Despite being the cause for the frenzy outside, her thoughts lingered elsewhere: in the folds of her lovely white day gown, in the beautiful roses beneath her window, and with her siblings, who would be there to support her as she became inaugurated as Halcyon's Crown Princess.

She regarded her reflection and smiled. She'd never been happier. Today was her day after all. As she absently played with the lacey gold choker at her throat, a sudden urge to rip it off overcame her. She pulled it down and there, around her neck, was a faint scar that encircled her throat. The longer she stared at it, the more she realized she didn't have a memory for it.

Why couldn't she recall suffering such a grievous injury?

The faint sound of glass cracking echoed in her ears. *The chambermaids probably just dropped a wine glass,* she reassured herself. *It's none of my concern.*

But her fingers kept tracing over the scar on her neck.

Something …

Something … broken …

"Focus!" she chided herself, shaking her head. "You're being crowned today for saint's sake!"

She let out a deep breath and relaxed her shoulders. As much as she tried to block out the commotion outside her room, she knew Beatrice and her chambermaids would be in soon to add the final touches to her hair and makeup. They had placed great care into Angelina's bath and wardrobe, assuring her skin remained radiant, her hair silky and her cheeks blushing.

The first morning light outlined her drawn curtains. It was still early enough that breakfast hadn't been brought yet, but it was no bother. Angelina's appetite had weaned to almost nothing. Meanwhile, her mind raced with possibilities. *What if I trip walking up the stairs to accept my crown? What if Tabitha embarrasses me for laughs? What if I stand in the wrong place?*

Angelina fell back onto her bed. Perhaps Piers would have some words to help ease her. She desperately sought his company, even if he still held some distance towards her.

She rolled onto her side. As her eyes began to close, her mind drifted to the girl in the pomegranate red dress from her dream. Why couldn't she recall the girl's name? Had she known her once upon a time?

A knock rattled across her door. Angelina, eager for a distraction, jumped up to answer.

"Oh, Beatrice, I—"

Tabitha shoved her back inside and shut the door before Angelina could say another word.

"Tabitha?"

"I haven't much time." She walked over to the window and peered out into the gardens. Outside, the distant sound of dog barks and shouting could be heard. "Are you okay?"

"Why wouldn't I be okay?" Angelina folded her arms. "Is something wrong?"

Tabitha regarded her from the window with a mixture of weariness and irritation. "What's your name?"

Angelina scoffed. "Very funny."

"This isn't a game," Tabitha snapped. "Tell me your name."

"Yes, because it hasn't been Angelina your whole life. Now can—Wait, what are you doing?"

"Hold still and don't blink." Tabitha held either side of Angelina's face and stared into her eyes. After a minute or so, her lips twisted into a scowl and she dropped her hands. "I knew it. He did something to you."

Angelina rolled her eyes. "Tabitha, really, I'm fine. I swear no one has done anything to me. Whatever it is you're on about, I really don't have time for it today. Piers will have my head if I'm late."

As if on cue, a knock rattled across the door. "Your Highness?"

"Yes, come in, Beatrice."

As Beatrice opened the door, Tabitha darted out swift as a cat. Beatrice looked at Angelina with a raised brow, but Angelina was too busy running her fingers over the shimmering ivory and gold bodice in Beatrice's outstretched hands to notice.

"Oh, Beatrice it's perfect."

As she poured over the golden layered skirts, Angelina soon forgot all about Tabitha's odd visit and her even odder accusation.

Her crowning was here.

Thousands of onlookers crowded together along the streets and balconies of Lordhaven.

Children waved crimson and gold streamers from their upstairs windows. Down below, the royal precession inched along Downing Way in their journey to St. Dahls cathedral. Bystanders surged against the storm wall of guards in hopes of glimpsing the lost princess through her carriage window.

"Remember, Your Highness," Piers reiterated. "It's just how we rehearsed. Smile and wave."

"The whole way?" Angelina said through her plastered smile.

"The whole way."

Angelina inwardly sighed but maintained her perfect smile and her genteel wave. When she finally lowered her arm several minutes later for a break, she said in a low whisper, "Piers, can I ask you something?"

"Of course."

"Did something strange happen to me?"

"I beg your pardon?"

Angelina shifted in her seat.

"Tabitha seems to think something happened to me. She looked frightened this morning. Upset. And I—" Angelina looked up to see Piers staring at her. "It's silly, but I took it maybe that was why her, Theo, and Madelyn were avoiding me."

Piers let out a sigh. "No one is avoiding you, Your Highness. And I assure you all is well. Everyone's emotions are running higher than usual, is all."

Angelina shifted her gaze to the window. Countless onlookers crammed together behind the stoic wall of guards. But behind the smiling faces she caught a glimpse of a sign the guards had missed.

DEMON was painted in thick black letters.

Angelina's breath caught. She'd seen that word before. A memory pulled at her, but the harder she tried to focus on it the more her head began to hurt. It didn't make her happy and she wanted to be happy. She wanted to stay warm and happy and safe.

Safe … happy … safe … happy … safe …

He did something to you.

The roar of the crowd invaded the carriage. Angelina pushed away the ill-painted sign in her mind and focused on a platoon of guards lined on either side of St. Dahls' towering gated entrance.

"Princess Angelina! Princess Angelina! This way! Over here! Princess Angelina!"

Piers held out his hand and shouted in her ear, "Follow me!"

Angelina was whisked from the comforts of the carriage to the largest and oldest cathedral in the kingdom. Inside, the ribbed vault ceiling rose high enough not even the light fully reached its corners. Two tiers of stained glass windows lined either side of the walls. Famous scenes from the *Book of the True Word* came to life within their panes, each more beautiful and bloodier than the last.

"Your Highness," Piers repeated, gripping her shoulder. "This way."

Angelina turned away from the windows and recognized a few of the faces from her lessons. Seated in the rows before her were dukes, viscounts, earls, barons, governors, and judges from all across Halcyon. In the balconies above, the other Sacred Seven families watched their future queen—yet another Chase—in silent judgement.

But it was behind the pulpit that stood the most powerful family of all—her family, the Chases. They formed a semicircle, with the Duchess of Chatwyn, Princess Ellen, her husband, Lord Gideon, Earl of Tyne and their five children standing on the left. On the right stood Duke of Maycot, Prince Roger and his wife, Lady Maxine, Countess of Harwell surrounded by their four children. And finally in the center of the chancel, standing above the rest was King Leonard and Queen Catherine. At their sides stood Madelyn, Theo, and Tabitha. Madelyn and Theo flashed weary smiles, but it was Tabitha who kept her eyes trained on the ground.

Heat prickled Angelina's neck. "Piers, I—"

"You can do this," he whispered in her ear. "You have to."

With a small nudge, he urged her forward. Arms held modestly in front of her, Angelina pressed on with reserve. A cold sheen of sweat clung to her back.

Warm and happy and safe.

"Your Highness." A tall woman with a cloud of dark, tight curls and warm honey brown eyes opened her arms. "May I welcome you to St. Dahls." The Vicaress Helena Vowl, Lady Bishop and head of the church, bowed and touched her right hand to her left shoulder. There, imprinted on her fingers was the First Ordinance, one of seven holy scriptures that swirled along her wrist and disappeared into her billowing white sleeves.

"By the kind hand of the saints above, you have been reunited with us, Maiden of Lordhaven," the vicaress proclaimed, her voice carrying through the cathedral with the might of a thousand wings. "May you rise with the blood of the Phoenix, your father, and soar with the blood of the Pegasus, your mother. For today we are given a gift of hope and strength with the return of the Duchess of Bethel, middle daughter of His Majesty King Leonard William Louis Chase and Her Majesty Queen Catherine Almira Lillian Chase. Now step forth, Maiden."

With the eyes of the nobility behind her and the eyes of her family before her, Angelina took a hesitant step forward. Above her towered the image of the Saint Father and his disciples at the First Miracle—the discovery of snake oil.

The vicaress spread her arms wide and tilted her head back. "Bring forth the strength of the Kingdom's Holy Warriors and Champions of Valor." With that command, the Knights of the Divine Crusade and the Knights of the Royal Order raised their swords. A man dressed in navy robes appeared at Vicaress Helena's side holding a white satin pillow. Atop it sat a magnificent tiara inlaid with diamonds and garnets, the royal jewel of the Chases. The vicaress took the tiara and held it above Angelina's head.

"With the power invested in me from the Saint Father and the kingdom of Halcyon as witness, I, the Reverend Vicaress Helena Vowl, Lady Bishop of Glasshern, proclaim this child, Angelina Joanna Brynn Chase, Crown Princess of Halcyon and Duchess of Bethel."

The cathedral resonated with applause. Everyone in the audience rose from their seats, tears welling in the eyes of several attendees. A brilliant flame of joy sparked within Angelina as the vicaress placed the tiara upon her head.

Suddenly, a familiar voice whispered into her ear. The girl in the red dress from her dream. *"Heavy, isn't it?"*

Angelina spun around, but only the applauding crowd was at her back. Her eyes immediately went to Audrey, why she couldn't say, but the delight in her cousin's impish smile sent goosebumps up her arms. Piers materialized beside her and intertwined his arm with hers just as the vicaress announced, "And now, Your Royal Highness, step forth into a new dawn. May the Saint Father's light guide you."

As Angelina took her first step forward as the official crown princess, she caught sight of her father and a fleeting glimpse of pride across his face. She smiled, but something within her felt different. Peculiar.

Resentful.

She looked away and once again found herself swept up in the moment of celebration. As she walked arm in arm with Piers, the echo of the audience's claps silencing her steps, a new emotion took hold of her. It wasn't until the doors of St. Dahls opened and they were met with the deafening roar of the cheering crowd did Angelina place its name.

Hope.

36

TOBIAS

"**L**ordhaven is quite a curious splendor. Only in the Bowery can I rub elbows with lords and beggars at the same table. I don't blame anyone who wouldn't find it to their tastes, but I imagine there are others who couldn't fathom in their wildest dreams of ever leaving. I must admit I haven't decided yet where I fall on the matter." – *Kitra Gillis, traveler, letter to her brother*

A fine, misty rain dampened Lordhaven just as Tobias left the train station. Burning coal and metal hung thick on the dewy air. He ducked beneath a nearby awning as the last few boarding passengers scuttled past to the screeching whistle of the next departing train.

He pulled out his two tickets to Debney. Months of saving gone in one five minute purchase. He sighed and tucked the tickets back in his pocket. The train gave one last screech as the porters pulled up the train car steps.

Just a few more hours and Lucy and I will be free of this place. Tobias sighed, leaning against the outside station wall. He stared up at the mottled grey sky, beyond the cramped flats stained by factory soot, the carved stone cathedrals with colorful glass eyes, and the sleepless pubs. Stray droplets fell across his cheek but he made no move to wipe them away.

A young man with light blond hair walked past with his mother. Tobias stared, thinking how similar he looked to Jóhann.

A bone reader who had come to warn Halcyon a monster from legend was hiding in its shadows. Tobias sunk against the wall, crouched on the balls of his feet. Jóhann shouldn't have mattered. He had helped him, hadn't he? Warned him to let his silly hero journey go and return to Soliljin.

But the image of the white-haired young man, Diðrik, slumped against the alleyway wall with a collar of blood seeping down his chest and the Seadevil spinning on his own hook waited for him when he closed his eyes. All fates awaiting Jóhann if he didn't leave Lordhaven. Tobias gritted his teeth together.

"Seven bloody hells," he cursed beneath his breath as he stepped into the rainy morning towards the Portkey.

A tepid breeze carried on Tobias's heels as he neared the Portkey. He slipped beneath the half-rotted partition and began to scale the ladder.

When he reached the landing he called out, "Oi, bedroll stealer! It's me!"

No response.

He can't still be sour can he? Tobias wondered. Maybe he was asleep. Tobias leapt across the rooftops, careful to pitch his weight forward given the damp landing and peered into his old flat.

"Jóhann?"

The room was empty. The only sign Jóhann had been there were the neatly folded blankets placed at the end of the mattress. On top of the blankets was a folded note.

Tobias grabbed it as dread gnawed at him.

"Tobias, thank you for everything. I hope our paths can cross again. I'm going to find Porter.

Yours,

Jóhann."

Tobias crumpled the note and tossed it into the corner. To hell with this, all of this.

"Bloody idiot!" Tobias bellowed, kicking the blankets. The outburst didn't make him feel any better, which pissed him off even more. He paced the room, staring at nothing in particular. So what if Jóhann ran off to fight storybook monsters? It wasn't his fight. He had his own problems.

But something about the whole situation wouldn't leave him. If it was the Seadevils targeting the voxossa, what was their motive for doing so? Was someone paying them for the hit? And if so, was it the same person that started the gang war? And how did the White Raven tie into their plans?

Just go to Debney with Lucy and be done with it, the logical part of his brain urged. He'd already stuck his neck out for Jóhann once and it nearly had gotten them both killed.

Venturing into Seadevil territory to go to the Drunken Jester in hopes of finding Jóhann was worse than a terrible idea.

Tobias stopped pacing. He unclenched his hands and stared at them for several minutes. Hands that had stolen to help feed himself and Lucy. Hands that had held pipes to knock out drunks for coin to live another day. Hands that carved out a pair of rare eyes to give Lucy the safe and mundane childhood he never had.

When he stepped out onto the ledge, the smell of garbage and rain wafted up from the streets below.

He was a Market Streeter and this was his turf to protect. *Let the bedroll stealer chase his monsters,* Tobias decided. *But the Seadevils aren't going to have him.*

The Drunken Jester was tucked away deep in the Bowery, a small area within the Trade District near Port Vale best known for their cheap kitten houses, rot gut barrel liquor, and an ever churning rumor mill thanks to the steady stream of sailors, traders, pirates and smugglers that passed through each day. But while the Bowery offered escape for those given the right price, it lacked the elegance and allure of the North Rim. The Bowery was a surly mistress who knew her worth and stated things plain. It was one of the only areas in Lordhaven the City Watch didn't control with an iron fist, lending an air of lawlessness that called out to the worst in the kingdom like a siren song.

It hadn't taken long for Tobias to find the Drunken Jester. Five sterlings for a dock hand's hat and another three for directions had been the best deal all day. Tobias lowered the brim of the cap to cover his curls. Although he was only a clobber and by no means anyone of importance, in the back of his mind was the gleaming red hook ready to impale him next.

Taking in a deep breath, Tobias crossed Hadley Row. At this early hour, the Bowery crawled with sailors and traders just finishing their night romps and lumbering back to the docks or shuffling to a kitten house to nurse their hangovers.

Tobias weaved through the crowded streets while narrowly avoiding stepping in horse droppings. The Drunken Jester was smaller than he expected, about half the size of Higdin's with a letterbox narrowness that forced people together. Every seat on the bar was taken except the last to the right. Tobias sat and waved down the barmaid.

"What can I do you for?"

"I'm looking for Edgar Porter. Know where I can find him?"

The barmaid raised a penciled brow as she laid a chubby hand on the counter. A pleasant floral perfume wafted off her.

"Aren't you a bit young for these parts, lad?" Her wine red lips quirked upwards, but her voice carried no malice.

"You know him or not? I promise I'll be on my way after."

The woman studied him for a moment then shrugged. "Fine, I'll bite. But information is for paying customers only. This ain't no charity house."

Tobias bought a cider that looked too brackish to be safe. Scribbled on a napkin beneath the glass was Porter's address. When Tobias looked up to thank the barmaid, she'd already moved on to another customer a few seats down. He unfurled the paper and saw it was a flat not far from Hadley Row.

You better be waiting for me alive and well, bedroll stealer.

Porter's flat was on the third floor of a nondescript brownstone on Tenley Street. A few potted plants lined the stairs of the building where a thin orange tabby slept beneath an awning, unbothered by the light but steady drizzle of rain. Tobias looked up and down the street. A few shops dotted the far end, but otherwise it was a quiet, unremarkable neighborhood.

Tobias traveled up the creaking wooden stairs until he reached the third-floor landing. He knocked on unit 1312. No response. He knocked again and waited.

"Jóhann?" he called. "Mr. Porter?"

Looking over his shoulder, he tried the door handle. To his surprise, it opened. "Hello? Mr. Porter? Jóhann?"

As soon as he stepped into the flat, he smelled the sharp tang of smoke. Something had burned not long ago.

"Jóhann?"

Tobias slowly stepped further into the flat. As he came out of the entry hall, something shifted in his peripheral. He turned and came face to face with Elspeth, one of five Market Streeter Commanders, perched on top of a table. Several folders and ledgers were scattered in front of her, with even more tossed on the floor. When she looked up from the papers in her hand, her unblinking eyes crinkled with her hidden smile.

"My, my, Tobias boy. You're quite far from your nest." She tutted. "Naughty, naughty."

It took a moment for Tobias to find his voice. When he did, it cracked with disbelief. "W-What're you doing here? Where's Porter?"

Elspeth cocked her head to the side. "I could ask you the same, no?"

"Save your riddles, croon. Where is Porter?"

Elspeth resumed looking through the papers in her hand. After a few seconds of unnerving silence, she finally said, "Not who you're looking for, though, hmm? No, no, not at all. You want the white haired one."

Tobias took a step back. How did she know about Jóhann? He'd been so careful to hide him away. Not even Ezra or Tavia knew about him.

"Was Jóhann here? Where did he go?"

"Taken to Kingtide's playroom, I'm afraid." Elspeth jumped down to the floor, landing on her feet with the grace of a cat. "Only a short jaunt through the sewers if you know the way. Perhaps the Lost Girls can help you navigate if they're feeling generous. Fickle, fickle, those little sewer rats."

She tossed a letter at Tobias's feet and resumed her shuffling. Tobias picked it up with a clenched jaw. "Now leave me, Tobias boy. I'm rather busy."

"Who is Kingtide?"

Elspeth regarded him with her wide, glassy eyes. A curious look came over her.

"Not sleeping well, Tobias boy? Do you dream of monsters? Or perhaps wolves?" She let out a shrill laugh. "Best mind your time. Yorin shall have you soon enough!"

Tobias fled from the flat, the letter clenched in his hand and the stench of smoke curled in his nose.

37

TOBIAS

"Little miss, little miss,
one day gone.
Waited out the night
and left with the dawn.
Little miss, little miss,
one week away.
Never to return,
in the sewers she'll stay."
– *Margot Little,* "The Lost Girls," A Collection of Halcyonian Nursery Rhymes, Vol. II

Tobias kept off the main streets until he reached the Theatre District.

Once he crossed the Dressell Bridge, his muscles began to relax. He was out of Seadevil territory. Thunder rumbled above him like the growl of an unseen beast. He sat on the steps of the Thistle and Twine bookshop and pulled the letter Elspeth had given him from his pocket. He read it, re-read it and then read it again for good measure.

Diðrik,

This will be my last letter. I'm being watched. Port Vale is no longer secure. Send your men to Hebdon Arch and ask for Ramil at the Portmaster's station.

Saints be with you.

E.P.

Tobias lifted his gaze. The street bristled with passersby. Dreary-eyed factory workers shuffled past preening mothers fussing after their children. A pair of smartly dressed men with waif thin moustaches and bright smiles passed him on the stairs and disappeared into the bookshop. Life continued to churn forward, even if Jóhann wasn't there.

Tobias folded the letter and tucked it back into his pocket. What had Elspeth been doing at Porter's apartment? Was she the one who'd been watching him? But the Market Streeters had nothing to do with the voxossa or their bone prophecy ... or did they?

Tobias stood and made his way to the Distillery. This time, he needed back-up.

Tavia and Ezra were playing Nines when Tobias returned to the Distillery.

Charley was asleep on the top bunk, his soiled boots from grave robbing tossed to the side.

"Back already?" Tavia said, looking over the rim of her cards. "Shouldn't you be helping Lucy get ready for her trip?"

"Aye, but first I need a favor. There's a friend who's been taken to the sewers and I gotta get him out."

Tavia and Ezra both replied, "The sewers?"

The words curdled in the air. Tobias winced, realizing how ridiculous he sounded. But the truth was so rarely neat. He filled them in on meeting Jóhann, their run in with the Seadevils, and Jóhann's reason for seeking out Porter. Ezra stared blankly at his cards, but Tavia, ever the sharp one, cast hers aside to focus on the absurdity at hand.

"So you're saying Jóhann, who came from Soliljin and claims to read *bones*, was looking for a merchant that knew some duke who agreed to pass along a message that the White Raven is in Halcyon? And he's been taken by a bloke named Kingtide to the sewers?"

"Wait, the White Raven?" Ezra interjected. "As in, the demon king Azavith? You serious right now, mate?"

"Look, I know it sounds like absolute rubbish, but that's what Elspeth said. There's also a room somewhere in the sewers that this Kingtide fellow goes to. That's all I know."

"Are you mad?" Tavia scolded beneath her breath. "If Marcellus found out you were anywhere *near* Port Vale, he'd have your head on a pike right now."

"She's right, mate," Ezra added. "This is courtin' death. If Elspeth is involved, Marcellus probably doesn't want anyone low rung knowing about it."

"So what am I supposed to do, Ez? Just let Jóhann die?" Tobias fired back.

Tavia began to say something but stopped herself. She glanced at Charley, who was now snoring, and motioned to the hall. When it was just the three of them, Tavia whispered, "I want to help you, we both do, but Deadeye and his goons are knocking on our door. It's bad timing. And what happened to you leaving town with Lucy? Are you seriously going to give that up to help someone you just met?" She folded her arms. "He could be lying, Toby. This could be some farce by the Seadevils."

Tobias ran a hand through his curls. "I know, but I can't just leave him, Tavia." The truth sat on the tip of his tongue as clear and sharp as a glass shard. But no matter how he tried to say it, how he tried to shift the words, only pain would follow.

My mum asked me to always look after Jonah and Lucy, but I messed up.

I fell asleep and he was gone.

I let Jonah get taken.

I broke my promise.

"Look, Jóhann's an idiot all right? Him and his mates got involved with some bad folks that he thinks are the White Raven and... I didn't help him when he asked," Tobias said with a sigh. "Now he's been kidnapped, and it doesn't sit right, okay? So will you help me or not?"

Tavia and Ezra exchanged glances.

"Rum Petey can cover our collection duties for today. He owes me a favor." Ezra looked over at Tavia who glared at Tobias.

"Ugh, you always have absolute piss poor timing, Tobias Flemming," she groaned, sulking back into Ezra and Charley's room. "Why can't you play saint *after* the Seadevils are sorted?"

"And where's the fun in that?" Tobias replied, unable to hide his smile. How lucky he was to count them as friends.

"Fine. Ezra, you go talk to Rum Petey. Tobias, lift some clementines from the kitchens. I'll meet you both at the sewer entrance in fifteen minutes."

"Wait, why do we need clementines?"

Tavia rolled her eyes. "For the Lost Girls, obviously. Unless you know your way around the sewers."

Tobias bowed his head. He didn't have the first idea about navigating the belly of Lordhaven, let alone avoiding the rumored terrors that lurked within.

"Didn't you used to live with them?" Tobias asked.

"I was just a tyke when they took me in. I barely remember it." Tavia shrugged her shoulders. "How scary can a bunch of runaway girls be?"

A putrid stench greeted Ezra and Tobias before the sewers came into view. Tavia had already removed part of the opening tunnel's large, rotted grate by the time the pair approached. Laying at her feet was a sign that read: NO TRESPASSING BY ORDER OF THE LORDHAVEN CITY WATCH. Out across the bay, barges ferried up and down the Dorne's shipping lanes. Thick plumes of smoke trailed behind them, smudging the greyish yellow sky with oily streaks.

Tobias peered into the dark maw of the sewer. Stagnant air cloistered around him like the hot breath of an animal.

"I already made our request. Now time to make the offering." Tavia leaned in and pointed to a small, makeshift altar. "There. Place the clementines on top. Then we wait."

Ezra clicked his tongue. "Are we sure they're going to help us and not just, I dunno, kill us and dump our bodies in the wastes for sport?"

Tavia smirked. "If you ask nicely, I'm sure they won't kill you."

Ezra looked at Tobias, who shrugged and stepped inside the tunnel, his steps echoing as he cut across a thin stream of water.

"I swear, if we make it out of this alive, I want a meat pie from the shop on King Street from *each* of you," Ezra called behind him.

Tobias took slow, steady steps toward the altar. It was little more than a makeshift shoeshiner's bench. A sign tacked to it read "MAY THEY GUIDE".

Tobias swallowed hard and set down the clementines. As he did, his gaze hooked onto the sign. *May they guide.* But what if they didn't? Or what if they guided you where you didn't want to go?

No, he was getting ahead of himself. This wasn't the time to let his nerves win.

As he began walking back—Ezra and Tavia bickering just a stone's throw away—a single sound made Tobias pause. A second echo reverberated behind him.

A second pair of feet stopping.

Tobias spun around to see a little girl around seven or eight standing near the altar, staring at him with wide, hazel eyes. In the half shadow of the tunnel, he could barely make out her pale skin, long stringy hair and tattered dress.

"You brought my favorite!" The girl reached into the bag Tobias had just set down and pulled out a clementine. She bit into it like an apple, skin and all with a grin of utter delight.

"I like you," she said between mouthfuls.

Tobias stood, stupefied, at the girl before him.

"You're a Lost Girl, right?" Tavia asked, coming up from behind. Ezra slinked in behind her. "That was ... fast."

"These are my favorite. I smelt them." She plopped the last bite of clementine into her mouth and chewed loudly. Sticky juice slid down her chin but she made no attempt to wipe it away.

"If you're not quick, you have to share."

"Top line manners down here," Ezra mumbled before Tavia elbowed him.

"You'll help guide us then?" Tobias interjected. "You can take us to Kingtide's playroom?"

The girl took another clementine and bit into it, tearing away the skin with small, sharp teeth.

"That's a very bad place," the girl said between loud chews. "Why do you want to go there?"

"Do you know the way or not?" Tavia snapped.

"Tavia, easy," Ezra murmured.

"What? Our offering was accepted. That should be good enough." Tavia leveled a glare at the girl. "Or is there a problem?"

The girl locked eyes with Tavia for a moment too long. She gestured to the first tunnel on the left. "You'll want to stay close."

"Why, there's not something down here is there?" Ezra's chuckles teetered into nervous laughter when the girl didn't respond.

"The sewer's secrets aren't ours to give." Another girl, a few years older than the Market Streeters, emerged from the depths of a far-off tunnel. She had smokey ebony eyes and slim braids tied at her neck. Unlike the younger girl's tattered dress, the young woman had a tailored cloak that buttoned at her throat and fitted trousers. Both were barefoot but traversed the slick sewer stone with practiced ease.

The little girl held the bag of clementines close to her chest. Like a feral sewer cat, she hissed at the older one. "You can't have any! I got them first! They're my favorite."

"You can keep them, Keeley. I won't tell."

Keeley narrowed her eyes and took another bite of the clementine in her hand. She clutched the bag to her chest as she ate.

The older girl turned to the others. "You'll have to forgive Keeley. She isn't a surface child."

"Are you a Lost Girl too?" Tobias ventured.

"Yes. And I'll take you to Kingtide's playroom. Keeley, off with you."

"But—"

"Skaazi bak tu."

Keeley flinched as if struck. "You don't have to be so mean, Mira." Keeley slunk past the group and skittered up a low wall, then hoisted herself into the darkness of an open pipe.

Tavia cleared her throat. "We didn't mean to cause any trouble."

"She knows better," Mira replied curtly, glancing at the open pipe Keeley disappeared into. "We don't normally approach Kingtide's space, and the young ones are strictly forbidden going near the area at all." Her gaze hardened. "His appetite for torture is bottomless. He doesn't mind us and we don't mind him, but I'll do my best to get you as close as I can."

Tobias stared into the darkness ahead. *We're coming, Jóhann.*

"So if you lot left society and came to live in the sewers," Ezra ventured, "and there's some torturer living here, too, why haven't you, y'know, taken him out?"

Mira didn't hesitate. "Not worth the trouble it'd bring us."

Trouble? Tobias wanted to press further, but Mira held up a hand. The group fell silent as she turned towards the cavernous dark behind them. She kneeled down, hand still raised, and slowly reached into her cloak. With her free hand she flicked a pebble into the darkness. It made a soft *plop* into the water and then nothing.

Silence.

Tobias's skin felt too tight. His eyes burned into Mira's raised hand as if it would somehow anchor him through the storm they suddenly found themselves in. Silence continued to press against them, tightening around their throats.

A sudden gurgling sound erupted from the darkness. The scratch of unseen claws against the slick, wet stone was swallowed by the splash of something heavy slicing through the river of sewer water. It was over in seconds. If Tobias hadn't seen the ripples trickle in from the shadowy depths ahead, he'd have thought the whole thing a trick of the mind.

"What *was* that?" Ezra squeaked.

"We have to move." Mira lowered her hand and stood. "Keep to the walls. And don't look in the water."

"Is it blind?" Tavia whispered.

"Only the front face."

Tobias swallowed down bile. Stopping meant death. He pressed forward into the cloying shadows, careful to inhale as few rancid breaths as possible.

As Mira led them down another passageway, something chittered overhead, scurrying along with the ceiling faster than Tobias could keep pace. Everyone kept their gazes trained forward. Staring into the darkness only invited it to stare back.

As they approached two tunnels, Mira motioned to take the left one. It was the smaller of the two and forced each of them into an awkward half crouch to move forward. Tobias's shoulders scraped against the sides of the tunnel and his lower back protested every step. He walked slowly to avoid catching Mira's heels, but nearly pitched forward when Ezra nicked the back of his ankle.

"Bloody hell, Ez, am I to carry you on piggyback?"

"Sorry, sorry. Just trying to keep close is all."

"Shut up, you two," Tavia hissed. "You want him to hear us coming?"

Mira was first out of the tunnel, then Tobias, then Ezra and lastly Tavia. Once they all gathered themselves, much to the relief of their backs and necks, Mira pointed to the second door in a long hallway leading to another waterway passage. A single snake oil lantern hung outside the door.

Kingtide was in.

Mira turned towards the trio. A nervous hitch in her voice betrayed her otherwise stony demeanor.

"Beyond that door is Kingtide's playroom. Should you survive, passage back to the surface will be waiting. May your saints be with you."

She disappeared into the darkness of the hall up ahead. Once she was gone, Tavia pulled out a knife from her thigh holster. "We have numbers and the element of surprise. I say we rush it."

Ezra searched the ceiling. "Maybe there's a vent or something we can sneak through?"

Tobias racked his brain for a plan, but panic, fear, anger, and excitement all jumbled together in his mind, drowning out everything and offering nothing.

But before he or Ezra could protest, Tavia was halfway to the door. Tobias snapped back to the present and readied his own knife hidden in his right boot. Behind him, Ezra swore under his breath. The door opened into a long, shadowy tunnel. A second door was open at the end of it leading to a room out of view. A faint light came from inside and the sound of an unfamiliar voice.

"Tough one, aren't you?" A shriek of laughter. "Brilliant, brilliant! Ah, it's so incredibly *boring* when they crack early. Now let's go again, shall we? What did those bones tell you, hmm? Where's that pesky little raven hiding?"

The trio slowly approached, but Tobias stopped in his tracks when he heard Jóhann's voice.

"Not your message to h-hear," he sputtered in a gravelly voice.

Kingtide tsked. "I don't think I like that answer."

Jóhann's gargled screams reverberated through the hall as if he were drowning. Tobias rushed forward, heart pounding in his ears, but Tavia was faster. She burst into the room, daggers raised and teeth bared. Tobias arrived only a moment before Tavia embedded one of her dagger blades into Kingtide's shoulder, just shy of his neck.

He doubled over and howled in pain, stumbling to the far wall and away from the group. He was all gangly pale limbs and taut, lean muscle, a wild mass of blond hair brushing over his sharp cheek bones. As Ezra rushed to Jóhann's side to free him from the table he was strapped to, instinct rooted Tobias in place.

Kingtide took a deep, ragged breath and pulled Tavia's dagger out with a grunt. "Oh, there's a does it."

He held the bloody dagger in one hand and clasped the wound on his shoulder with the other. Suddenly, his blood quivered and retracted back through his fingers and up his arm. When Kingtide lowered his hand, the wound and any blood that had been there was gone.

"Fateshifter," Tobias murmured. *Seven bloody damn hells.*

"Got me good there, little miss." Kingtide's yellow-toothed grin split his face in two, his green eyes gleeful. "Aiming for the neck were you? Mm, I could tell. Good on you. No pansy games. Straight to the bloody reaper!" He doubled over with laughter as nausea rippled through Tobias's body.

"But if you're gonna bite to kill, love, you let go when the job is done." Kingtide's hands shot out in front of him. In the next breath, Ezra and Tavia were both doubled over, hands at their throats, gasping for air as blood filled their lungs.

Tobias shuddered. *He's going to kill them.*

The clarity was sudden and absolute. It was beyond reason or logic or hunch—it was instinct. It was survival.

White hot pain pressed behind Tobias's eyes. It raced down his nerves like a flash fire until every inch of him thrummed with it. Muscle and bone shifted beneath his skin and the rippling pain forced him to the ground on all fours.

A guttural snarl bellowed through the room, but Tobias heard it as a far-off echo. His mind had sunken beneath the unseen depths of his subconscious as a wolfish beast rose to take his place.

A hungering madness with two dark moons over its eyes.

Tobias' hulking body lunge forward, his razor-sharp teeth slicing through Kingtide's flesh and piercing through bone, but it was a distant feeling. Those were and were not things he had done. There was no joy, no pleasure, no disgust.

Only instinct.

His mouth was sticky and hot. The taste of salt and copper spread across his tongue and down his throat. From within the deep recesses of himself, he watched through a distorted lens as he tossed aside what remained of Kingtide. He heard the fateshifter's body hit the wall with a thud and felt nothing. He sensed hundreds of eyes watching him from the shadows, ancient things that smelled like no scent he could place, yet he was unafraid. When he looked over his shoulder, Tavia's stared back in horrific rapture. Ezra lay crumpled on the floor, alive but unconscious.

Jóhann stared at him from the table, his bloodshot eyes almost sorrowful. His throat was too sore to give his words voice, but Tobias read his lips. "*Come back.*"

And then all was dark again and Tobias was rising, higher and higher, with breath hot in his lungs and blood sharp in his mouth.

38

Nathaniel

"And she pleaded, with trembling lips, to not forgive her deeds for they were not wrong. The White Raven had shown her truth. She was grateful. There was nothing to regret." – *Official statement from Father Hermon Parlow, holy officiant to the sentencing of Hazel Barnett to the pyre, the 22nd of Bloomleaf, 1707*

A dense fog clotted the neighborhood of Carnberg.

Nestled on the southern edge of Lordhaven's Garden District, streetlamps dotted the muted corridor, their flickering snakelight illuminating the golden family crests emblazoned on each iron gate. Nathaniel was grateful for the clouded skies, relieved of the headaches prolonged sunlight sometimes caused duskborn.

His carriage came to a halt in front of a nondescript two story townhouse nestled between two sprawling manors.

Brown door, chipped paint. No knocker. Dark brick exterior, Nathaniel repeated in his mind. The townhouse was frustratingly plain, but Sampson's warning had been clear: unlike its neighbors, the townhouse faded from memory if one looked away long enough. Holding onto its details and shape in one's mind would help to "ground" it.

"We've arrived, Master Trevet," Anders said through the driver's partition.

"Thank you, Anders." Nathaniel stepped out just as another carriage emblazoned with a double swan crest ambled past. The Walcrofts, a highborn family with ties to the Order at least three generations back. Nathaniel grimaced as the carriage disappeared around the corner. A sobering reminder he had to move quickly lest Claude's plan come to fruition before he could secure the eternal heart.

Nathaniel walked up to the front door, surprised to find it unlocked. As he opened it, a musky, earthen odor assailed his nose. A wooden stairwell rife with age and sag bent into a sharp left that led to a barely visible door upstairs. The stairs creaked beneath him, but it was Nathaniel whose breath rattled with each step he took. By the sixth step he was hunched over, winded and sweaty.

As Nathaniel struggled to catch his breath, he noticed a handful of small runes carved into each step: the work of a particularly gifted soothsayer. One who had knowledge she shouldn't.

An older woman with long, silky grey hair stood at the top of the stairs. Layers of tasseled shawls in various shades of indigo draped over her thin shoulders. An apathetic look crossed her wrinkled face.

"Not fond of visitors, Lady Cavall?" Nathaniel called up to her.

Lady Cavall said nothing at first, only continued to stare down at Nathaniel as if he were a stain upon her rug. "If you're too weak to overcome a simple runic inscription then you're not worth talking to. Get on with it then or leave. I needn't care either way."

She closed the door behind her. Nathaniel fought the urge to snap her in two and instead pushed on against the runes. In no world would he, Nathaniel Trevet, be bested by some enchanted stairs and let Claude have his way.

When he finally reached the top, nearly twenty minutes later, Lady Cavall opened her door and reluctantly stepped aside. Her eyes, a waxen blue, were like two spring moons staring into the darkness, clear and all-seeing. Up close, something in her movement spoke of strength, as if she only appeared aged by some trick of the light.

"I greatly appreciate you meeting with me, Lady Cavall," Nathaniel said once he'd regained his composure. "You'll have to forgive my forwardness, but I abhor your stairwell."

Her thin red lips curled back, caught between a snarl and a smile. "I find those with a great enough need fare the journey. Come now, you've taken up enough of my time as it is."

Nathaniel followed behind Lady Cavall. Silk scarves of varies shades of fuchsia, violet and magenta hung over most of the antique furniture. Candles covered nearly every tabletop, but only a handful were lit. Nathaniel immediately wished for the outside air instead of the stuffy confines of the soothsayer's flat, but he didn't dare ask her to open a window. It would be all too easy for a watcher, vora or chimney sweep to overhear and sell the information to the highest bidder.

Lady Cavall led him to a table draped in silk tapestry.

"Tea?" she asked as he took a seat.

"No, thank you."

"Funny, your mum always denied tea, too." When she returned to the table a few minutes later, she took a seat across from Nathaniel with a cup of tea that smelled of honey and elderberries. Between them was a wooden board with an amethyst triangle embedded in its center. A peculiar feeling came over Nathaniel when he looked at the board as if it possessed its own power.

"Is this the board you used during my mother's readings?"

"Yes." She eyed Nathaniel curiously. "You're familiar with spirit boards then?"

"I've never seen one like this. It's quite ... plain."

"Hmph" Lady Cavall grunted, looking off into the distance. "Those silly imitations used by alley tellers in the Rim aren't part of any real craft other than thievery and pomp. A true spirit board must have certain traits or else it's useless."

Candlelight glinted off Lady Cavell's myriad of gold rings. Gemstones were nestled into some while others had runes carved into them. Her eyes, focused on a distant point, suddenly fixated on Nathaniel once more. Her words pierced like thorns through skin. "You went through a lot of trouble to find me. Not many would have the gall to use a vora."

"I have friends in high places."

"Clever. But know I only took your request out of respect for my prior patronage to Lady Trevet. Voras are absolute pests for spiritualists and the wards against them are terribly troublesome and expensive."

"Feel free to forward your next service bill to my residence." Nathaniel cleared his throat. "Now, there's someone I wish to find and I believe you're the best one for the task."

Lady Cavall was silent a moment before replying. "Did your mother speak of her readings to you?"

"No, never."

"She was a very private woman. I see she's shaped you to be the same. Quite the number of secrets you must have carried all these years." Lady Cavall leaned back in her seat, lifting her chin and studying Nathaniel's youthful face. "How very curious indeed."

Nathaniel looked down at the spirit board. "Are you able to commune with the souls a raven-eyed takes?"

"No." Lady Cavall took a sip of her tea. "Once a soul is absorbed by a raven-eyed, they become locked within their host until the raven-eyed dies. The only way to commune with one is to have hand-to-hand contact with the raven-eyed host."

Nathaniel frowned. *Of course this wouldn't be simple.* "Fine. What about someone killed but not absorbed by the White Raven?"

Lady Cavall was silent for several seconds. Her voice fell to a harsh whisper. "Do you understand what you're asking of me?"

"Yes, I—"

"But do you *understand*, Mr. Trevet, the gravity of what you're asking of me? Of yourself?"

"I'm asking you," Nathaniel replied evenly, "to seek out a victim of the one who calls themselves the White Raven. A task, I should think, you're more than capable of handling."

Lady Cavall held Nathaniel's gaze without a word. Finally, she took another sip of her tea and replied, "There are some things best left buried. I warned your mother against such pursuits, but she didn't listen." The shadow of a smirk flinted across·Lady Cavall's face. "You have a good life, Mr. Trevet. Fine clothes, wealth, youth, influence. Such precious things to waste on something as fickle as curiosity."

Nathaniel's eyes darkened. "My dear Lady Cavall, please do try to understand I only came here today to hear of your terms and the truth I seek. I'm rather pressed for time and your suggestions only slow me further. Find a victim and I'll be gone from here."

Suddenly a scratching noise sounded from overhead. At first subtle, it rapidly intensified until the whole upper floor was riddled with the clamor of something running from one end of the room to the other, dragging its nails across the wooden floorboards. But just as quickly it stopped and silence fell upon the flat.

"As I said," Nathaniel repeated with a coy smile, eyes flickering to the attic, "I'll be glad to be on my way as soon as we're done. With utmost discretion of course."

"I'll need some of your blood for the reading," Lady Cavall replied, ignoring his jab. "Otherwise, I can't help you."

Nathaniel's nose scrunched. Unfortunately, his mother's old soothsayer didn't seem the type to be swayed by sterling. "Fine, but you'll need a strong bowl."

"This spirit board can handle even pure duskborn blood." She produced a silver knife from a hidden harness beneath her shawl's sleeve. "Now, raise your wrist over the board."

Nathaniel did as he was told. "A trinket of the goblin market, I take it? My mother mentioned meeting you there before becoming your patron."

"Keep nosing around and I'll have you repeat the stairs."

Lady Cavall made a small incision across his wrist. A few pale red droplets appeared before the wound repaired itself. She repeated this two more times until the amethyst was covered in a thin coating of Nathaniel's blood. To his surprise, the amethyst and surrounding board stayed intact.

"You're not so far gone yet," Lady Cavall said, looking at the blood pool. "Oh, don't look so concerned. A proper spirit board is meant to handle all blood types. Duskborn aren't even the worse of it."

As she wiped Nathaniel's blood off the blade with a cloth, the fabric slowly began to be eaten away as if touched by acid.

"Before we begin, understand I make no promises. The path leading to the White Raven is smoke and glass, there one moment and gone the next. It doesn't make itself known often, and when it does, it tends to play with its victims to the point of madness. I will do what I can."

Nathaniel nodded.

"And what you may hear, I can't say or speak to its truth. The spirits are fickle and at times desperate. Sometimes even vengeful. As honed as my powers may be, I can't say for certain who will answer my call, if anyone." Lady Cavall took a deep breath and looked up. She laid her hands over the spirit board and chanted, "I offer this blood token for the divide to open."

Something upstairs shifted. The sound of chains being dragged across the floor rattled above them. Nathaniel's jaw clenched.

"Bring forth my call and let my words be heard across the spiritual rift. I offer this blood token for passage and my body as vessel."

Lady Cavall reached for the triangular amethyst in the center of the board. The blood slid up and around her fingers like red tendrils. A faint glow emanated from her hands, shielding her flesh from the ravenous duskborn blood. The air grew heavy. When Lady Cavall lowered her head, only the whites of her eyes remained.

"The divide has been opened. All can now be seen. We shall begin."

Her gaze remained unblinking as she murmured, "I seek word with those whose lives were ended by the White Raven. Reveal the path to yourselves so that I may lend my voice to your truths." The candle flames flickered around the flat. A strange weight settled in the air as Lady Cavall began to twitch. Nathaniel's fangs slid down behind his canines.

Suddenly, Lady Cavall's hands gripped the sides of the table. Her body arched backwards as she struggled to hold onto the sides. She winced, her face contorted in a silent howl of pain. With a powerful jolt, her body relaxed and her head slumped forward.

Silence.

"Lady Cavall?"

Instead of replying, Lady Cavall began to hum a tune. When she lifted her head, Nathaniel saw a serene smile on her face. She strolled around the room, a childish glee to her steps, and started to sing:

"There she sits atop her chair

With eyes so dark and skin so fair.

As she rises with the Sun,

Watching from her to-wer.

"Climbing up so gingerly,

The noose is waiting patiently.

Gazing out towards the sea,

Watching from her to-wer.

"Now the morning light shall bring

One less child for the king.

Dressed in blue and never free,

Watching from her to-wer."

Nathaniel hurried to Lady Cavall's side. He grabbed her arm, forcing her to look at him. "Lady Cavall, enough of this trickery. What do the spirits say of the White Raven?"

"The White Raven ..." Lady Cavall's face contorted into a menacing mask of its former visage. "Poison! Bird of poison! Haunting, haunting, always haunting!" She gripped the sides of her arms and dug her nails into her flesh until she bled. "Haunted Elizabeth! Killed her! Never forget, never forget! The king hides its heart! Burn it, burn it! Kill the White Raven!"

Lady Cavall collapsed. Nathaniel rushed to her side, touching the side of her neck and feeling a faint pulse. He gently scooped her up and laid her on the lounger, draping a blanket over her. Lying there, she somehow looked frailer than before.

The clawing on the upper floor returned. It was gaining fervor, a mad sort of desperation with such force Nathaniel feared whatever it was would fall through the floor at any moment.

He gathered his things and hurriedly left the flat. The stairs proved no trouble for anyone going down, thank the saints. As he stepped into the rescinding fog, a group of young boys with post caps carried back their unsold bundles of penny papers. Lordhaveners carried on as if nothing was amiss around them. As if the townhouse that wanted to be forgotten didn't hold monsters and secrets that would tear their normalcy asunder.

Anders opened the carriage door. "Pleasant visit, sir?"

"Satisfying," Nathaniel replied tersely.

As the pair traveled down the dampened streets of Carnberg back to Thornwood, the events in Lady Cavall's flat played over and over in his mind. The White Raven, Claude, Victoria Whitmont, the Chases ... Nathaniel was certain now the eternal heart was the connecting piece he'd been missing. If Victoria and Claude meant to take the throne and use the eternal heart to keep it, certainly the newly crowned Princess Angelina would be their next target if the White Raven didn't reach her first.

"The heart has to be with her," Nathaniel mumbled to himself. "The crown princess is the key."

He leaned back and closed his eyes. Lady Cavall was right. His life could be considered good. Comfortable, even. But it was a well fabricated illusion as fragile as glass. Everything had come with a price.

I warned your mother against such pursuits, but she didn't listen.

What had his mother been pursuing? The White Raven? The eternal heart? Or something else entirely? The day scarlet lung had taken her, there had been no struggle, no outward signs of lingering pain or bloody coughing fits like those struck with the illness usually suffered. She had died rosy cheeked and clear eyed.

Priscilla Trevet had been a woman of many secrets. She knew there was another world beneath Lordhaven. A face beneath the mask, terrible and divine, that spoke of promises and traded in impossibilities. She'd shown him a glimpse of that world, gave him a taste of what it had to offer. The deals that could be made.

The path of smoke and glass. The path to the White Raven. If he were to find the eternal heart first and harness the power it promised—the chance to finally become his perfect self— to claim the throne, he had no choice but to follow the path all the way down, wherever it may lead.

39

—◦○◦—

SYBIL

"He was named Felnor in his fourth year of life, once it was certain death would not take the babe, for no son of Isameine and Hadrin had shown the strength and courage of Felrak the Unbeaten until he." – *Leopold Dunston,* The Great Heroes of the Dark Age

It had been days since Sybil had seen Priya.

Not that she minded walking alone to school, but how long would she go on avoiding her? As Sybil neared Lycoris, the wind began to pick up and a stray raindrop ran down her cheek. When she wiped it away, she caught a glimpse of Priya heading up the steps. Adriana was beside her.

"Priya!" Sybil called out. "Priya!"

Priya didn't turn around. Had she not heard her? Sybil hurried forward, but the clog of students between them was too great. By the time she finally made it to the entryway, she'd lost sight of her friend.

"Miss Vorn."

Sybil turned to see Professor Nera Rossi standing behind her, dark golden hair brushing her crossed forearms and amber eyes narrowed. Professor Rossi towered over most in Sanctis in part to her Arcadian ancestry, but it was the elaborate sigil tattooed over her right eyelid that always unnerved Sybil. A strange energy emitted from it that reminded her of death mana, but different. Older. Malevolent.

"The Headmistress wishes to see you. Follow me." Professor Rossi didn't wait for Sybil's response before striding past her.

Sybil glanced down the hall. A few students lingered, but Priya was long gone. She sighed and followed Professor Rossi in the opposite direction. As they neared the Administrative Wing, her curiosity grew. She'd never been inside the Headmistress's office even after returning to school following the trial.

"Stuffy and pompous," Tianna had once described it, sometime after her fourth tardy to class. "It smells of books and tea and horrid age."

But now sitting in the Headmistress's office herself, Sybil found the room quite comfortable and not at all stuffy. The walls were fitted to the brim with leather bound literature, some spines more worn than others. Certificates of masteries in magic study and maps of the kingdom crammed the walls. Sybil tried not to let her eyes linger too long, but the idea of spending even a single afternoon in the Headmistress's library was intoxicating.

Headmistress Catrin Seaver looked up from the file she was reading and extended her hand to the open seat across from her. She was a slight woman with practiced poise and delicate features. Her crown of white hair was meticulously pinned atop her head, showcasing the netted garnet choker about her wrinkled neck.

"Welcome, Miss Vorn. Please have a seat." She gestured to a bald man with a steely gaze and wrinkles just beginning to show around his eyes. He made no acknowledgement when Sybil nodded to him. "This is Chancellor Walsh. The High Council had a few questions they wanted to discuss with you."

Sybil's heart pounded. It was no coincidence the High Council had called her mother in after the blood wolf attack and now sent a member to Lycoris. Professor Rossi closed the doors behind her and stood off to the side, arms folded.

Yorin, please watch over me, Sybil silently prayed.

"You must be curious why you've been summoned here." Headmistress Seaver folded her hands in front of her. Although she only had one good eye—her left one had been replaced by bluish moon glass years ago—her gaze was no less penetrating.

"Before we begin," Chancellor Walsh interjected, "have you been approached by anyone in the last few days, Miss Vorn?"

Sybil shook her head.

"Good. Now, I was told you were attacked while you were in the forest? By a wolf, is that correct?"

Sybil glanced at the Headmistress, who nodded for her continue.

"Y-Yes, that's right. My friend, Priya and I were training and um, were attacked. By a wolf."

"That must've been awfully frightening," Chancellor Walsh said, his expression unchanged by the news. Could he see through her lie? Did he know it was really a blood wolf, a creature she shouldn't have ever been able to kill on her own?

"How did you manage to escape?"

Sybil shifted in her chair.

"Magic," she replied, tacking on a smile for good measure. "My training helped, too."

"Of course," Chancellor Walsh replied with mock friendliness. "But not with your own magic, correct?"

Sybil's stomach dropped.

"There were several witnesses that testified hearing a terrible screech that morning. Abnormal mana spikes were also detected by the Sentinels around the same time. The source of the spike was traced back to a large, charred area covered by recently summoned foliage."

Chancellor Walsh put on a pair of glasses before looking down at his notes.

"Your friend, Miss Priya Majumdar is a Willowfang with botany specialty. You and Mr. Heath Tanner, who I'm told assisted transporting you, are both Dawnslayers with necromancy specialty, which begs the question Miss Vorn, who was there that used flame magic?"

Sybil broke into a cold sweat as Heath's words echoed in her mind.

"When I found you, the blood wolf was already dead. Scorched until there nothing was left. And your hands, the palms were blistered. Burned."

"I'm sorry. I don't remember. Someone must've come by when we passed out. It all happened so fast." Sybil cleared her throat, turning to Headmistress Seaver. "I'm sorry I can't be of more help."

"Miss Vorn—" Chancellor Walsh began but the Headmistress held up her hand.

"That will be enough, Titus."

When she shifted her gaze back to Sybil, her expression softened. "I understand it must have been a terrible experience for you, but it is of great importance to let us know if you remember any additional details."

Just then, a cluster of voices could be heard outside the door. Sybil picked out her brother's voice even before he barged into the room with two junior assistants on his heels.

"Headmistress Seaver, ma'am, what is my sister doing here?" Cal demanded.

One of the junior professors, a recently graduated fourth year whose name sat stubbornly on the tip of Sybil's tongue, pushed up his glasses along the narrow bridge of his nose. A thin sheen of sweat coated his forehead. "I'm sorry, ma'am, we tried to stop him."

Professor Rossi stepped forward, her ashen grey eyes a smoldering storm. "Kingsley, Daniels, out! And you," she growled at Cal. "You may speak with the Headmistress after she has concluded talks with Miss Vorn. Return to class at once."

Cal ignored her. His gaze flickered only briefly to Chancellor Walsh. Sybil sensed mana gathering around him, no doubt his water magic bubbling beneath his skin ready to unleash on anyone who stood in his way.

"Cal, it's fine. Go back to class," Sybil said through clenched teeth. Her mouth soured with the words she wished to say, but with the Headmistress and Chancellor Walsh sitting opposite her, she held her tongue.

"I ask again, ma'am, why is my sister here? The High Council cleared her return to Lycoris. My mum oversaw everything."

Headmistress Seaver nodded. "Yes, she did. However, the matter at hand is your sister's inappropriate use of magic outside of supervised studies to harm another student while on school grounds."

Sybil felt the floor give way beneath her. Blood pounded in her ears as she tried to make sense of the Headmistress's words and the utter shift in questioning. She stole a glance at Chancellor Walsh, but he remained an impassive bystander wholly uninterested in correcting the Headmistress.

"What?" Cal shook his head. "No, that can't —"

"Dean Carlyle came forward while your sister was recovering to report the altercation. Witnesses confirmed the assault, in addition to the use of Miss Vorn's magic to further intimidate." Professor Seaver turned a calm, yet withering gaze upon Sybil. Her mouth fell into a frown. "I'm incredibly disappointed to learn of this behavior from one of our top students, especially a Head Girl. As Headmistress of Lycrois, I hereby denounce your admittance to this school for the remainder of the academic year, including preliminary testing for the Trials of Six. You may apply for readmittance evaluation next spring."

"Headmistress Seaver ..." Sybil's voice failed her. She doubled over, willing the tears back. This wasn't the time to cry, she had to fight, to plead her case, to—

Cal gripped her shoulder. "Understood, ma'am. I'll escort my sister home."

Sybil bit her tongue as she stood and excused herself. She paid no mind to the hushed whispers and disapproving glances of the two junior professors. She passed by them with eyes trained forward, matching Cal's hurried footsteps and shaking shoulders.

When they were off the academy grounds and nearing the edge of the main square, Cal snapped.

"What were you thinking? Gods, Sybil, do you have any idea the mess we're in? Mum's gonna kill us both!"

"Don't you think I *know* that?" Sybil shouted back, running her hands through her hair. She paced across the square, focusing on nothing and trying to think of something, anything, to fix her expulsion. *Gods, I need frost.*

"Chancellor bloody Walsh was in the Headmistress's office hearing that you attacked Dean Carlyle!" Cal kicked a patch of dirt, sending more than one pebble flying. "Shit!"

"He and his cronies attacked me first, thanks for asking." Sybil shook her head. "It's absolute rubbish I get expelled for punching him when it wasn't even a fair fight! They tried to kill me! And Chancellor Walsh was there to ask about the attack in the forest. The Headmistress never mentioned it until you came in."

"So she's lying then, hmm? You didn't attack Dean?"

"No, that's not—no, I did, but that's not the point."

Cal shook his head. "They're probably telling Mum right now how we're gonna be banished or killed or whatever because of you. *Again.*" His mouth curved into a snarl, spitting out each word like a child flinging stones. "I wish you'd never came back!"

"You don't mean that." Sybil reached for Cal's arm but he pulled away. "Cal, I'll fix this, all right? I promise. I just need a chance to see the Headmistress and explain what really happened."

"You can't fix anything, Sybil. Stop telling me you can!"

People were staring now. Cal didn't seem to notice, but Sybil felt their eyes fixated on her, her failures laid bare for all to see. For all to judge. Her stomach coiled.

"Cal, please let's just go home. I really need to go home." The anger she'd shoved down in the Headmistress' office was bubbling through her cracking surface, rising to her neck and rippling through her fingers. An anger threatening to boil through her very skin. Becoming a Major meant finding the truth. It meant clearing her name. It meant understanding how she had a memory of harming Major Quinn. She needed Cal, needed Lycoris, needed everyone to believe her.

"Cal, please, I need to go home." Tears blurred her vision. "I can't think. I can't be here right now. Please...."

"Everyone knows what you did and we suffer for it every day," Cal shouted. "Just admit you killed them, Sybil!"

"I didn't!" she cried. Hot tears slid down her cheeks. "I didn't!"

"Gods, just say it!"

Sybil's chest constricted until she could barely breathe. A torrent of shame and rage surged through her body as the weight of everything she'd ever held finally came crashing down. She looked up at Cal through watery eyes. How could she love him—love Sanctis—so much when they hated her just the same?

My fault, she silently berated herself as something pulled back on a distant, unseen shore. *Always my fault. Always always always always—*

Failure.

I'm a failure.

Sybil let out a piercing cry as brilliant green flames burst from her hands. They snaked above her head and twisted into a canopy of fire.

It was the most beautiful thing she'd ever seen.

For a moment, all was quiet in her head. The world and its terrible weight fell away and left silence in its wake. But when Cal's eyes met hers and betrayal stared back at her, rage—white hot as the flames above her—coursed through her blood, incinerating all reason and guilt. It nourished her, fed her, *became* her.

Hate me then.

She flung her arms wide. The flames fanned out from the fiery mass overhead, reigning down like leaves from a tree of fire.

The world rushed back all at once in a cacophony of screams. Passerby that had looked on while she was being reproached now fled in terror, scrambling for cover while others grabbed small children and ran for their homes.

Cal didn't move. His eyes were wide, glassy things seized by the fantastic horror raining down all around him. When Sybil ran past, he made no move to stop her.

Sybil continued running. She didn't dare turn around. If she did, her guilt would surely swallow her for good. She crossed Delwitch Bridge, now pocketed with hungry flames, as the air grew heavy with smoke.

When she stopped beneath Felnor's Archway to catch her breath, she noticed the curtains were drawn on every home. They had all been deemed guilty for something at some point or another, but today it was not for this.

Her body shook violently. Dread swelled in the pit of her stomach as her mind tried to process what had just happened. Short, clipped breaths darted from her mouth. Somewhere, deep in her heart, she knew she had made an irrevocable choice. Tears streamed down her face in unrelenting rivulets.

"What have I done?" she whimpered.

"Oh, I'd say you have some idea." Cain leaned against a tree a few paces away. A knowing smile curled his shadowy lips. "Tell me, how does it feel to finally let it all go? Was it everything you hoped it would be?"

Sybil looked down at her hands. They were blistered and still pink with warmth. Gods, she was going to be sick. "This isn't right. It *can't* be right. If I had a second affinity, it would've already shown years ago."

She studied Cain's yellow gaze and in the writhing shadows found herself at a crossroads. "You know what's wrong with me, don't you?"

Cain tilted his head, regarding her.

"Right and wrong. Good and evil. Arcanics and unseers. All silly little names that fateshifters gave immense powers beyond their realm of understanding. Magic simply *is*, Miss Vorn. It is beyond category, shape, time or space. Didn't the Forsaken teach you fateshifters anything before their banishment?" Cain's sharpened fingers thrummed against his cheek. "Now the real question is what will drive you more: hunger for knowledge or fear of the unknown?"

It struck her then. This is what Lady Ilva tried to hide. What Headmistress Seaver was trying to find. What Major Quinn had seen in the very end.

"No ..." Sybil whispered, shaking her head as memories of Major Quinn's charred body pushed to the surface. Cain howled with laughter. His teeth sharpened and his eyes glowed a sulfurous yellow.

"Run, riverborn," he bellowed in a deep, ancient warble. "Run and never look back!"

Sybil ran towards the forest faster than Felnor himself.

40

SYBIL

"More than any rifle or sword, family is the strongest armament. Where a lone ship would sink, a fleet will persevere." – *King Walter Rowland Chase, inaugural address, Lordhaven, Halcyon 1822*

Sanctis haunted Sybil.

When she finally eased into a fitful sleep that first night, flames rained down like stars and blood wolves waited beyond the black trees, their mad eyes following her.

Waiting for her.

She called out for Priya, for Tianna, for Lady Ilva, for Cal, for her mother, for her father. She called until her voice cracked and her throat burned. But no one would answer. She ran and ran until she reached her room. She grabbed her father's journal, only to find a single word scribbled across every page.

Traitor.

Sybil didn't sleep after that.

When she couldn't run any longer, she walked as far as her feet would carry her. She spoke to no one and avoided the main roads. When her stomach growled, one thought seized her: *Run, riverborn.*

She kept moving.

A storm caught up with her on the third day. Lead grey clouds snapped with lightning but still Sybil forged ahead.

Only Sentinels and death waited behind her.

A spell of vertigo suddenly overcame her as a roar of thunder boomed overhead. She leaned against a nearby tree and tried to shake it off. She didn't have time for this. She had to keep moving.

She pushed off the tree and stumbled forward, gritting her teeth. Moving, she had to keep—

"*Poppet.*"

Sybil opened her eyes. She was on one knee staring at the muddy underbrush of the forest. When had she fallen? She tried to look up but the pain and dizziness stopped her. The outline of a figure hovered in the distance, but she couldn't make out their features in the rain. Only the brief familiarity of the figure's strange and malicious mana tugged at her fading mind.

"Help me...." she mumbled as her eyes rolled back and she hit the ground. Overhead, the storm raged on, rife with fury.

"Remember poppet: the north belongs to the mountains and the south belongs to the king. Everything else belongs to the sea."

"But Papa, why don't we go north to Soliljin, away from the king? Couldn't we make more friends there?"

"There are no friends to be found on the other side of those mountains, my dear."

"Are there monsters there?"

In the distance, waves crashed against the shore.

"Papa?"

Silence.

"Papa...?"

"Run, Sybil!"

Sybil shot bolt upright, sending her spiraling into a wave of dizziness. She winced just as a pair of hands pressed against her shoulders.

Standing above her was a woman around her mother's age with a white scarf tied over her dark blonde hair.

"My word." She stroked Sybil's dark hair with a feather light touch. Her eyes were the pale blue of robin's eggs, their corners pinched with concern.

"You've seen something quite awful, haven't you?"

"W-where am …?" Sybil couldn't finish the sentence. She touched her throat, frowning.

"There, there. Don't force yourself to speak if it hurts too much." The woman reached for a glass and held it to Sybil's lips. "Here, drink this. It's tea."

Sybil did as she was told and took a sip. It immediately soothed the rawness.

Before she could thank the woman, her mind and body once again slipped into a deep slumber.

When Sybil next awoke, the woman was gone and a young girl was in her place.

She had the same dark blonde hair, but instead of being tied behind a scarf it fell in golden waves around her shoulders.

"Oh, you're awake!" She set down her needle and thread and leaned in closer. Notes of cinnamon and juniper tickled Sybil's nose. She laid the back of her palm on Sybil's forehead and Sybil nearly jerked away from the coolness of her touch.

"It's all right," the girl said. "I'm only standing in for Mum. I'm Kate. Kate Abcott."

Sybil's eye caught the crossed silver staffs hanging from a delicate silver chain against Kate's throat. Familiarity nudged at her, but then Kate pulled away and she lost the thought entirely.

"How are you feeling?"

"Better."

"Brilliant! Mum'll be so pleased to hear it." Something in Sybil churned hearing that word. *Mum.* Her heart began to quicken. The fire, oh gods, the *fire*.

Kate squeezed Sybil's hand, mooring her.

"What's your name?"

Sybil paused. "Esther."

"Esther," Kate repeated, turning over Sybil's middle name on her tongue. "What a lovely name. It's a pleasure to make your acquaintance, Esther. Although I'm afraid it's under rather poor circumstances."

She grabbed a glass from the bedside table. "Here, would you like some water?"

Sybil nodded and nearly finished off the glass in one gulp. "The woman from before. She's your mum?"

"Mhmm. She runs a bookshop in town, so I take to looking after you while she's away." Kate looked down at her hands, suddenly sheepish. "Well, that's not entirely true. My younger sister Liza looked after you the previous night but only for a bit. She's rather easily frightened."

"Frightened?"

"You had some awfully fitful dreams. Calling out for your mum and da. Gave Liza quite a fright." She chuckled, but hurriedly cleared her throat and lowered her voice. "Were they traveling with you, your parents?"

"Um, yes. They were. But we were … separated. And then the storm hit." Sybil sank deeper into the bed. "I don't remember much after that. Then I woke up here."

Kate frowned. "You poor thing. It must've been terrifying being out there alone. Lucky Benny came across you when he did."

"Benny?"

"Stanley Baker's hound. He's absolutely precious. He and Stanley were hunting rabbits when Benny found you. You were in a dreadful state when he rushed you in. Mum took to your side all night bringing down the fever." Kate squeezed her hands together. "I'd never seen her so worried. But her mum, Grandmum Edith, had been the best nurse in Brightpool and she learned everything from her. Mum's brilliant with patients."

Kate stood, smoothing down her soft pink day dress. "Are you hungry? Can I get you anything?"

"No, I'm fine, thank you," Sybil replied. In truth she was famished, having been surviving off the odd bits of berries she could find on her travels. But she didn't know Kate or her family. What if they had already sent word to the High Council about her whereabouts? She had to leave as soon as she could and reach Lordhaven. It was the only place beyond the High Council's reach.

A knock rasped across the door.

"Kate, is that you?" A young woman poked her head in. "Is she awake?"

Kate beamed. "She is! Esther, this is my older sister, Liza."

Liza's expression soured as she opened the door fully. "Must you say 'older'? Why can't I just be your sister?"

Unlike Kate who was all round cheeks and soft curves, Liza was sharp edges and dark eyes. She stood half a foot taller than Kate but standing next to each other Sybil could see where their similarities had diverged over time, taking them on two different but not so far off paths.

Had people seen that between herself and Cal? Or had time changed them too much to tell anymore?

Traitor.

Sybil's hand curled into a fist beneath the covers, hidden from the Abcott sisters.

"Well, I'm happy to see you're awake. We were worried with the fever and all." Liza peered down at Sybil with an unreadable expression. "Where had you come from? Is there any family we can send word to?"

"She was traveling with her mum and da when the storm separated them," Kate piped in. "Absolutely dreadful."

"Yes, thank you, *Kate,* but I think Esther can tell it herself."

Kate shrank back. "I'm sorry. You're right, go on."

"We were only passing through," Sybil added, her voice still a bit hoarse. "Traveling to Greyfell for business but we hadn't prepared enough for the storm. I don't know where my parents are."

Kate looked at Liza with downcast eyes, but Liza said nothing. Sybil clutched her fist tighter, willing the panic inside her to calm. Did Liza know she was lying? Had she been to Greyfell and found Sybil missing an accent or a mannerism?

Finally, Liza said, "Kate, why don't you talk with Stanley? He and those Beesley raffs he runs with can comb the forest for signs of her parents."

"On it!" She pulled Liza into a tight hug. "I knew you'd have a brilliant idea."

Liza rolled her eyes. "Yes, all right, just go then already."

Once Kate left, Liza asked Sybil, "Can you walk?"

Sybil slowly got to her feet. She had been changed into a thin cotton spun dress. Liza handed her back her clothes. They were in a neat pile and smelled of fresh air and rain, but an undercurrent of smoke still clung to them.

She clutched them close to her chest.

"Your boots are near the door. When you're changed, come downstairs."

As soon Liza closed the door, Sybil leaned forward and rested her head against her pulled up knees. It was all so surreal. She should be waking up in her own room, having breakfast with her mother and Cal, going to Lycoris with Priya and Tianna, but instead she was ...

A headache throbbed behind her eyes. She winced, wishing more than ever for a bit of frost to clear her mind. She needed to focus. She had to make her way south, away from anyone who might recognize her and alert the Sentinels.

She slowly changed into her clothes and made her way down the stairs, the squeak of each step announcing her presence before she made it even halfway down.

The Abcott home was small, but cozy. Yellowed family photos lined the sparse walls and hand-stitched quilts hung over the well-worn loveseat and chairs that made up the seating area. A small kitchen engrained with the smell of bread and vegetable stock was situated in the back. Only an old table propped up with books and adorned with five chairs separated the two spaces.

Sybil looked around but didn't see anyone.

"Kate? Liza?"

Just then, she heard laughter coming from outside. She opened the front door and found Kate talking to a young man around seventeen or eighteen. They were standing at the other end of a plush green yard bordered by a squat fence and yellow and white flowers. Liza was standing off to the side of Kate, a tight smile on her face.

When the young man saw Sybil, he waved and ambled up the walkway with Kate. Liza trailed behind them, her expression caught between bored and annoyed. Sybil noticed the young man walked with an awkward, impish stride as if he hadn't quite grown into the changes of adolescence.

"Best of mornings," he greeted with a wide smile. Up close, he had a smattering of freckles across his tanned face and eyes the color of almond shells.

"Esther, was it? I'm Stanley Baker. Pleasure meeting you."

Sybil nodded politely. "Likewise."

"Blessing of the saints we found you when we did. Kate was in such a state you'd swear we'd need some of that infernal spellcraft to pull you back from the brink."

Sybil stared at him as he and Kate laughed.

Infernal spellcraft.

Had he really said that with a smile? A knot coiled in her belly. Despite their light banter and the idyllic setting, something Sybil couldn't quite name shifted in the wrong direction, as if a shadow had been cast over their picnic. Her whole body went rigid with the blow of his words in a way she'd never felt before. Othered. Unsafe.

They're not your friends.

"You all right then, Esther?"

"Don't be daft," Liza snapped at Stanely. "She's still reeling from her ordeal, clearly. She only just awoke today."

"Stanley is going to help look for your parents," Kate interjected with a bubbly smile. "Right, Stan?"

Stanley scratched his ear, a blush smoldering his cheeks. "Right, right. Gonna round everyone up and be out there soon. We'll find 'em for you, Esther, don't worry."

Sybil swallowed hard. "Thank you."

"What's this now?" said a gruff voice.

Sybil nearly jumped back. She hadn't heard anyone approach, let alone the burly giant of a man standing behind her.

His face was masked by a wiry black beard streaked with grey. Two narrowed eyes the deep, golden brown of a forest during Harvestgrain stared back at her. But it wasn't his stony gaze that made her take pause.

It was the shimmering air of mana around him.

"Da, this is Esther, the girl mum was tending." Kate nudged Sybil. "Esther, this is our da, Arthur Abcott. Don't worry, he only looks like a brute, but he's a charm, I promise."

Arthur's gaze hardened. "Esther, was it?"

"Y-Yes, sir."

"Praise be to the Saint Father," Arthur said. "Truly you were in his graces to pull through that fever."

Suddenly, it came to her. The necklace Kate wore—the crossed staffs. She *had* seen it before. It had been the same symbol that emblazoned the cover of the only book she knew Mabel never displayed in her personal library. The one kept beneath her bed, hidden from the prying eyes of old councils and even older gods.

The Book of the True Word. The holy text of Ascendism.

They don't know he's a fateshifter, Sybil realized.

When she looked up at Arthur, realization clear in her eyes, a tight smile lifted the corner of his mouth. He remained in the doorway, unmoving, as if barring something sinful from his home.

"Welcome to Brightpool, Miss Esther."

41

Sybil

"**W**ANTED:** First edition of REVEL'S WAR. Last seen in Lord Kendrick's manor. Forgeries not accepted. Must be without damage or stain. Leave in green post box on Colter Street with address for payment." – *Anonymous patron, The Jester's Hand request board, The Bowery, Lordhaven, Halcyon*

Life at the Abcotts became a mundane dream.

Irene Abcott tended to her in the mornings, preparing her breakfast and a cup of chamomile tea thick with honey and thistle berry juice to fight off the cough and fever. In the evenings, Kate took over and recited the day's events in long-winded detail, often with a myriad of hand gestures and very few breaths taken in between.

It became a comforting cycle. She never saw Ruby, the middle Abcott daughter, but heard of her on occasion from Kate's recounts. Arthur Abcott never made an appearance again much to Sybil's relief. Irene and Kate were plenty of company in their own way. If loneliness ever crept in, Sybil would close her eyes and find comfort in the quiet arms of sleep.

But when night fell, the terrors would find her.

When Kate bid her good night and the house fell into a quiet slumber, Sybil waited with bated breath as the hours slowly passed. She imagined Cain rising from the shadows of the forest, darker than the night itself, to loom over Brightpool.

"There," he would tell the Sentinels, pointing to the Abcott house. "You'll find the traitor there."

Night after night, moon after moon, she waited to be found. Waited for the Northland ghouls to snatch her away and take her back to the pain and ash she'd left behind. Waited to see the confusion and hatred twisting her mother and brother's faces when she returned.

But resistance burned inside her. It hid her fear behind a snarl and kept air in her lungs when panic threatened to squeeze them dry.

It became the voice she had lost.

I won't go back.

Sybil waited for her captors every night. But it was the ninth night that Sybil, having nodded off, awoke to find not a Sentinel, but Arthur Abcott standing in her doorway. He was outfitted in a soot-stained apron, thick pants and work boots. She sat upright with a start.

"Follow me," he whispered gruffly, then turned and left.

Sybil blinked slowly. Her gaze affixed to the space Arthur had just been. Or had he? Had she imagined him? She rubbed her eyes. Maybe she finally had lost her mind in a sleepless stupor.

She slid out of bed and peered into the hall. A sliver of moonlight from the hall window guided her to the stairs. She carefully made her descent into the dark foyer. At the back of the house, a door was left slightly ajar.

She slipped through and followed a short path to the side of a small workshop behind the Abcott home. Arthur sat on a bench awash with moonlight. He held a sword in his hands, inspecting the blade at various angles, turning it this way and that. Behind him, a forge sat cold, but the workshop walls reeked of smoke. Sybil went rigid. Memories of a sky on fire and the hollow look in Cal's eyes bubbled to the surface.

She pressed them down and took a deep breath. One, two, three deep breaths. *Not here,* she told herself. *Not now.*

"Where was home?"

Sybil snapped back to attention. "E-Excuse me, sir?"

He sighed. "I said, where was home? North? West?"

"West, I suppose."

"You suppose?"

"I've never traveled elsewhere. Until we left for Greyfell."

"I see."

A long silence stretched between them, filled only by the shrill chirping of crickets and faint echoes of chatter from the Bell & Barrel, the local pub Sybil had caught glimpses of from her window.

"Do you always work in the middle of the night?"

"Sometimes." Arthur balanced the sword as he spoke, as if weighing its heft against his own words. "Helps me think. Clears the head."

He brought the sword to eye level. Sybil watched him stare down the length of the blade as he slid two fingers from hilt to tip. Her eyes widened as the metal rippled with life and white-hot runes carved themselves into the blade wherever Arthur had touched.

The glow of the runes lingered for a moment longer. White faded to red then orange and finally to black before disappearing without a trace. The blade returned to a smooth polish. A sword without the faintest etch upon its surface.

Sybil leaned forward, looking from the blade to Arthur. Her breath caught in her throat. *Such skill.* "You're a Willowfang."

Arthur grabbed a cloth and began polishing the blade.

"And you're no mere traveler to know that name." He looked up at her for the first time. Her stomach hardened. Something primal gnawed at her, a gut feeling she'd just said the wrong thing to the wrong person.

"I'm familiar enough," she stuttered. "My parents knew of them, I mean."

"Did they now?" Arthur stopped polishing. "Then I take it we won't be finding them anytime soon, eh?"

Sybil said nothing.

"Doesn't matter, I s'ppose. Everyone has their reasons. Life owes us nothing, after all. I'm not here to judge you." He gazed down at the sword in his hands. "Some of the oldest stories say magic could shift the very fate of the world. It's how the term 'fateshifters' came to be. Arcanics hold the power to change the fate of the world. But where there is power, death will always follow."

Memories of black trees and fiery rain. The cries of the fearful and the wails of the dying. The laughter of shadows and the taste of ash.

Her power had shifted the very fate of Sanctis and all its inhabitants. Control kept Sanctis safe. But without it... death will follow. Is this what the High Council had feared? Why so many in Halcyon hated fateshifters?

Follow the rules. Don't get upset. Mind your manners.

Swallow anger. Swallow sadness. Swallow confusion.

Swallow, swallow, swallow.

It's your fault if you choke.

Sybil felt Arthur staring at her, as if he could see her thoughts laid out like an open diary. She clasped her hands together to expel her nerves.

"Magic is potential incarnate. Nothing good or bad, just is. But without direction, well ..." He laid down the sword. "When I first met you, I'd not seen so much mana surrounding a person in years. Are you prepared to give it up then?"

"What?" Sybil shook her head. "No, I mean, for now I—"

Arthur raised a brow. "For now?"

"The Sentry holds an annual public hearing that's open to anyone. I'm going to make a case. My father was planning to attend before ..." but Sybil couldn't find the words to finish her thought. "We were going to go after they conducted business in Greyfell," she lied.

"Going to storm Lordhaven and change it all then, hmm? Sway the king and his dogs not to hang you from the gallows and charge admittance for the show? How noble of you."

Her stomach coiled with rage, but instinctively she pressed it down, squeezed her shoulders inward, smaller and smaller until her anger was smothered back into the darkness. She tucked a wily strand of black hair behind her ear. She needed to focus. Gods, if only she had a little frost.

"I should get back. It's late."

Arthur said nothing as she stood to leave. He walked past her to a small table near the back of the workshop. On the work bench was a long black sheath decorated with a golden ivy filigree. As soon he slid the sword into its casing, Sybil could feel something in the air quiet, deaden almost.

The magic was gone. Silenced.

"Iron to bind, iron to hide," Arthur whispered loud enough for her to hear, "so death may not follow."

The following morning, it was Sybil who was awake, jovial and upright, when Irene came through the door. A new resilience sparked in her after talking with Arthur.

"Oh my, someone is up rather early," Irene said with a smile, laying down the breakfast tray on the desk. "How are we feeling today, dear?"

"Much better, thank you Mrs. Abcott."

"Wonderful, I'm glad to hear it." She laid both her hands over Sybil's. "You really were on the brink but saints willing here you are."

"It's all thanks to you and Kate. I'm truly grateful, really. For everything."

"Oh, it's nothing at all," Mrs. Abcott said with a wave of the hand. "Gah, look at me getting all misty-eyed like a schoolgirl." She laughed as she dotted the corners of her eyes. "Well, let's get you fed and dressed, then. I have some errands to run with Kate and Ruby over in Belton End, so I'd appreciate it if you could assist Liza in the bookshop today."

Sybil beamed. "Of course!"

Irene patted her on the arm. "Thank you, dear. And I hate to mention it, but the search party hasn't been able to locate your parents yet."

Sybil bowed her head, hoping her downturned expression would be enough. "I understand."

"I'm sure they're well, though. Perhaps they got lucky and happened across help like you did. We'll ask around while we're in Belton End, don't you worry."

Irene gave Sybil's arm one last squeeze. As she was about to leave, she paused in the doorway. "Oh, and Esther, did Arthur happen to say anything to you the other day?"

"No, nothing at all," Sybil lied. "Is everything all right?"

Oh gods, did she hear me leave the house last night?

Irene hesitated for a moment, and Sybil caught something in her expression shift ever so briefly. Sadness, perhaps? Regret? But just as quickly the moment was gone and Irene was heading out the door, all smiles and leisure again.

"Be sure not to strain yourself, today. Be well, dear."

After she left, Sybil wondered if she had seen anything in Irene Abcott's expression at all.

Liza was waiting at the landing when Sybil left her room a short time later.

Outfitted in a buttercup yellow petticoat and skirt, matching parasol and ringlet curls, Liza looked better suited for a stroll through town with the local gentry than consigned to a used bookshop desk.

"Well, let's get a move on it then," she snapped, striding towards the door. "We haven't all day."

Sybil quickened her pace. The moment she stepped outside, the glaring sun forced her to shield her eyes. But feeling the warmth on her skin, the breeze in her hair and the birdsong reminded her of better times.

"You all right?"

"Huh?"

Liza titled her parasol. "Are you having trouble? I mean Mum said it might be a bit much for you being out and about, but I figured it might help."

Sybil lowered her hand from her eyes. "You asked her if I could come with you?"

Liza huffed. "Well, you looked positively pathetic lying there day after day. Personally, I'd been driven mad by now."

Sybil beamed. "Thank you so much, Liza."

"Yes, well you can thank me by cataloguing our new wares. The dust is horrendous on good fabric." Liza paused then rolled her eyes. "Oh, don't give me that look."

"What look?"

"Don't you think I know bookshops are dusty things? But places like Brightpool will have you believe practicality is everything, including how you dress. And you know what? It's not. Not for me, anyway. Never will be either." She lowered her voice. "But don't tell my mum I said that. She'll go absolutely feral."

Sybil winked. "Your secret's safe with me, promise. And I think you look really lovely."

Liza smiled smugly and Sybil fell in step behind her as they left the Abcott house and walked the short way into Brightpool proper.

A warm wind carried through the pastoral town. Chickens scuttled past Sybil's feet as giggling children with ruddy red cheeks and bright eyes pursued them. Squat, thatch-roofed cottages thick with moss dotted either side of the road framed by wild, colorful gardens that hid reading benches and tadpole ponds. Narrow brick walkways strewn with ivy vines and potted plants snaked between each cottage. Sybil wished to explore them all, half imagining some led to warm, happy homes and others to fantastical worlds unseen.

And then she saw it—in the center of the town was a small pond rimmed in a crown of ankle-high rocks and wildflowers. She smiled, eager to cool down from her walk.

Apple red fish with black-tipped tails no longer than a tack darted through the clear water. Sybil slipped out of her shoes and sat down on the bank. As she was about to dip her feet in, Liza came from behind and snatched her arm back.

"What do you think you're doing?" she shrieked, fending off gathering stares with a shaky smile. She nodded toward the lake. "That's the Father's Pool. You can't just go putting your dirty feet in there."

"The Father's Pool?" Only then did Sybil notice the pond was free of bathing bodies or children playing. There wasn't even a bucket to gather water.

Her eyes lifted to meet Liza's. A mixture of concern and shock stared back at her.

Shame rippled through Sybil, burning her from the inside.

Traitor. Outsider. Traitor. Outsider.

"You know, from the *Book of the True Word*?" Liza shook her head. "Remember how it says on the last leg of the Saint Father's ten-year journey he bathed in a sacred pool and the water healed all his wounds?"

"Oh, right, of course. Sorry, my head's still a bit foggy." Sybil slipped her shoes back on, careful to keep her eyes down lest Liza see through her lie.

"Well, Poolers believe this pond to be *that* pool." She lowered her voice. "They even went so far as to bloody named themselves after it. 'Brightpool.' Can you imagine? It's beyond dreadful." She laughed and drew back up to full height, twirling her parasol. "I mean, honestly, I bet it doesn't even work, but it makes a nice story for tourists."

Sybil had also heard tales of healing pools from Lady Ilva. One of her favorite stories was of Grenda, a Dawnslayer princess born from rain and sunlight, who prowled the skies atop her dragon and guarded the Sun from thieves. During a storm, the winds became too strong and Grenda fell from her dragon's back to the earth below and died. Her body created a small crater where she fell, and the hole filled with the rainwater that coursed through her veins like blood. The water possessed her powerful healing magic, which healed any wound or illness of those who drank from it. But unlike the Father's Pool, legend claimed Grenda the Fallen's healing pool could only be seen at the end of a rainbow by the injured or sick in the calm following a storm.

Sybil found it odd that if the Father's Pool carried such powerful magic, then why weren't all of Halcyon lined up to take some for themselves?

"Has anyone actually drank from the Father's Pool?"

Liza shook her head. "Saints no. It's protected by the governor's edict for emergency approved use only. But visitors from all over Halcyon, Arcadia, and Bronwen visit on Saints Day."

"But what if it's real?" Sybil protested. "What if it can actually heal?"

"Not like more of it can be made if it did. Besides, what if it can't? Either way, it gives Poolers very real coin that can fill stomachs and heat homes." Liza shrugged. "Seems good enough to me."

Something about Liza's answer didn't settle well with Sybil, but she let it go. She was risking enough bringing up the topic.

A short walk from the Father's Pool was a small bookshop nestled between a tailor's shop and a pharmacy. A worn wooden sign hung from its doorway that read: Used Books & Antiquities.

Liza unlocked the door and stepped inside. A bell dinged a note of her arrival. Sybil stared, her mouth agape. Her fingers itched to touch everything in sight. She picked up a book nearest her from a shelf along the wall. It had a bare leather cover worn soft by years of readers. The title read: *Birds of the Bronwen Coasts, Vol. I* by Dr. Richard Prather.

"Welcome to the shop. I'll show you the catalogues." Sybil carefully slipped the book back into place, her eyes marveling over the shelves towering above her brimming with books waiting to be opened.

"Coming," she replied, her grin stretching ear to ear. The story of Grenda the Fallen crossed her mind as she passed through the aisles, catching up to Liza.

The storm had passed.

The calm had settled.

She had found her healing pool.

42

—◦—

TOBIAS

Tobias leaned against the open window of the Portkey flat and stared out across Fenwater Downs.

The sun crawled higher in the smoky, predawn sky. Tobias rubbed his eyes. Tiredness persisted like an ache. When his stomach growled, but he barely registered it.

Two days had passed since Kingtide was left for dead in the sewers. Two days since Tobias had turned into a blood wolf. His eyes grew heavy again, but the moment they closed the distorted view of Kingtide's mangled body waited for him.

His eyes snapped open.

"Dammit," he muttered, shaking his head. How he wanted to see Lucy then. Had she eaten? Slept well? It'd only been a day since he had seen her off to their aunt's house in Debney, but the unease of making yet another promise followed him like a specter. And returning to Lordhaven was another reminder of the unspoken clock ticking away on his sanity.

"Is this what you didn't want Ezra seeing?"

Not yet. He rubbed his eyes again.

"We're sick, Toby."

Not yet.

"And there's no changing that."

Not yet.

"Tobias?"

Tobias jerked his head up. "Bedroll stealer. 'Bout time you finally woke up."

Jóhann sat up. "You saved me."

"Aye, something like that." The easy answer was he had settled the guilt gnawing at him. He'd been there for Jóhann when he needed him. But even easy answers bore their own troublesome questions.

"May I touch your hand?"

"This again? Seriously?"

"Please." Jóhann's voice was meek, but steady.

Tobias sighed and swung his legs around. "You're a right pain in the arse, y'know that?" He laid his hand in Jóhann's. "If I wanted to off you, I would've done it already. I highly doubt the White Raven would waste their time watching you sleep for two days."

Jóhann sighed and let Tobias's hand go.

"Thank Halvar."

Tobias took a seat across from Jóhann. "I found a letter in Porter's apartment. I went there looking for you after you left." After a pause, he added quietly, "I think something happened to Porter before he could send it out. It warned your mate Diðrik to not come through Port Vale. Said someone was watching him."

Jóhann nodded solemnly. "Kingtide mentioned something about our mission. He knew. I don't know how, but he knew."

"Look, there's a chance they may still be out there. No one has sighted the White Raven, er, at least, well, you know. Except for the usual loons and honey-eaters."

Jóhann gave a weak smile. "You're a true friend. I won't forget what you did for me."

"Pft, don't go thinkin' we're mates or anything," Tobias huffed. "I just wasn't going to let you die on my watch is all." He slid down beneath the window and let his arms drape over his knees.

"So, who was that Kingtide bastard anyway?"

"I don't know, but he was a powerful heks."

"Heks?"

Jóhann pondered it a moment, then responded, "I believe you call them fateshifters here, yes? Those who can wield magicks." He lowered his eyes. "Kingtide could manipulate blood, which I suspect is a strong control of water. It filled my lungs, almost like I was submerged in Stjernevann again."

Jóhann voice softened. "I was chasing after my older brother one winter morning. He had taken one of my toys out of jest, but in my haste I didn't hear our mor yelling for us to come back. Then the ice gave way and the water overcame me so quickly." Jóhann shivered. "I hated being in that room. Kingtide looked so pleased with himself. Like it was some cruel game."

A powerful fateshifter who could drown people where they stood. Surely it would be easy enough to take out a merchant like Porter or a bone reader like Jóhann. Tobias mulled over the idea. Were the Seadevils just a ruse to cover his tracks? But why now? Why just kill voxossa?

"Kingtide was looking for the White Raven, right?"

"Ja. He wouldn't stop until I gave up their location. I don't know why though."

An unease settled over the room. Outside, the din of penny paper boys making their shop rounds and the screech of horse carriage whistles sounded below. Lordhaven was stirring awake.

"That was your first time, wasn't it? Turning, I mean."

"Don't," Tobias snarled.

"I didn't mean—"

"Stay as long as you need, but after that I'm done with this voxossa business, got it?"

Jóhann stood up from the bed. "Where are you going?"

"To do what I should've from the start. Gut some fish bastards and end this stupid mess."

When Tobias stepped out onto the rafters, a sticky heat wrapped itself around him.

He nimbly made his way across the gap and slipped down the ladder. Just as he landed on his feet, Tavia pulled away from the opposite wall. She was in a brown vest, blouse and page boy trousers. Her curls were pinned beneath her cap.

"So this is where you've been holed up." She craned her neck and whistled. "Saints, I can't believe you'd ever come back to this place."

Tobias's voice hardened. "What're you doing here?"

"Come on, Toby. Don't be daft. You haven't been around since the fight in the sewers." She nodded towards the flat. "How's he been?"

"Fine. Alive at least."

"Good, I'm glad." Tavia folded her arms. "Roderick's been asking around about you. I told him you'd taken sick and he backed off, but that won't last long."

"Thanks for that."

"Thank me by coming back already. Ezra's been asking about you too."

Tobias's stomach clenched. *I'm sorry, Ez.* Looking after Jóhann and dodging his questions was easy enough, but Ezra was a different matter entirely.

"You don't get to just run away and sulk. We're family, Toby. You need to talk to him. And Lucy."

"And what good's talking done, huh? What's that supposed to solve? I'm handling it."

"You don't get to take this on all on your own," Tavia fired back. "You can't keep shutting them out. It's not the remedy you think it is."

"Piss off, Tavia." As Tobias turned to leave, the bite of Tavia's dagger against his throat froze him in place.

"Since this is the only way to get your attention, hear this." She pressed the blade ever so slightly, but it was sharp enough to leave a trickle of red in its wake. Tobias gritted his teeth.

"I'm here for you, whether you want me to be or not. I know you're scared. But the wolf can't be stopped, got it? The disease will take our dreams, then our bodies, and then our minds." She pressed her forehead against his back. "It may have gotten to your body, but I won't let it take your mind. I'll end you before that happens."

She lowered her knife and stepped back. Tobias rubbed his throat and looked at her with a mixture of hurt and murder in his eyes.

"Going to kill me then? Is that it?"

"I'm not asking your permission," Tavia replied. "You know what it means if blood wolves are allowed to live too long."

The image of wanted posters calling for his head flashed through his mind. Mobs storming Higdin's, the Distillery, and the hideaway above the Portkey. If he was found out, no place would be safe. Suspected blood wolves didn't get the spectacle of Iron Square's gallows like fateshifters or the theatrics of the pyre like duskborns. They were shot on sight, no questions asked. Any constable would be drunk giddy with the opportunity to take out a blood wolf and a Market Streeter in one go.

A promise is a promise.

He couldn't give up. Not yet. He had made a promise to protect Lucy. He couldn't fail their mum. Not again. He would see to it they both left Lordhaven safely.

"Give up if you want to, but that's not the Tavia I know. And that's bloody well not me either."

"It's not about giving up, it's—"

"—not standing still," Tobias interrupted. "Stand still and you die."

Tavia pinched her brow and sighed. "Why are you so damn stubborn?"

"Because I know it's what Rhody would say if she were here."

Tavia's neck grew red.

"That's not fair," she grumbled, folding her arms, but a faraway look softened her expression. "Besides, it's not as if she'd ever return for someone who's sick with wolfbite. She deserves better than me."

"Don't say that. You know she still loves you." Tobias touched her arm. "We're allowed to live, all right? We're allowed to exist."

Tavia jerked her arm away. "And at what cost? It's selfish and dangerous and cruel. You tore Kingtide to bloody ribbons. Can you really tell me we should exist after *that*?"

"That was different. I did it to protect you and Ez. He was going to kill you both."

"Do you think you'll always have that choice? Don't be stupid. The sickness won't stop. We won't always have control."

"And what of the Monarchy? Or the Sacred Seven, eh? What of them? Do they get a pass because they don't turn into beasts when they kill innocents?"

"They're a necessary evil to keep society running," she scoffed. "Blood wolves are different."

Tobias bowed his head. She was afraid, and yet she remained loyal to a fault. Loyal to a system and its rules that didn't care about her as a human or a blood wolf. How could she not see that?

"I won't let you give up on yourself for this saintsforsaken kingdom."

"I won't give up on you either." Tavia gripped the hilts of her daggers. "And I won't let you suffer."

The morning carried on a groggy reluctance as the heat picked up.

Tobias was halfway down Hadwick Street, turning over his conversation with Tavia and wondering if Marcellus would let him help Vivian and the twins, when a carriage driver stepped in line behind him. Besides Tobias, only factory workers, housemaids and shopkeepers were out and about at this hour. The exact kind of group that minded their own business, for they had foremen, landlords and ladies of the house to answer to. It didn't pay for them to intervene when a boy was suddenly approached by a carriage driver with ill intentions.

By the time Tobias realized someone was behind him, Anders had already grasped Tobias's shoulder and invoked a paralyzing influence over his mind.

Follow me, young sir, an unfamiliar voice beckoned Tobias within his own mind.

Tobias didn't try to flee. He was aware of wanting to run, but neither his mind nor body responded. He was blocked from any control. But this wasn't a change of guard like with the blood wolf. No, this was paralysis. Thievery.

Magic.

The wolf stirred within him, a beast awoken to action. Anders tightened his hold on Tobias's shoulder and the animosity of the blood wolf quelled. He led Tobias to a sleek black carriage parked a few steps away. Its ivory curtains were drawn, but Tobias could make out the silhouette of a person sitting inside.

"Step in, young sir."

Tobias did as he was told. As soon as he slid onto the plush seat, Anders closed the door behind him.

Sitting on the other side was a young man in his early twenties. He was devilishly handsome, crafted by charm and favorable features, but a danger lurked in those blue eyes and sharp smile. Tobias had seen that look a dozen times on a dozen different men. The North Rim was full of people like him.

Insatiable hunters.

"Good morning, Tobias." The man said his name with an air of familiarity Tobias would've decked him for had he control of his arms.

The man frowned when Tobias didn't answer. He knocked on the driver's partition and Anders appeared once more. "You can release him now, Anders."

"I'm afraid that's not wise, Master Trevet. I sensed blood wolf power within him, sir."

"Is that so?" the man raised a brow. "Interesting. Regardless, release him. If he misbehaves, I'll snap his neck." A smirk pulled at his mouth. "Do you understand, Mr. Flemming?"

Anders moved his fingers and Tobias gasped for breath. He glared at the man but made no move to leave the carriage. He wasn't eager to lose control again.

"And who in the seven hells are you?"

The stranger leaned back in his seat. "Ah yes, where are my manners? Nathaniel Trevet, your new employer."

"New employer?"

"I don't care to repeat myself, so do try to keep up," Nathaniel said, recrossing his legs. "There was a theft in High Hampton recently. A certain pair of eyes went missing from a young boy's skull. Terribly unfortunate for everyone involved, I must say. Unless of course you have the eyes to return to me."

Speech had suddenly left him, so Tobias shook his head instead.

Nathaniel frowned. "Tsk tsk. I paid very good money to the Jeweler for that procurement, and now it's in the wind. It seems only fair I'm compensated for what you stole, wouldn't you agree?"

"I don't know—"

"—much, I know," Nathaniel interrupted, boredom dampening his tone. "Luckily for you, I already have a new item in mind I wish to procure. In two days' time, Albert Hoyt will be hosting the Summerillia, Halcyon's largest ball of the season. You're going to attend this event and locate a book with a sun and moon emblazoned on its cover from his personal collection. Do this, and I'll see to you and your sister's protection."

"Protection?" Tobias replied with an air of snark. "Protection from what? And how do you know me? Or that I was even in High Hampton?"

"Fail me and your debt will grow." Nathaniel's charming smile did little to warm his words. "And I always collect what I'm owed, one way or another."

"You didn't answer my questions, highblood."

"I don't need to, Mr. Flemming. An employer isn't beholden to the whims and wants of his employee. But in the spirit of our new working relationship, I'll humor one of your requests. As a sign of good faith, if you will. You'll come to find I'm quite an agreeable boss."

Nathaniel cleared his throat. "A couple of days ago, a fateshifter was killed here in Lordhaven. I believe you know the one—Oswyn Spettle." Nathaniel paused but Tobias's blank expression remained unchanged. "Doesn't ring a bell? Perhaps you may know him under his other name: Kingtide."

Tobias's face fell. *How does he know so bloody damn much?*

"Mr. Spettle was a criminal and deserved his fate, but he was a leashed criminal. And the man holding that leash is on the Crown's payroll." Nathaniel tilted his head, watching Tobias as a cat would a cornered mouse. "I trust that even you know the king doesn't like to share his toys. What do you think he'd do if he found out a lowly thug broke one of his best ones?"

"N-No, you're wrong." But even Tobias didn't believe his own words. The pieces were slotting into place. Nathaniel could be lying, but Tobias's gut told him otherwise and instinct had gotten him and Lucy this far.

"I'm afraid I have another appointment, so Anders will be in touch tomorrow for your measurements. I strongly recommend you be at this very spot tomorrow at 7:00 a.m. sharp, but the choice is yours. Keep in mind I will take your absence as a breach of our verbal employment contract. I'll have Anders provide a print copy to review at your leisure as well as reading accommodations if needed."

Tobias spit at Nathaniel's feet. "Piss off. I don't bloody work for you, got it? Not now. Not ever."

Nathaniel leaned in close. Tobias's eyes went wide as two needle-sharp fangs slid down behind Nathaniel's canines.

"Let me state it for you plain then. I will sell you and your sister's whereabouts to the highest bidder. The Crown. Deadeye. The City Watch. Theatre surgeons. Blood wolf trophy hunters. Traffickers. Murderers. All of them. Rest assured the auction will be swift and by the end of it there won't be a sewer, house, or hole you or your sister could hide in where they won't find you. I will personally see to it you never rest, you never stop, and you only eat and drink enough to stay alive. Do we have an understanding?"

Tobias nodded, speechless. This was no mere highborn. His tailored three-piece suit, his trim form, his posh speaking—it was all a ruse for the well-groomed duskborn beneath. How old Nathaniel really was Tobias could only guess, but he knew too much to be anyone less than dangerous. Information was power. Names even more so. Money was merely the tip of the iceberg.

Nathaniel knocked on the window and Anders opened the carriage door.

"I look forward to working together, Mr. Flemming."

Tobias said nothing. As Anders closed the door and snapped the reins of the black mare, a ribbon of dread spooled out in the street behind the departing carriage.

One end was tied around Nathaniel's finger, and the other was wrapped around Tobias's throat.

43

NATHANIEL

"The First Child, their name Isomol, bore the face and instincts of the gods. Broken first was their mind, for they knew too many things; second was their body, from which the seven instincts—Greed, Lust, Gluttony, Pride, Wrath, Envy, and Sloth—fled from Empyris, realm of the gods, to Chthonis, realm of the dead. It is there Umbrin, God of Souls and Trickery, offered the seven instincts a deal." – *Archscribe Hashmir Almrid Charellia*, Legends of the Dawn Age

As the Summerillia approached, a strange calmness settled over Nathaniel.

Claude had shown his next card in play—Victoria Whitmont—and it was a powerful one indeed. Princess Angelina had also emerged from the dark recesses of the kingdom and with her, a soul stealing monster from legend. While their entrances had changed a few things, the goal remained the same.

For the Mayfair Plot to be a success, Nathaniel would need access to Princess Angelina. The Summerillia was his best chance, and once he disposed of her in one of the countless rooms of the estate and secured the eternal heart, he was to meet with Dr. Rubin Debenham, one of the best surgeons in Lordhaven and known for his discreetness at the right price. From there, Claude, the Malsik, Victoria and the Chases would be dealt with in short working order.

What he was not about to do was give any hint of his doubts to Rose or Samir. He called no meeting to discuss what had happened at Lady Cavall's and sent no correspondence. He stayed at his residence in Thornwood and took no visitors.

He only needed to wait for the Summerillia festivities at Chersey Hall two nights hence. If Claude were to make any sudden moves, Nathaniel assured it would be when the whose-who of Halcyon was in attendance and not a moment before.

Patience, he had whispered to them after the party at Galbrooke's. *Trust me.*

But that had been before his visit to Lady Cavall's. Before he was aware the White Raven and Princess Angelina were connected.

Nathaniel pinched a morsel of venison between his fingers. The puzzle pieces before him were small and many sided, but no matter—he already had an idea of the larger picture. Even without the raven eyes that pesky Market Streeter stole, Nathaniel trusted Anders's findings on the boy. If all went well and the Market Streeter succeeded in his task, Nathaniel would soon have a means of mastering the eternal heart and thus securing his title as Halcyon's immortal duskborn king.

He reached into the gilded cage before him. It stood nearly as high as the ceiling itself and spanned the length of the guest room wall. Eribus, a miniature Stalvik dragon no larger than a cat, moseyed over to the bars. With practiced restraint he took the morsel, never biting Nathaniel's fingers.

"There's a good boy," Nathaniel cooed.

Eribus's scales shifted to deep aquamarine. Also known as a bismuth dragon, miniature Stalviks were one of the few remaining relics of the Golden Age. A testament to the magicks and wonders of a bygone era brimming with ambition. A reminder that even dragons, once the titans of the arcane hierarchy, could be tamed with enough patience.

Everything can be brought to heel.

Suddenly, Eribus's scales flared to a fiery ruby. His spiny tail snapped back and forth as a low growl reverberated from his heated throat.

"Eribus?"

Nathaniel followed the dragon's golden eyed gaze to a corner on the other side of the room. He reached into his jacket pocket. In a blink, he pivoted, fangs barred and pistol drawn.

Nothing.

Nathaniel titled his head, shifting his gaze from Eribus to the corner. His scales hadn't reverted back to their normal dark green.

Nathaniel kept his pistol raised. "Who goes there?" Sunlight and shadow began to shift and Dolly materialized from a shimmering nothingness.

"You have an awfully funny way of greeting your guests." She peered around Nathaniel and pointed at Eribus. "I don't believe he likes me very much."

"By the gods, Dolly." He retracted his fangs and put away his pistol. "I almost killed you."

She giggled. "I'm very good at hiding. I doubt you could've found me."

"What are you doing here? And how did you even get *in* here? This is the third floor."

"Silly, I came through the front door of course." Dolly shook her head. "Really, Nathaniel. You don't think I've sprouted wings now do you?"

Nathaniel didn't know what to believe anymore. He'd heard of Dolly's disappearing abilities, but up until now she refused to use them around him.

"So, this is what the Forsaken granted you in exchange for your tongue? You can, what, slip in and out of places?"

"It was a *gift*," Dolly corrected with a sigh.

"A silver tongue unable to lie isn't much a gift."

"Was I supposed to not have a tongue at all then?" Dolly crossed the room, hands clasped behind her. "And I never truly disappear. I simply weave together light and shadow to make it seem that I'm not really here, there, anywhere really." She smiled at Eribus. "But there's no fooling a dragon. They're so clever! And he's so small, too. Oh, he's simply adorable, Nathaniel!"

Nathaniel stepped between Eribus and Dolly, blocking her view. "Why are you telling me this now? You never spoke of your abilities when I asked before."

Dolly frowned. "The howler ... I'm almost certain it understands what I'm saying. It just watches me, you know? It never moves. It never blinks. Sometimes I wonder if it even breathes." She shivered. "I hate looking it. How could Dr. Loveney ever create such a foul creature?"

"The howler?" Nathaniel shook his head. "There's no howl—" but then he understood. Of course King Leonard would want one of his best assets protected. It was how she could remain safely undercover in one of the most popular kitten houses in Spade Alley. Even a Watcher would be no match for a howler's speed and paralyzing bite.

Clever.

"Do you conceal it?" Nathaniel probed.

"Yes, I must. At all times."

"And it's handler?"

"Never far."

Nathaniel had only glimpsed a dead howler once in a private surgical theatre session, but it was enough for a lifetime—black, bulbous eyes; a disproportionately wide, beak-like mouth curved into a perpetual grin; three rows of tiny, razor-sharp teeth to latch onto skin all set in an oddly human-like face and contorted hairless, human-like body. Even if law demanded they remain cloaked in the royal colors while in public with their constable handlers, a howler's predatory crawl alone was enough to unnerve most people.

"I swear it tells Dr. Loveney things," Dolly murmured. "And of course she wouldn't hesitate to tattle to the king. She's never forgiven me for not volunteering to be one of her test subjects."

Dolly shook her head as if to ward off a memory. "I didn't mean to startle you or little Eribus earlier. I simply came to tell you I found the King's non-royal son, Leander, like you asked. It was safer to show you in person. I also found something else you might find interesting but first take this."

Dolly reached into her clutch and handed Nathaniel a folded piece of paper. It was a hastily written letter penned by one Sir William Batterford to Mr. Douglas Tillings. Nathaniel raised a brow. He recognized those names—both were members of the Houndstooth Gentlemen's Society with known affiliations to the Sentry.

So, Leander Winslett had traveled in highborn circles. Nathaniel had never personally corresponded with the Winsletts, but their shipping fortune was well known throughout Lordhaven.

"Douglas, there's been an accident," the letter began. "Pruton misfired during last weekend's hunting expedition and Leander ... Well, the poor boy didn't make it. I've made arrangements with Colton, Georgina's brother—good man—to settle the matter with the local constables, but we need your boatman's services to handle the rest. Trust Colton's district will have your favor come the next cabinet run. Your utmost discretion during these trying times is greatly appreciated. With best regards, William."

Nathaniel looked at the corner of the letter. No date. Given Victoria's sudden appearance, this could only have been a few weeks old at most. Another accidental death. Another body swept beneath a rug threaded in favors.

Nathaniel opened Eribus's cage.

"No, don't!" Dolly cried, but he held her back with his free arm. "Please, I stole that letter from Bennett's office. He'll know it was me! I'll be punished!" Her eyes went childishly wide. "The king will be furious with me!"

Nathaniel turned away from her. "Tell Bennett you have new information. Victoria Whitmont intends to kill Princess Angelina with the full support of the Order of the Boar behind her. She's already orchestrated her fellow step siblings' deaths. That should get his attention."

He extended the letter in front of Eribus, careful to stand to the side. He balled his other hand into a fist. As he brought it down, Eribus spewed a stream of blue fire on command and within seconds, the letter was gone.

Dolly collapsed onto a cushioned bench.

"Bennett will have my head ..." she murmured to herself.

"Tell him what I told you and you'll have nothing to fear," Nathaniel said, his voice firm. "Victoria admitted herself she plans to seize the throne. Now all that remains is the rest of her family."

Nathaniel's mind raced. The Order was playing with a viper. If Victoria was as methodical as her trail of carnage warranted, Claude would either have a puppet queen or be struck dead in the process.

"You said you had something else for me?"

Dolly absently reached into her clutch again and removed a postcard. The golden Teatro Paradiso in Arcadia's capital of Fiore gleamed like a torch against the velvet night. On the back, neither postmark nor address were present. The unaddressed message read, "The accords will burn first."

Nathaniel hesitated before asking, "What is this?"

Dolly gathered her things and stood. "Bennett had it wedged underneath that letter. I...I don't know." She cradled her arms, digging her nails into her elbows. "Arcadia wouldn't declare war on us...would they?"

Nathaniel gripped both of her shoulders. "Dolly, go back to the Blue Rose. I'll be in touch. And repeat not a word of this to anyone. Tell Bennett what he needs to hear and not a syllable more. Understand?"

Dolly nodded, her face weary. "Nathaniel, promise me you'll be careful, too. And no more with this White Raven business. You swear it?"

Nathaniel flashed his signature sly smile. "Of course."

He glanced out the partially shaded window. Beyond the sooty rooftops of Lordhaven loomed Dutchenson Castle, a legacy of liars and brutes behind its walls, unaware their end was creeping ever closer.

As soon as Dolly exited the room, Ivan stepped inside. Eribus scuttled to the furthest corner of his cage, his scales shifting to black and his tail curled defensively around him.

"You're unwise not to use the girl to get that book," Ivan said, his voice contorted into a fiendish screech. "A mad spy is better than a thieving child with wolfbite. Especially if war is sailing to your shore. A mighty risk you're taking."

When Nathaniel looked over his shoulder, the shell of Ivan stood in the doorway, only this time, yellow horizontal pupils cut across Ivan's normally vacant black eyes.

"If I needed the opinion of a parasitic demon, I would've asked," Nathaniel quipped. "And one measly postcard confirms nothing. Now, return to sleep, Salvamot and let Ivan resume his duties. Eribus needs his cage tidied."

Salvamot grunted. "You wouldn't have even known Albert Hoyt possessed *Aeternus* if it hadn't been for me. If you fail to kill the princess before Victoria—"

"Do you take me for a failure, demon?" Nathaniel interrupted, barring his fangs. "The eternal heart will be mine and your precious host will be protected once I've secured the throne as discussed. Dare to insinuate failure in my presence again and I'll deliver you and Ivan to the vicaress myself."

Salvamot blinked back a rebuttal and softened his features. "Understood. Hopefully for you and the child thief the White Raven is occupied with a full dance card."

Nathaniel paused. His eyes slowly narrowed. "How do you know the White Raven will be at the Summerillia?"

"I don't. Sir." Salvamot smirked, hands clasped behind his back. "Just a hunch."

44

—◆◇◆—

SYBIL

"As Queen, it is my duty to protect the people of the Avalon Isles—Halcyon and Bronwen. Fateshifters are citizens and therefore the very people I'm sworn by duty to protect. The Sentry can't simply pick and choose whom they wish to serve. They serve the people. *All* of them." – *Royal correspondence from Queen Minerva Chase to Sentry House Leader Trudie Nettleton*

Sybil squinted against the early afternoon sun.

The grass was soft beneath her, the blades tickling her ankles. The smell of soil and field weed hung on the warm, stagnant air.

"There." She pointed at a passing cloud. "That one's a cat. See the ears?"

Kate frowned. "I don't see it. Oh, but look at that one! It's shaped like a prince! And that one over there could be the lovely princess on his arm." She rolled onto her side and looked up at her older sister.

"What do you see, Ruby?"

Ruby lowered her sketchbook and pencil and looked up at the sky. Her face fell into a frown.

"Clouds." She resumed sketching.

"We all know that, silly. But what do you see in them? You know, like animals or people, that sort of thing?"

Ruby let out a long sigh. "Must we, Kate? You know I'm not good at this."

"Yes, we absolutely must!" Kate fell back on the grass and winked at Sybil. "Ruby always comes around one way or another," she whispered. "Just like Da." Kate studied the sky with the focus of a hawk.

"That one!" She pointed to a particularly puffy cloud. "What do you see?"

"No fair. You're choosing clouds for me now?" A smile tugged at the corner of Ruby's lips.

"Because you choose the dull ones."

Just then, the sound of a bell rang across the fields. Kate sat up with a start. "Oh, no I lost my time! Bye for now!"

Sybil pushed up onto her arms and watched in puzzlement as Kate hurried towards the Abcott house. She turned to Ruby, who had paid her sister no mind and was quietly humming. "What does the bell mean?"

Ruby glanced over at Sybil as if waking from a daze. "The wha—Oh, it's the bell from the school hall. Stanley will be coming 'round to help out da soon. Kate always makes an absolute fuss if she doesn't have lunch made for the three of them." Ruby shrugged her shoulders. "I dunno why she troubles herself. Stanley has been sweet on her since they were kids. Mum is afraid he might grow tired of her though."

Sybil understood wanting to please someone regardless of the shape it left you in. And yet hearing Ruby speak of her sister's actions left Sybil wondering if maybe she'd been wrong. What if in her attempt to do everything expected of her, she'd done nothing for herself at all?

"I think it's sweet of her," Sybil replied, eager to lighten the mood. "It's rare to find people who are so honest."

"Did you have a sweetheart back home?" Ruby asked, resting her chin on her hand. Her brownish green eyes stared at Sybil curiously.

Sybil inhaled sharply. Love was a distraction and distractions were dangerous. She hadn't given up everything to prove herself as the best in her year to lose it because of her heart's whims.

"Well, no, not really ..."

Ruby smirked. "Don't worry, I'm not like Kate. I promise I won't ask you when you plan to wed and what names you've chosen for your future children." She rolled her eyes. "As if we all want those things anyway."

Sybil had never given much thought to a future with someone, let alone having children with them. It just wasn't something she cared about. If it happened, it happened. If it didn't, she didn't think she'd be sad over it.

Suddenly a voice cut across the clearing.

"There you both are." Liza approached with bundles of yarn in various shades of reds, golds, browns and whites in a basket beneath her arm.

"By the saints, Ruby, don't tell me you've been doodling in that silly book of yours all morning."

A blush spread across Ruby's downturned face. Before she could answer, Liza held out the basket of yarn.

"Mum told you yesterday to take this to Mrs. Gordon first thing, remember? You should've been there an hour ago."

"I-I'm sorry, I forgot. I was having a chat with Esther and Kate ..."

Liza's gaze flickered to Sybil. Her lips pursed into a scowl and Sybil tensed for an argument, but Liza shifted her focus back to Ruby.

"Really, Ruby? Blaming your forgetfulness on our guest and your little sister?" She shoved the basket into her sister's hands. "I won't tell Mum but be quick about it. She'll be cross at all of us if word gets back you were late. And you," she said, looking at Sybil. "You're coming with me today."

Sybil and Ruby exchanged confused glances and Liza let out a groan. "Am I expected to run the bookshop by myself *and* finish your cataloguing?" She turned on her heels with a huff and headed towards town.

"That'll be today, Esther!" she hollered behind her.

Sybil shot Ruby a sympathetic smile and hurried after Liza. Once they reached the used bookshop a short time later, Sybil went straight to her box in the back corner of the shop. She picked up the ledger—her last entry being *The Yellow Swallow*, a collection of poems she had made a note to read with several other titles—and resumed cataloging by title, author, quantity and quality of the newly arrived books.

Not an hour later, the click clack of Liza's boots echoed down the aisle. "I have to run a quick errand, so I'll need you to run the register while I'm gone."

Sybil looked up, her brows furrowed. "I've never run register before."

"Well then, today's your lucky day. It's hardly any trouble at all. Just make sure to double check your coin counts and you'll be fine, I promise."

"Wait, I—"

But Liza was already halfway to the door. Sybil scrambled to her feet, panic rising in her gut. She'd never had to count coins before. Sanctis didn't operate with the crown's currency since they were largely cut off from Halcyonian society. Any sterlings that did manage to circulate were largely kept to the larger traders or the Council. Most goods and labor between Sanctinites were bartered or traded for by an agreed value between both parties.

Sybil's palms began to sweat. *Calm down*, she reminded herself. *She said she'd be back soon.*

She walked behind the counter with sheepish steps, her eyes darting around the empty shop. She folded and unfolded her hands until she annoyed herself and dropped them to her sides.

"Get it together," Sybil said aloud. "It's just a shop."

Just a shop. A bookshop. In a normal, Halcyonian town. The dream flinted before her, if only for a moment. What if this were *her* shop? In a town *she* lived in, all on her own? A warmth bloomed in her chest, a mere flicker of a flame, but gradually it grew until her arms tingled and her lips pulled into a smile.

A future. Normal, quaint. Gods, even idyllic. She looked down at her hands. Not blood soaked. Not tinged in fire. But hands that had reached and reached and reached and still came up with nothing.

The *ting* of the doorbell cut through her thoughts. "Hello, welcome!"

"Sybil?"

Sybil's stomach dropped. There was nothing to say. There was everything to say.

"Sybil?" Priya repeated.

There had always been ease between them. But now Sybil heard the fear cracking Priya's voice into shards.

Gods, what have I done?

Priya was a shell of the best friend she'd left behind. The shadows of sleepless nights lingered like stains and her clothes hung a bit looser than before. But it was the flatness behind her eyes like a candle snuffed out that tore Sybil's heart.

I did this to her.

Sybil bowed her head and bit the inside of her lip.

"Don't bite. It's fine."

Sybil reflexively let the inner skin of her lip go, then flashed an annoyed look at Priya. "How did you find me?"

Priya chuckled and smiled despite herself. "Hello to you, too."

"You didn't answer me."

Priya's smile fell away. The false ease they'd shared was gone, replaced by the valley of unspoken truths between them.

Could they survive the fall?

"It's a compass the Sentinels have that traces mana by a blood sample. Like calling to like." Priya ignored the horror on Sybil's face. "I know it sounds awful, but it's only for security. Please, Sybil. Please come back."

"No." The words left Sybil's mouth before she could think about them. They looked at each other in surprise.

"You can't really mean to stay here. It's not safe outside Sanctis."

"If I return, they'll kill me, Priya. I—" The words caught in her throat. She couldn't bring herself to say the rest.

"I'm a Dawnslayer," Sybil finally whispered, fighting back tears. "I know who I am. And I know what I need to do."

"So you'd live a coward's life then? Hide amongst the unseers and wait for the Sentinels to find you?"

"I have a plan."

"No, you don't."

"*Yes*, I do. I'm fine."

"You're not *fine*, Sybil. You haven't been fine since your coven was killed. None of us have." Priya approached the counter, her eyes glassy. "Your mum begged the Council not to send the Sentinels. She convinced them that I could bring you back to answer for your actions. Peacefully." Priya frowned. "But that was a lie. I can't bring you back. Only you can do that." She grabbed Sybil's hand and searched her green eyes. "If I don't return with you, Cal has sworn to come in my place."

"What?"

"There's something you don't know. The High Council has a secret watch committee in Sanctis. Each family is required to have a member keep watch on what goes on around them. They're called scouts. Most are children or teens so they can train to be Sentinels when they graduate from Lycoris."

Sybil tried to take back her hand, but Priya only tightened her hold. When their eyes met, Sybil knew her best friend well enough to know this was breaking her.

"I was assigned to be my family's scout. The Sentinel assigned to my case said I was chosen so Anjali could focus on her studies. She showed more promise than me. More value to Sanctis and the Council." A bitter laugh left Priya's mouth. "I absolutely hate it but what choice did I have? I couldn't let Surjan take my place. He's so young." She lowered her voice. "I'm so sorry, Sybil. I know this all sounds terrible, but I promise we'll talk to the Council together. Please, just come back with me."

Sybil withdrew her hand, and this time Priya didn't stop her.

"I can't go back there. What, so I can be watched by my family and reported on? And they call *me* the monster."

"You're not a monster. You never were."

In that moment, their friendship laid itself bare and Sybil saw with painful clarity that Priya would go into that unspoken valley with her, plunge into the abyss hand in hand and brace for the fall, together. And Sybil wanted a hand to hold hers in the dark. Gods, she wanted it more than anything. She was tired of being alone. Tired of questioning her sanity in the fight to keep her head above water. But the idea of ruining someone else's life stirred her anger and fanned the flames around her heart.

I'm sorry, Priya. I can't break you, too.

Sybil took a step back. "Maybe you're not as good at judging someone's character as you thought."

"Sybil, don't ..."

"Just go home, Priya! Leave me alone."

"If you don't come back, it'll just prove to them they were right all along about you! Do you want that? Because my best friend would *never* give up that easily."

"Then you weren't listening." Sybil shook her head, hot tears behind her eyes. "They already made up their minds about me when I came back and my coven didn't. How was I ever supposed to fix that? How was any of it fair?"

Just then Liza strode through the doorway. She froze, her eyes darting between Sybil and Priya then back to Sybil. "Oh, a friend of yours?"

"No," Sybil replied, exiting from behind the counter without a second glance in Priya's direction. "I'm sorry but I'm unwell."

Sybil left the bookshop as Liza's voice called out behind her. She walked as fast as her feet could carry her and all too soon she was running from Sanctis again.

Tears poured down her cheeks in hot rivulets. She cupped her mouth to keep in the screams, but she couldn't stop trembling. She was coming undone again.

Stop—

Stop—

Stop this!

She took in a deep breath and rubbed her eyes with the palms of her hands. One breath, two breath. Deep in. Slow out.

She lowered her shaking hands.

And there, across the way, leaving his workshop was Arthur. They stared at each other in silence. Sybil's mouth hung slightly agape.

She looked away first and bolted into the Abcott house. She rushed upstairs, closed the door and let out a shaky breath. Arthur didn't matter. None of them mattered. She just needed to clear her head. Yes, just like the frost would've done if she had any. She needed a lie down, a quick one, and everything would be fine.

When Sybil drifted off to sleep, Sanctis was waiting for her.

Flames devoured everything she'd ever known. As she watched, a hand slipped into hers. Priya stood beside her, her face streaked in tears, watching a cottage burn to ash.

"Why are you burning our home?" Priya asked.

"I had to."

Priya dropped her hand and walked towards the burning cottage. Sybil tried to follow her, to stop her, but her feet wouldn't move. When she tried calling Priya's name, her voice was gone. She grabbed her own throat in disbelief as Priya watched from the burning doorway. Flames charred the ends of her dark hair and bubbled her skin.

"Come to me, Felnor, my beloved."

Sybil's eyes flew open.

She was being pulled out of bed by strong hands. The hands of a Sentinel. She tried to move, to scream, but just like in her dream her body refused to cooperate. Her voice was lost. Something was binding her mouth.

That's when she realized the stranger wasn't a Sentinel at all.

They wore an all-white uniform, but it lacked the elegance of the Sentinel robes. Thinly tailored cotton long sleeves and pants. Cruder, but no less cruel.

"Careful," one of the men warned. "Could be a biter."

Sybil swiveled her head to see another man approaching from the hall. He was in the same crude white uniform as her captor. He snapped a pair of iron cuffs on her wrists.

Panic seized her. She couldn't pull mana, couldn't summon her grimoire, couldn't feel the dead. *I can't spellcast. Oh gods, I can't spellcast!* Her eyes darted around the room looking for someone, anyone to help her. But there was no one.

The men each took an arm and hauled her to her feet. She bucked and clawed at skin but to no avail. When she was dragged past the Abcott sisters' room, she screamed their names as she kicked, desperate to buy time. But if they heard her garbled pleas, no one answered them.

Outside, the night air was unusually cool.

Arthur stood in front of an unmarked carriage. A porter sat up front, staring straight ahead.

"Are you certain of this, Mr. Abcott?"

Arthur didn't look at Sybil as the men in white brought her up to the carriage.

"Yes. Such a young, impressionable mind is prone to troubling thoughts. I'm afraid only proper rest and silence will treat her hysteria. My wife and I have done all we can for her niece."

Sybil tried to scream again, tried to dispel the lies Arthur spewed to these strangers, but her protests came out as little more than muffled whimpers behind her gag.

"We shall see to it Miss Abcott receives the treatment she needs in Lordhaven, sir."

The man reached into his coat pocket and removed a syringe. He popped off its cover and flicked it a couple times. Sybil tried to squirm away, but the men in white gripped her tight enough to bruise. She let out a shrill cry as the needle pricked her arm. Seconds later, tiredness weighed her down like heavy furs.

She turned to Arthur as darkness crept at the edges of her vision. When she looked past him, she caught the flutter of his bedroom curtain and Irene's figure pulling away from the window.

"Liar," she whispered against her gag. "You..."

She fell into the abyss, headfirst and alone.

Sybil awoke with a heavy head.

When she went to move her arms, she couldn't. Afraid she was still under whatever the man in white had given her, she tried turning her head.

Oh, gods.

She was shackled. Iron cuffs bound her wrists to the bed. When she tried to move her fingers, they were oddly numb, as if not properly attached to her body. Fear surged through her racing heart.

A door clicked opened and Sybil jerked her head in the direction of the noise. A woman in a white uniform walked in. Although she didn't appear more than thirty, her eyes bore a tiredness only elders usually carried.

"W-Where am I?" Sybil said in a hoarse voice.

The nurse frowned.

"Mansfield, dear. Mansfield Sanitarium."

45

SYBIL

"A crown is a sword as a grimoire is a mirror." – *Scrollmaster Jhaeros Tartaro, excerpt from* Aeternus

The first thing Sybil learned at Mansfield Sanitarium was that everyone was being watched by someone.

The patients were being watched by the nurses. The nurses were being watched by the guard stationed in every room. And the guards were being watched by the patients. A cycle of watching. A season of waiting. For what, Sybil wasn't certain, but the tension pulled at her like the undercurrent of a stream. She stared down at her bowl of paste and winced. The line cook had called it porridge, but Sybil was convinced the grey, goopy mass was mortar.

"You gonna eat that?" A girl a little older than Sybil nodded towards Sybil's bowl. Her light brown eyes were wide with alert. She reminded Sybil of a small forest creature darting out for an acorn. "Well? Are you?"

Sybil shook her head.

The girl grabbed the bowl and started shoveling the porridge into her mouth. Grey mush dribbled down the side of her chin, but she didn't seem to notice or care. Sybil sank back in her seat and rubbed her eyes. The sharp metallic smell of her shackles gave her pause.

Iron to bide, iron to hide.

Arthur had betrayed her. She had worked hard to mind herself and it still wasn't enough to convince him. *Why am I never enough?* Her stomach coiled with anger, heat writhing inside waiting to—

"You can't use magic here," the girl snapped. She licked her lips and started picking at her cuticles. Two empty bowls sat between them.

"I know." Sybil held up her wrists. "Iron nullifies mana."

"Are you mad I ate your porridge? Because I asked you and you gave it to me."

"No, I don't care about the stupid porridge."

The girl's gaze flickered to the white uniformed nurses mulling around the tables, smiling and assisting patients. She turned back to Sybil. "My parents sent me. What about you?"

Sybil paused for a moment, then replied, "Me too."

She felt a pang of guilt for lying, but the feeling quickly hardened into an indifferent numbness. She had to get out of Mansfield.

"I'm Birdie. What's your name?"

"Esther."

Birdie's eye twitched as a smile flickered across her face. "No, it's not."

Sybil stared at Birdie with new suspicion. *She has cuffs on. How can she be using magic?*

"What do you mean it's not?"

"You're lying," Birdie chirped. "That's not your name. And your parents didn't really send you here." She lowered her voice until it was a harried whisper. "Magic isn't all we have."

Before Sybil could respond, a nurse materialized beside them with an unnerving smile. A uniformed guard nearly twice Sybil's height lingered behind her.

"That's enough socialization for the morning, ladies. Perhaps you can carry on with more banter over tea later, hmm?" She gestured for Sybil to rise. "Come now, Miss Abcott. Let's get you back to your room."

Sybil glanced up at the guard and bit back her protest. Birdie watched in silence as Sybil was led out of the gathering quarters.

When she returned to her room, a short, thin woman in a lab coat she'd never seen before was waiting for her. She had long black hair hastily pulled back at the nape of her pale neck and dark eyes hidden behind wire rimmed glasses. Messy bangs framed her angular face but did little to dim her piercing gaze. Standing beside her was a tall man with fine, dark hair and a fitted lab coat. Both kept their hands tucked away in their coat pockets.

"Hello, Miss Abcott. I'm Dr. Lillian Loveney and this is my lead assistant, Farhan Shah. A pleasure to meet you."

Her voice carried all the warmth of steel. As if sensing the weighty silence to follow, Nurse Turlow turned her beaming smile towards Sybil.

"Esther, Dr. Loveney is visiting you today with a wonderful opportunity."

Dr. Loveney's mouth set into a thin line. "As I've stated before, Sharla, it's unnecessary to refer to this as an opportunity. It's a research program. *My* research program."

"Of course," Nurse Turlow replied. "My apologies, doctor. I meant no offense. It's just that we find patients tend to be rather nervous when its termed so ... *clinically*." Her shaky smile faltered under Dr. Loveney's rigid gaze. "Our aim is to ensure a smooth transition from Mansfield to ..." but she let the words die in the air.

"Right then." Nurse Turlow clasped her hands together. "I'll just let you two get on. I'll be out in the hall if you need me."

Dr. Loveney said nothing as she watched Nurse Turlow depart. Farhan remained vigilant, a stoic shadow of his boss. Once the door was closed, Dr. Loveney's attention pivoted to Sybil.

"Have you heard of the Horace Project before, Miss Vorn?"

Sybil's breath caught in her throat.

"How do you know my name? Are you with the Sentinels?"

Dr. Loveney lit a kell and took a deep drag. "No, and I haven't any interest in your supposed crimes if that's your concern. Now, have you heard of the Horace Project?"

Sybil's heart still raced. "No, ma'am."

"It's a study of arcanics and how their abilities may benefit those not in possession of a sacral nervous system." She blew out a plume of smoke from the corner of her mouth. "Unseers, I believe we're referred to as in your community."

Sybil's mouth fell open. "You study fateshifters? Here, in Lordhaven? And you're not imprisoned?"

Farhan chuckled but Dr. Loveney remained aloof.

"The Monarchy is rather generous with their pardons when the work is being done for the kingdom's benefit," Farhan replied. "Dr. Loveney is the head researcher of the Royal Medical House at Dutchenson Castle. She doesn't care much for titles, but I assure you her skill warrants it."

It was then Sybil noticed his extended fangs capped by a gold-plated brace that stretched across his top teeth. A duskborn. She stiffened but kept her face as neutral as possible. She couldn't afford to cross him, not without her magic.

"You shouldn't be concerned about Farhan. He's no more dangerous than you are in iron shackles."

Sybil's eyes went wide. She knew that voice.

She whirled around to see Professor Nera Rossi leaning in the corner of the room. Gone were her floor-length Lycoris robes and in their place was a rustic orange and gold bodice and skirts. Sybil took a double take. Professor Rossi appeared more as a Lordhaven high lady than a semiotics professor.

"P-Professor Rossi?" Sybil stammered. "How—?"

Nera crossed the room and nodded to Dr. Loveney and Farhan. She took a seat across from Sybil and gestured for her to sit. Sybil sank into her seat, mouth agape.

This can't be real....

"Let's start with you first." Nera leaned forward. "You fled Sanctis under distress and came to stay with Arthur and Irene Abcott. It was there Miss Priya Majumdar approached you. You refused her proposal of surrender and that night, you were forced into Mansfield custody at the request of Arthur Abcott. Is that correct?"

The air grew heavy with chill and kellweed smoke. Sybil ground her teeth together as she searched for her voice.

"Yes, ma'am. Are you here to take me back?"

Nera smirked. "No. I'm here to recruit you."

"Recruit me?" Sybil sneered. "You mean to be a scout? Cal not cooperating then?"

Dr. Loveney pinched the half burned kell between her fingers as she took another drag. "Wrap it up, Nera. I haven't all day."

Nera's gaze flickered between the doctor and Sybil. The sigil imprinted over her eye shimmered for the briefest moment, leaving Sybil to question whether she'd seen it happen at all. Farhan continued to observe in silence.

"No, not for Sanctis. I was tasked with the assignment of observing Sanctis and the High Council's governance on behalf of King Leonard." Nera smiled, almost wistfully. "Don't look so surprised. You're Head Girl. Smart. Cunning. Focused. You must be when there's blood on your hands."

Sybil shot to her feet. Her shoulders and arms trembled as she pointed a shaking finger at Nera. "You're the traitor here. Not me."

Nera rose. "You killed your major and lied about it. I spied on the High Council and lied about it. Another way to tell that tale is you defended yourself when Major Quinn was injected with a serum containing blood wolf saliva and attacked you. I recruited the

High Council's blacklisted fateshifters to serve the Monarchy in exchange for proper compensation and legal freedom. What if I'm not a spy, but a liberator? What if you're not a traitor, but a victim? There are always two sides to everything, Sybil."

Nera closed the gap between them. "I'm asking you to become a spy for the Monarchy. In exchange, you'll get the answers you seek from the High Council. I'll see to it personally."

Sybil's eyes welled with tears. She backed away from Professor Rossi until she collided with the wall. She sunk to the floor as the adults watched in silence.

Professor Rossi ... a spy ... Major Quinn ... turned ...

"As it is a recruitment," Nera continued, "it's your decision if you wish to participate. But I would strongly urge you to consider your position. You're immensely powerful. It'd be wasted here."

"And if I choose not to?" Sybil mumbled, her fallen tears salty in her mouth.

"Then you'll remain here at Mansfield until Arthur Abcott signs off on your release," Dr. Loveney replied. "Or you perish. Whichever occurs first."

Sybil's eyes went wide. "W-What do you mean perish? Am I going to die here?"

Dr. Loveney frowned, tossing down her kell and stubbing the butt out with her heel. "The politics of humans—arcanic or unseer—dictate violence is bound to occur in confined dwellings such as this. Try not to look so startled, Miss Vorn. It's statistics, not divination. Your true concern would be figuring out how to maintain a positive response to this facility's treatment. Anything less may result in a permanent surgical solution." She tapped her forehead. "No more magic after that."

A loud buzzing rang in Sybil's ears. Arthur was never going to come back for her. If she didn't leave as a spy, she'd remain trapped forever as a patient. She looked down at her shaking, shackled hands.

"Fret not, poppet," her da's voice reminded her. *"A grand adventure awaits, and one must never turn their back on such marvelous timings."*

Two sides to every story. Two ways to tell every tale. *Become the spy or stay the patient. Become the traitor or stay the victim.*

"What happens if I join?" Sybil asked. "Will I ever be able to leave?"

"After initial training, and should you survive, yes, you may eventually leave. But if you're successful," Nera said with a smile, laying a firm hand on Sybil's shoulder, "then the Monarchy will have additional opportunities for you. Consider the Jackals your new coven of sorts."

Additional opportunities? For a fateshifter? In Lordhaven? It sounded like a child's tale. Something her father would've been over the moon to hear. When had Halcyon made such progress towards accepting fateshifters? And how had news of it not reached Sanctis?

What else has the High Council not been telling us?

Sybil took a deep breath. A new coven. A new chance. A new story.

"I want to join."

Relief brightened Nera's features. Dr. Loveney smiled for the first time, a child with a new toy. But Farhan looked suddenly somber, his pensive eyes darkening.

"Excellent." Nera held out her hand. "Welcome to the Jackals, Miss Vorn."

46

ANGELINA

"If war is to be believed, love is a rather dangerous thing." – *Orseta di Zorzi, Dionora, translated by Iseppo Balbi*

As the sun dipped beneath the horizon, lamplighters emerged from their dwellings of squander to illuminate Lordhaven.

Scores of carriages snaked towards Stone Hill in the heart of the Garden District. One such carriage, elegantly understated in black and gold, drew more stares than the rest. Inside, Angelina, clad in a glistening silver crescent mask and deep sapphire blue gown, watched in delight as Lordhaven came alive in the shadows just beyond the carriage window.

Her journey to her first gala as Crown Princess took them past Tenley Park, where highborns strolled the promenade by day and lovers sneaked away to by night; the windowless Fraiser House, a gentleman's club upon whose roof crows and stone statues sat side by side with mischief in their eyes; and the gleaming glass manor known as the Bathes, the gathering place of creatives to whom beauty was but everything. Finally, along the upscale Leaby Street, tucked away atop Stone Hill was the Hoyt's estate, Chersey Hall.

Angelina pressed her gloved hands against the glass, mouth agape. She expected Dutchenson Castle to be grand—it was a castle after all—but Chersey Hall was far larger than she ever imagined a private residence could be. Its frontage alone boasted over thirty windows. Two stone stairways bookended the large landing leading to the front set of doors.

"Saints, it's magnificent."

"It's one of the largest estates in Halcyon," Madelyn added, her golden filigree mask shimmering as she spoke. Some of the strangeness had fallen away from her voice, as if Angelina's Crowning had shifted something inside her. "And by far one of my favorites to visit."

"Are you sure Chersey Hall is your favorite and not just Lord Mason?" Tabitha teased from behind her emerald and gold butterfly mask. Madelyn shot her a glare, but Tabitha only smirked.

"Who's Lord Mason?" Angelina asked.

"No one," Madelyn quickly replied. "Just a friend. Lord Hoyt's eldest son."

"*Unmarried* son," Tabitha clarified.

"Now, Your Highnesses, if we are to have teatime gossip I advise bringing a teapot next time," Piers chided, his sapphire blue mask, adorned in diamonds and feathers to match his peacock feather collar, lending him a buoyantly regal air. "Otherwise, let us focus on the task at hand. It is the Summerillia, after all."

Beneath the brilliant indigo sky, the black and gold carriage finally made it to the front of Chersey Hall. Piers disembarked first, followed by Madelyn and Tabitha. Finally, Angelina stepped out and into a waking dream.

The night air was rich with the sweetness of moon blossoms and resonant sounds of a violin. Beyond the spiraling staircases and glistening chandeliers of the entryway, Angelina stepped into Chersey Hall's grand ballroom. She watched, transfixed, as masked attendees swept across the dance floor, hand in hand. Jesters scuttled about, coaxing those too shy to dance to the main floor and arousing laughter from those too bubbly in the head to hide their grins. The air was rife with risk as the fantastic creatures of the ball spoke boldly beneath the anonymity of their sequined masks.

"Isn't it all rather romantic?" Madelyn beamed. "I love the Summerillia."

"I can't believe Theo would want to miss this," Angelina replied, her attention flinting from one spectacle to the next.

Madelyn shook her head. "Too many people. It does quite number a on him."

Angelina wasn't surprised. It was as if all of Halcyon were crammed into the sprawling mansion.

Piers leaned closer to Angelina and whispered, "The hosts will come around soon. Best ready yourself."

"But how will I know it's them if everyone is in masks?"

Piers chuckled. "Oh, my dear you'll know. The Sacred Seven are anything but subtle. The Hoyts most of all."

As if on cue, a blond man with strong angular features arm in arm with a short, cherry brunette woman emerged from the crowd. They wore matching gold and bronze griffin masks that only partially covered their faces.

"Your Highnesses, Lord Astley, so glad you could make it to our little soiree," the woman said, flashing her brilliant white teeth. Her gaze not so casually slid over to Angelina. "Oh, and this *must* be our dear Crown Princess returned at last."

Angelina's brow furrowed. "Returned? I—"

"Welcome Your Royal Highness," the pair said in unison. The man bent forward in a bow and the woman dipped into a courtesy as if Angelina hadn't said anything at all.

Piers cleared his throat. "May I introduce Lord Albert Hoyt and his wife, Lady Myra Hoyt."

"We're so honored to have you here with us tonight," Albert gushed, the tinge of red in his cheeks peeking beneath his mask when he smiled. "Our family has been deeply aligned with the Chases for generations and we hope you find yourself at home here within Chersey Hall."

"That's very kind of you both, thank you." Angelina gave a small bow as the Hoyts strode away to greet another couple. Piers, his own peacock feathered mask rimmed in emerald and sapphires, shimmered beneath the light.

"Piers, why did Lady Hoyt say I just returned? I haven't gone anywhere."

"Pay it no mind," Piers replied, waving away her question. "Just a turn of phrase. The wasps of Lordhaven shall be swarming you now that the hosts have made their introduction. Best we refresh ourselves while we can."

"Why don't you let Tabitha and I take care of Angelina," Madelyn interjected, slinking her arm through Angelina's. "It's a far better look, don't you think?"

"A chaperon is embarrassing, Piers," Tabitha added, threading her arm on Angelina's opposite side.

Piers's mouth pressed into a thin line. "Sorry, ladies but I have strict orders from His Majesty to not let the Crown Princess out of my sight. And lest you not forget I too was a teenager once upon a time."

Tabitha rolled her eyes. "Don't worry, we'll stay in your sights. And I promise you needn't worry." She lowered her voice, but even still Angelina caught the menace in her words. "You already clipped her wings."

Tabitha turned and pulled her sisters along after her. Angelina looked back to see Piers frozen where he stood, his jaw clenched.

"A bit much, Tabitha," Madelyn said beneath her breath once they were out of earshot.

"Hardly. He knows everything that happens in Dutchenson. Dr. Loveney's little pet Farhan wouldn't have acted on his own and you know it. Father would have her head if he knew."

Madelyn pulled Angelina and Tabitha into a nearby alcove. "*We* don't know anything," she said in a harsh whisper. "I'm asking you nicely, Tabitha to please just drop this for tonight and let's enjoy ourselves."

Angelina looked between her sisters. Curiosity and confusion swirled inside her, but she hesitated to give it voice. Instead, a familiar warmth overcame her, blanketing her mind in a dreamy haze and reminding her she was happy and safe, not scared and confused.

Reminding her she was Angelina Chase.

"I agree with Madelyn. Let's—"

"Good evening, Your Highnesses."

A tall man with slicked back brown hair in a burnished gold fox mask stood before them. At his side was a black haired woman only slightly shorter than her partner in a ruby and lace encrusted cat mask.

"Apologies for the interruption, but I'd be remiss if we didn't give our regards to Halcyon's dearest family." The pair dipped into a bow and courtesy, respectively. Angelina's neck flushed hot watching them. Beneath their refined grace and honeyed words, they exerted a pull, an urging as primal as the call of the forest. It tempted her, whispered for her to follow.

A headache creeped into the back of her head. Shadows ... she had followed shadows once upon another time into a place she wasn't meant to go...

"Nathaniel Trevet, and my date, Miss Rose Blakely."

Rose smiled. "A pleasure, Your Highnesses."

The headache deepened. But Angelina was lost in the curl of Nathaniel's crooked smile and the curve of Rose's perfumed neck. The shadows beckoned.

"Don't trust them," a familiar voice growled in her ear. The girl in the red dress from her dream. A sharp pain pierced the side of Angelina's head. She winced through gritted teeth.

"Are you all right, Your Royal Highness?" Nathaniel reached out a hand to steady her, but Angelina took a step back.

"I'm fine, thank you," she said with a shaky smile. Almost immediately the pain disappeared as if she'd dreamt the whole thing.

"We must be on our way." Madelyn took Angelina's arm. "I'm afraid my sister is a bit overwhelmed with the excitement of the evening. It was a pleasure meeting you both."

"Likewise. We do hope you enjoy the Summerillia." Nathaniel eyed Angelina curiously, and she could've sworn a hint of amusement flash across his face. "It promises to be a most interesting night."

After Nathaniel and Rose departed, Madelyn gripped Angelina's hand. "Are you sure you're all right? Do you need to lie down?"

"Maddy, really, you're worse than Piers," Tabitha scoffed. "Clearly, she fancies him just like everyone else." Tabitha cast a glance down the hallway and smiled. "I mean you can hardly blame her. He is the most *interesting* bachelor in Lordhaven."

"Interesting and attractive can't hide controversy, which is the last thing any of us needs to worry about right now," Madelyn reminded her.

Tabitha smirked. "I never said attractive."

Madelyn's cheeks flushed as Angelina and Tabitha exchanged knowing grins.

"The dances will be starting soon. Let's get some refreshments, yes?" Madelyn spun on her heels and dragged her sisters along with her.

"Why is he so controversial?" Angelina asked.

Before Madelyn could respond, Tabitha piped in, "Rumor has it he is the illegitimate great grandson of Remus Trevet. You see, Remus was in a courtship with Madalena Cioli, who was the lady of the season, but he was secretly having an affair with Priscilla Lethe, Madalena's best friend. When he and Madalena broke off the engagement it was in *all* the penny papers. Remus and Priscilla were rumored to have had one son who apparently died very early leaving the Trevets without an heir. Then Nathaniel appears all these years later claiming to be that son's grandson and—"

"Really, Tabitha," Madelyn interrupted, "if you spent as much time on reading every gossip column as you do your music sheets, you'd be selling out concerts at Dorian Hall."

Angelina squeezed Tabitha's hand. "Tell me more later?"

She'd missed this closeness to her sisters. Now that her Crowning was done, she would have her family back and all the oddness of the last week would be forgotten.

No more strange dreams. No more beckoning shadows. No more ominous voices. And no more headaches.

The girls stepped into the main ballroom and Angelina lost herself in its storybook rosewood and gold walls, columns of overflowing bouquets and tables laden with dainty cakes and fruits.

As the evening pressed on, it was easy to sneak sips of juniper wine when Madelyn wasn't looking and steal dances with Tabitha when Angelina tired of masked strangers. It was easy to forget one day she would rule over those around her instead of waltzing with them. And if she caught glimpses of a familiar girl in the crowd, outfitted in a pomegranate red dress with a ribbon tied around her neck, she pretended she didn't because tonight was her night, her moment, her dream. Tonight she was Angelina Chase, Crown Princess, free of worry, safe in the swirl of the quadrille.

But the future couldn't be denied so easily. Someone—a dance partner perhaps?—said something to her but their words sounded worlds away. All else fell away except the young woman in the red rabbit mask standing against the back wall, watching her. She had pale blonde hair and wore a dark red dress in the fashionable cage style. Her matching red rabbit mask covered the top half of her youthful face.

She lacked the opulence of those around her, yet Angelina couldn't look away. Unlike Nathaniel and Rose whose allure drew her in, the young woman in the rabbit mask seized her completely. A dull ache spread across her chest.

Don't look don't look don't look don't—

A feeling of familiarity cut through the haze, but Angelina couldn't quite place it. She took a step forward as her mind grasped for the memory and her fingers brushed against her throat.

Something broken...

The young woman reached out a hand, beckoning.

"Come with me."

The music swelled with each step Angelina took, sending chills down her neck. She was nearing a precipice. The ache in her chest morphed into the pelting of a thousand wings against her ribcage. One more step and she'd leave the dream behind. A single tear rolled down her cheek. Something inside her pleaded for her to stay, to bask in the ignorant bliss just a bit longer, but her heart urged her forward as if of its own volition.

It wasn't a need born from love or hate. No, this was older.

This was a reunion.

Angelina took the young woman's hand. She drew Angelina close and there, within that deep violet gaze, a memory stirred sudden and clear. The dream reverberated and the false warmth slipped from Angelina's skin like a thread unspooled.

"My, my." The young woman frowned, her face pale and lovely, and traced a finger along Angelina's cheek. "I'm afraid this won't do. I need you to be ready. War is coming, and the Prince of the Night Court will be a great foe indeed." Her gaze bore into Angelina, the violet of her eyes shifting and swirling to impossible depths. "It's time to wake up now, Julia."

The sound of glass shattering erupted around Angelina. As Farhan's glamor withered, memories flooded her mind all at once. Fear, sadness, anger, confusion—all the negative emotions the glamor had suppressed rushed through her, drowning out everything else. Hatred burned hot behind her eyes. Tears clouded her vision for the ignorance—the bliss—torn from her.

Then a single memory came to her like a burst of light in the dark. Something someone had told her. A warning she was supposed to remember.

"The White Raven is coming for you."

Angelina spun on her heels and dashed from the ballroom. Her heart throbbed with each traitorous step she took from the young woman in the rabbit mask. She'd betrayed it, betrayed her own body, but she couldn't explain how or why. None of that mattered though. She needed air. After stumbling through the maze of corridors and masks she finally found a set of doors leading to a courtyard. She tore them open and hurried down the steps until stone gave way to grass.

She inhaled a large gulp of air and sank back on her heels. The stars glistened above her like jewels against the darkness. She sucked in another deep breath. Waves of anger submerged the surreal meeting with the young woman. Only a single thought pressed to the surface.

Piers had betrayed her.

She wanted to scream, to cry, to run, to curl into a ball and disappear. How utterly stupid she'd been to trust someone *assigned* to watch over her. Even now she knew why he had done it, but it did nothing to dampen her fury at him and herself. She had let the queen rattle her at her coronation party and in the process lost her chance to escape through the ghost tunnels and board the Borealis. All because she had been afraid.

Now she had a name that had grown into her like a weed, choking off her own until it'd fallen off the vine, a crown that demanded lies, and a family that wasn't hers.

Her fingers dug themselves into her palms, eager for the release of nails on flesh, but her gloves buffered her skin. Her eyes welled with tears.

I'm so bloody damn stupid! Idiot! Idiot! IDIOT!

"Your Royal Highness?"

A young woman a couple years older than Angelina with long, wavy dark hair and deep blue eyes stood off to the side. Her emerald and gold gown draped around her narrow shoulders and bloomed into a tapestry of lacey golden flowers and latticework, a perfect complement to her golden half sun mask. She kneeled and extended her hand. "You can borrow my kerchief if you want."

Angelina sniffled and nodded. "Thank you."

"Is there someone I can get for you?"

Angelina shook her head. "I'm here alone."

"Well, I was just getting my carriage drawn around front. Can I take you somewhere? I'd hate to leave you in such a state."

It was now or never. Perhaps her original plan could still work. She could pawn her dress and jewelry for a train ticket to Sheffield at least and figure things out with her family from there. Anything to get out of Lordhaven while Piers and the Chase sisters still believed she was under Farhan's influence.

"Yes," Angelina lied. "I'd love that, thank you." Suddenly remembering where she was and the manners expected of her station, she added, "Sorry, I don't believe we've met. And you are?"

The girl smiled sweetly, almost confidently, as she extended her hand. "You can call me Victoria. Victoria Whitmont."

47

NATHANIEL

"At first, he believed it to be a dove perched across the way. But as sleep left him and the clarity of the morning sun set in, the beak became longer, the talons sharper, the call shriller. It was no dove watching him, but a raven, white as snow." – *Elora Jemison, "The White Raven", folk story*

The moon hung low in the sky, hovering over Lordhaven like a silent god.

Nathaniel watched from a nearby balcony as guests milled about on the front lawn, eager for a little air and a short reprieve from dancing. He tipped back his glass and let the rich red wine slide down his throat. The Hoyts owned several vineyards in Arcadia and the benefit of attending the Summerillia was access to their vintages. His gaze lifted beyond the dreamscape to the capital beyond, bathed in shadow at the feet of Dutchenson Castle.

Come on, you bastards. Make your move.

Claude, Victoria, the Sacred Seven, the Malsik ... each one stood at the ready to make a grab for power the likes of which many had never seen in their lifetimes. But then there was the White Raven, the path of smoke and glass, the reading with Lady Cavall, the Ravenhood, the eternal heart ...

The promise of power for himself.

When would the roads cross? And what would happen if they did?

Nathaniel took another sip of wine as the music from downstairs crept through the windows. He'd seen nearly every member of the Order in attendance, but Victoria Whitmont had yet to be seen.

He swirled the wine in his glass. He and Rose had swept the entire first floor already. Not even Samir had seen Victoria.

"What is that little viper up to?" he murmured to himself.

As if on cue, a large mahogany carriage drawn by two beautiful chestnut horses meandered down the cobbled drive and stopped at the front landing.

A porter opened the doors as Victoria Whitmont emerged from Chersey Hall in a stunning dark emerald gown. A golden half sun covered the top half of her face. As the porter assisted her down the steps, she looked up and locked eyes with Nathaniel. She smirked and within seconds was gone, ushered into the carriage. But it was her companion trailing a few steps behind that caught his breath.

Princess Angelina Chase.

Nathaniel abandoned his wine and retreated into the manor. As he drew closer to the grand hall, the warmth and music all heightened, enveloping around him like a cocoon of luxury. Taking one side of the curved staircases, he spotted Rose exchanging hushed whispers with Reese Ward, a cousin of John and Daniel Ward, the Iron Barons of the Hamptons.

He cursed Victoria's ill timing and hurried past the pair, making a note to circle back to Reese once he was done with Victoria. It'd been ages since he'd seen that teasing smile, always eager for a bit of mischief.

But another attendee suddenly caught his eye on his way to the front doors. A young woman in a dark red dress with a half rabbit mask eyed Nathaniel as she reached for a flute of bubbling wine. Pale blonde hair swept down her back.

He stopped. Had he seen her before? Why did she look familiar? Nathaniel racked his brain but couldn't remember. A guffawing laugh broke his pondering and he turned. Tyson Hoyt, Albert's younger brother whose mask was hanging half off his face, clapped Albert on the back and exchanged a joke with three other gentlemen. His cheeks were already sweaty and red with drink.

Then it hit him.

The handmaid Renzo described at the theatre. The one who was with Victoria at Kendleston Manor.

His desperate gaze went to the door, the hope of catching up to Victoria dwindling by the second, then cut back to the rabbit masked young woman. If she really was Victoria's companion, then he would drain every ounce of knowledge she carried. Each step he took pulled him further and further away from the haze of the party. Masked bodies pressed against him. Somewhere over the din of the music Samir called his name, but he ignored it.

Nathaniel reached the hall in time to see the third door on the right close. He entered a large drawing room adorned with soft blue lounge chairs and a setting table. A large oil painting of a group of cherubs playing amongst a sea of wispy clouds hung over the mantle. Off to the side of the room was a partially open door.

She must've gone through there. Nathaniel crossed the room and entered a smaller one. A hand-carved rocking horse painted a brilliant purple was in a far corner next to a stack of wooden colored blocks in different shapes. A small table and chairs were positioned in the center, perfectly in view of the sprawling courtyard in the center of the mansion. Nathaniel frowned. Was he being made a fool?

He exited the nursery and found himself back in the hall. Behind him, the warm glow of the chandeliers and jovial banter beckoned him.

When he looked back, a slip of red disappeared around the corner.

A shy one then. Perhaps she wanted away from the prying eyes of Victoria and the other highborns to discuss matters. Fine, he could play along with her little game.

As he turned the corner, a masked couple walked past him. Up ahead, the young woman slipped into the last door on the right. The sound of music carried through the hall, faint but growing. Nathaniel followed her, passing by portraits of Hoyts throughout the century, each more pompous than the last, until he reached the right-side door.

The smell of old pages and leather greeted him as he stepped into the largest of Chersey Hall's two libraries. Rows upon rows of books filled the walls floor to ceiling, the gold lettering of their leatherbound spines shimmering in the slants of moonlight. Deep green walls not filled with books were home to more portraits of Hoyts adorned in medals and jewels. History, it would seem, only remembered those that succeeded or were too wealthy to be forgotten.

Nathaniel took slow steps amongst the books, his eyes comfortably sliding between the darkened spaces to catch sight of movement. But the young woman in red was nowhere to be found.

"No need to be afraid. We can discuss matters here." Nathaniel's offer was met with silence, followed a moment later by the closing of a door.

He hurried towards the back of the room and caught a whiff of lavender hanging in the air. Perfume. He then noticed a note tacked to the wall. In small boxy letters it read, *Getting closer, little rabbit.*

Nathaniel's heart skipped. *Little rabbit*. Only one person—one goddess—had ever called him that when she proposed a deal that would give him the power he craved. The one person who tricked him into signing over his soul to become a duskborn in a twist of cruel fate.

Moxra, the Goddess of Dreams and Nightmares.

Nathaniel tore the note from the wall and crumpled it in his fist. He exited the library and found himself in a new hall leading to two large doors. Marble busts of Remiclus and Aeth—scholars from before the time of kings—were positioned on either side of the doors.

His better sense told him to turn back. Rejoin the gala and the bliss it promised. After all, the young woman couldn't be Moxra. He was still very much alive and entitled to his soul. Perhaps she was a pawn of the goddess sent to keep an eye on him.

Curiosity pulled at him with an unrelenting tug. Regardless of who she was, if someone knew of his past—the deal he'd made—who had told her if not Moxra herself? The young woman would tell him, one way or another. Then she would confess Victoria's plans down to the time of day.

And then he would end her.

He tucked the crumbled note into his jacket and opened the doors. The sweet and sensuous air of roses and sweet peas immediately washed over him. The mansion's second ballroom was smaller than the first but steeped in no less opulence. Rosewood walls were strung with gold and ivory silks. Masked guests swept across marble white floors to the steps of the midsummer march as a full orchestra performed from the far side of the room. Overhead, a giant diamond chandelier glimmered like Chersey Hall's own private crystalline sun.

Guests not dancing sat at a cluster of gold and ivory clothed tables, their banter and laughs nearly as loud as the orchestra. A legion of gold-masked waiters wove through the maze of tables silently topping off each glass. As usual, the Hoyts had spared no expense.

Nathaniel lingered against the back wall when a gold masked waiter approached him. "Excuse me, sir, but I was asked to tell you your immediate audience is requested in Mr. Hoyt's study."

"Was this requester dressed in red and wearing a rabbit mask?"

The waiter nodded. He pointed to a pair of doors on the other side of the room.

"You'll want to go through those doors and up the stairs," he instructed. "Mr. Hoyt's study is the last room at the end of the hall, sir."

Nathaniel thanked the waiter and hurried out of the ballroom. He smiled as he ascended the stairs, his fangs itching to be released.

Caught you.

The door to Hoyt's study was ajar. An orb of ensconced snakelight shone from within. The music downstairs fell away with each step he took until it was nothing more than a distant whisper, eclipsed by the stillness of the hall.

Nathaniel slowly brushed back the door. The study was empty. White walls were cluttered with oil paintings of the surviving Hoyts. He looked over Albert's desk but it was clean. He made a note to help himself to the drawers on his way out. As he continued looking over the room for the young woman's whereabouts, one of the shelves caught his attention.

There was a slight opening in the wall, barely a crack, but it was there. Nathaniel pressed against the shelf with his shoulder, and it gave way to a secret passage.

How did she know about this? he wondered as he entered a dim hall.

When he reached the end, he opened a second door to a small waiting room. Dark violet walls surrounded him on all sides. Two white chairs stood opposite him. Between them, on a small wooden side table, garishly red in the dark room, was the young woman's rabbit mask.

Nathaniel picked it up. An invitation. No, that didn't feel right. A *promise*. But of what he couldn't say.

To his left, one final door lay ajar.

He walked through and was greeted by a crackling fireplace. Moonlight poured through the room's single window, illuminating the otherwise black room. A small ebony clock hung on the wall, chiming the arrival of the twelfth hour.

The young woman kept her back to Nathaniel, holding her arms in front of her as she stared at the portrait above the mantle. He took a step closer to her, his ears buzzing.

"Are you familiar with the Dance of Seven?" Her voice was pleasant but controlled, and carried a hint of an accent he couldn't place.

"I can't say I am," Nathaniel lied.

His eyes followed hers to the painting.

"On the surface," she continued, "one would see seven ballerinas dancing on a circular stage, an enraptured audience at their feet, surrounding them on all sides. Trapping them."

Nathaniel took another step closer. Firelight danced off her pale blonde hair that hung loose down her back.

"Some believe the ballerinas are the seven deadly sins enchanting the audience. Which would mean the audience wouldn't be the hunters at all." She turned to reveal a lovely face framed by high cheekbones and pale, grey eyes. "They'd be the prey."

Her thin red lips pulled into a smirk as she sauntered over to him. "What do you think?"

She was close enough now Nathaniel could smell the traces of lavender on her skin. His eyes slid down her face and rested on her exposed throat.

"I think the fable of Isomol says it best. When the First Child's heart was taken from their body, the seven instincts fled to the underworld of Chthonis and forced to remain there, far away from the human hearts they could touch. But Umbrin made a deal with them. They then attached themselves to human souls in hopes of being reborn in the human realm. Woven into our very nature."

Nathaniel didn't pull back when she slid a gloved hand over his arm. "But it's a story I'm sure you're quite familiar with already, Moxra."

The young woman laughed, rich and sharp.

"You mistake me for a dreaming one. I'm no god." She leaned in closer, her breath hot on his neck. "I'm their end."

"Then how—?"

She slid a finger over his lips. When she pulled back, tilting her head ever so demurely, he caught a glimpse of the firelight in her eyes.

For a breath, they were deepest violet. The violet of a raven-eyed. Her smirk deepened, a fox hidden behind a rabbit's mask. "I heard you've been looking for me, Nathaniel Trevet."

Before he could utter her name—speak of the fable, the lie, the curse, the promise—*the White Raven*—her lips were on his and he was lost in the softness of her mouth.

Her hands slid through his hair, pulling him towards her, a ballerina drawing her audience ever closer. And just as quickly she pulled away, a lingering breath between them, and angled her exposed throat to him. Her eyes, pale grey once more, locked onto his.

"Take it."

Every fiber of him seized with relish.

Consume her.

Devour her.

Take her power.

Take it all.

His fangs unsheathed in one second and sunk into her throat the next. But if she winced when the duskborn blood rushed into her, Nathaniel didn't hear it. Blood sweeter and richer than any wine he'd ever tasted slid down his throat. A rapturous warmth coursed through his body like a pulsing desert heat. Gravity held no law over him. He was lighter than air, untethered to time or space.

The darkness took him first. He wasn't certain when his body hit the floor, but the pain came much, much later. Seconds, minutes, hours, he couldn't say when. The sensation of frostbite started in his throat first then spread out across his skin like a contagion, biting and merciless. Needles pressed into his arms, legs, and face, slowly converging into his pores and piercing his muscles, releasing the festering darkness beneath.

He finally understood. She was releasing him. The crackling flames, the red rabbit and the ebony clock ticking, ticking, ticking melded together. He couldn't stop it, but he tried, oh he tried.

A dream was unfolding before him, living and breathing, unlike anything he'd ever seen.

The blood, his mind screamed at him from far, far away. *Poison ... bird of poison ... ancient thing ...*

Nathaniel seized on a sudden moment of clarity. Water bubbled in his mouth. No, not water. Foam. Red swirling in the white. He tasted the iron in it spewing over his dribbling lips.

Panic choked him. His body shook uncontrollably, but just as quickly the warmth returned. Beyond his syrupy gaze the dream bloomed once more. His mind took him away from the black room and his frost-bitten body and foam-soaked mouth.

The White Raven picked up the red rabbit mask Nathaniel had dropped. Once she refastened it, she kneeled beside him.

"Do you see now?" asked the White Raven. "You're not fit to be a vessel for my heart, little dreamer. Not as you are now. But we are nothing if not creatures of change, aren't we?"

She stepped over his convulsing body and shut the door behind her. The hands of the ebony clock continued their steady march forward, ticking away each second of Nathaniel's descent into blissful madness. When the White Raven's blood finally released him, the clock face disappeared. In its place was a large violet eye staring down at him.

Still in a dream, Nathaniel reminded himself with all the clarity he could muster. He struggled to sit up right, hindered further by an unrelenting headache and vicious nausea.

Then a voice, splendid and terrible, spoke with the gentleness of a mother from somewhere behind him.

"Fear not, little rabbit, for I have a new deal for you." Moxra's voice contorted until only the sharpest edges of her words remained. *"It's time to clip those raven's wings."*

48

TOBIAS

"I believed that brief, timeless dream during my girlhood was just the imaginative folly of a child. But after years of travel, I'm certain people have carried memories of those fantastical revels here to our world. I've seen variations of the same dances in ballrooms across all the major cities—Lordhaven, Fiore, Amani, Svaberg, and Kolbua. It can't be a coincidence. Dolly Theall wasn't lying." – *Anonymous citizen, Street Watch box testimonial, City Watch Records Department, Lordhaven, Halcyon*

The opulence of Chersey Hall loomed before Tobias, brilliant and otherworldly.

He had told Tavia to watch over Jóhann and buy him some time with Ezra. The plan from there was simple: find the book for Nathaniel, drop it off at the designated meet with Anders, sell off his tailored suit, board a train to Denby to gather Lucy and use the money from his suit to escape together to Bronwen.

No more gangs, no more blood, no more monsters.

He double checked the lockpicks in his fitted jacket pocket—tailored suits truly were a gift from the saints, damn that pompous duskborn—and headed up the stairs to the party.

Nathaniel had said he was looking for a book with a sun and moon emblazoned on its cover in Hoyt's personal collection. Anders had elaborated further on their carriage ride to Chersey Hall:

"The book will be in a locked glass case in the junior library. When you enter the manor, go up the stairs and follow the main hall to the end. Discretion will be an utmost priority should you hope to succeed."

Tobias parsed Anders's unspoken warning: *No one will be coming for you.*

That was fine. Tobias would get in and get out. Anders would pick up the book that evening and all would be settled. He'd leave Lordhaven behind once and for all. The city had taken enough from him and his sister. No more.

Soon, Lucy. Wait for me.

As he stepped onto the landing, he glanced over his shoulder to take in the gardens one last time. He had seen his share of impressive manors while catching rats in the Garden District, but nothing compared to the shining jewel that was the main Hoyt residence.

Nicknamed "the Pink Garden" during the summer months, it was divided into several small areas partitioned off by cleverly shaped box hedges and stone walls. Each area was themed, and various flowers and sculpted shrubbery were brought in from all over the world to fulfil the vision of Myra Hoyt. Pink rose bushes blossomed at the feet of shrubbery elephants; swan shrubs swam in a lake of pink peonies; pink lilies graced the wings of hummingbird shrubs locked beak to beak.

While staring at the Pink Garden's splendors, he suddenly realized he knew nothing of *true* wealth. This was not the kind one accumulated in a lifetime. Nor was it born solely from the twin pillars of hard work and uplifting others praised by Ascendism. This was rooted deep beneath the earth where only darkness and rot resided.

This was untouchable. This was terrifying.

Tobias hurried inside. Months of prowling the North Rim made him nimble on his feet and easy to lose in a crowd. But as he made his way to the middle stairwell, his eyes hungrily drank in the sights. The decadent spread of roasted meats and vegetables, towers of sugary pastries, and bowls spilling over with fresh cut fruits.

Masked waitstaff floated through the crowd like golden phantoms, filling glasses to the brim with wines they could never afford to taste themselves.

For the briefest moment, Tobias flirted with the idea of succumbing to the lure of the Summerillia. No one knew him here and what's more, no one would care to. Lordhaven's gossip mill ran thick in the summer season. He would merely be a gnat beneath their masked noses.

When will you ever pass through these doors again?

The thought was both chilling and inviting. Nathaniel had granted him access to see the world from the highest reaches of Lordhaven.

And the view was bloody damn marvelous.

"Excuse me, young man. Do you—?"

"Sorry, I'm in search of my brother," Tobias blurted. "Please excuse me." He slipped beside a couple and made haste to the stairwell. He could hear the man's voice call out behind him, but he didn't dare stop for the world.

Dammit, Tobias chided himself. *This is a bloody job. Get in, get out.*

He couldn't risk being seen, noticed or saints forbid, caught. He had to be a ghost. No one was coming for him. Saints, no one even knew where he was or who he was with. When had the lies piled so high?

It wasn't Jóhann's fault but shifting the blame made Tobias feel better. It started with him after all, hadn't it? Him and his pitiful face and heroic ambitions.

What a damn waste.

The upstairs hall was quiet, but not without guests. Lovers tucked away in corners exchanged low, sultry whispers. A group of men lowered their voices when Tobias passed them, their sharpened gazes following him like spotlights until he was out of ear shot.

More noises were heard behind closed doors, some jovial and others not. But Tobias only had eyes for the last door at the end of the hall. He glanced over his shoulder as he slipped a pin from his jacket. Anyone who bothered to look his way would assume he already had a key, maybe even tasked by Albert Hoyt himself to fetch something for his guests to fawn and coo over.

As he assumed, the door was locked but easily gave way with a few practiced twists of the pin. Tobias slipped into the room and shut the door quietly behind him. The library itself was dark and smelled of must and cedar.

Not wanting to risk a light being seen from the incoming guests or footmen below, he used the moonlight to peruse the room. Glass cases were nestled between the shelves and in a couple of the corners: a gilded knife inlaid with precious jewels; a stone carved with strange, rudimentary symbols; a petrified wooden hand; a pearlescent scale perfectly in balance. All collector oddities bought with stories of grandeur woven into the price, Tobias was sure.

He pressed on. Maybe Anders had gotten it wrong and the book was amongst the hundreds that lined the shelves? He prayed to all above and below it wasn't. The longer he was in Hoyt's library, the less chance he had of making it out of Chersey Hall at all.

As he approached the nearest shelf, a momentary groan froze him in place. It was soft, almost a trick of the mind, but Tobias's instincts knew better. He slowly peered over his shoulder, a deer alert to footsteps.

There, hidden by the darkness, was a small alcove tucked away beyond his line of sight. Someone, a woman, began breathing heavy.

"Collin, we should return soon ..."

"Should we?" Collin teased. "I quite like it here instead."

In clear view of the lovers was another glass case. In the center, nestled between an intricately carved wooden stake and a golden fox figure was a mauve book with a golden sun and silver moon on its cover. Collin and his date hadn't noticed Tobias's presence yet, but they surely would if he went for the book.

Nathaniel's steely calm voice echoed in his head. *"I will sell you and your sister's whereabouts to the highest bidder."*

Going to Nathaniel empty handed wasn't an option. Tobias crept toward the case. The knife in his pocket reminded him there was always a way out worse come to worse, but perhaps if he bluffed his way through ...

The moment he turned the corner, he and the woman locked eyes. She was slow to realize his presence at first, but within seconds realization dawned across her heart shaped face.

"Oh, saints!" she shrieked, pushing Collin off her and pulling up her cotton under-dress. Both of their masks were discarded on the floor.

Collin shot to his feet first. He was of average build and height with sandy brown sideburns and a strong chin. The same strong jaw possessed by Albert Hoyt in the few portraits Tobias had seen on his way to the library.

"Collin ... Hoyt?"

"Yes, and who in the seven hells are you?"

Saints dammit all.

"I-I apologize, sir, I didn't mean to interrupt." Tobias nudged closer to the case. "Your father requested I fetch a certain piece from his collection. A few of his guests were rather keen to see it."

"Is that right?" Collin stepped closer, an ugly sneer on his face. "So why didn't you announce yourself then at the start?"

"Collin, don't be a brute. Just let him be on his way."

But Collin ignored her. His eyes gleamed with smug delight. Tobias gritted his teeth. He was nearly upon the case and yet it might as well have been across the room.

"I think we have ourselves a dirty little peeper." He barked a mirthless laugh, his face contouring with amused cruelty. "Father not paying you enough to catch a show in the Rim then? Pity. Let's say I ask him for a raise for you, hmm?"

Dammit dammit dammit.

Tobias couldn't stall any longer. Collin wasn't going to let him off easy. Bringing up his father meant Tobias would be found out for a thief and a Market Streeter in front of nearly every highborn in Lordhaven. Even on the slim chance he made it out alive, either Nathaniel or Marcellus would end him themselves.

Dammit!

Collin was nearly on him now. Tobias let him take another step and then his fist locked with Collin's nose. He stumbled back and wailed in pain over the woman's scream. Tobias ignored them both and drove his elbow through the glass and snatched the book.

As he spun around to flee, a strange, gossamer haze hung over the door.

What in the seven hells?

"I'll fucking kill you!" Collin roared. Blood ran down his chin and stained his shirt.

On instinct, Tobias regained his composure and rushed forward, but when he reached for the door handle his fingers found no purchase. The handle was gone. His momentum carried him through the door just as Collin grabbed the back of his jacket collar.

The pair stumbled and landed on the ground with a heavy thud. Tobias was flung to the side, falling hard on his shoulder. He winced but quickly righted himself while Collin staggered on his hands and knees to do the same.

"W-What the—?"

Nightingales fluttered overhead, jumping from one tree branch to another. A brilliant golden pink sky stretched high above them. The air was pleasantly warm, but not overbearingly so, and reminded Tobias of those late summer afternoons in his childhood when he'd lie down in the fluffy grass of a nearby field to nap until his mum called him for supper.

Collin looked back at Tobias and pointed to the sky.

"You're seeing this too, right?"

"Aye ..."

"What in the saints did you do, peever? Where's the bloody damn moon?" Collin closed the gap between them in an instant. He grabbed Tobias by the shirt and pulled him close enough to smell the wine on his breath.

"I didn't do anything!" Tobias yelled. "I swear it!"

Something shifted behind Collin's eyes and his expression grew dark.

"You're a fateshifter, aren't you? Huh, demon scum? Think this is some sort of joke then? Think yourself clever? *Do you?*"

A melodic voice cut across the clearing. "Oh, I wouldn't provoke that one if I were you, sir."

Tobias and Collin both turned to see a short, pudgy man in tradesmen's garb and boots leaning against a nearby tree. He was on the younger side of middle age, with bright green eyes and a short, dark red beard framing a rosy-cheeked face. Several silver rings lined his fingers.

"Who are you?" Collin spat. "And where are we?"

The man made no move to answer Collin's questions. He continued to watch them with the languid ease of a cat observing mice scuffle.

When his emerald gaze shifted to Tobias, a strange unease crept over the Market Streeter. The same gossamer filaments he had seen over the doorway danced in the man's eyes at just the right turn of the light. But when Tobias blinked, the feeling—and the filaments—were gone.

The man smiled, revealing a row of tiny sharp teeth.

"You took a nasty stumble there, boyo," he said, nodding at Collin. "Let me take you back to the party."

Collin glared at Tobias before tossing him back to the ground and stalking off to the man's side. "Take me to my father at once. I'm in need of a word with him about who he employs."

Tobias grabbed the book beside him. When he got to his feet, the short, pudgy man was gone.

In his place was a lithe figure close to seven feet tall. The stranger's dark red hair fell in short waves around his pointed ears and silver circlet. His once plain rings were now adorned with polished gemstones in an assortment of colors. Gone also was his tradesmen's outfit. In its place were billowing silver and black robes that perfectly complimented his smoky, alabaster hue impossible for any human to achieve. A hue made only more jarring by the red rose bursting from the cavity where his right eye should've been, its thorny vine growing from behind his ear, snaking down his throat and disappearing into the skin of his partially exposed chest.

Whether because he was drunk or upset, Collin didn't seem to notice the stranger's transformation. But when Tobias blinked, the stranger had returned to his short tradesmen appearance.

The tradesmen grinned and held a finger to his lips.

Tobias grabbed the book and ran the other way. And there, saints be, was the same gossamer door. He ran through with all the might his legs could muster and nearly collided with the bookshelf upon his re-entry. He jerked to the side at the last moment and managed to bump his uninjured shoulder against the bookstacks instead.

His heart pulsed in his ears as several books toppled to the ground. There wasn't enough air to fill his lungs no matter how many gulps he took.

When he finally managed the courage to look back, half expecting constables to burst into the room, the library door stood closed, normal and wooden. No gossamer. No strange light. No indication it had been anything other than a normal door at all.

Collin.

He had left him with ... that ... Tobias shook his head, reeling from those tiny sharp teeth and emerald eyed stare.

He gripped the side of the book. It hadn't been damaged in his scuffle with Collin, but there were faint traces of dirt on its front cover. The book had been outside. *He'd* been outside. He'd fallen in the dirt and stood beneath a twilit sky. But how? He was on the second floor of Chersey Hall and it was well into the night.

The woman and her mask were gone, but Collin's mask was on the ground. Which meant Collin was still there, in that other place.

Tobias rushed to the window. The moon hung full in the sky. He nearly sighed with relief until he looked down. The front drive was free of carriages. But that was impossible. It had been clogged at least three miles deep when he had arrived not even an hour before. He looked over at the clock mounted on the wall opposite and his heart sank.

Two hours had passed since he ran into Collin and his date.

Two hours had gone by without a trace.

A noise brought him reeling back to his senses. Standing in the alcove Collin and the woman had been moments before was the red-haired tradesmen. Tobias reeled back, pressing himself against the library's window.

"Woah, there. Didn't mean to startle you, boyo," he said, holding up his hands. "But if you're going to pass through a door, you'd best have the good sense to close it." A grin crept across his face. "One can never be too careful who or what may come through."

Tobias clutched the book to his chest.

"W-Who are you? And where's Collin Hoyt?"

The man shrugged. "I'm a simple stranger. And your friend is still in Ilrith."

"Ilrith?" Tobias shook his head. "What're you talking about? We're in Lordhaven. He was just here and then—"

The red-haired man cut him off. "My business is in trade, boyo, not cartography." He gestured to the book Tobias held close. "Let us say the copy you're holding there is a fake. If you can find the real one for me, I'll trade you for it."

It isn't mine to trade, Tobias almost said, but instead replied, "For what?"

"A golden apple from Yorin's garden."

Tobias recognized the name. He'd seen it etched into makeshift shrines tucked behind shop counters and shadowed alleyways. A hedge god of arcanics. Tobias backed away towards the door.

"You're some kind of fateshifter, then?" he said in a low, harsh whisper. "Is that why you looked different before?"

A shadow passed over the man's features and his green eyes narrowed to slits.

"If I were so lowly as that, would I bear the mark of the Rose Court?" he snarled, holding up his right hand to reveal a silver ring etched in the shape of a rose in bloom. The very same Tobias saw bursting from the man's eye socket.

Tobias glanced at the door behind him. "I'm sorry, I-I didn't mean to offend."

The stranger's features slid back into a mask of composure.

"I forget myself sometimes. Apologies—?" The man's brows lifted with the open-ended question.

"Tobias."

Gossamer threads flickered in the man's green eyes as he crossed into the moonlight, an air of smugness cloying to him.

"Tobias, then." He clasped his hands behind his back as if holding Tobias's name just out of reach. "You see, I trade in rarities, both physical and mythos. Allow me to let you in on a little secret about Yorin's golden apples. Legend says they grant the eater great knowledge, but they also have unique properties that keep blood wolf madness at bay."

Tobias's eyes went wide. His heart thrummed in his chest as he struggled to grasp the man's words.

"A cure? There's a cure?" he said in a fervent rush.

"A remedy," the man corrected.

I can be healed, Tobias thought, suddenly overwhelmed by the urge to cry and dance all at once. *Saints, I can be healed!*

Tobias grabbed the man's arm with his free hand. "Where do I find this book? Please, sir. Please tell me."

The man considered Tobias a moment before pulling his arm free. "The Malsik was the last known person to see the real one. Start with him. When you know more, open the next woven door you see. I'll be waiting."

The man stepped out of the moonlight and slipped between the shadows. There one moment and gone the next. Tobias stood, mouth agape, at the space where the man was only seconds before. His gaze fell to the book in his hands. He slowly opened it to the first page. In tall, wispy letters read *Aeternus* by Jhaeros Tartanos.

Curiosity pulled at his fingers. The next page had but a single sentence: "Within these pages I lay forth what I know to be truth." The pages that followed were written in a strange scripture Tobias had never seen before. By the tenth page, a handwritten note in the margin caught his eye. It read: *Fey runics?*

A chill crept over him. Fey. He only knew of fateshifters to be feared magical wielders, but were there others? Tobias was certain the red-haired man had used magic to some extent, but it was strange.

Like a trick of the light.

The clock on the wall chimed midnight. Tobias tucked the book beneath his arm and looked out the window at the moonlit grounds. Somewhere out there, Lucy waited for him in Debney, unaware the glint of a golden apple outshined the path leading to her. Somewhere further still, a red-haired traveler waited on the other side of a gossamer door.

And somewhere close, the groan of Lordhaven's roots tightening around Tobias reverberated in his ears, leaving the shards of a shattered promise once again at his feet.

49

ANGELINA

"When wolves hunt, they are methodical, patient and observant. Death is not swift; it is earned." – *Dr. Lucia Viscardi,* The Wolves of Tomini: Hunters of the Eastern Arcadian Ridgelands

"Do you have a destination in mind?" Victoria asked as she dabbed her lips with coloring. The snap of her pocket mirror closing nearly made Angelina jump.

"Um, the Brunswick Theatre," she replied, recalling Martha yammering on for days about a show she'd seen there for her fourteenth birthday. Guilt surged through Angelina. *Martha is … Oh saints, she's …*

Angelina bit down on the inner flesh of her lip until the pain stilled the growing grief. Her mask remained, pretty and free of troubles.

"Oh, a fan of the arts?" Victoria's eyes brightened. "Me too. I simply adore a good performance." She removed her silver half sun mask, revealing the kind of beauty artists craved to capture. But it was the miniscule details that made Angelina's skin prickle. The confidence in the curl of Victoria's mouth, the angled nose and keen blue gaze. She recognized those features, knew the face that had worn them so well.

Emily.

Suddenly, the carriage slowed to a stop. Angelina looked between Victoria and the door as it opened. A golden masked man carrying a young woman with pale blonde hair and wearing a red rabbit mask stepped inside. Angelina covered her mouth to bottle the scream in her throat, her hands trembling as the man propped the rabbit-masked blonde in the seat next to her. As he fell into the empty seat beside Victoria, Angelina dared a glimpse at the young woman slumped against the drawn window beside her.

"I take it introductions have already been made." Victoria cast a sidelong glare at the golden masked man, who Angelina recognized as part of the wait staff from the Summerillia.

"Get out!" Emily screamed in her ear.

Angelina dove for the door, but the golden masked waiter grabbed her throat with one hand and blocked the door handle with the other. Angelina's eyes widened. This close she could see the brilliant violet eyes staring back at her from behind the waiter's mask. The same eyes that had woken her from Farhan's control.

"Naughty girl," the waiter tutted. "I wouldn't listen to her if I were you."

"Y-You hear Emily?" Angelina croaked.

The waiter laughed. "Of course. She's a part of you just as you are a part of me." He released his hold on her. Angelina fell back into her seat, grasping her throat and coughing. "And one day," he continued, an amused sneer cutting across his face, "you'll come to hear the rest of them. One by one. Your own eternal chorus of souls."

"You're the White Raven, aren't you?" Angelina sputtered, pushing herself further into her seat. She looked at Victoria, whose steely expression remained unchanged.

"So I've been called," the waiter responded. "But you can call me Alice." His gaze slid to the shell of a young woman beside Angelina, her glassy grey eyes staring into nothing. "She was quite fond of that name."

The waiter's eyes suddenly glowed a deep violet. In a blink, the young woman sat up as the waiter slumped to the side, his head hitting the door with a loud thud. Angelina screamed and plastered herself against the window as the young woman in the rabbit mask turned to face her. Her violet eyes glowed as if lit from within before shifting to a dull grey.

"There's still much to be done before the Twilight Gate can be opened," Alice said. She smirked, her red lips like blood against her mouth. "I wonder who you'll decide to be when that time comes."

The carriage continued through the Theatre District and past the wharfs onto Corvin Bridge. The dual towers on either end loomed like wrought iron wardens forever bound by the elevated constable walkways between them. The black waters of the River Dorne ebbed far below as the carriage neared the first tower, the South End checkpoint.

Angelina tried and failed to steady her breathing. Her head reeled with passages from the *True Word* about Azavith, the Demon King of a Thousand Faces. His treachery against humanity with the First Sin—a spell to conjure fire, an everlong addiction to magic disguised as a miraculous gift to humans. The continued deals for powerful magic in exchange for devotion in life and one's soul in death. All crimes Angelina had hung for in Iron Square.

"But you're a fable," Angelina protested, her head spinning. "The Saint Father, the seven disciples, they—"

"Ignorance is Halcyon's heritage," Alice cut in. "While it may provide comfort, it doesn't make it a kindness towards you."

Angelina sank into her seat. The White Raven was a prophecy of doom to come. A harbinger for the rise of a great war. The undoing of humanity itself. Was that somehow tied to the Twilight Gate? She shook her head.

"No. No, you're wrong. There's magic, but not like *this*."

Victoria cleared her throat. "I understand this is a lot to take in, but we'll be arriving soon. Try not to dwell on it too much."

Angelina pulled the curtain aside and gasped. "No, no, no. Where are you taking me?"

"Dutchenson Castle, of course," Victoria quipped, studying her nails. "Although you'd have known that had you ever been to the Theatre District. We passed it ages ago."

Angelina paled as the carriage came to a stop. After a brief conversation with the driver, the checkpoint guard waived the carriage through.

"Your father—" Angelina began, but before she could finish Victoria added, "—is King Leonard, yes. Honestly, what have you been doing all this time that you couldn't even parse my identity the moment we met?"

"Pots and kettles, Victoria," Alice chided, wagging her finger. Victoria huffed but said nothing further.

The carriage approached the North End checkpoint. Angelina picked up a muffled exchange of voices when the driver's partition suddenly opened. A stern-faced woman with dark eyes and curly hair pulled back beneath a constable's cap stared back at them.

"Lady Victoria, the grounds have been secured. We'll be arriving momentarily."

"Thank you, Maribeth."

Angelina snuck a peek behind the curtain as the carriage pulled forward. Only a few paces away, the guard tower's snakelight lanterns illuminated several dark pools of liquid. Laying in the furthest pool was a severed arm.

Angelina jerked back against her seat, but the cry that left her throat pierced the silence as thoroughly as any scream.

"If you haven't the stomach for war, you have no business being a Chase," Victoria sneered.

"And what, *pray tell*, gave you the idea I asked to be a part of any of this?" Angelina fired back. "Your business with the king isn't mine."

Victoria leaned forward, her lips pursed into a mock pout. "Do you want to go home? Hmm? Is it too scary for you?" Her face fell, all mockery hardened to a focused point. "Grow up. It's pathetic."

"Fuck you," Angelina spat.

Victoria rolled her eyes and let her simmering gaze slide to Alice with unspoken resentment.

"She's a feisty one," Alice said with a grin. "I like her. And you are a twat."

"Piss off," Victoria snapped as the carriage came to a halt. "Oh, finally. Thank the saints."

A moment later, Maribeth opened the carriage doors. The waiter slumped forward and hit the ground. Victoria stepped over him using Maribeth's outstretched hand as leverage, followed by Alice and finally Angelina, whose eyes widened in muted horror and awe.

The base of the castle loomed like a massive, thousand-eyed stone beast from its clifftop perch. A forest of towers crowned in ribbed spires protruded from the castle's center, each connected by intricate ironwork and braced by skeletal buttresses. Snakelight lamps lined either side of the tiered stone stairwell at the base of the Noble Seat, a small village between the North End checkpoint and Dutchenson Castle.

Moonlight illuminated the bodies scattered through the Noble Seat. Angelina recognized the crimson and black uniforms worn by the castle guards, but a handful of others were dressed in loose red trousers tied with white sashes over their partially bare chests. Each one was adorned in an intricate array of bone arm cuffs, necklaces, bracelets and anklets.

"What happened here?" Angelina asked as she fervently swallowed against the rising bile in her throat.

Victoria strode past the fallen guards, the hem of her soaked gown leaving a bloody trail and stood in the center of the Noble Seat. Seconds later, several pairs of reddish orange eyes gleamed from the treetops of a nearby tree. Three hooded figures dropped down and landed effortlessly on their feet. White owl masks shielded the upper half of their faces.

"Welcome, Lady Victoria," one of the figures said without bowing. "Your audience awaits."

Angelina watched Victoria march toward Dutchenson Castle with shoulders drawn back and head held high. She never faltered as she ascended the very steps Angelina hadn't been allowed to tread as a prisoner. The very steps that now belonged to her as the Crown Princess.

But for how much longer?

Angelina fell in line behind Victoria, followed by Alice and the owl-masked figures. The stairs opened to a large, circular courtyard littered with more guardsmen corpses. Stab wounds and slashes marked their last moments. Angelina kept her eyes trained ahead and refused to look down even when she stepped into what she told herself was a puddle.

Two phoenixes rising from the ashes flanked either side of the nine-foot doors leading inside the castle, their brilliant tails and puffed out chests stained by blood splatter. A rose window overlayed with iron latticework nearly as wide as the doors beneath it gleamed like a miniature sun from the snakelight within the castle. But there was no warmth to be had. This was, after all, no home.

Victoria shoved open the doors. Standing several feet ahead in a half circle were several men and women clad in a mixture of highborn fineries and bright red tunics and loose trousers Angelina didn't recognize as a fashion of Halcyon. Perched high above in the shadows of the inner sanctum were several pairs of reddish orange eyes watching in silence.

But it was the man kneeling in the center of the circle and woman, slain beside him, that caused Angelina to gasp.

"Your Majesty!" she cried.

King Leonard looked up, revealing a bruised right eye and a deep gash across his left cheek. Blood matted his beard and stained a corner of his mouth. Behind the king stood an owl-masked figure holding a bloody dagger to his throat, its cobalt blade curved into waves.

"As promised," the figure said evenly, "King Leonard left alive and Queen Catherine slain by the requested dagger."

"Thank you, Beza." Victoria smiled. "The Watchers truly are worth every sterling."

"Is that it, then? Don't get your way so you side with these *fiends*?" King Leonard's brittle laughter filled the inner sanctum. "Really, Victoria. Do you honestly think you're the first to use supernaturals to threaten the Chase legacy?"

Victoria's eyes narrowed. "That's your problem, Father. You only see someone's use. I see their potential." She looked up at the Watchers scattered high above and the duskborn surrounding those below. "A shame you never saw mine."

"Don't be absurd," King Leonard replied, his voice as gruff as his appearance. "Every Chase has their place in this kingdom, be they royal or bastard. I saw you exactly as you were meant to be—the Crown Princess' spare." He met Victoria's resolute gaze with his own. "Be unsatisfied with your title. I would never fault you for that grievance. But to align with duskborn, especially those of a rival land, and threaten this kingdom's future because of your childish whims I *cannot* forgive."

King Leonard reached for Queen Catherine's limp hand and squeezed it. His attention shifted from Victoria to Angelina's.

"You are a phoenix with the shadow of a raven. That is your— " but Beza dragged the dagger's blade across King Leonard's throat before he could finish. With a muffled gurgle, he fell across the queen, the growing pool of blood beneath him staining her amber and gold dress.

Beza's unblinking gaze held Angelina's for a breath too long. Beneath the fear and shock muddling Angelina's thoughts, a singular urgency gnawed at her the longer she stared into those owl-like eyes.

Pay attention.

Victoria made her way to the fallen king and queen. She kneeled and took King Leonard's golden crown, rubbing her thumb over the blood speckled diamonds for a moment before speaking. "By law, this now belongs to you. But it's not what you truly desire, is it?"

One of the duskborn from the half circle, a short, brutish man clad in a tailored navy suit, stepped forward and handed Victoria a sealed scroll.

"I know you had a life before this. A family and friends far from here. Well, here is your chance to have it back." She unsealed the scroll to reveal a legal document. "Sign this and you'll return to Temmings as Julia Sheffield and I become Queen of Halcyon instead. We'll both get what we want."

Angelina gaped. "You're lying."

"No, I'm not," Victoria replied, impatience sharpening her tone. "I want legally binding proof that you've relinquished your claim to the throne. Clean and simple. I'm not interested in spending all my resources trying to convince an entire kingdom their beloved missing princess is actually a fake." She glanced down at King Leonard's corpse. "Nor do I intend to give my uncle or aunt room to unseat me. I may have friends in high places, but as royals, theirs are higher."

Angelina was silent for several moments. Finally, she shook her head and replied, "No, the throne isn't yours. Tabitha will— "

"—never see the throne," Victoria cut in. She rolled the scroll down further to show a single signature above a second blank line. "Tabitha has already forfeited her claim."

"Liar. You forced her, didn't you? Where is she? Where's Theo and Madelyn?"

"She made her choice and they're no longer your concern," Victoria snapped. "Now, it's your turn—join Tabitha in a comforted exile or return to your grave."

Return to Temmings or die again. A weighted silence fell over the castle. Angelina stared down at her feet until her eyes went cross. She once again found herself in the forest frozen before a monster. The faces were different—Victoria's instead of Billie's—but the truth of them remained.

"I never outran him," Angelina whispered to herself. Her heart fluttered in response, and she swore she heard Alice snicker, as if they'd already become one, vile being. As Angelina's head lifted with dawning realization, she noticed Emily standing partially behind Victoria, a black ribbon tied around her neck and a coy smile on her lips.

Emily is dead, Angelina reminded herself. Martha too, perhaps even Dorothy. Everything she loved, everything she knew, existed alongside the terrors and monsters the adults around her convinced themselves were myth and superstition. Or worse, tried to will away with lies and prayers in the hope it wasn't one of theirs that was taken or eaten. And just as the truth of Billie had haunted her, Victoria's shadow would follow her back to Temmings and gnaw at her until nothing remained but a single question: *What if I hadn't run again?*

Angelina took a deep breath. Every pair of eyes focused on her.

"You can have the throne, but I won't be returning to Temmings." She lifted her chin higher, willing her voice to steady. "Train me to become the blade that kills the Night Prince."

Confusion and anger flashed across Victoria's face. She glared at Alice, lips twisted into a scowl, then turned back to Angelina.

"And what makes you think this is a negotiation?" Victoria replied.

"Ignorance won't protect my family and pride won't save your throne. War is coming, isn't it?" Angelina extended her hand. "Kill me if you truly want. Or let us help each other save Halcyon. Then we can part ways and never see each other again."

Victoria regarded Angelina's outstretched hand but made no move to take it. Her gaze flickered to Alice then back to Angelina. It was a risk, Angelina knew, but if the Chases had taught her anything, it was that whatever beat in her chest was too precious to lose.

Victoria's nostrils flared as she straightened her posture. "Don't think for a second I don't see this farce for what it really is. You can't let go of the riches and power, can you?" Victoria stepped forward, a dark gleam in her eyes. "Don't think I won't hesitate to end you."

"Likewise," Angelina replied with a smirk. No more running. No more hiding. This time, she would stand tall and bare her teeth just like the monsters around her.

Acknowledgements

Thank you for taking the time to read this story. It has been with me for over a decade and I hope you enjoyed it enough to continue the journey.

To my family, who shaped me into the writer I am today. Mom, who showed me the world of books before I even knew what reading was, thank you for giving me the outlet I needed to explore literary worlds. Grammy, thank you for always encouraging me to keep writing and giving me plenty of laughs between moments of doubt. Dad, thank you for pushing me to never settle for less than the story I wanted to see no matter how long it took. I'll always be grateful for the drive and patience you bestowed me. I miss and you Grammy every day, but your teachings make the journey a little easier.

To my husband, Christian, thank you for being my rock, my safe space, my #1 fan, and my iced coffee supplier. This book literally would not have happened without you and your feedback, and I'm forever grateful to have you here with me on this incredible adventure.

To my friends, who kept me sane while I figured out how to do this whole author thing and cheered me on the whole way. I cherish every single one of you always.

To my sister Lyndsay, who made me believe all those years ago I could be the best writer ever. I'm not there yet, but I'll keep trying. THWW forever!

To my wonderful cover artist Ashley, thank you for taking a chance on me and my rambling ideas and mood boards. You're an absolute artistic magician and TDG wouldn't have come to life without your brilliant design and insight.

To my lovely editor Carrie, thank you from the bottom of my heart for taking the time to help me learn, grow and become a better writer. The developmental editing process is a beast, but you made it seem seamless. TDG is where it is today because you cared so deeply and I couldn't have asked for a better editor to work with as a debut.

To my AMAZING beta readers, thank you thank you THANK YOU for taking the time to read early versions of TDG! Everyone's feedback was invaluable and forever appreciated. Michaela, your insight is top tier and I'm so lucky to count you as a friend. Gabi, I can't thank you enough for the support and enthusiasm you showed this story. Love you all!!!

To Jen, the best fated friend ever, I finally did the damn thing! Hope you thought it was pretty cool.

To the Wildborn, thank you so much for being such a supportive writing space and a retreat for the good and bad days. Love you all!

To the bookish community, your insights, advice, sprints, and encouragement were invaluable while I navigated the self-publishing waters. I truly appreciate all the creators and readers taking the time to make this a supportive and knowledgeable space that is accessible to all.

And finally, thank you to Libba Bray, whose *Gemma Doyle* series introduced tween me to gothic fantasy and planted the seeds of what TDG would eventually become.

Angelina, Tobias, Nathaniel, and Sybil's adventure continues in Book 2...

But first, a deeper look into how a young woman of bastard birth became a queen.

More details coming soon!

About the Author

Olivia Danson always had stories to tell. Drawing found her first thanks to her artistically gifted father. But when she was told at ten she couldn't become a painter when she grew up because that was silly (it's not) and not a "real job" (it is), her journalist-inclined mother showed her how to craft stories with words instead of paint. This turned out for the best because while writing is hard, perfecting hands is indeed much harder (she swears one day she'll let pockets go).

When she's not writing, Olivia can be found playing video games, reading (duh), binging anime, snuggling with her dogs, or lurking the aisles of a bookstore (usually over-caffeinated and partially covered in dog hair). She currently lives in Texas and *The Darkest Glass* is her debut novel.

You can find her @thebiblionaut on social media platforms.

www.ingramcontent.com/pod-product-compliance
Lightning Source LLC
Chambersburg PA
CBHW020521110726
47899CB00004B/1198